WHITE KING AND THE SEAT AT THE TABLE

WHITE KING AND THE SEAT AT THE TABLE

A NOVEL INSPIRED BY CURRENT EVENTS

BY

LEE KESSLER

Brunnen
PUBLISHING

Early Reader Comments

Like the gasp of instinctive adjustment when entering cold water, the reader palpably reacts as real-life, real-time events and people begin to be recognized. Kessler, known for her "God's eye view" perspective, brings into sharp focus the murky, muddled connections of seemingly unrelated happenings and their effect on our country and world. As the plot and characters move briskly between cities and continents, intentional destruction and soulless, malevolent future plans—across all aspects of society on a global scale—are revealed. Truth is revealed, both damning and liberating. The hero himself realizes that "What you cannot face will bring you down. But what you do face, you have a chance of defeating." An intense battle ensues to change the course of events. The battle plan's creation itself is ingenious, enlightening, and a true example of Kessler's talent for analysis and storytelling. While deeply frightening in its plausibility and urgency, this "peak heart rate" thriller is also hopeful, humorous, touching, and inspiring. But most importantly, it is a harbinger and call to action—quickly—for all who care about the preservation of our very humanity—indeed, our "humanness."

—"Sam" Warner, Former NASA Public Affairs Specialist and Health Care Administrator, Florida

Lee Kessler has done it again! Inspired by current events of the 2020s, she has, once again, been able to bring clarity—through her prophetic style of writing novels—to the roller coaster ride that America has been on since early 2020. The author is able to help the reader assemble all of the puzzle pieces together into a clear picture of enlightenment.

I was hooked from the opening chapter and found myself unable to put the book down. Much in the same way when Netflix loads 10 episodes of your favorite drama series, I kept wanting to dive into the next chapter to see what twists and turns were coming.

For those of us who consider ourselves patriots in the United States and notice the cultural shift and sense an undercurrent of evil that threatens to destroy us from within, Lee Kessler articulates a proverbial warning that will shake readers to their core.

I can only hope that the ending of "White King and the Seat at the Table" is a harbinger of a better tomorrow in America.

—Vincent Rush, Owner, Rush Business Group, LLC , Ohio

Lee Kessler has done a great job with "White King and the Seat at the Table." I found myself not being able to put the book down. It is very compelling and thought provoking. Looking at current events through the lens of this book, I was thankful she offers a solution. Read and be stirred!

—**Jeff Moore, Motivational Speaker and Entrepreneur, Texas**

Having read the first three books in the "White King" series, I knew I was in for a ride, through fictionalized storytelling of history in the making. But in this latest installment, "White King and the Seat at the Table"—coincident with almost daily shifts in the world as we have come to see it unravel—I was not prepared for the dramatic highs and lows of emotions I experienced as I traveled with old and new friends and old and new enemies.

The pace had its ebbs and flows, from thoughtful perceptions of disquieting signals in otherwise-tranquil moments at national monuments to high-intensity, high-alert rapid-fire actions and international intrigue. There are questions always present of who's doing what to whom, especially since everything Kessler writes mirrors real-time events. How do we prepare for what's coming?

In fact, this story touched so deeply with concerns I have about the future of our country, and for the future of life itself, I found myself crying for several pages. I was almost losing hope, like our protagonists must have felt at the unimaginable task ahead, and then finding relief and hope again in the pages that followed with the unbelievable—yet oddly well seated in reality—solutions! By the end, moments of despair turned to hope and a regained belief in the inherent goodness of men and the ability of individuals to work together to reclaim the freedoms for which so many, past and present, have fought and died.

An inventive, deeply personal writer, Kessler has the courage to share through fiction what she has observed and analyzed with breathtaking accuracy. She does not depend on outside sources for her analyses, preferring her stories to unfold with the depth and breadth of her own research and ability to pervade her characters' personalities in order to predict their actions and intentions. Her unwavering belief in the basic goodness of people everywhere inspires her to look for solutions to the problems we face as offered through her protagonists.

With so much bad news surrounding us, the question remains: What can any of us do about it? "White King and the Seat at the Table" provides both the reality and the answers! A book for all generations. A book for now. Today's nightmares, tomorrow's solutions.

—**Tanii Carr, Author and Ocala Horse Consultant, Florida**

Right now, multiple aspects of our world are not just divisive, they're downright frightening. Will we ever achieve harmony? If it continues to worsen, can the world survive? Is it a coincidence that so much got so bad so fast? Open the cover of this clairvoyant book and discover the deceitful, vicious truth fully displayed through fiction by this brilliant author. The bonus is a "map" for how it can be turned around and an ending you've just got to read.

  —Marcy Sanders, Nonprofit Founder and Counselor, Florida

Once again, master storyteller Lee Kessler has crafted in "White King and the Seat at the Table" a suspense-filled, truth-based thriller that makes us seriously rethink what is happening right before our eyes—what we read, hear, and see about politics, business, and world affairs.

In the fourth in the "White King" series, the characters uncover and take us through the spider web of deceit, lies, and propaganda known as Perception Management (PM), used by those who covet power and a seat at the table to ensure their agenda—the Great Reset—at any cost.

Through mainstream media, social networking platforms, commercials, film, TV, education, radio, internet and more, Kessler brilliantly lays out how Perception Management teams are wielding the tools our population relies on for the truth. PM insidiously changes how and what we think. While PM is widely known and used in politics, the misinformed general public is unaware of being played by spins that are outright lies, deepfake videos, misdirection, and planted news stories.

I believe it is every citizen's right and duty to look behind the "curtain" of what we are being subjected to in this brave new world of Perception Management in order to truly understand how our freedoms are being eroded. Lee Kessler's book, though fiction, reads like an enticing nonfiction work.

  —Eileen Drillick-Batson, Marketing and PR Consultant
    and Internet Entrepreneur, Florida

Seldom does a work of fiction contain an urgency factor, but this new book by Lee Kessler exposes an evil that is currently eating our culture alive. In great detail, it reveals a very real plot to enslave the world, and it inspires effective action by people who wish to remain free.

  —Tom Solari, Award-winning Filmmaker and Screenwriter
    ("America!" and "In Search of Liberty")

This is the story of America, Americans, and a future being planned for us. Thirty-five years ago, I was given my first insight into this future world by my business mentor, Bill Britt. It was not comfortable to discuss it then, and it is not comfortable now. But these are unique times.

George Washington said, "Truth will ultimately prevail where there is pains to bring it to light."

This book is dedicated to Bill Britt, who was a visionary business leader and courageous man. He challenged me to look. It is my hope that what I "found" will bring some truth to light for you. And it is my prayer that you, too, are willing to look.

CHAPTER ONE

"*I*'m sorry, my friend, that it has come to this," James Mikolas said to the statue that dominated the Lincoln Memorial. Standing at the feet of the titan who had withstood so much nearly two centuries earlier, James felt the familiar comfort he gained whenever he came to visit the man he referred to as "my old friend, Abe."

In recent months, this former CIA analyst and field operative had been awash with a sadness he could not shake. His normally analytical mind would become fuzzy when he attempted to make sense of the sudden and almost complete collapse of law and order in the land he loved. James felt he was boxing with a shadow—that there was something, or someone, shrouded in the darkness that was manipulating and causing it all.

Moreover, he felt as if he had failed Abe somehow, as if the freedoms that had been so hard fought for, and hard earned, by earlier generations were hanging by a thread. He had hoped that merely seeing the image of his hero would provide some clarity, calm his mind. Regrettably, that had not happened. Nothing could have prepared him for the gloom and darkness that enshrouded the Capitol and the entire National Mall. Once a beautiful, memorial park dedicated to the men, women, and conflicts that had shaped the American character, the National Mall now was neglected, surrounded by fence, and only a few were walking along its reflecting pools and pathways.

A slimy, dark-green moss was growing in the waters that once shimmered in the almost-milelong reflecting pool that stretched from the Lincoln Memorial to the Washington Monument, making it appear like a literal swamp. Benches were in disrepair, and weeds were beginning to dominate the once-velvety grass that stretched to the Capitol building at the end of the mall.

He had heard that the statue of his hero had been defaced. Yet, as he stood there, it appeared undamaged, albeit not the shimmering white stone he was used to. The memorial itself, however, was "decorated" by a vandal's spray paint. Expletives and historically inaccurate, inflammatory slogans had been painted, left to stand as a 21st-century comment. James wondered why the man at the White House would not order the National Park Service to clean, restore, and open this mall.

He knew the answer, though, and that is why he had journeyed here—hoping to gain some insight and soak up any wisdom that might linger spiritually from the man who had saved the nation long ago.

"You should probably start making your way to the exit, Mr. Mikolas," the park guard said politely. James was a familiar face to the older guards. They had seen him many times over the years and had enjoyed conversations with this mysterious man from the CIA, who seemed to have such an odd affection for the statue of Abraham Lincoln. The younger guards merely thought him a bit eccentric.

Today, the guard James knew as Patrick was especially solicitous. There was no way he intended to offend, or rough up, a man he knew to be friendly.

Patrick's admonition shook James out of his reverie enough to answer. "Yeah, I will Patrick. If it's OK with you, I will just sit a while on the steps. You know me. I like to enjoy the sunset and the view down the mall."

"Sure, take your time. We don't lock up or anything, but the mall isn't safe after sundown anymore—even with us here." Patrick's voice trailed off, as he, too, remembered a brighter time in America's history. Respectfully, he stepped aside and went on about his final rounds for the day.

James turned and sat at the top of the stairs, enjoying the same view Lincoln enjoyed. It was true about the sunsets. There was nothing James enjoyed more than sunset time at the memorial along the Potomac River. Though the sun set in the west behind the memorial, it left the mall awash in an alpine glow. At that time of night, everything was quieting down, still and hopeful. The light caused the magnificent white Capitol dome to almost sparkle before it would slip into the midnight blue ascending on the city. Shortly, the streetlights and lights of the Capitol would come on. It was usually then that James would rise and walk his way past the Vietnam Veterans Memorial to an exit.

So, today, he sat there. It was a chillier day than he expected, so he pulled the bill of his cap a little farther down to protect his forehead, and he pulled his scarf up to protect his neck and chin. *Ah, that's better*, he thought.

It was then that he saw a lone man walking toward the Lincoln Memorial. The man had an odd gait, as if one of his legs was shorter than the other and it caused him to wobble from right to left. He was well dressed in an expensive topcoat and a plaid scarf—the likely colors of a clan. The man seemed familiar to James, however, so he continued to watch him as he got closer to the foot of the memorial on the right-hand side. Not wanting to be rude or to make the man uncomfortable, James turned on his surveillance skill set and pulled his cellphone out of his pocket, still keeping his eye on the man while pretending to have a conversation on the phone.

To James' surprise, he did not come up the stairs. He got close enough, however, for James to recognize him. He was indeed familiar. In fact, James had worked for the man years ago. He was John Brannigan, the former head of the CIA. Brannigan disappeared right below the stairs, to the right. James knew there was a door down there—a small, unobtrusive door that no one would notice. Whatever was behind that door was dwarfed by the approach to the beautiful memorial that had been erected. James doubted that anyone ever asked what the black door was and where it led.

It led, in reality, to a small museum underneath the Lincoln Memorial. A few rooms held information on the construction of the memorial, and additional quotes by President Lincoln himself were carved in stone, covering the walls. It was small. And one would have to know it was there to find and enjoy it.

James' heart started to race just a bit, causing a slight shortness of breath. He recognized immediately that it was the sign he was onto something. All his career—both in the field and as an analyst—his body always seemed to signal him with a racing heart when he was coming up on something of significance and danger. It had been a long time since he had felt that. For months now, he had experienced merely a sadness, a heaviness, brought on by the state of affairs in the nation he loved.

But now, he leaned forward slightly, recognizing something was wrong and that he needed to be alert. It was at that moment that two other men approached the memorial—one from the Foggy Bottom side, the other from the Korean War Memorial area. Each was well dressed. Each looked like anyone who might work in Washington on K Street or in one of the many buildings nearby that housed the hundreds of thousands of bureaucrats whose machinery kept the government running.

One thing James concluded was that they were not tourists. They walked with purpose. They reached the memorial at the same time but did not seem to know each other. Nonetheless, they, too, disappeared through the black door.

By now, James' heart was racing. There was no mistaking the tell-tale signal that he was on top of something. So, he waited. The guard came by one last time, waving to him from the bottom of the stairs. "I'll be just a while longer, Patrick. I'm enjoying the quiet actually. So unusual to see no one here."

"I understand, Mr. Mikolas. Hardly anyone comes here anymore. You just remember what I told you about it not being safe."

"I will. Thanks."

The guard left, presumably heading to the quiet and security of his home.

Still, James waited. About 30 minutes after the three men had entered the bowels of the Lincoln Memorial, they came out. Not wanting to attract their attention, James began to take photos down the mall in the direction of the Capitol like any other tourist. His camera had a wide angle, which he touched lightly to make sure he could capture these men on camera, as he did not want them to be alerted to his presence in any alarming way. Brannigan was a discerning and cunning CIA chief. Mikolas despised him, but he knew the man's talents, and he did not want Brannigan to recognize him if he happened to look up the stairs at the man taking photos.

As it turned out, Brannigan did not notice. He was quite jovial— gleeful actually—and seemed to almost glad-hand the other two. Whatever the three had done or discussed behind that little black door, they all seemed happy and in agreement, without any fear of intervention. *Like men who have just concluded a major deal,* James surmised. *What are you up to, John Brannigan? And who the hell are you two?*

The men split up and each exited as they had arrived. Dipping his chin even farther to avoid being recognized, he was confident that he had caught each of their faces in the string of shots he had taken. When they all were gone, he rose, dusted himself off, and took a quick glance at the images before he repocketed the cellphone.

He had indeed gotten them. Though he did not know who they were, his training told him that whoever they were, they had chosen to meet in a secret spot, at a time of day when no one of any consequence would see them, let alone hear them. And James Mikolas, who had faced some of the worst villains in the world over the last three decades, knew in his gut that these three were engaged in something he had to know about.

Looking at the smiling faces of the two men he did not recognize, James said under his breath, "Who are you? And why are you here?"

James could not know then, but that photo—taken during a chance observation of three men—would change the course of history. Today, however, all James knew was that he had to find a way to identify the two unknowns.

Chapter Two

*B*rannigan verified the elevator to the Lincoln statue was locked. *I don't want any surprises tonight.*

He had selected this small, unobtrusive space for the meeting he had hoped for, and worked for, his whole career. Even if someone did manage to walk in while they were talking, he knew that he would have plausible deniability as to why there were people under the Lincoln Memorial after normal hours.

He wasn't really concerned about that, however. Other than the lone tourist at the top of the steps, there was almost no one in the National Mall now. He smiled, proud of the covert work he had done to get the people themselves to enclose, behind fencing, the very monuments and memorials they cherished and had brought their children and grandchildren to view in generations past.

Easiest way of all to erase history, he thought. *Get people to react to some problematic event, and the solution they impose becomes the goal you desire.* John Brannigan had made a career out of manipulating people's minds and emotions in order to bring about behavioral changes he desired. Long ago, he had set upon a goal of being one of the great influencers in the world. As a second-generation Irish immigrant, he was raised within the Catholic faith and was educated mostly by Jesuits. His family was of modest means and imbued in him a sturdy work ethic.

When he was a boy, recovering from a polio attack that left him still somewhat wobbly and arthritic, he had been confined to his room for months. With no siblings, his mother had bought him puppets. Her son seemed to have a keen imagination, and a flair for drama, so she had encouraged him to occupy himself with puppets. And John Brannigan had done just that. He had a gift for storytelling and, regrettably, a natural contempt for what he referred to as the "ordinary man."

Day after day, he would create stories where the strong character vanquished the weaker, less bright, characters in his story. "The Common Men," as he referred to them. It wasn't long before he, as the puppeteer, had realized that if he could do that with puppets, he could likely do it with actual people. By his teen years, he had become fascinated by the writings of Karl Marx and later Saul Alinsky and other authors who used disinformation and manipulation to create change in a society. In his mind, they were master puppeteers.

That hobby his mother had encouraged to help take her son's attention off his weak legs and the pain had unwittingly given birth to a man who viewed himself as smarter than anyone else, capable of turning any scenario into one in which he won. His mind and storytelling ability gave him a natural superiority, and that sense of being the smartest kid in the room outweighed any physical deficiency he might have had.

His burning ambition took care of the rest. Intelligence and counterterrorism were natural playgrounds for his intellect and sense of adventure. Today, he lived a dual life. One life was a sought-after commentator who nightly was able to come to people through their news networks and—like that puppeteer from the past—tell them the story he wanted them to believe. No one challenged his assertions successfully because he masked them behind his career credentials as one of the nation's top intelligence chiefs.

The other was a life in the shadows. No one was close enough to him to know his true thoughts, let alone his true machinations. He had always gotten other people to do the dirty work, the brutal work. He himself could never be linked to some of our nation's most damaging subterfuge—perpetrated against any opponent of his and against the American people themselves. He made sure he had "clean hands." He was a smug bastard, and he knew he was about to be rewarded.

The other two arrived a few minutes later, right on time. Brannigan stepped out of the shadows of one of the exhibit rooms and into the light of the main vestibule. The meeting would be short, and he wanted to see who he was dealing with. For John Brannigan had not called this meeting. He had merely set the location for maximum invisibility. Having no idea who or how many men would be meeting him, he was relieved to see only two.

"Mr. Brannigan?" The man who spoke had a sonorous voice and an impeccable appearance. It was obvious he lived and engaged at the highest levels of business and government, was a man of means, and was succinct in his communications.

"Yes." Brannigan answered and added, "Are you Mr. Schmidt?"

The man nodded and extended his hand. Schmidt then assumed control of the meeting. "You are Peter Loren, I gather?"

The man he addressed was younger than Brannigan and Schmidt, perhaps only 40 years old or so. John Brannigan knew who Peter Loren was but did not let on. He decided to hold his cards close to his chest for a bit.

"Yes, sir. At your service." Loren smiled and extended his hand as well.

Schmidt complimented Brannigan on the selection of the location, smiling at the irony of them starting something in motion that would cement the end of America's influence in the world and doing it in the bowels of the Lincoln Memorial.

Then, he said, "I know we all want this to be brief. Do you two know each other?"

Loren was the first to answer, seeming to defer to Brannigan. "I think everyone in America knows John Brannigan, sir. He has become quite the media darling in recent years. But we have never met personally that I remember."

"Quite true," Brannigan responded, then continued. "I don't remember having met you in person either."

"I come from Paris, originally. Worked there for some time with a PR firm until it was closed. Then, I began my own. For the last few years, my primary client has been a company whose influence in the media and on Capitol Hill has been profound. You might call them a disinformation group, and I help them with their spin and with their image. That's all."

It was said with such a finality, despite the mystery of who the group was, that Brannigan smiled because he and Peter Loren were, in fact, working for the same organization. The group was like an octopus, with tentacles extended outward in many directions, and participants chosen for their expertise. Though they knew each other's names, most had never met in person. Until Peter Loren said his name, Brannigan had not made the connection. They each had different roles, and Brannigan had told himself often that whoever this Peter Loren is, he is very talented.

"Well, now that you have at least met, let me get down to the purpose of our brief meeting." Schmidt resumed control. "You know who I represent, correct?"

Brannigan and Loren nodded. Emotionally, both were excited and anticipatory. Each knew something wonderful portended for them. Yet, each maintained the decorum and calm exterior one would expect of men who apparently both dealt in intelligence.

"My employer did not want to send any form of communication that might be traceable. He's concerned that your agencies and personnel tend to leave entirely too much on laptops and in emails. Sloppy, frankly." He laughed briefly, signaling that he was poking lightly at them but that it was a just a little warning.

All three laughed, agreeing that was indeed the case. Too many incompetent underlings, all puffed up with their own self-importance, had left a few too many trails in recent years. They had been easy to discredit or to "disappear" however. Brannigan and Loren recognized that Schmidt was not here to elaborate. He was here for another reason.

"I am here to extend an invitation to you both to meet Ernst Schweiner in this location two weeks from today." Schmidt handed each of them a small piece of paper. Upon examination, it did indeed hold an address. "You do not need to arrange any accommodations. Just arrive at this airport. You will be met there and taken to Mr. Schweiner. I would plan to be out of the country for perhaps a week or two, and dress for cooler temperatures."

This was it, the moment Brannigan had hoped for since he was a young man. All that he had done. Everyone he had manipulated, deceived, and used had led him to this moment. He had just received an invitation to a seat at the table. In all of the world's history, the men at that table would rank among the most powerful. Knowing the speed at which the United States was unraveling, he believed now that Ernst Schweiner, the founder of the Global Commerce Forum, was about to assume control of the nations of the earth. And that he, John Brannigan, had made it to that table. It was a proud day. Only his eyes betrayed an Irish twinkle.

Peter Loren, on the other hand, was demonstrably excited. His stunning and totally effective guidance in the art of Black Propaganda had helped the Democracy Preservation Project undermine the entirety of the news media outlets and forums in the United States—and had immersed politicians unwittingly in the greatest Information War Game ever attempted. He felt no remorse. After all, politicians are the easiest to dupe, given their natural tendency to place self above country. He knew, and had been taught by his mentor, how to exploit raw ambition.

Always in the shadows, never in the limelight of the Democracy Preservation Project, Loren's role in the demise of the Constitutional Republic known as the United States of America could never be traced. A shadow warrior, he knew he could never be identified as complicit, and he knew now that his genius had helped that group accomplish its missions—and had earned him a seat at the table.

"Well, I see you took that well," Schmidt chuckled. "Not entirely unexpected, I assume?"

"No, but a great honor, nonetheless. I look forward to serving," Brannigan said.

"Likewise," Loren added.

"Excellent, gentlemen. We have a great game afoot. And I personally anticipate your contributions. Mr. Schweiner looks forward to meeting you."

Brannigan then moved the other two back to the door, switched off the light in the vestibule, and all three exited into the imminent twilight overtaking the Capitol dome. In their congratulatory frame of mind, none noticed the man seated at the top of the stairs taking photos. None knew what was about to be discovered.

CHAPTER THREE

*A*ri swatted away a fly that had been buzzing around his head and eased himself into a booth in the diner. *It's been quite a few years since I have been here,* he thought. *Wonder if they still have that lemon meringue pie James served me...*

Ari Ben-Gurion's thoughts were interrupted by a brassy, bossy voice. "What'll you have, mister?" Looking up, Ari recognized the woman from years ago. He might be getting old now, but his memory was good, and he couldn't help but remember this diner's owner.

It was comforting somehow to know that some things hadn't changed. Her diner hadn't. She hadn't done a lick of redecorating or updating in 20 years. And as he looked up at her and smiled, he could see her figure was still bosomy and her hair still red—albeit with some gray showing at the roots. Nonetheless, she had that same welcoming smile.

"I'm Ari Ben-Gurion."

"Well, pleased to meet you, Ari Ben-Gurion. I'm Sadie. I own the place."

"I remember that, Sadie. My friend, James, had me meet him here a long time ago, and he—knowing that I have a fondness for sweets—introduced me to your lemon meringue pie. I don't suppose you still serve that?"

Sadie cackled, "Honey, I'd go out of business if I didn't serve that! Why, I'd have a damn mutiny on my hands." Ari nodded in agreement. "So, I gather you'd like a piece."

"Absolutely, Sadie," he said, daring to be just a bit familiar by calling her by name. "And one for my friend, too."

Sadie looked around and said, "Well, if you mean James, he usually sits in the booth at the end. I'll bring it to you there. I'm sure he'll be along." Ari took the hint, got up, and re-seated himself in the end booth, where he could see the full length of the diner.

He pulled out his phone and started looking at photos, concentrating on one in particular that seemed to be a closeup. Not even noticing James arrive, he was surprised when James suddenly plopped two pieces of pie on the table and slid in beside Ari.

"Thanks for coming, my friend!" James said.

"It's an honor to be invited back to the famous Cape Fear River area, and to one of the most memorable haunts in the neighborhood," Ari responded.

For a moment, the two old intelligence and espionage operatives just sat, staring ahead. It didn't seem they had much to say. Truth was both were examining mentally what this meeting might portend. James picked up his fork and dove into the pie. Ari grinned and followed suit. They ate in silence. It was not that they had nothing to say to each other. But rather, each man had led a lonely life, ferreting out bad guys from the old days of the Soviet Union up to their retirements.

Ari, who was Israeli intelligence and an officer in the Mossad, had met James when James was a field operative for the CIA, a post he had held for 30 years and which put him into Eastern Europe and the Mediterranean. Later, after James was moved back to Washington to serve as an analyst, the two only infrequently crossed paths—mostly when James needed something from Ari.

James' analyses had saved the United States from a multi-tiered terror, pharmaceutical, and international banking conspiracy that had unfolded from 2001 to 2011. It had been the best, the most dangerous, and the most heart-breaking work of his career. But it had led to a surrogate family—two boys whose courage and goodness had done the heavy lifting. Those boys now lived in the West, and James, after his official retirement, had not had much opportunity to see them.

But the dark path the United States was on now, and what he had accidentally witnessed at the Lincoln Memorial in Washington, D.C., haunted James. He hoped today that Ari had come through for him. Ari's presence in Cape Fear confirmed that he had.

"So, I gather you liked my photos from my vacation in Washington," James broke the silence. His racing heart gave warning to the fact he had indeed come upon something of significance.

"Oh, yes, James. Lovely. Some of the best sunset shots I have seen." Holding up his camera, he showed it to James, commenting on the photo he had been studying. "Such a contrast to the darkness of the city, and the pastel bathing of light into that darkness. I'm impressed. Who knew you were such a photographer, especially using a cellphone."

James said nothing, just continued to eat his pie. He waited.

Wiping his mouth after devouring the last bit of crust, Ari added, "I had to deliver this information in person, James. There are still electronics surveillance eyes watching me, you know. Every key stroke cyber-shadowed. How I miss the days before we had to use an email, computer, or phone. So much easier to just pick up notes in a park, in the dark." They both laughed.

James knew there would be no folder today. He had prepared by bringing a small notebook, which was in his shirt pocket. That was a signature tool of Mikolas. Through the years, he had always carried a small note pad to jot down theories, ideas, and projects that needed attending. Today, as in years past, he had pad in hand as he looked now at the photo Ari presented in front of him.

"I took the liberty of zooming in on the photo with the three men," Ari began. He had switched gears, and the briefing had begun.

"I'm all ears."

"This one, you know, of course. John Brannigan." James nodded, and Ari continued, "Well, the other two are very interesting." Whether he paused for dramatic effect or just to gather up some courage to address the next revelation, James couldn't tell. But not even James was prepared for what Ari said next.

"This man is Peter Loren. We had him in our system in some archive files after a raid on a public relations firm in Paris. Took me awhile to positively ID him from photos from the raid."

James could hardly breathe. Looking straight at Ari, he asked, "What firm, Ari?"

"ST & Associates."

Memories came crashing in of his identification of the propaganda chief for Al Qaeda, Samir Taghavi. Taghavi had been killed in Venezuela by a team James had recruited. He had been found running a sex-trafficking slave ring and was taken down by a team requested by James and paid for by the investor who had bankrolled several of his past projects to ferret out terror operations. Samir Taghavi was dead, but not before he had penetrated and nearly destroyed one of the largest media empires in the United States—Walker News Group.

"James, our government overlooked Loren because Taghavi seemed to have set up a slick PR operation where the entire Paris office was legit. Yet, hidden within it was the Al Qaeda cell of propaganda operatives

Taghavi had recruited and trained." Ari shifted position some to take pressure off his right hip, which acted up sometimes in the humidity. An old war wound.

"PR laundering," James scoffed. "Better nowadays than money laundering!"

"Yep. It's an information world, my friend. Whoever controls that controls us." He continued. "In any case, this man's photo was taken, along with other employees, as we were executing a search warrant from Interpol. Taghavi had flown the coop, but Loren and his PR people seemed to have no awareness of the other nefarious operations. We gave him a pass. But we archived the pictures."

James wrote his name down, knowing he would have to figure out where Peter Loren worked now. He didn't have to wait long.

"James, Loren's firm is in Washington, D.C." Mikolas looked up at Ari, questioning. "Once I identified him, and remembered him, I felt bad. So, I did a little internet search of my own. He's the owner of PL & Associates."

James laughed, almost barked, "Well, that apple doesn't fall far from the tree!" The ironic reference to the name of his predecessor's firm, ST & Associates, hadn't escaped Ari either. He nodded.

"All right, James, here's where it gets real interesting." Again, Ari paused. "Do you remember years ago when I was scouring photos taken at a World Health Organization event on Lake Zurich? And we spotted a photo that got published in the local newspaper of the director of the WHO with a man we did not know?"

James thought he was going to be sick. *This can't be happening again! Surely, not another nest of undercover villains!* James was numb.

Non-plussed, Ari continued. He seemed to relish his discovery, taking little note of the ashen color James had turned. "Well, among the photos where we spotted Phillipe Monet, the finance guy from Geneva who you later concluded was Ayman al-Zawahiri hiding in plain sight, those blessed archives had a photo of *this* man." Ari pointed to the third man in the photo James had taken. "His name is Rutger Schmidt. He is personal attaché to Ernst Schweiner."

"Who?" James asked, truly not recognizing the name.

"Schweiner is the founder and head of the Global Commerce Forum. Also from Geneva, Switzerland. The photographer back then caught both of them doing a Champagne toast at the event on the lake."

James had recovered now and was fully in gear as the former CIA analyst. "Interesting," he commented. "Back then, no connections were obvious, not possible to instantly spot. But today's photos may have surfaced a nexus of some kind from long ago…"

"Yeah, that's where I would start, my friend. Just a little too coincidental for my liking." Ari laughed. "You know me. Swinish suspicion."

"This is excellent, Ari. I am grateful for you, and for this information. I need to learn more about this Peter Loren, and about Schmidt's employer."

"James, if your photo captured those three together—in today's world of governmental resets—there is something going on. This one is going to be dangerous, James."

"How so? Why more than the others?"

"Because, the string you pull may lead to Ernst Schweiner. That's all." Ben-Gurion paused, then said, "I want in on this one, James." Before James could demur, he added, "This may be the toughest game you and I ever play."

James thought about it for just a second and nodded, rocking his whole body. "Agreed. I'll be in touch, Ari. First, I need to research this Ernst Schweiner and his Global Commerce Forum." With that, the two rose and parted company. A quiet meeting between two friends over pie, with only a small notebook to document the conversation, was about to unleash a whirlwind against the largest assault ever perpetrated against the free peoples of Earth.

Neither James nor Ari knew it then. Nor did they know the consequences. It was just as well.

CHAPTER FOUR

"*D*amn it!" James exclaimed, as he pulled yet more floorboard up, only to find another snake cowering beneath. Seeing it was not poisonous, he took his shovel, scooped it up, and dropped it into the river about 25 yards away. "Count your blessings," he said as the snake easily swam away. Flooding on the Cape Fear River had been intense during the hurricane, but his own home was far enough up a knoll to protect it from complete destruction.

He was thinking he would have another month of repairs to siding, flooring in the bedroom area, and the back porch—if you could call it that. He paused for a moment, overtaken by memories of Andy and Brian and the first time Brian had come seeking sanctuary. It seemed so long ago, yet it had been just a decade since he and the boys embarked on the hunt that had saved America from complete economic collapse. He smiled at the magnitude of what they had done.

Kelly would have welcomed repairs to this place, he thought. A little too rustic for her taste…He changed the channel quickly on any memories of his beloved Kelly, who had died as collateral damage in their pursuit of the terrorist Ayman Al-Zawahiri and his devastatingly deadly minions.

Mikolas had kept pretty much to himself since his retirement from the CIA, and from the entanglements his analyses had created. He was content to occasionally stop by Sadie's to have some of her pie, but the rest of the time he spent fishing, reading, and occasionally watching TV. It was his sole connection—other than his cellphone—to the world he had once been so influential in.

But that had all changed after spotting the three men in Washington and learning from his Mossad friend, Ari, who they were. Further research into Peter Loren and Rutger Schmidt's boss, Ernst Schweiner, revealed frightening yet plausible global scenarios.

For almost two years, he had struggled with the feeling he was boxing with a shadow, trying to identify a hidden attacker. Often, he walked in the woods to get clear of the feeling that he was trapped in some kind of spider's web. Spiders' webs are annoying if you don't find the spiders. No matter how many times you wipe their gauzy pattern away, it keeps coming back. And that was the feeling James had had since former CIA Director John Brannigan had begun threatening the then-President of the United States.

It was bad enough in James' mind that a former director would openly criticize a sitting president. But the day he saw Brannigan look directly into camera, referring disparagingly to the president in the second person, not the third person, he knew in his gut that something was wrong. If you are going to criticize someone, you generally say something like, "he did this, or they did that…" But to say, "You did this, and you did that…" is very personal and something he knew Brannigan was schooled enough to never do. James' antenna had been up ever since, and he had made it a point to try to catch the man by monitoring him on TV. The day that Brannigan said, "Stay tuned, Mr. President, stay tuned," James wondered if the Secret Service was listening and speculating as to the nature of what sounded like a direct threat. They may not have been listening. But James was. That was the beginning of his boxing match with the shadowy world he had once been part of and which he had happily left. In view of current events, though, he now realized it was a world he was going to have to re-enter.

Researching Peter Loren confirmed for James that the military Fifth Column he had theorized as having been implanted into the American media was real. Only now, however, was he coming to understand just how securely it had grabbed hold. He had hoped that the last financial crisis, and the emergence once again of Walker News Group, would have stifled any lasting degradation of the media. He was wrong. Loren's influence extended to the Democracy Preservation Project and their tentacles and personnel pervaded all of U.S. politics.

In the world of the military, a Fifth Column is a force planted inside the country you are about to attack. It is there to sabotage and break the solidarity of that country, so an external attack can occur and be successful. In recent years, it was the essential American free press that had been infiltrated, thus making it possible for propagandists to wreak havoc on an unsuspecting public—at least, that is how James Mikolas viewed it.

His agitation today was that he was not in that game anymore. His connections were mostly retired, and unlike many others, he had given up his security clearances when he turned in his paperwork. He had hoped to just live quietly and not be in the thick of nefarious plots ever again. It was not to be so, however.

James had already linked Brannigan to the former head of Australian intelligence and the MI-6 agent whose confession, now declassified, had established that the whole infamous Russia Dossier was false and had been created for political interference.

Seeing Brannigan with Loren and Schmidt had started James analyzing. And for the first time in months, he felt he was no longer boxing with a shadow. Hidden pieces of information had just surfaced, and a germ of a theory began to formulate. Paying no attention to the setting sun, or the evening chill, he read his notes over and over. Each time, the theory seemed to open doors and illuminate dark mysteries that the American public was struggling with.

By dawn, he knew what he had to do. Packing just a duffle bag, his phone and his laptop, James loaded the small trunk of his prized Mustang convertible and started out. Stopping by Sadie's to grab a piece of her apple pie, he smiled at her and placed a $100 bill on the counter. "Sweetie, it's too early in the morning for me to have change for that!" she said.

"No need, Sadie. That's your tip." She started to protest, so he jumped in, "I'll be gone a while, so I am tipping you in advance! You can make me a fresh strawberry pie when I get back." She winked.

He stopped in town only long enough to email Ari that he hoped to see him soon.

He knew who he had to see. And he guessed they'd be glad to see him, but not glad about what was written on the note paper he had folded and slipped into his breast pocket.

First, however, he drove out of his way to Washington to see his friend Abe. The city was occupied by troops, so he parked across the Potomac at the foot of Arlington Cemetery. Standing at the grave of Kelly and her husband, Greg Weir, he looked across the river to the Lincoln Memorial.

"Old friend, I don't know if I will see you again." He breathed deeply, taking in the fragrances of incipient spring along the Potomac. "This one is pretty serious this time. And if I am right about this, I don't know if you and I will be able to keep company anymore. So, thank you, my friend—for who you were then and who you are now."

A few minutes later, James rose, strolled downhill through the headstones of men who had died for us, fired up the Mustang, and headed west to Los Angeles.

CHAPTER FIVE

*A*ndy smiled as he watched his 3-year old daughter, Faith, running around at her birthday party. Reagan had chosen an emerald-green dress for her, which he knew could not survive the rolling in the grass and the cake that would be coming. *Ah, well, that's for Reagan to deal with,* he thought. *I just hope the photographer catches at least one photo of her before she shows her true tomboy colors!*

Equally aggressive, though much less steady on her feet, was Hope Carver. Brian Washington Carver had always followed the lead of his friend Andy, and shortly after Andy and Reagan were married, he proposed to Alicia Quixote, much to the relief of all their friends. At the time he first met her, Alicia Quixote was WNG's star TV anchor. She had accepted, and now they, too, had a little girl. Hope wasn't quite 2, but she already showed the signs of the athletic prowess her dad possessed. Nothing seemed to deter her, and no tumble seemed to intimidate her. She would get right back up and charge ahead. Today was no different, as she chased Faith around, trying to grab something that Faith had in her hand.

Andy winced, guessing that it was going to be a real hoot watching Faith open gifts and eat cake with her pursuer Hope around. And he knew that Hope was in her "mine!" stage. He relished the idea of watching to see if she ended up with his own daughter's gifts. Faith was naturally generous, and they had taught her to share, but he wasn't certain she'd be too good about it today. Chuckling under his breath, he nodded for Reagan to take over the supervision of the two, and he headed out into the side lawn overlooking the Pacific to spend some time with Brian.

"Hey, man, this is still fun," Brian said as he looked out over the serene blue ocean as it intersected the horizon. "I never get tired of this view. So glad I bought this place when we had the chance."

"Yeah."

"You still in love with the city lights?"

Andy laughed. "Yes. Reagan and I both like the sparkle. I love to think of all the stories out there, millions of them. Each light represents a household, a story."

"Geez, Andy, you sound just like your wife!"

"Hah!" Andy laughed. "I could do worse. What do you want, me to sound like you?"

Brian paused for a moment, sighed, and said softly, "No. But I wonder, do you miss it, Andy? Do you miss the work we did to help save this country?"

It took Andy a moment to answer. "Sometimes…but I'm so damned grateful that we don't have to save the place for the first time in 10 years that I'm at peace. I know there are still bad guys out there, but somehow it seems we did our part. I'm enjoying my 'early retirement'!"

"Hell, you're 38, for Pete's sake! We're both too young to retire. I don't mean from the company. We're a good team at gaming. I mean from the adventures."

With that, the two friends who had saved the entire world from a financial Armageddon a decade earlier, enabling the United States to right itself and rebuild, stood side by side, absorbing the afternoon California sun and the occasional breach of water by whales about a mile off the Pacific Palisades cliff.

Andy was the first to hear the rough sound, and he recognized it immediately. Many times over the years, he had heard that Ford Mustang. But today, it was incongruous. For a moment, he thought he was imagining things, that the memories he and Brian had been sharing had evoked the sound of James Mikolas' car. The last time he had heard that rumble was on his wedding day, nine years earlier. That was the day James said his goodbyes and drove off to his beloved cabin on the Cape Fear River. James had admonished Brian to follow his heart with Alicia. That idea had been seconded by Bud Walker and Jessica Ranger. Bud Walker was still at the helm of Walker News Group, and Jessica, though still running her financial empire, was now his wife.

It had worked out well for all of them. The only bittersweet memory was of James—alone, having lost Andy's mom, Kelly. She and James had been each other's second chance. Kelly Weir was a casualty in their fight against tyranny. She had been innocent collateral damage as their analysis had closed in on the mastermind of Al Qaeda. His long arm of vengeance had reached James Mikolas. It had stolen the only love of his life, and it deprived Andy of the joy of having Kelly ever see her granddaughter.

There was a flood of emotion rising in Andy now. It was interrupted, however, by the sound of the car again, seemingly getting closer.

It couldn't be, could it? He turned just as James rolled up in the convertible—top down, as always.

Running to him, he gave James a big bear hug, barely letting him get out of the car. "Oh my God, James, it is you! I thought I was hallucinating there when I heard this old gal's rumble." He patted the car affectionately, as if seeing an old friend.

James smiled. "Yep, some things don't change."

At that moment, Brian noticed James, yelled to Reagan and Alicia, and came running. They weren't far behind, each holding a daughter. The reunion was sweet, yet tentative. For a moment, they didn't know how to act around each other.

Andy broke the silence. "James, we sent you an invitation to the party, but to be honest with you, we thought you would, at best, mail a gift. It never occurred to us you would come…"

James' face scrunched a bit with confusion. Then, looking at the decorations in the yard, he suddenly remembered it was Andy's daughter's birthday. Somewhat sheepishly, he said, "Oh, you know me. I forgot, to be honest with *you*." He looked down for a moment, then added, "Didn't even bring a gift."

"James, don't worry about that. She's got more packages to open than she will have the patience or strength to accomplish." Let me introduce you to Faith Kelly Weir. He turned her to James. Immediately, Faith's green eyes sparkled, and she grinned mightily, even though she was meeting a complete stranger.

James was speechless. Not only was she a precious little girl, but she looked exactly like her grandmother Kelly. His heart ached, and he had to take a deep breath to hold back tears as he looked at Kelly's namesake. "She's beautiful…how old?"

"Three today," Reagan answered. "And she really likes you." Knowing to change the subject, she said, "But you haven't met Hope either."

Brian and Alicia took the cue and offered their daughter for James to cuddle. She went willingly into his arms, and he stroked her smooth dark hair and admired her unique beauty. "So, you two finally did get together. I am so happy about that. That was quite a time, wasn't it?"

They all nodded.

It was then he noticed Bud and Jessica. Almost doubting his eyes, he asked, "You, too? Are you two married?"

"Yep. Living on the ranch in Montana. You look good, James, a lot better than the first time I saw you!"

"Hah," James barked. "Well, that time you were drunk, and I had a gun in your face." They all laughed.

As the laughter abated, Andy was the first to speak. "So, James, why *are* you here?"

At that moment, James answered by reaching into the breast pocket of his sport shirt, pulling out a folded piece of paper. Andy knew immediately what that meant. He shook his head as if to ward off the inevitable. Then, he mustered the courage to ask the question he knew the answer to. "Is that another one of your theories?"

James nodded, handing the folded note to Andy. Unexpectedly, Reagan intervened. Putting Faith down, she grabbed for the paper, defiantly saying, "No! Andy, for God's sake, don't read it. Every time James pulls one of those out of his pocket, we nearly get killed. Please…"

Her plea failed, however. Andy had too much of a history with James to ignore the simple piece of paper he now held. He knew in his heart that James would not have driven across the country, driving straight to him, unless there was something very important on that paper.

Opening it, he started reading. Its content caused him to inhale quickly, as if he had been struck in the stomach, and then to exhale deliberately and slowly. There was total silence in the group as they stood around. Even the two little ones seemed to sense something had changed.

Turning toward the ocean, he gazed out over the tranquility that had been his and Brian's life. He looked to the left slightly, smiled, and offered the paper, which he held gently between two fingers, up to Brian. Brian snagged it. He said nothing as he read it. Silence hung over them all. Brian turned to Alicia, as if to say, "I'm sorry, Babe." Turning back to James, he asked just one question. "Are you sure?"

"Well, that's my theory. But I can't shake it. All my instincts and experience tell me it is real."

Bud asked if he could see it. Handing it over, Bud, Jessica, and the two wives all read it, passing it from one to the other. None knew how to respond. Andy was the first to speak. "You know what this means if it is true, James?"

"It means our Constitutional Republic will be dissolved and the 'Great Experiment' of self-governance ends, Kid."

"Well, this should be challenging," Andy said.

Brian looked to his partner and said, "Yeah, but I am not sure how we can help. I don't know where any of our skill sets fit in. We make computer games, you know."

"Yep, I know, Pal." James used the affectionate name he had for Brian. "But I somehow think the same Grandmaster Chess Champion skill sets Andy used years ago to figure out what Al Qaeda was really up to may come in handy here," he said, referencing the title Andy held at age 18 when James had first sought him out. "You boys are both good at data analysis. Anyway, I don't know what choice we have. I didn't know where else to go. Obviously, I couldn't take it to the Agency."

Andy nodded. Turning to Reagan, he softly said, "Sorry, Babe. I have to help him." Reagan was a mom now, wanting only to enjoy their life and raise their daughter. But she was also a patriot. She owed her life to James Mikolas. His daring rescue plan had saved her and Alicia from the clutches of an Al Qaeda-run slavery operation. Reluctantly, she loosened her hold on her husband and nodded assent.

Bud Walker broke the tension with an absurdly obvious comment, "So, I gather this is going to be dangerous?"

"More than the last time, I'm afraid," James responded.

"Well, in that case, we all need some cake. After all, we came here to celebrate this little one's third birthday. And I, for one, don't want to spoil the celebration for these two gorgeous girls. Can't miss the gift opening, you know." Stroking Faith's copper hair, he added, "She's a lucky kiddo. She has all of her family here today. Come to think of it, these two angels are the only ones here with parents. The rest of us are all orphans. No family but each other."

It was true. Everyone there, except Faith and Hope, had no mother or father. They were indeed orphans. And they were about to confront an adversary on a centuries-old mission—an enemy with an astonishingly complex strategy. It was an enemy arrogantly confident that no one could untangle the web of intersecting personnel and tactics. An enemy that smugly knew it could not be defeated.

CHAPTER SIX

*H*e'd stayed a few days. *Probably longer than I should have,* James thought. *I just don't want to leave.* He looked out over the Pacific Ocean again, admiring the silver-grey water today. A fog hovered over the shore still, and he wondered if it would lift before he pulled out. Turning back to the house, he walked into the great room with its 20-foot glass windows. The others were there. They quieted when he walked in.

Andy was the first to speak. "Well, what are our marching orders, boss?"

James laughed and looked around at Andy and Brian, their wives, and Bud and Jessica. "Well, believe it or not, I have a plan. It's a non-plan, plan. But a plan, nonetheless. Seeing the quizzical looks on their faces, he continued, "I'm going to roll out today for the East. My first task is to meet with my counterpart in Mossad and work out what his role will be. Since I am former U.S. intelligence, and do not have clearances anymore, I expect a lot of what we will learn will come from him."

"And as for us? What?" Andy asked.

"Reagan, Alicia, you'll be happy to know you are not part of this one." Before they could interrupt with any disagreement, he added, "You gals need to hold down the home front. Keep things as normal as possible. And if anyone comes asking about me, tell them I came for the kiddo's birthday. I doubt they will, but…well, you know."

Alicia nodded. "I can do that!"

"Andy, Brian, your role is the game. In the end, it's the game that can save the day."

Brian leaned into James. "All right, man, but what's the game? What are we making here?"

"Damned if I know," James spat it out. "Until I can get into deeper research, I don't really know what we are dealing with here." He paused. "But I can tell you this. I have to find out who is really behind this overthrow of our government. I don't know for sure who they are yet, but I have a clue. The three men in the photo are the beginning of the string I need to pull."

"So…what do we do in the meantime?" Brian asked.

"Whatever I find, and whoever the players are, the only thing likely to save us is for your game to unite the people of this country. Somehow… get them to stop hating each other. My theory is that the enemy is attacking through propaganda warfare and is camouflaged behind the incendiary polarization of the people of this country. As long as we are pitted against each other, we can't fight *them*."

Andy and Brian got the gist of that. They looked at each other and smiled. James had seen that smile many times before, as these two partners seemed to have the ability to fix on a concept at the same time—a meeting of the minds. That expression "pitted against each other" would provide a major clue in the coming months. But today, it was just an off-the-cuff response of James Mikolas.

"Sorry, guys, that's all I got now."

Andy assured him. "It's fine, James. We can start. You let us know when you figure out who everybody is supposed to be united against. We can do the rest."

James exhaled, looked at the floor, and then said, "Now, here's the tough part." They all seemed focused on him, so he continued, "There will not be any communication by phone, text, email, nothing electronic." He stopped for the full import of that to sink in.

Bud was the first to understand. "Surveillance?"

"Yep, Bud. I think all of us need to assume that we are under 24/7 surveillance electronically. You probably won't be. But at this point, I have to assume the conspiracy is pervasive. In all likelihood, I will not be 'reading' anyone into this."

"How are you going to get info to us, James?" Bud asked.

"The age-old method used in the Mideast still today. By messenger. If our old friend Ayman Al-Zawahiri has used it for 20 years, and we still haven't found him, I can do the same. Bud, let me ask you. Is Walker News Group still up and credible?"

"Sure. Absolutely. If you get something, we will cover it. You just let me know when."

James nodded and then turned to Jessica. "Yours may be the most active part, Jessica." She cocked her head and shot him a look that said, "What are you getting me into, James?" To reassure her, he said, "Actually, it's your private plane I may need the most."

She let out a sigh of relief, laughed, and said, "No problem with that, James. You can use the plane anytime you need it, and as often."

"Good. Good. Moving around on private aircraft is a lot safer for me. No security check-ins, not so many cameras. But what I will need the most is Vince McCoy. Do you know where he is?"

Jessica did, in fact, know where the mercenary she had used as an extraction expert was. And she knew who was with him. The last time they had all been together had been when Vince, Hector Rodriguez, and Brian had successfully rescued Alicia and Reagan from a sex-trafficking/kidnapping gang in Venezuela. Perhaps, the most terrifying moments of her life had been waiting out that stealth raid, while at the same time praying that Andy's direct presentation to the President of the United States—of a solution for the world's leaders—would stop the global financial Armageddon that was to be unleashed from the Repository of International Transactions in Basel, Switzerland.

A consummate professional, Jessica knew Vince McCoy would likely want in on this, too. "They are in Venezuela. I don't know the mission. I just know he and Hector went there to surveil someone."

"Hector is with him?" James found that such an odd combination. Hector was a boy from Compton who had volunteered to help find the women, but who was truly a street kid."

"Oh, yeah!" Brian explained. "He and Vince partnered up after you last saw them. Man, who knew Hector had 'skills?'" He laughed.

"What?"

"Turns out Hector's not just a gamer. Right, Andy?"

Andy nodded.

James had no idea what they were talking about. "What skills?"

Andy and Brian spoke almost simultaneously. "James, we'll let Vince explain it to you. But do you think Vince McCoy would take in a partner and risk his 'jobs' unless the guy was good at something specific?" The answer was obvious. He would not. *I wonder what the hell Vince determined Hector had an aptitude for?* James asked himself.

"But you think these are skills I might be able to use on this project?" he asked.

"Well, since it seems you don't even know yet, James, what the project is exactly, I don't know," Andy answered. "That's why you should work that out with Vince."

James knew he was just going to have to live with that mystery for a while. Turning to Jessica he asked, "Can you get them?"

"When do you need them?" Jessica asked.

"Damned if I know," James blurted. "I'm in a complete mystery on the timeline here. If only I knew what those three men had talked about…" He thought for a moment, calculating how long it would take to get home and to reach Ari. "I'd say a couple of weeks. If they can do it."

"I'll try, James." She added, "How do I reach you?"

James handed each of them a mailbox address in Arlington, Va. "I'll check it every Friday." Then he added, "If anything goes south, Bud, your sports editor will get a message for you. Reads, 'Hunting trip off.'"

The room fell silent as everyone introverted into their own thoughts about the content of James' note. He didn't want to leave. But every day he stayed west was a day he could not be pursuing the connection between Loren, Brannigan, and Ernst Schweiner. He shook hands all the way around, even with Reagan and Alicia, telling them to give the kiddos a kiss from him when they got up from their nap.

The two smiled and said they would. As James got in the car and started to back out, Andy ran up. "Good hunting, James."

"Thanks, Kid." *He's something, that kid. Let's just hope I can give him the material for one hell of a game!*

Driving straight through, James made the trip to a small motel in Arlington in three days' time. He was dead tired but eager to get into the hunt. So, he stopped by the franchise mailbox location a block away and opened his box. There was one envelope inside. Opening it, one page in block print read, "Brannigan and Loren headed to Dinkelsbühl, Germany. Reason unknown."

James drew a deep breath to buck himself up. *Damn, I hate being behind before I even start! Let's hope Ari's on top of them at least.*

He pocketed the note, returned to the small motel room, and crashed. All he remembered thinking before he passed out was *I'll figure this out tomorrow.*

CHAPTER SEVEN

*T*he medieval fortress town of Dinkelsbühl in the area of Germany known as Bavaria had never enjoyed a reputation for nefarious deeds or infamy, except perhaps in stories from the brothers Grimm, who lived and wrote in that area of the world. It is said to this day that elves and trolls inhabit the dark, lush woods throughout the area.

That, however, was not the reason the city is still surrounded by a moat and has a drawbridge that is drawn up every night—sequestering the residents and visitors inside the walls, parapets, and towers of the old town. The town crier still walks the streets every night with his lantern, signaling the time and ensuring the safety of those secured inside. In the daytime, children still play on the wall that encircles the city, reenacting in their fantasy battles between knights and dragons and scenes of knights protecting the fair damsels they loved.

The streets are still cobblestone pavers, and the town winds up a hill with slight switchbacks to make climbing a little easier. Rows of attached houses from medieval times are in remarkable restoration. All with four to five stories and steep roofs that drop nearly three of those stories, each house has been painted a different and vibrant pastel color. Most of the windows are adorned with window boxes overflowing with seasonal, colorful flowers. A day in Dinkelsbühl is like a day inside a rainbow.

There are shops, hotels, and restaurants renowned throughout the region for their wares and extraordinarily sophisticated and savory cuisine. One cannot go wrong visiting this town and enjoying a step back into another time, a time of romance and chivalry.

But, for some men, it was a sanctuary of perfidy—the place they came to secretly plot the final victory over the inferior underlings that populated the Earth. These were men of destiny, as far as they were concerned. Born superior and privileged, it had been their life's mission to set this world straight and bring the order needed to launch into a new world.

It was a world few of us could even imagine, let alone bring into existence. If we did conceive of it, we would flinch and retreat from it. But not this group. The man at the helm had other cohorts. There were others who enjoyed a seat at the table with him, but as he had grown older and smarter, he recognized he would need allies that were unique to the 21st century if he was going to render the governments of Earth and their sovereign nations powerless. So, he was inviting a new team to sit at the table.

The inescapable charm of this medieval town was a great camouflage for the devastation that would be unleashed from behind its walls in the coming months—with the town crier having not even a scintilla of awareness of what had been loosed. It would occur among the laughter and singing at biergartens, among classical piano at the elegant restaurants, over the raucous laughter of children, and in the quiet of night as the town's gas lanterns turned on at dusk and the bell of the crier could be heard tinkling as he strolled reassuringly through the narrow streets and through ancient arches.

The first auto to arrive was a saffron yellow Citroen. The car had a driver only and had left Amalfi, Italy, the day before. There was nothing remarkable about the vehicle or its driver, except that he came out of a magnificent villa set up in the hills overlooking the Amalfi coast, not far from Portofino. Clearly, the driver liked speed and was familiar with the winding coastal road. He had made it past Lake Como and into the Swiss side of the Alps before he had stopped for the night. He did not seek an expensive hotel, but rather an ordinary hotel in an ordinary town. There was nothing ordinary about the man, however.

He was Serge Pilaf, and he owned and controlled the most powerful technology and internet platforms in the world. Whether it be search engines, web browsers, or social media, it was all within his purview. Though still a young man by Ernst Schweiner's standards, his wealth made it possible for Pilaf to implement any type of assault he wanted against a competitor. And he was clearly smarter than—and out of the reach of—regulatory agencies in any country, including the United States.

The Citroen crossed over the drawbridge just before it was being raised for the night. It was dusk, and the lights were now on in the town.

Driving to an older private residence on the far side, near the north wall of Dinkelsbühl, he could see its five stories of pale pink and the tower it seemed to be attached to. Remembering the directions relayed to him, he knew he was at the right place when he spotted the illuminated clock at the top of the tower.

The house had a large arch on the first floor, wide enough for cars, so he drove easily into the arch, disappearing into the shadows. "Mr. Pilaf, we have been expecting you," a doorman said, retrieving Pilaf's bags from the trunk.

"Thank you. I am glad to be here." Handing the man a generous tip, he added, "It's been a long day. Is there room service of any kind?"

"Most definitely, sir. I am fairly new here, but Herr Schweiner has a chef on hand at all times. You may consider him at your service." Pilaf smiled and thanked the man.

He did not notice the tourist who was descending the steps that led to the parapet and ramparts. That man had arrived in Dinkelsbühl earlier that day and would become a fixture in the town for the summer.

Just before Ari Ben-Gurion dispatched the letter James Mikolas would find in his mailbox about the whereabouts of Brannigan and Loren, he placed a call to his man in Dinkelsbühl. Right when Aaron Alon was preparing to walk over to the house from his modest room near the center of town, he received the call. The boarding house with utility apartments allowed each tenant to have a phone in their room. They were land lines, not cellphones, and the owner of the house was almost apologetic for not being more up with the times and technology. For Aaron Alon, however, the land line was perfect. He was part of the Israeli intelligence agency, Mossad, and they had had interest in this particular house for some time.

His partner, Ari Ben-Gurion, was on the phone. "Aaron, Schmidt flew in from JFK to Zurich this morning. Loren and Brannigan arrived just now from Dulles. They rented two different Audis, one blue, one green. Schmidt is driving the blue, and Loren and Brannigan appear to be sharing the green. They are driving north along the lake."

Aaron digested that for just a second. Knowing that Ari was in the United States, he asked, "Is someone following them if they leave Switzerland?"

"No. One of our team spotted them at the airport and are following only as far as the border. If they cross over near Lake Constance, I know where they are headed."

"To me?"

"Yes. You should encounter them later in the day—if Dinkelsbühl is the destination."

"Understood. I have been exploring the town and definitely have eyes on the house and tower."

Neither used any of their affectionate Hebrew salutations. Ari merely said, "Good, good, I am glad I was able to alert you. Aaron, two of them are dangerous, you know?"

Aaron nodded, though his friend could not see it. "Yes, I know. If your analysis is correct, we have two information warriors traveling together. Should be interesting."

Ari paused, then added, "Keep your distance, Aaron. Brannigan, for sure, will recognize anyone he sees more than once—especially in a non sequitur location."

"Yeah, I understand. Loren, too, you think?"

"Yes. Consider them combatants. I am not sure my American friend is convinced of that yet. But they earned an invitation, didn't they?"

With that, they hung up, and Ari sent the letter to James Mikolas' mailbox.

CHAPTER EIGHT

*E*ach man came down to a drawing room that featured a side credenza stocked with a coffee urn, tea pots, exotic tea choices, croissants, jams, jellies, and yogurt. *Typical European light breakfast,* Brannigan thought. *Certainly hope I can get out for a brat, potatoes, and something sturdier.*

However, before he could do any more silent complaining, his attention was drawn to a photo wall. Holding his coffee cup and pretending to be casually walking around with it, he strolled over to the wall and began to look at the photos. They seemed to be laid out in somewhat of a chronological order, with a recent picture of Ernst Schweiner and the current head of the Global Wellness Organization, known as the GWO. Brannigan knew for a fact from intelligence data he personally had reviewed over the years that the GWO was involved in many of the control mechanisms that had been set in place in Europe—and most definitely was involved with the recent pandemic.

It was a series of photos in the middle of the wall that pulled his attention, however. They seemed innocuous scenes of the house, life in the town, and the surrounding countryside taken in the late 1930s and early 1940s. Nazi flags and symbols of the Reich adorned the town square, and many vehicles parked inside the town's walls bore the flags of the German military. *Not surprising though that the Nazis were here. Bavaria was one of their starting points.* Still, he felt it odd that Schweiner would have chosen to commemorate it, including the house they were staying in now. *I guessed that all along about him,* Brannigan thought. *He's an economist and his insistence on a global partnership of government and big corporations felt like a 21ˢᵗ-century version of the definition of fascism.*

Brannigan was interrupted, however, by the entrance of Rutger Schmidt and Ernst Schweiner. "Good morning, gentlemen, welcome to my home—or I should say my family home!" Peter Loren and Serge Pilaf set down their plates and moved to greet Schweiner. Brannigan, too, turned away from the wall, following the other men. It had not escaped Schweiner, however, that Brannigan was surveilling the room.

"I trust you all had a good night's rest in our quiet Dinkelsbühl," he fawned a bit. "You'll have time to explore some of its fascinating elements later, and perhaps I will be able to even show you some of its secrets."

None of the men knew quite what to make of that, but it was, in fact, Ernst Schweiner's party, and they were there at his invitation. So, they simply smiled. Schweiner waved his arm about as if to encourage them to take in the room and its furnishings. "I lived here as a young boy, and I couldn't bear to part with it. It holds a lot of the heritage of my country and is a harbinger of things to come. You can see it dates back considerably."

Indeed, it did. The house itself was probably 200 or more years old, with restorations and updates over the centuries, so today, it was a comfortable place to reside, or at least to visit. The walls had rich woods as wainscoting. Above were tapestries woven with coats of arms of past generations in his family. There was even the clichéd standing armor and helmet that some ancestor no doubt had worn in one of Germany's many skirmishes for territory.

In the center of the room, near where Brannigan had wandered to observe the photo wall, was a commanding oval table. It was solid mahogany wood, with thick, carved legs that were not just at the ends, but spaced about three feet apart under the table. They were undoubtedly holding up a very heavy piece of wood. There were eight seats at the table and still room for more.

Loren's mind was racing in anticipation of the imminent meeting. He almost had to pinch himself to be certain he was even in the room. For 10 years now, he had been simply following through on the plans and instructions of his mentor, Samir Taghavi. His mission was to undermine completely the American free press. That was one of the institutions the United States and its citizens revered the most and relied upon almost exclusively for information in order to govern. Taghavi had learned how to manipulate the minds of others from perhaps the best and most creative propaganda and information warfare master in the world, Ayman Al-Zawahiri.

No one in this room knew of Taghavi's real identity as the propaganda chief for Al Qaeda, let alone his close relationship and guidance by the man who intended to implement a remote mind control on the whole of the American people. Taghavi had been discovered and eventually killed, but not before his student, masquerading as the head of a public relations firm specializing in public policy organizations and the steering of influence, had mastered the trade himself. Peter Loren was a Black Propaganda warrior of the highest rank and skill, and his primary client was an organization whose daily briefings to every major news outlet and to members of Congress and their staffs had driven every headline from 2016 to the present. Remaining in the shadows, his skillful implanting of lies, diversions, misdirections, and misinterpretations of data had rendered the U.S. media uncredible.

Loren knew that much of the material provided to his client, the Democracy Preservation Project, had been given to him by the intelligence community, where it would be concealed in a maze of hidden communications. Not until the meeting at the Lincoln Memorial, however, did he realize that the clearinghouse for all of the disinformation he himself had helped distribute was John Brannigan. *He's a stealth operator working right out in the open now—boldly,* he thought. And that could only mean that Brannigan must feel it was safe to do so.

Peter Loren did not trust John Brannigan. It was a mistrust well placed, as time would reveal. But for today, he was relieved to have been chosen and eager to hear what Schweiner had in mind for the future.

Pilaf was unusually subdued. Normally brash and loud—despite his appearance as almost a latter-day Howard Hughes—he had learned long ago to just shut up and listen when in a new environment. That skill, coupled with his brilliant mind and visionary capability to create technologies that could lead the world, had served him well.

Just as Schweiner took his seat at one end of the oval table, and Schmidt at the other, two other men entered the room. Everyone recognized Cedric Cornell, one of the directors of the GWO, but Schweiner made the introductions anyway. He also took great pains to introduce a man the three newcomers did not know. A bookish, yet elegant-looking man, he was introduced as the head of Decu-Hehiz, a Swiss pharmaceutical company specializing in psychiatric medications. The two looked like they belonged together. Both had round bodies, round, slightly balding heads, and round spectacles. There was indeed a connection between global wellness and Big Pharma, and these two could be poster children for that alliance.

"All right, gentlemen," Schweiner began, "if you have had enough repast, let us get right down to business." Each man took the seat designated by his place card. "You all have been chosen for leadership. You three," he said, pointing to the newcomers, "have been given a seat at the table. The other members—and they are numerous—you will meet in more public forums. They are representatives of relevant governments and global commerce in Big Tech, Big Business. Some are from the most prestigious and historical families in Europe today. They have their part to play."

He paused to make certain he had everyone's attention. Satisfied, he then said, "But you here will be the vanguard. You are the chosen ones who will bring about the 'Great Reset.'" Those simple words, spoken with no more emotion than one would have demonstrated while planning a neighborhood barbecue, were about to change the direction of the entire world and the course of history.

Schweiner leaned back in his chair, crossed his legs as he often did when taking the stage in a forum somewhere on Earth. As a renowned economist and thinker, he was a highly sought-after keynote speaker among the world's intellectuals and elites. He knew he had to lay this out today, in outline at least, so that the plan could be refined and ultimately triggered.

"I want to get right to the point, gentlemen. There is no time to waste, certainly no longer time for delay. It is time for us to set this planet right and put all of humanity in the desired position of being governed by those most suited." Ernst Schweiner had a noticeable habit of tilting his head back and up slightly, forcing him to look down the bridge of his nose in order to talk with those around him. It gave him an imperious demeanor. Rather like an emperor, he peered downward at people—even at these men he had chosen and, in many cases, had even groomed.

"Time is short. Action is needed now," he said.

"And why is that, Ernst?" Cedric Cornell abruptly interrupted.

Schweiner breathed in through his nostrils, smiled slightly, and turned very slowly toward the man.

"Well, there is a much greater sense of urgency in the last four years than ever before. Our plans have been materializing, the world changes we desired have been occurring, but something changed. You ask why *now*, Cedric? Our age, plain and simple. Look at us." He waved his hand magnanimously in the direction of each man at the table, as if he were putting them on display.

"With the exception of Pilaf, Loren, and Rutger here, we are in our 80s or, if I am generous with some of you, our 70s. And that means that if this mission is to be carried out according to our vision, it needs to be done now." It was true. The men at the table were, in fact, aging out. They had worked their whole lives for this moment, this seat at this table, and all were far nearer the end of their lives than the beginning.

Then, realizing that statement might be somewhat offensive to the newcomers, he explained. "It's not that we do not have the second team in place. We do. You all are around 40 and can clearly carry on for another 40 years. But your motives may be different from ours. They might not be as 'pure,' if you will." Watching each man closely, he saw that, though they were quiet, all were listening. No one moved, and no one challenged. *Sehr gut, that is how it should be,* he thought.

"You will undoubtedly be able to carry through technologically. I have no doubt of that. But it is my desire that you understand *why* we are compelled to do this and that you *feel* my passion—and the passion of the others as well." If any of the men had had a sense of humor, they would have laughed at the incongruity of that statement delivered with a complete dead pan expression. Ernst Schweiner may have been a brilliant engineer and economist, and he may have created a pervasive and menacing organization, but he was not known to possess much emotional range. Other than his somewhat supercilious attitude and arrogant demeanor, he would have fit into any polite company at a prestigious university.

"No, this reset needs to be done—according to my vision—and it needs to be done now! We are almost there, my friends. You can feel it. People are racing headlong into technology, into virtual reality more than reality, embracing digital monitoring, and surveillance of nearly every aspect of their lives. They have been almost anesthetized by popular culture and drugs, and the millennial generation is ripe for the taking. They cannot think, and they are just now reaching for *us*—happy that we will do their thinking for them."

"Then, why the urgency, Ernst?" Cornell still pressed. "I must be missing something."

"It's those damned Brits and Americans! They are fouling everything up! The Americans more than the Brits, but the people of those countries have been a thorn in the side of the world order we would like to see for as long as I can remember. When I was a boy, I saw this stubborn, independent spirit of 'those people' literally prevent us from bringing about a higher state of man."

The men at the table were quiet, surprised by this uncharacteristic outburst and not quite certain where he was headed. Except for Brannigan. He knew. The last five years in the United States had indeed been a handful for him, too. No matter what brilliant piece of disinformation and sinister conspiracies he concocted and sold to the press and to government, the American people seemed to be choking on it, instead of swallowing it easily.

Brannigan must have nodded because Ernst leaned forward and said, "You know what I am talking about, don't you, John?"

"Yes, I think I do."

"At first, I thought it was just that American leader, and I could not discern why on Earth any of them would follow him. We expected to take him down quickly, did we not, John?

That's a dangerous admission he's eliciting from me, Brannigan thought. *But I'm here, aren't I? Safe, I think.* He answered, "Yes, I thought it would be simple. But I misjudged, gentlemen. I should have known when Brexit won in the United Kingdom that something was happening."

"Exactly!" Schweiner said with considerable animation now. That animation got everyone's attention.

"We *all* missed it. True, we were able to stall the British prime minister, until that delay aggravated the Brits and they picked someone even worse." He spat it out, as if he were clearing his pallet of something distasteful. "But those damned Americans. Who could have known that they would revert so quickly, and so fiercely, to their self-reliance and individuality? Instead of being controlled by *us*, spouting *our* 'message,' they went back to their 'rule of law and equality for all' stronghold. Sickening…We had wrested them away from their Constitution, and their Founders, with education!"

Ernst rose and refreshed his tea with some additional hot water, then came back to the table. "So, we must neutralize the people of the United States. Hear me on this. I am not talking about the government. I am talking about that rabble that keeps insisting they know better and should govern themselves. Once we have rendered them impotent, we will be able to govern and proceed to that glorious moment when we can create our transhuman, our superman!"

It was quiet in the room. Each man was examining the reality that the American people in the last four years had become unruly, demanding freedom and opportunity. For those older in the room, the Americans of today resembled all too closely the generation of Americans that had crossed the ocean and defeated the most powerful military and political machine ever created. Ernst Schweiner had despised them then and thought he had covertly vanquished them. Yet, something had changed, and he knew he had to destroy that change.

Loren, oddly, broke the silence. "Strategically, I can add, if I may, that all we have to do to render the Americans impotent is to do what an early mentor of mine taught me. The truth is, if you try to force the Americans to agree with you, to submit and let you control them, they will never do it. You punch an American in the face, he punches back. Surely, we have seen that in the last decades. And we all had to watch that with their former president."

Schweiner encouraged him to continue. "No, you must get the American to choose—on his own—your control. If he chooses it, he will not resist. And that is in the purview of myself and Brannigan for sure."

Ernst smiled, *I was right. Right to pick this one.* "And that, Peter, is why you have a seat at the table. This war, my friends, will be an information war. And he who controls the information controls the world." Turning to include Serge Pilaf, he smiled and said, "And that, Serge, is also why you are here."

Though the men appeared somber and reflective, there was the feeling of an undercurrent of exhilaration. While their countries' scientists worked with capitalist funding to develop enticing and opportunity-opening transformation of humans and machines, the information war that would enable the new superman to emerge was winnable.

They all knew it. They were closer than they thought. Schweiner was perhaps the most exuberant, for he knew now he had the right men in the right places—and the time was now. The end of United States' global domination was at hand.

Deciding to delay giving the men their "marching orders" for a while longer, he said, "Gentlemen, how about a stroll along the wall and the moat? I think the air will refresh us all, and there is a charming wine house that is just bringing in the May wines. Let me be the first to introduce you to one of Germany's great traditions."

As they exited the house like ducklings following their mother, a tourist on the steps of the wall's rampart stepped aside, smiling. At the foot of the stairs, he took one last photo of the lush green area and managed to get all of the men in the photo as well.

CHAPTER NINE

James had received a message in his hotel room in Washington to meet Ari at the Mayflower Hotel. Deciding that it would be best to attack this enemy from behind enemy lines, James had taken a room at one of the newer hotels near Capitol Hill. It had not been difficult to reserve. If anyone had wanted to deliberately decimate the city, tourism, and the Washington, D.C. economy, the events of the last 18 months had been perfect for the task.

Jessica had come through as the investor she had always been on projects involving James, Brian, and Andy. Though James himself did not have money that would have afforded a prolonged stay in the District, and basically just had what any government employee's retirement benefits would be, the generosity and bankrolling of this operation by Jessica Ranger were much appreciated.

She had placed an ample amount of money into his North Carolina bank, in a reserve account. In her line of work, she had come to be circumspect. She knew he would need funds, but those funds needed to appear as if they were his own money—socked away during his years of service. It was plausible, for James Mikolas had never married. He had no children. He lived a modest life. It was believable that he had merely hoarded the money. The old Mustang that he refused to let go of added an even greater air of authenticity to his being a money saver, not a spender.

As he walked from his hotel to the Mayflower, that oppressive gloom and heaviness he had experienced before was palpable once again. *I wonder if Ari has word from his man in Germany. Who is there? How deep does this go?* He had many questions and was grateful to have received a summons from his friend. It would relieve some of the suspense. James did not like being on the sidelines, never had. He was an action man who was smart enough, though, to know not to take action until you knew the situation and had a plan. He hoped Ari would be able to help with both.

Ari Ben-Gurion did indeed have information on what was transpiring in the Bavarian Alps, and more importantly, he had vital information on Peter Loren. Ari was not hard to locate. Ben-Gurion was seated in the restaurant, facing the entrance. He was focused on the éclair the waiter had placed on the table and did not notice James until he was standing in front of him.

"James, James, please sit down. I have much to share with you."

"Are you talking about your pastry, Ari?" James joked.

"Hah! Not likely!" Ari grinned. "Something much better."

"Good, but first, may I ask you something?"

"Of course. What?"

"Do you ever eat healthy?" James teased.

"Always, my friend, always. A Mediterranean diet is very healthy. So, these are my little indulgences whenever I am in the States. And no matter how much you rag on me, I am not surrendering that right!"

James relaxed and sat back in his chair, looking admiringly at this counterpart, who had always been there for him. He was grateful to Ari and hoped he could repay him someday, in some significant way. That wish would be fulfilled, but James had no way of knowing about it now.

"You know, Ari, this is my first time in this hotel," he said as he looked around the restaurant and out through the magnificent glass partitions to the lobby. There was an old-world grandeur coupled with a modern elegance in the main floor layout. "Most in Washington refer to it like President Truman did, 'the second-best address after the White House.' I know a lot of shenanigans have gone on here over the years…"

Ari nodded. "But for us, James, this restaurant is best known for power lunches and for being the watering hole of politicians. I have information for you, but I want to begin to establish a presence here. Don't want to seem like a tourist, you know."

At that moment, the waiter noticed that another gentleman had sat down with his guest, and he approached the table with two leatherbound menus, one for wine and cocktails, the other for lunch. James accepted it graciously and asked the young man if there were any specials today. "Yes, sir, they are printed on the removable page in the center of the menu."

"Thank you. Give me a moment to look. And in the meantime, a gin and tonic."

"I didn't know you were a lunch drinker, James," Ari observed.

"Not typically, no. But if we are establishing a presence here, I want to fit in, not stand out." Looking at the menu, he selected a sole dish with white grapes and almonds, then handed both menus to the waiter when he returned with the drink.

"Well, here's to the game, Ari!" James raised his glass to toast. Ari, having no drink except a glass teacup, raised it to the toast.

"And to victory, my friend."

About 30 minutes later, when James had finished eating, Ari explained to the waiter that he could clear the table and that they would be talking for a while. For the waiter, that was the signal that another one of the myriad power lunches he had observed was about to begin. And it was certainly his clue not to disturb the two men.

When he was out of earshot, Ari came straight in. "I believe I have the source haven for your Mr. Peter Loren. His company's main client—and for all we know, his firm's only client—is the Democracy Preservation Project. He moves in many circles, but all the circles overlap, and this one organization provides security and anonymity for Peter—and all others who play games of deception in order to take control."

Wiping his mouth and placing the napkin on the table, James leaned in slightly to be able to hear everything, without requiring Ari to speak too loudly. He had pulled out his small notepad, and leaning in concealed the pad somewhat in case he wanted to take notes.

"The project started in 2017, founded by a Congressional aide who apparently got tired of the political games and the nauseatingly slow process of change through government. He sped up the results considerably. Basically, James, the DPP feeds information/disinformation about investigations and dirt to the national media and to Congressional investigators—the folks members of Congress rely upon and trust to give them accurate information so they can fulfill their Constitutional duties. At least that's what these dupes think."

"That's sobering from our perspective, isn't it?"

"Oh, and the DPP also briefs federal law enforcement. We have confirmed that the briefings are daily."

"Garbage in, garbage out…" James' voice trailed off as he grasped the power that a central disinformation agency would have. "And Loren? Is he part of that group?"

"No, he is not. But you will find him camouflaged in the world of the project's founder. He's the public relations guy for the project—an outside consultant, if you will. He's the spin guy, and he will be in the shadows, hiding in plain sight, much like our Paris 'friend,' Samir Taghavi."

James took a long sip of his gin and tonic and said, "So, information comes to the Project. He spins it for their purposes and attack lines and directs them where to 'release' the lies—who to target. And he creates the marketing buttons so that the recipient can't resist embracing the information. Well, that certainly speeds up the distribution process, doesn't it?"

Ari nodded. James continued, "So, simultaneously, each day federal law enforcement, Congressional staff, and all major media are receiving the same lie at the same time, packaged in the same language." James stopped, but he was definitely thinking with this. Suddenly, he laughed, "Well, that certainly explains why all these news outlets sound like parrots of one another!" James seemed to be thinking about something, so Ari waited. When James' attention returned to Ari, he continued. "Hard to believe the American free press is reduced to basically being stenographers, taking dictation, printing it, and then mimeographing it for each other."

Looking at it further, he said, "So, he's the man who shaped the whole narrative of the last four years. He's smart enough to know human nature and that the various individuals could be counted on to perform according to their own personal ambitions and objectives."

"He's one dangerous operator, James, a real credit to his mentor. And a real problem for us."

"If Samir Taghavi was his mentor, then indirectly Ayman Al-Zawahiri is also. Do you think Zawahiri is involved?" James asked.

"I don't know. It doesn't matter at this point, though. This problem is real, and it is *here*." Ari let that sink in. Both knew the situation had morphed into something far bigger than the machinations of an Al Qaeda terrorist. He added, "There are a lot of vested interests here, James. A lot of people are benefiting: global corporations, politicians, governments, Wall Street, China…this is big."

James said nothing. He simply nodded.

"One last question. What is Brannigan's role in the Project? Do you know?"

"Yes," Ari sighed. "And that is why I called you here."

"All right, let me have it."

"Brannigan creates the story, sets the tentacles for its expansion, leaks the story through 'anonymous sources,' and then—using his credibility within the U.S. intelligence community—he takes it to the DPP. He, of course, has 'clean hands.' He has the tools to make stuff up whole cloth, disguising it so well, it appears authentic."

"That's quite a tangled web, Ari," James' voice exposed a level of dejection.

"James, you and I have lived inside this game our whole lives. We know Information War is deception."

"For sure, but it's disheartening when it's coming from inside our own group!"

Ari reached across the table and patted James on the arm. "My friend, one thing my country's intelligence team knows—which enabled us to find this information for you—is that it is *always* an inside job. And we have had *all* of your top intelligence people under watch for years."

"I don't know whether that is comforting or not. Israel watching…all politically necessary, I expect."

"Yes."

James noticed that his heart was racing now, though, and that was the familiar sign that he was over the target. "I don't suppose you have some good news for me, do you?"

Ari broke into a grin. "As a matter of fact, I do. Brannigan, Loren, and Serge Pilaf are all still over in that medieval city in Germany. They have been joined by Schweiner, Schmidt, and two others you will be interested in. One of the directors of the GWO and the president of a Swiss pharmaceutical company. They may be expecting someone else. We don't know. Whatever, their parley continues."

"OK, OK, thank you." James was relieved to know he had a bit more time to establish a plan to intercept the three Americans at least. Preoccupied, he put only passing attention on Ari's comment that it is always an inside job. It would be some time before the possibilities of that would sink in, giving rise to a new theory—and, ultimately, to a path out for all Americans.

CHAPTER TEN

*B*rannigan was standing on the rampart, enjoying the early-morning air. As he scanned the forest out in front, he looked down at the moat, spotting Peter Loren sitting on a bench along the water. He appeared to be tossing something into the moat. *Ah, ducks,* he thought. *He's an unusual man, this Peter Loren.*

Glad that he had found Loren alone, he went down the stone steps near him and approached. "Good morning, Peter."

"Good morning." Motioning for Brannigan to sit, he offered him a piece of bread as if to allow him to feed the ducks as well.

"No, no, you go ahead," Brannigan demurred. "But I am glad to be able to talk with you a bit before we go into today's summons by Ernst."

Loren said nothing. He just turned and looked at Brannigan. "I wanted to tell you, Peter, that you are the best I have ever seen in my years. I've known a lot of information warfare people, propaganda experts…it's part of my trade. But your work in the United States over the last five years is stunning."

Loren smiled and said, "Thank you. It was fairly simple actually, given the data, and especially the corrupted data, you provided." He laughed. "Though, I must say I wasn't totally sure who was getting the information to the DPP. I surmised it had to be someone inside, with deep connections, who could navigate the web of intersecting agencies. I guessed it might be someone providing it to you, then you filtered it and selected what you knew to use."

Brannigan nodded. "Yeah, no question being formerly at the top of the intelligence clearinghouses, and having access to counterparts in the UK and Australia, helped. It's also a lot easier when the United States has so many intelligence agencies that the right hand doesn't always know what the left hand is doing. A lot of turf war possibilities, if one plays his cards right."

"Seems that way." Loren hesitated for a moment, then added, "Well, it appears you played yours right. After all, here we are in Dinkelsbühl."

Brannigan knew their private time might be short, so he dove right in. "Strategically, what I saw you do—and which I admired by the way, not even knowing who you were—was this. We fed data to the project, some true, some false. And then I would see that data—if true—perverted. You flipped the evaluation of the data. Things worthy of criticism you praised and things worthy of praise you criticized—at the same time, using an emotional tone guaranteed to incite or inflame. The false information we supplied I saw embraced as true and distributed without question." Considering it even more, he continued, "And it wasn't just one news distribution outlet. It was all of them simultaneously. You created competition, and they did all the dirty work for us."

"Exactly. The key for me was to get the same message repeated over and over again at once so as to impinge upon the public." Loren stopped and then laughed. "Kind of a perverse brand-name exposure."

"So, where did you learn to do that?"

Loren saw no reason to be cagey. He suspected that Brannigan might know something of his background anyway and was testing him. "I had a very good teacher, in Paris."

Peter watched Brannigan scrutinize him, so he knew he had to provide more. "Samir Taghavi owned a public relations firm in Paris. My staff and I handled a myriad of clients in finance, advertising, hospitality—basic PR stuff. Advertising, of course. But I learned strategies from Samir. Ironically, most of them he taught me defensively, so that we could protect our clients from the Black Propaganda that gets spread in the compete-and-destroy world of business. Seeing that the strategies worked to defend our clients, I personally realized they could be deployed in the reverse as an offensive tactic."

"That makes sense. Intelligence/counterintelligence…it's just a question of motive, objective."

Loren nodded in complete agreement. "Well, through the years, it became necessary to engage in offensive propaganda against one of our client's competitors. Turns out we were good at it."

"Lots of people are good at that. What was different about you?"

"We were just skillful at the manipulation to the point the recipient didn't realize the false information, but even more importantly, didn't spot how it was compromising their reason, spurring on emotion. People don't make good decisions through emotions. So, we were just good at subtle but powerful mind manipulation. Emotion, you know…"

"And Taghavi knew all this." It wasn't said as a question, but rather a confirmation. Secretly, Brannigan knew that the PR team for Al Qaeda was masterful and, in his opinion, over the years had cleaned our clock in the world of Black Propaganda. He himself liked that field the best since it involved the spreading of lies to harm or destroy people and organizations.

"Yes. For me, John, certain basic strategies are paramount. Tactics may change, but the strategies are constant in my approach. Whether the target be a business competitor or, in recent years, a political opponent. What I added to the mix in the United States was this. I just wantonly prey upon the base emotion of fear. I work with the biases I know people have, and I get them to hate. Hate is a powerful tool. Frozen in hate, one's reason is easily overcome. My specialty is 'stimulus-response' PR, anchored on hate." It was said with complete dispassion, no moral assessment whatsoever.

Brannigan seemed to be enjoying this "shop talk," so Peter added, "You're an information warrior, John. It's all about divide and conquer, the big tactic there being a lie told often enough becomes the truth. And even better, the truth so outrageous it can be made to be dismissed as a lie. That's the big one." Loren was smiling now. "Yep, that's the one that makes it almost impossible to disentangle the pile of lies and distortions. Even if someone figures out the truth, as soon as they articulate it, it is easy to discredit them, knock them down, and, in doing so, knock down the truth." Loren was proud of his recent work and decided to tout it. "You take the political scene in D.C. these days. Truth is surfacing and being revealed, but we equate it to domestic terrorism, and the salivating media cancels the truth. The truth is now a lie. And the public absorbs it."

Looking at the surroundings, John commented, "Well, those strategies and tactics didn't get created here, but they certainly were embraced in this area of the world. And used."

"It's elementary, actually, isn't it, John? The Trojan Horse of coming as a friend, and then implanting something that will destroy from within, is no new military strategy. What is different is the information technology of today that makes it almost completely certain I can overwhelm reason with too much data. And what Samir taught me was that once one source embraces the false data, let's say, other lazier sources just copy it.

Invited plagiarism, if you will. I just knew enough to exploit the greed and laziness of the competition. Simple, actually. My goal was always to help the DPP destroy the targets they selected, using the information that—I know now—was coming from *you*."

Neither man spoke for a moment. Loren tossed the last of his bread to the insistent duck in front of him.

"Well, that creates somewhat of a symbiotic relationship between you and me, doesn't it, Peter?"

There was just a flicker of hesitation in Loren's answer, which did not go unnoticed by Brannigan. "Yes. Yes, I guess it does, John."

"We accomplished a lot, so let's keep it that way with whatever Ernst has in mind for us, all right? You and me, we need each other." Peter Loren did not know whether he was being subtly threatened by Brannigan or subtly propositioned. He didn't have to wait long though. Brannigan offhandedly added, as he rose to return to the inside of the walled town, "I met Samir Taghavi once."

Not waiting for Loren's response, he continued. "Yeah, at a ranch in Montana, many years ago. I was fly-fishing, doing some hunting. He was an invited guest of Bud Walker, head of Walker News Group. Do you know them?"

"Yes. Well, I know of them, at least. They're pretty hard to influence now. My mentor had a lot to do with the decline of that network back in the day, or so I am told."

"You were told right."

Where's he going with this? Peter asked himself. He felt uncomfortable being on the receiving end of what might be a veiled threat. That was his purview, and up to now, he had gone unchallenged.

"Interesting. The infamous Samir Taghavi was your mentor. Well, well, all I can say is that Al Qaeda always was better at propaganda than they were at fighting! Quite a coup your man pulled off. Yours is even greater. You took all the networks down. He must have been one hell of a teacher," Brannigan slapped him on the back.

Deciding to play this close to his vest now, Peter had not quite concluded whether Brannigan was friend or foe. "Like I said, John, the principles are the same. It's just a matter of who you work for. Who you are applying them for—or against."

Brannigan nodded, and the two made their way back to the meeting Ernst Schweiner had called for noon.

When Brannigan and Loren walked into the room they had been meeting in, Rutger greeted them and said, "Today, we are meeting in a somewhat more private area. Follow me, please." He led them through the kitchen and into the butler's pantry, opening a door masked by a large shelf of baking supplies. They proceeded through a short passage into a square room.

Brannigan realized this had to be the inside of the tower attached to the house. He had wondered what was in the tower and how one accessed it. That architectural feature of a large medieval home attached to a tower had caught his imagination upon his arrival the previous week.

The others were already there, seated in a room without windows, illuminated by huge hanging oil lights, and encased by thick, stone, unadorned walls. The room was stark and imposing. Brannigan and Loren sat next to Pilaf, who was his usual silent self. *No electronic surveillance possibilities in here,* Brannigan concluded. *This must be it, why we were summoned here.*

"Are we late?" Brannigan asked. "If so, my sincerest apologies for holding up anything."

"No, not at all. Rutger told me you two were spotted feeding ducks along the moat."

Peter responded first. "That was my doing, I'm afraid. Frankly, I had snuck a roll out this morning, planning to nibble on it myself, but I ran into a flock of ducks that were ravenous and insistent. John came along to give me support," he joked.

Everyone had a good laugh at their expense. Ernst Schweiner smiled, thinking, *So typically American!*

"Ach so, gentlemen. Let us begin what will be the meeting defining our mission from here forward. As you notice, we are in different quarters today." Everyone acknowledged comfortably. "That is done for your security, as well as mine. Nothing said here today leaves this room. It will not be discussed even with other members of the GCF when you meet them. Though 'players' in our little game, they are not privy to the longer, more imperative goals. You are. And that is why we are here."

The five men in that room, not counting Rutger Schmidt and Ernst Schweiner, were about to receive a mission that would transform life on planet Earth in almost unimaginable ways. Each had a role to play.

None knew that role yet. Each felt the trepidation soldiers feel as they are being given the mission, and the details of the mission, before a military engagement.

The plan was foolproof, except for one obstacle in its path. Just one. That obstacle had to be removed in order for Ernst Schweiner to implement the plan he had worked on for all the decades of his life. He believed these men, separately—and in concert—could achieve the final objective. He intended for it to occur while he lived. An old world was ending, a new one was beginning.

"The first day we convened, I explained some things to you about the sense of urgency and why there are no more decades to slowly simmer the frog. Today, I am going to take you to the next level—a higher level. I hope the 'altitude' doesn't sicken you." He laughed.

CHAPTER ELEVEN

*E*rnst Schweiner peered at his cohorts over his wire-rimmed glasses, tapping his fingers together as he pondered just how to begin. A kind-looking gentleman, his upper lip overlapped his lower one in the center, as if they were pursed. His superciliousness added to his appearance of looking down at people. All combined, it made him appear somewhat effete.

This Swiss elitist's presentation irritated John Brannigan. He was more of a ruffian, dressed up in suits for Congressional hearings or TV appearances, but a brawler, nonetheless. But he knew not to let appearances fool him, and his gut told him they were all about to encounter the *real* Ernst Schweiner—not the one economic forums around the world were used to. He was right.

"Other than the unacceptably large amount of death and destruction that came as a result of the thinkers of the Nazi era in my country of birth," Schweiner started, "there was a great deal to be said for the pursuit of a higher man, if you will." He paused for a moment as if examining a picture in his mind. "Yes, the vision of a super-human was something they pursued. Eugenics was just such an unacceptable way to achieve it. But the dream is still there, and advancements in science have now brought into reality—or near reality—the possibility of such a human. Gentlemen, this is an idea whose time has come."

"You have heard me speak about the fusion of our physical bodies with our digital selves. I've opined often on this subject." He paused to see if they got what he regarded as his little joke. Only Schmidt did, and he dutifully laughed to signal the others to follow suit. They did.

"But I wasn't dreaming, my friends. Brilliant men all over this world for decades now—each in his own field—have brought us to the brink of the greatest advancement in human evolution of all time. What happens next determines the rest of man's history. Today's the day for you to learn what I see and what your role will be in it."

Serge Pilaf leaned back in his chair now, turning his head to fully observe Schweiner. "Ready, Serge?" Ernst asked.

"Yes, most decidedly."

"We will witness a combining of robots, artificial intelligence, virtual reality, and humans in the imminent future. The incipient elements of it are being embraced whole-heartedly by the world's population, particularly the Americans. Notice how easily they embraced computer games, making them the favorite pastime in that country. Notice how that elevated into virtual reality goggles, where their own eyes are taking them into a different reality, one that becomes real to them, the more they wear them. Notice how the game of chasing a cute, animated figure out into the environment has engaged not just adults, but also all their children, in the act of literally stepping into a virtual world—actually, physically moving *their* bodies in a game created by others. Notice the full-on embracing of the artificial intelligence of named household assistants who perform tasks and answer questions. Notice the desire for robots. First, a simple little one to clean your house. Now, dogs for you to play with. And even robots that deliver medications in hospitals and tell jokes to entertain patients. I'm told they now have maître d robots, politely seating you at your table.

"Notice the headlong charge for self-driving vehicles, which remove the person from any responsibility for the motion or the consequences of that motion. Notice the acceptance of transgenderism without the blink of an eye—save for the wailing of religious types. Who can tell me why the speed of these technologies becoming commonplace is accelerating?"

"It's a marketing issue. The convenience of these things and the placement of one's ego in the realm of the progressive and advanced. The privileged." The answer was so swift and so certain that Brannigan's head snapped toward the man who had spoken. Peter Loren simply looked at Ernst Schweiner, paying no attention to the others.

"Brilliant, Peter, brilliant!" Schweiner always did love engaging with people of intellect who could also see a brighter future.

Ernst continued his tutorial. "You see, these are the preludes to a conflation of all of these technologies into a human being who is part robot, lives in virtual reality as well as reality, who relies upon the data and input of another intelligence to think and reason. In short, a trans-human, a superior being that has combined all the superior elements of these technologies. This human will be capable of not only controlling all other humans on Earth, but will also be capable of traversing the universe and becoming the dominant force wherever that trans-human engages. And the domination of the peoples of Earth, who are, in fact, inferior and incapable of making choices that allow for the welfare of all others, will be breathtakingly simple."

Pilaf involuntarily interrupted, "Whoever controls the data, and the information flow, controls the others."

"Exactly." Schweiner was becoming noticeably more excited. He seemed to savor every morsel of this almost sci-fi world picture he was painting. "Now, here is the problem, however."

He had the attention of everyone, even Brannigan, whose expertise was more in mind control, brainwashing, and some other more mundane types of cyber warfare. The one thing he could totally identify with, however, was the fact that whoever controlled the information could control the world. Nations could succumb in the face of digital subterfuge.

"It will be a few years before this amalgamation is fully implemented— and *accepted*. That's the key, to get the people to accept the very thing that renders them controllable. Without that, we cannot bring about the world of peace and stability that we desire. Mere humans have demonstrated throughout man's history that they cannot be trusted with their fellows."

"And we can?" Brannigan asked.

"Yes, John, yes. The men with a seat at the table can lead the world."

"And what is the problem, Ernst?" Rutger reminded his partner that his enthusiasm had caused him to drift off the trail somewhat.

"Thank you, Rutger," Ernst smiled at his colleague. "The *problem* is the Americans—a particular class of them. We need a few years. We had everything progressing swimmingly, until the Populist Movement in the United States. It threatens everything, frankly."

He heaved a deep sigh and continued, "At first, I thought it was coming from the reprobate the Americans elected as president. We brought everything we had to bring him down, and he did not fall. So, it took me quite some time to realize *he* was not the obstacle, really. He was a symbol of the obstacle. The obstacle is the American people themselves. Peter, do you follow?"

"Absolutely. The work I did was to covertly compromise the free press.

With that as a propaganda tool, under the direction—it appears—of our colleague to my right..." he nodded his head toward Brannigan. "And spun by me and targeted with laser precision at the mind, and at certain groups, there has been an erosion. But you are correct. There is a very large segment of that country who cling to this notion of self-reliance and independence. Consciously, or unconsciously, they will resist—in the long run—the world being ruled by us here today, let alone this 'trans-human' you are describing."

"I have a question," Cedric Cornell interjected. "Who is the one with a seat at the table who is responsible for bringing about the merging of all of this? You know, creating the new creature, if you will."

"No one at the table. It is not necessary. The people developing these technologies are brilliant in their own right, greedy in their own right, and arrogant in their own right. If getting a 'seat at the table' brings them more money and power, they may try for it. But right now, their game is the challenge of it in and of itself, as well as their wealth. I doubt they are putting attention on whether man will embrace the new superman. They are creating it simply because they can. But all of those corporations and their brain trusts are under the Big Tech umbrella, and that is the purview of Serge here!"

This seemed to put everyone at ease a bit. They were a little unnerved at something no one had brought up until now. Not Brannigan, however. "So, who is the seat at the table for—the empty chair we have all been looking at?" He pointed to an eighth chair, which was conspicuously empty.

"Aha! That is there in case we do need someone to help us make the final charge. All right with you, John?" The tone was menacing despite the saccharin smile.

"Yes, Ernst, this is your game. Far be it from me to tinker. I was just curious, that's all." That seemed to satisfy Ernst.

"So, my friends, how do we get 100 million Americans to submit? That is the question."

Again, Peter dove in. "You don't force them to it. Your birth country, Ernst, is evidence enough of that, I think. And recent politics. As I have mentioned before, I think, you don't ever hit an American directly in the face. You punch him, he will punch back. You simply get the American to choose it themselves. If the American chooses it, he is not submitting, he is embracing. Big difference in the American psyche."

"But are we not doing that already?" Pilaf asked.

"Yes, but the pace is too slow." Ernst responded.

"Well, then, if there is not time for enough Americans to willingly accept this shift in leadership to a new, evolved human, then you attack directly. Just don't punch him in the face." Peter's answer befuddled a few at the table, but not Pilaf.

"Peter's right," Pilaf said. "You do it covertly, not so much with mind control as Brannigan might lean toward. You do it with information. You cut them out. You block the flow of information, both directions. You block what Americans can see or learn about, and you block any ability they would have to communicate outbound, let alone organize themselves." He decided to drive his point home in order to establish the supremacy of the territory he was in charge of. "We did that on the infamous January 6 riot. The huge victory for us is not that there was a riot, and not that there was violence magnified and driven into the public psyche by John and Peter's teams, but the victory is something that went completely unnoticed. We successfully blocked the video from the President of the United States from reaching the people in a time of emergency. We held it for more than an hour—all justified."

Pilaf stopped to assess who might now see the importance of that. Then, he continued, "Think of it. Not the man. That's the distraction and manipulation my colleagues are expert at. Think of what the action represents. Think of the office itself. We successfully over-rode the authority of the *President of the United States*, and no one noticed. We made it impossible for the leader of the free world to communicate! And we did it with impunity."

"Thank you, Serge. I agree." Ernst said, retaking control of the meeting after that impassioned utterance by Serge. "We are going to take control by keeping half of the United States completely unaware, by the absence of information, and the other half completely impotent, even if aware. The two opposing realities will cause the Americans to destroy themselves."

"Violently?" Brannigan asked.

"Perhaps. That's up to them. But frankly, it is not necessary. Americans do not have to die. America does not have to burn. America does not have to die. It just has to be rendered impotent in the global game we are playing. Without that rugged individualism they espouse, we will prevail easily."

Rutger pointed to a clock on the wall, the signal for a little repast.

Ernst offered, "Let us adjourn for an hour or so, and when we reconvene, I would welcome your input on some strategies or ideas that you have. You know, not just the idea, but perhaps who walks point? Who is next in the sequence of events we are creating? Who or what is the fallback? What is your role? We'll game it out a bit in concept and see if it lines up with my vision. Good idea?" Each nodded.

The whole group seemed relieved to be out of the bunker-like environment inside the tower. Adjourning to the dining area, each remained a bit apart, occasionally conversing with one or more of his new colleagues. Given the magnitude of the plan, most frankly resorted to cocktail party chitchat to release some tension. An hour later, Ernst suggested they reconvene in the tower.

"Gentlemen, I trust you have been revived a bit by our mid-day meal and are ready to resume." Not even waiting for a response, he continued, "I do realize that you all have not likely collided in your professional arenas before, and it was my hope that by bringing you here to this private and totally secure facility—and giving you a few days together in this bucolic setting—you would get to know a little about each other before we deploy back to our own environments. Are you getting to know each other?"

"Well, I learned Peter likes to feed the ducks," Brannigan joked.

They all laughed at that earlier reference. The idea of those two feeding ducks was incongruous, given the gruesome nature of their work. And it brought levity to the table.

Peter didn't know whether to be embarrassed or not. Somehow, he didn't think that was exactly what Ernst had in mind with them "getting to know each other." But he was a good sport and said, looking at Brannigan, "That is so true, John. Given the chance, you will find me enjoying life's simple pleasures."

Peter then commented, "I learned that Serge is likely a very good poker player."

"Really, what makes you say that?" Serge responded.

"It's your poker face. In all the days, all the meetings, I have had no idea what you are thinking at any given moment." All of them seemed to connect with that observation. They nodded in a benign silence.

Ernst broke the silence. "What we are about to discuss is all going to happen simultaneously. *We* are going to have to attack from all directions at the same time and with all of our resources. This movement in the United States must not be allowed to expand. Quite the contrary, it must be destroyed. All the people involved must submit, and there is no time to lose." He paused for effect to let the solemnity of that statement settle in. "We have planned and worked for 70 years to bring about a better world. And though Peter and Serge here were not even born then, and have exploded into this arena with star quality, I personally will not see the mission fail."

It was quiet in the room. Each man now felt quite comfortable, for their own aspirations were in complete alignment with Ernst, and the opportunity to be the ruling class was within reach.

"We will use divide and conquer and get one group to conquer the other. Less messy and less expensive for us," Ernst said with the delight one has when placing a cherry on top of a Charlotte russe, creating a magnificent concoction.

There had not really been any debate. Though some mystery remained about the role of the "empty chair" in the room, the others knew what they were to accomplish.

"Cedric, you have done brilliant work with the pandemic. Frankly, you have kept everyone guessing, shifting gears, fearing each other, reviling each other, and suppressing the economies of all the major players that threaten us. The stunning twists and turns you and your Chinese and American compadres have created need to continue." Suddenly chuckling, Ernst added, "And the best is—the fact you are not even the head of the GWO gives plausible deniability to you and all your team.

The man nodded that they would continue. Ernst suddenly asked another question. "Are the Chinese prepared with something else in the event the world starts to right itself prematurely? We must keep people down, separated from each other, afraid of each other, and afraid of the future."

"Yes, they have several iterations of this weapon—which Peter has successfully promoted as 'variants'—and an additional one or two capable of being released, rendering the target of the virus incapable of avoiding its effects. I want you all to understand, though, that I have a personal distaste for biological warfare—too many things can go wrong. But the Chinese are invested and are very useful."

"Why is that?" Brannigan asked.

"What is it always about, John? Money, power…they have their own world vision, I would guess," Cedric responded.

"Can it compete with ours, thwart ours?" Brannigan continued.

"No, John, it can't." Ernst interjected abruptly. "We have ways of handling the Chinese if they get out of line." Ernst Schweiner was an extremely confident person, so confident in his own ability to lead that he did not notice Brannigan look down briefly, compose his face, and look back up. That oversight would cost him dearly.

Peter's explanation was the most involved because it involved several different military strategies turned into an information warfare arena. The most innovative—and, assuredly, the most dangerous—was to turn America's strengths into weaknesses. He paid particular attention to converting righteousness into self-righteousness because he knew what a person was capable of when on a self-righteous path and how vehemently and purely emotionally he would defend his actions.

Another was to use a long-standing propaganda tool, turned into an art form by Goebbels 80 years earlier: a lie told often enough becomes the truth. He had already achieved remarkable success with that one and had even bragged about it to Brannigan earlier that day.

And conversely, another in his portfolio of deception and misdirection was telling a truth that was so outrageous it would be dismissed as a lie because the hearer could not embrace the truth of it easily. Given man's natural mental laziness, it would be easier to dismiss a truth. And that would effectively stop any presentation of evidence that ran contrary to the story he would continue to implant.

"We have already succeeded in turning their precious free press into a propaganda instrument—basically worthless to the people, except as a way of inciting the people to disavow their other First Amendment rights. The strength of freedom of speech will be turned into weakness, as we define and control what is acceptable speech." Looking to Serge, Peter pointed a finger. "You will be the one to bring that about. You are now the arbiter of acceptable speech." Ernst was a little surprised at the independence Peter displayed in turning directly to Serge rather than to himself. He decided to let it go, for now.

Continuing, Peter said, "I will see to it that the message coming through on any platform you control is geared to engender the emotions of fear and hate. Then, you take it from there. You will naturally become the Minister of Truth." Peter smiled.

John Brannigan knew his role was to create such subterfuge and interconnecting false intelligence that all U.S. and foreign intelligence agencies would be befuddled. Each would be working on different theories and premises—his goal to sow confusion and make it almost impossible for any of them to interconnect data or the significance of that data. Moreover, it was his job to wholesale manufacture data that would smooth the way."

"It's evident, is it not, my friends, that Peter and John are going to carry the lion's share in the United States?" Ernst asked. "Serge, you correctly identified that you are assisting with the distribution with John's material once it has been taken by Peter and is ready for penetration into the public. The technology platforms—in all forms—are essential to the information reaching those targeted."

"*And* my ensuring that nothing reaches them that we do not want to reach them…" Serge added.

"Quite true. You are the fallback position. You are both the vanguard and the safeguard. Nothing is consumed by anyone on this planet without it passing through the Big Tech companies, whether they are wittingly or unwittingly doing your bidding." Serge nodded his complete agreement with Ernst. That degree of power was inflating, and Serge Pilaf seemed to virtually expand in size as he sat in his chair. What he had created technologically and business-wise was real. Now, he fully realized that what he had created was understood and being utilized in immense and important ways. Emboldened a bit, he sweetened the pot. "And once we have battened down all the hatches there, then my other companies that are creating the elements of the cyborg, the implants capable not only of reading one's mind, but also of dictating commands, the virtual reality implants—all of that—will be able to run unfettered."

"Exactly," Ernst added. "We will have turned the Americans' moralizing and talk of 'ethics' into muted babbling."

Clearly, Brannigan's role in creating false evidence, leaking that evidence, and providing ammunition to the DPP put that information indirectly into Peter's hand. In the coming months, the United States would suffer greatly from this unholy alliance. Divisiveness and diversion would rule. And Brannigan had one other ace that the others did not. He had blackmail folders on everyone who would be involved in this move against the United States.

Characteristically quiet, but nonetheless involved, was Cedric

Cornell. Ernst had complimented him on his victory in handling the virus. But there was more. He knew that one of the ways to get people acclimated to being controlled—and even desiring it—had been the restrictions placed upon them during the global pandemic of 2020. He had learned a great deal there, and he seemed to have been immune to any action by a country affected by his handling of the global issue. Plenty of people were angry with him. But none had successfully assailed him. He could clamp down the globe, if need be.

And I am one of only two here who can bring China to the table, he thought. *I wonder if they even know just how big a part China can play in this new world with its super humans?*

The role of the president of Decu-Hehiz was simple. Rudi Iseli was to be ready with any amount of psychiatric medications necessary to subdue a population that might become physically unruly. He had been down this path before and was personally grateful that his efforts had not only been noticed by Schweiner, but were also going to be rewarded. *After all, it's not like I am the only Swiss pharmaceutical company! Wonder why Ernst chose me?* There was a reason, but it would be some time before his role in super vaccines would be revealed to him, let alone the others.

"Well, well, well, this has certainly been productive!" Ernst exclaimed. "We are only beginning this full-on assault, but we can return to our normal lives and venues, I believe. You know what we are trying to accomplish and who is responsible for what. Do each of you have secure video-conferencing capability?" They all nodded. "Good, in the future we can do our planning using technology. It will not be necessary for us to be seen together. We live and work in our own arenas, right?" He smiled that supercilious smile. "I will signal our next meeting by a text to each of you, and Rutger will convey the conferencing information."

Continuing, he said, "Should anything untoward happen that compromises your operations, use this 'keep' as your fallback location. You all know how to get here. And you all know how to find this room. You would be safe here, if need be." A silence fell over the room, as the conspirators recognized the gravity of their plan. It had been talked about for eons, dreamed about by men through the centuries, and now—in this century—it would come about. The prospect of subjugating an entire world's population was daunting, but doable. It was time to leave.

Before they parted to head back to their respective missions, one question was raised by Pilaf. "I have to say, this is the most extensive, comprehensive, potentially volatile conspiracy one could imagine. This, frankly, is like either a sci-fi movie or a true vision of the future that can be. It crosses into corporations, governments, politicians, media, medicine, banking, education…all of it. How do we know that the various now-anonymous 'players' will play their part? Clearly, none of us can do this by ourselves. This is very deep and very broad."

Schweiner did not hesitate. He knew the answer to that question. He had always known it. It was what he was gambling on and why he knew he would very soon be leading a group of powerful individuals who would bring on man's evolution into the inevitable future. "That is simple, young man. They all want a seat at the table. That's the simplicity of it."

CHAPTER TWELVE

*T*he private jet lifted off from the airstrip near Ovando, Montana, shortly after sunrise. There was a beautiful opal sky over the Bob Marshall Wilderness that bordered Bud Walker's ranch. The flight manifest showed three passengers and a pilot, with a destination of Manassas, Virginia. A pre-Revolutionary War country estate just outside that small Civil War town had an airstrip on its back 100 acres sizeable enough to handle small jet traffic for wealthy travelers.

The jet belonged to Jessica Ranger, who had been the primary investor in a small gaming company called Carver & Weir. Wealthy in her own right, long before that investment, her wealth had increased massively as Brian Washington Carver and Andy Weir's company had become one of the most successful private ventures in that industry. More than money, though, her association with James Mikolas and "the boys," as he referred to them, had led to her reconnecting with and marrying Bud Walker, the now-retired owner of Walker News Group.

Today, she was escorting two of her "operators" to the Washington, D.C. area. James Mikolas had asked her to find these two and have them ready to assist him. Vince McCoy was a surprisingly effective mercenary, specializing in rescuing kidnap victims. His young associate, Hector Rodriguez, had volunteered to help on a rescue a decade earlier. His participation, though untrained, had led to a great success and to the rescue of Alicia Quixote and Reagan Lynch from a human-trafficking ring. Those two women were the future wives of Carver and Weir, respectively.

So, McCoy and Rodriguez enjoyed "family" privileges with all parties. McCoy was trusted implicitly by James Mikolas, and Rodriguez was trusted implicitly by Vince McCoy. And today, neither knew why they were on board—only that Mikolas had said he needed them. That was enough for McCoy.

"Jessica, did he give you the mission? Are you involved?"

"I am not involved, Vince," she answered. Then, reconsidering, she added, "Save for being an investor like always and supplying my plane as needed."

Vince was not satisfied with that but knew he would have to wait until they connected with Mikolas in D.C. A few hours later, they landed easily amid the lush green farmlands of Virginia. Exiting the plane, they were greeted only by a farmhand who tended the land and maintained the house. Guessing that this was an additional one of Jessica's properties, the two men accompanied her to the house. She settled them in and told them a letter from James had said he would talk with them that evening.

The three were sitting on the front porch of the old home, enjoying the evening air and the noise of crickets, when they saw headlights turn into the driveway and approach the house. They did not recognize the car, nor the driver, until James got out of the car and approached them. He smiled but was overall very subdued.

"Thank you for coming, Vince," he said, shaking his hand. Vince nodded.

"Hector, wow, I am very happy to see you here. Surprised to see you, but happy!"

"Wherever I go, Hector goes. He's got skills." Vince said, winking at Jessica and James.

Ignoring that for the moment, James asked, "Jessica, may we go inside?"

She nodded and led the others into the farm kitchen. Each took a seat at the table, and she set out some elegant snacks and offered each a drink. To her surprise, they all took a pass on the alcohol but scarfed down the snacks. "I didn't know what to expect, or who would be staying, so I am not as prepared as I normally would be," she said apologetically.

James waived it off and said to Vince, "Before I get into anything, tell me what you mean by 'Hector's got skills.' It's the second time that has been said to me." Turning to Hector, James added, "They tell me I need to hear about it from you." Looking at Hector more closely, he said, "But, I must say, you look fantastic. Vince put you through some image consulting?"

Hector laughed heartily. "Yeah, as a matter of fact, he did." Rolling up his left arm sleeve, he pointed to an area that had once had a gang tattoo. "Pretty good work, isn't it?" James surveyed the arm and realized that an expert plastic surgeon must have done this. Hector Rodriguez was a big guy. He carried a lot of weight due to muscle and height, and the biceps of his arm—nearly the size of an ordinary man's waist—had had tattoos all around the circumference. There was no sign of any of them, no ghost of a former tattoo, anywhere.

"Why?" James asked, wondering why Hector had it removed.

"Because Hector needs to be able to work in any arena and not be spotted still brandishing his former life." Vince continued, "Especially if we are operating south of the border."

James nodded and changed the subject. "So…is it language skills then?"

Vince smiled, looked to Hector and said, "Shall I tell him, or shall you?"

"You go right ahead, man. Me? I can't wait to see his face!"

James had had enough of the mystery. He threw his hands up in a gesture of surrender. Vince laughed and said, "It's simple, actually. Obviously, Hector has language skills, and brute force skills, but I discovered something else after he asked if he could just hang out with me."

"Don't forget to remind him about my gaming skills," Hector coached.

"Am I telling this, or are you?" Vince teased.

"I remember very well that Hector was the one Brian chose to test his first game on. And frankly, Hector, if you had not done that, and experienced the change you did, I doubt we would have gotten out of Compton alive that night."

"You got that right, bro! You had balls comin' onto our turf. But that 'White King Rising' game turned a lot of things around…." His voice trailed off. Hector Rodriguez had a naturally appreciative sense of self. Gang or no gang, he was loyal to those who helped and protected him. And he had not one ounce of racial prejudice in him.

James knew that. *He still has that child-like faith quality,* he thought.

"Anyway, as it turns out, Hector got to spend some time with one of my surveillance guys," Vince explained.

"Physical surveillance?"

"No, electronic and digital. I have to be able to find out where the target of the rescue is located and who the bad guys are communicating with and being paid by. You know, 'background' essential to the mission." He smiled.

James was listening. "It wasn't a couple weeks into it that my guy came to me, explaining almost in fear of losing his job, that Hector here is a natural hacker." Hector grinned and high-fived Vince.

"Are you serious?" James asked.

"As a heart attack, James. He can hack into almost anything, and we trained him then also in the art of setting up electronic surveillance."

It took a moment for that to sink in and for James to realize he indeed had skills that would likely be very useable. Turning to Hector, he asked, "So, Hector, have you offered your skills to the FBI, intelligence community?"

Hector shook his head no.

"Why not?"

"Well, first of all, I don't much trust 'em." He frowned a bit and added, "And second, I don't think I'd pass the background checks, you know, former member of the 118th Street Gang."

James doubted that and made his skepticism known to Vince. "Vince, sure, they would. How do you think they recruit their 'white hat hackers'? They were most always 'black hats' first. They either had an epiphany or the price was high enough to get them to turn."

"I know that, James!" Hector forcefully answered. "I know that." He was reluctant to add anything more.

"What he's a little shy of telling you is that—in addition to not wanting to expose any of us in the background check they would do on him—he felt he'd be homesick. You know, we're the only family he's got." Vince paused.

It was a truth so simple James had almost missed it. Hector Rodriguez had lived in a shed in a backyard until his unlikely "adoption" by a notorious Compton gang's leader. He was the only Hispanic in the gang, and the members had had to fight often simply because of Hector's ethnicity. Hector Rodriguez might have had a lot of faults, but ingratitude wasn't one of them. So, he remained loyal to the gang's leader, DeShaun Williams, and later to Brian Washington Carver and Andy Weir. That totally unlikely alliance had led him to Mikolas, Jessica and Vince.

A calm came over James. As he examined why he felt at ease with this news, he realized that every member of this crew had a core decency and respect for one another, regardless of color, history, education, or money.

However it had happened over the last 20 years, this was a true team. And the calm James experienced came from his realization that maybe they did have a fighting chance. *Maybe we can just pull it off...manage to save this sad, beleaguered country after all.*

He sat quietly, looking from Hector to Vince, then back to Hector. "I totally understand, Hector.

And I'm glad you're here. Real glad." Hector grinned. James added, "Did you, by any chance, bring your gear?"

Yeah, bro, I sure did. Everything I need."

A few hours later, James left with Vince McCoy in the passenger seat. He was about to check in at James' hotel, and though he did not know it yet, the plan James outlined in concept would thrust Vince McCoy into one of the greatest intelligence operations ever attempted.

Hector was told to remain at the farm, out of sight until called for. Before they left, Jessica had insisted on showing them the small airplane hangar in the back area. It appeared to be just a normal hangar to keep a small jet secured, but inside, James spotted a T-4 pipe. That alone indicated a tremendous amount of communication could come and go from this shed. *This woman never ceases to amaze me,* he thought.

He had asked, "Does anyone know about this?"

Her response was reassuring. "No. But if they find out, it's natural, isn't it, that the head of a global news agency would need a lot of communication ability, even if he was just taking a retreat to his eastern home?"

"I don't suppose it is a secure line?"

"James, you know it is! Dedicated and encrypted!" she joked. "How on earth could they work on confidential workflow that is about to become breaking news?"

This is all good news, James had told himself. And as they drove away, he was grateful Vince McCoy was with him.

CHAPTER THIRTEEN

John Brannigan was having a rough night. Lying in bed for hours, he had been unable to fall asleep. Even getting up to check the windows and doors of his Georgetown brownstone hadn't assuaged the sense of apprehension he felt.

His long career in intelligence/counterintelligence, and his top-level participation in most of the dirty tricks perpetrated by the United States in recent years, had left him almost "the man who knew too much." Counterbalancing that with war games played against the United States by other nation states had resulted in feelings of disorientation from time to time. *When was the first time this wave of suspicion began recently?* he asked himself.

Rewinding the last few weeks of conversation, his mind came to rest on one in particular. Like a ball settling on the roulette wheel, there it was, a conversation he could not shake from his mind. There was something about Peter Loren that made Brannigan very suspicious. It was not his effectiveness in virtually destroying the American media—that was something Brannigan truly did admire. The mental picture Brannigan was looking at was something far less sinister, yet that is where he was stuck.

While the two sat along the moat in Dinkelsbühl and Loren fed the ducks, Loren told him who his mentor had been. Brannigan knew about Samir Taghavi from files released years ago, after Taghavi's cover had been blown, and it had been revealed that he was a high-level Al Qaeda operative. His cronies at the FBI had informed him about what they had discovered.

I know the Israelis gave him a pass. I know we did, but something doesn't add up, his thoughts turned back to Loren. One of the traits of those who have secrets of their own is that they wonder what secrets everyone else has. And that was haunting John Brannigan. He had a secret. For that reason, he suspected and feared Peter Loren.

He had, in fact, met Samir Taghavi one time—at Bud Walker's ranch in Montana. He had revealed that fact to Loren to test him, to see what his response might be. Loren had shown no signs of a reflexive response. *Yet…here I am thinking about you, Peter Loren.*

That settled it. *I'm going to find out **more** about you—without anyone involved with us knowing it.* Brannigan justified that in his own mind by telling himself that it was the only fair thing he could do for Ernst. "After all, he gave me a seat at the table. I need to protect this little group—and my seat. We can't have any imposters at the highest level." With that proclamation, he gulped down the remainder of the Chivas Regal he had poured himself and went back to bed.

The next day, Ari was the late arrival at the Mayflower Hotel. James was already waiting for him at the bar, sipping the gin and tonic he had selected as his daily drink. This was his third visit to the hotel bar, and the staff now seemed to view him as a regular. He had asked the bartender to bring over some mixed nuts. "Want some?" he offered Ari.

"No, thanks." Ari looked around the bar, seeing that they were the only two seated at the bar itself. Another man and woman had their heads together, flirting, in a corner booth. But beyond that, they had the place to themselves.

"I have something for you, James."

"The list?"

Ari nodded. James had asked that he be given the full list of attendees at Ernst Schweiner's little summit. "I picked this up at the Embassy this morning. It came in from Tel Aviv."

James opened the brown envelope and started scanning the list of names. It was shorter than he had expected. And he didn't know if that was a good sign or a bad one.

Ari changed his mind about the nuts, grabbed a handful, and, with his other hand, pointed to something on the sheet James was holding. "You see, of course, Brannigan, Loren, Schmidt, and Schweiner. But the next three arrived from Switzerland."

James knew Serge Pilaf, of course. The sheer magnitude of his wealth and influence made him a recognizable figure anywhere in the world if one followed technology. "Where is he now? Do you know?"

"Yes, he returned to his villa in Amalfi, Italy, stayed a couple of days, and returned to the United States last week."

"Is he here in Washington?" James asked.

"No. He went straight back to the Silicon Valley. You'll have to sort it out from there."

James nodded that he understood Ari would not have creds to engage in surveillance in the United States. Continuing to study the list, he finally said, "CIA, public relations, Big Tech owner, and the head and second of the Global Commerce Forum..." He stopped. "Hmmm. If it weren't for the CIA component, this could have been just another high-level business meeting."

"Exactly, James." Ari concurred enthusiastically. "Brannigan's presence throws a wrench in the mix."

"So, the next two are one of the directors of the Global Wellness Organization and a pharmaceutical executive." James was still trying to assemble a picture. "Nobody else?"

"Nope. As far as our people saw, that was it. Maybe someone else was there beforehand, but if so, we didn't see them. We started surveillance once Schweiner went on the move and your two birds flew to Zurich."

"It's Brannigan, Ari. He's the outpoint here." James laughed, putting the sheet back into the envelope. "A mystery. You have any theories?"

Ari shook his head no. "Just a gut hunch." Pausing to order what James was drinking, he then added, "You're going to have to figure that out somehow on your own."

"I know. I have an idea, given who you told me Loren is and who his main client is in Washington. I did a little digging on that crew!"

The two paused for a bit, looking into the mirror behind the bar as they sipped their cocktails. "Well, James, I don't have a theory, but I have some advice," Ari volunteered.

"I'm all ears."

"Stay on Brannigan. That's the entry point." Ari hesitated and then decided to add, "You know as far as Israel has always been concerned, the fact that a member of the Communist Party rose in the ranks of U.S. intelligence and eventually became Director of the Central Intelligence Agency has never sat well with us. We've just never been able to reconcile that oddity."

James nodded.

"For the longest time, I thought he might be a Soviet spy, trusted and burrowed deep in your intelligence apparatus. At least, until recently, that's what I thought."

James wasn't going to be able to let that go. "What changed your mind?"

"Oh, well, I realized it's been a long time since the fall of the Soviet Union. Russia's not a Communist country. The Soviet Union was. Kind of a 'duh' moment—as you Americans say—wasn't it?" He chuckled.

James, too, appreciated the joke, until Ari jumped off his stool, put some money on the bar, slapped James on the back, and said, "So, I guess one should ask who are the Communist countries today, right? Who would value a Party member on the inside in the U.S.?"

Seeing that James had frozen for a moment, he said, "A little food for thought, my friend—that is, only if you are the suspicious type!"

Still focused on Ari's parting comment, James made his way to the dining room. Vince McCoy would be joining him soon, and he wanted to get his usual table. The restaurant was set up with tables designed for one to see and be seen. Those tables allowed for other diners to easily observe who was also in the dining area. The prestige and status of the restaurant was such that just dining there added credibility.

On the perimeter walls and in the corners of the restaurant were more intimate seating areas for those who did not want to see and be seen. Overstuffed chairs and ottoman-like coffee tables in front of each chair allowed diners to sit more discreetly, away from the eye of everyone, and enjoy a more comfortable sitting experience.

"Is your friend joining you for lunch, Mr. Mikolas?" the maître d asked.

James smiled and said, "No. But someone else is joining me, so there will be two of us."

Happy that he was a frequent enough patron to be referred to by name, he realized he had been successful in installing himself in the Mayflower Hotel's regular clientele—at least for meals. He took his usual seat, and, though he had a different waiter today, the new fellow seemed to know he would want the gin and tonic.

"You're new?" James asked.

"No. But I usually work the dinner hour. Ronald had a dentist appointment, so I am covering for him. He briefed me that if you came in, you like a gin and tonic."

"Thank you,…?" James' voice trailed up, indicating he needed the fellow's name.

"Bruce, sir."

"Thank you, Bruce. It's just that kind of service that has prompted me to stop in so often. There is someone joining me. Mr. McCoy. I have no idea what he drinks, let alone will want to eat, so we will both need menus then."

Before James finished the sentence, he saw McCoy entering the restaurant. *He's got such a preppy look with that navy blue blazer, khaki slacks, and blue shirt,* James thought. *Looks like he belongs at any firm in the area.* McCoy asked the maître d a question, and the man nodded, pointing out James at the back of the room. He then escorted Vince to James.

"Thank you." McCoy smiled at the maître d. As he sat down, Bruce introduced himself and asked Vince what he would like. "I'll start with an Arnold Palmer, if I may."

Casually looking around the room, trying not to be an obvious gawker or political celebrity stalker, he said, "Nice place, James." Without waiting for a response, he added impulsively, "Could we be any more visible? This place is like a fishbowl with all these glass walls," he observed, nodding in the direction of the etched glass that separated the restaurant from the opulent lobby.

"Nope. That's what I wanted. Take a look at the menu, Vince. They've got excellent food here, and we can linger as long as we like."

"Lingering"—as James referred to it—may have been encouraged here, but the service was nonetheless fast. Knowing that Senators, Congressmen, and lobbyists might be in need of a good meal, but on a restricted timeline before heading into their afternoon's activities, the hotel prided itself in providing exceptionally fast service, without encroaching on conversations or one's need for privacy. At the same time, the hotel valued the opposite type of patron—the one who wanted to spend a considerable time there and have leisurely conversations.

James and Vince chose the "serve us quickly and we will continue our meeting" path. "That was a very fine small plate, James. Much obliged for the recommendation," Vince said.

"You bet. Now, let's talk a little business." The noise in the room had ramped up quite a bit as the tables had filled for the lunch crowd. James preferred it that way for what he was about to say. "Vince, Ari Ben-Gurion and I are working on a theory that a cabal of unlikely bedfellows is planning an attack of great magnitude on the United States. Not just government institutions, but the people themselves."

McCoy leaned in a bit. James continued, "What I need you for is to surveil one of the conspirators in our theory. He's intel himself, so whoever does this has to be really circumspect and convincing."

"I see. Does this involve a snatch and grab? A hostage-taking?" Extraction?"

"Hopefully not, but I have to be prepared to move in any direction necessary. We're too early in our investigation yet for me to really know." He paused for a moment, seemingly scrutinizing some mental picture. "I need someone stealth, an 'unknown' in these parts."

"I understand, James. No one from intel themselves."

"Exactly."

"So, who is the target?"

"John Brannigan." James stopped, waiting for McCoy to respond. All Vince did, however, was whistle lightly under his breath.

"Jesus, James, that guy is probably wired into every spook and covert operator on the planet! He's a relic from the Cold War, isn't he?"

"Yeah, the latter part of it anyway. He's been through a lot—rose through the ranks. He's retired now, of course."

"You know that for sure?" Vince challenged.

"Well, let's just say he doesn't keep offices at Langley anymore. He has a lucrative contract at one of the networks. But it's another crew he's supporting that is at the core of the attack. Theoretically."

"James," McCoy interjected, "are we talking criminal enterprises or something else?"

"Something else, real white collar...I'd place them in the category of opposition research, dirty tricks, disinformation, but embedded and accepted at the highest levels of government and media. I have reason to believe he's been promoted recently into a global cabal's inner circle." James watched Vince listen without flinching and continued, "That's why I have to find a way to get an inside man. He will remember that he knows me from before. I don't know if he will remember or care about the skirmishes we had along the way. But he seems to be using other assets than the typical agency ones he used to rely on."

"Got it." Vince McCoy did indeed understand. He said nothing, but James could see the wheels of an idea turning in Vince's mind. He took a deep breath, held it, then let it out slowly and fully. "Well, it may turn out to be a good thing I brought Hector along…"

James nodded.

Suddenly, a mixture of frustration and curiosity overtook Vince, and he blurted out, "The fact I'm an outsider is a good thing, a plus point. But…it's also a huge drawback, isn't it?"

"Meaning?"

"You're talking about an inside man here! If he doesn't know me from any arena, how the hell am I going to get close enough to him to even surveil, let alone get on the inside?!"

"Beats me," James said. The absurdity of the answer just hung there, until both of them laughed, appreciating the irony of playing a vital game, coming from behind. The truth was that neither of them had a clue how this might unfold. James only knew he needed a U.S. partner who was smart and savvy. He needed someone creative and able to improvise in tough situations. Vince was that partner. James knew what he needed here was a "Hail Mary" pass, or whatever those men in Germany had cooked up would be unleashed. He knew that in his gut. He had two possible "receivers"—Vince McCoy and Andy Weir. In his spirit, he sensed that somehow—between himself, Carver & Weir, and McCoy—there was some hope. *At least that's what I believe,* he told himself.

The tides of war throughout all history have turned sometimes on sheer luck and sometimes on divine intervention. James would never know for sure which one of those intervened at that moment, but the tide did indeed change.

As he looked past Vince McCoy toward the restaurant entrance, John Brannigan walked in unaccompanied.

CHAPTER FOURTEEN

*B*rannigan wasn't paying much attention when he came into one of his favorite Washington, D.C. haunts. His mind was still on Peter Loren and the queasiness he felt about the man. *Probably nothing,* he thought. *Here I am talking queasy. Jesus, you'd think I was James Comey with his queasy feelings!*

That thought was enough to shake Brannigan out of the dumps, and his interest in a good lunch rebounded. Looking across the room while waiting for his meal, he noticed two men sitting about 40 feet away, near the back of the restaurant. One had his back to him, but the other was facing him, and he looked familiar to Brannigan.

Brannigan was a natural schmoozer and had navigated his way through the changing tides of favor in D.C. for more than three decades. Even without his espionage interests, he had always wanted to know who was who—and who he might cultivate for his own purposes. So, he stared at the man until he began to place him. Then, it dialed in for sure, and he remembered who he was. *Son of a gun, that's Mikolas, I think. Haven't seen or heard of him in years.*

Whether it was genuine curiosity, or simply that John Brannigan didn't have anyone else to talk with that day, he decided to get the man's attention. He waved one hand, hoping to catch James' eye. It worked. James spotted him, recognized him, smiled, and nodded. *I think I'll just go say hello.*

"Vince, Brannigan's coming over here. Let me assess this," James said under his breath.

"All yours, James." Whether McCoy was surprised by this turn of events or not, no one would have noticed even the slightest change in his demeanor.

"James? James Mikolas?" Brannigan asked.

Rising, James said, "That's me." He put his hand out to shake Brannigan's. "I thought I recognized you but didn't want to intrude…"

"Well, that's the difference between us, Mikolas. You don't intrude, and I don't hesitate to." He laughed at his own joke, then looked down at Vince McCoy.

"Sorry, John, this is a friend of mine from out west, Vince McCoy." James completed the introduction as properly as he could. "He's spending a few days in the District, and we ran into each other at my hotel. Must have used the same online hotel site," he joked.

"Pleasure," Brannigan said as he shook McCoy's hand.

Recognizing an opportunity, James decided to seize the moment. "Are you alone, John? If you are, why don't you join us? We're just sitting here, reminiscing."

Brannigan was secretly relieved they suggested sitting together. Truth was he wanted to know what Mikolas had been up to and if he was still with the Agency. If so, he might be useful. But he was also curious about the dapper friend. *If he's with Mikolas…I wonder what he does.* "You know what? I'm by myself and would enjoy some company. Thanks for offering." He took the chair to Vince's left and signaled to the waiter to bring his setup to this table.

The next few minutes were spent with Brannigan poking around to find out whether James was still with the Agency, retired, or working as a contractor now. He hadn't known Mikolas well—too far down the food chain in the hierarchy for him to have paid much attention, but his recollection was that Mikolas was a good analyst with quite an independent streak and guts. He vaguely remembered something about Mikolas pissing a lot of folks off when he tried to stop President Bush from going into Iraq. Though he had been right about the WMD being a trap, Mikolas had let his superior carry the message. And it never arrived. *Too bad he didn't have more of a killer instinct,* Brannigan thought. *He might have climbed the ladder.*

"You actually are retired then?" Brannigan asked.

"Yeah. Thirty years was long enough, and I missed my fishing hole."

"Where's that?" Brannigan asked, smiling.

"Down on the Cape Fear River. Real good catfish in that one. And nice folks. Most of my life, I was in the field, John, and never did settle down at all. That camp of mine is the closest thing to it."

"You been there, Vince?" Brannigan asked unexpectedly.

"No, never have. Sounds peaceful though," Vince answered, almost regretfully.

Brannigan picked up on that. "How did you two meet up, if you don't mind my asking?"He ordered another scotch and soda to appear to not be paying too close attention.

James responded first. "Well, John, I had a friend who needed help. His girlfriend ended up getting kidnapped by one of the human-trafficking rings out of Mexico City. The kid was desperate and had no idea who to call."

"I would have thought FBI would have wanted it," Brannigan offered.

"Me, too, but for some reason, they didn't seem to take it seriously. She was a human rights activist, and, I don't know, maybe they didn't give a damn. I don't know. All I know was he came to me."

Brannigan understood that phenomenon actually. Most Americans held a much higher view of their federal law enforcement's capabilities than was warranted, as far as he was concerned.

James continued, "Anyway, I had never handled anything like that. But I knew a woman who was a business investor out of LA. I took a long shot and asked her if she could help or if she knew of anyone. Turns out she did."

"Knew someone then, huh?" Brannigan engaged.

"Next thing I know, she brings Vince to me." James nodded toward his friend.

Brannigan turned his attention once again to Vince. "Vince, what do you do? Negotiate for kidnap victims in Central America? I understand Mexico City is a hub, and it is big-time organized crime."

James said nothing. This was the perfect opportunity for Vince to take over. He sensed Brannigan was asking questions for more than just idle curiosity. James wondered if Vince had tipped onto the cat and mouse game Brannigan might be playing.

Whether he had or not, Vince easily carried on. "No. I'm not much of a negotiator. Usually, I'm called in when negotiations fail."

"So, you don't work for one of those London insurance firms that insure against kidnapping for corporate execs?"

Vince shook his head no, adding a little hint of disdain. "I've always been freelance. It's a difficult business, and I need to set up my own methods. I'm the locate-and-extract guy."

"Ahh," Brannigan was very interested now. "Human surveillance or electronic?"

"Both. As needed."

Brannigan thought that over for a moment and then said, "I wouldn't have guessed. Extraction guys usually blend in more," he referred to Vince's blond hair and blue eyes.

McCoy laughed. "Hah. One of my talents, Mr. Brannigan, I seem to disappear in the landscape. Always have."

James decided to chime in. Not knowing where Brannigan might be going with this, he decided to try to steer the conversation a little more. "Anyway, he lived up to his reputation. Found the girl and got her out…"

Brannigan was observing Vince more closely now. He nodded his head and smiled. "Friends ever since, heh?"

"Well, we don't run into each other much. Let's just say I have a healthy respect for Vince's talents. And hope not to need them again." James laughed.

Unexpectedly, Brannigan took the conversation in a different direction. "Tell me, Vince, you know who I am, right?"

"Yes, sir. I do now, at least. I've seen you on cable TV, after you retired. Why?"

"I was just wondering where you got your training? Were you with the Agency? Or some other intelligence group?"

Vince shook his head no. "I'm ex-military, special forces in the Gulf War. There were all kinds of things we were locating and extracting back then." Vince grinned. His blond hair, with a sprinkling of gray, and those piercing blue eyes were typical of many Irish. And Vince had the charm to go with it.

Brannigan laughed. "So true! If America only knew!"

Vince chose to ignore the remark, smiled, and added, "Anyway, after I got out, I realized there might be a need for those skills and a way for me to be my own boss."

"Very nice," Brannigan offered. "I like it when we can carry some of what we know out into civilian life and make a go of it."

I bet you do, you bastard! James thought. *I wonder what you have sold, and been paid, to have earned your seat at the table.*

"How 'bout you, James? Converted any of your skills?"

"John, I was happy to leave that all behind me, to be honest with you. The game kinda wore me out."

At that moment, Vince rose and said, "Gentlemen, if you'll excuse me for a moment. I'm going to head to the restroom. Be right back."

Brannigan kept his eye on McCoy, watching as Vince asked a waiter for instructions on where the restroom was and then headed through an arch. Turning back to James, he leaned in and said, "Mikolas, is he the real deal?"

"Let's just put it this way, John. If I got myself kidnapped, I'd want him to be the one hired to find me."

"That good, huh?"

"Yeah."

"What makes him better, do you think?"

James pondered it a minute and answered, "My guess is because he doesn't have a background in intelligence—you know, isn't all caught up in that network. Not that they're not good..." Brannigan waived it off as if to say he understood and agreed.

James continued. "Every group's got its procedures, policies, hierarchies, and resources. Doesn't leave much room for creativity. I think him being an outsider, relying on the network of support he developed just for himself, puts him a cut above. At least, that's my hunch. Anyway, he's good. And...he's fearless."

Brannigan was listening intently. "Was he SEAL team?"

"I think so, but maybe Delta Force. You better ask him. I never did. It was enough for me that he showed up when Jessica Ranger called him, and he was willing. It was a while ago, you know?"

"Sure. Sure. You know, I think I know Jessica Ranger."

"Yeah?" James feigned pleasant surprise.

"Well, not know her, really. I think I met her at some event here in D.C. a few years back. She's married to Bud Walker, right?"

"I think I heard they got married. She wasn't when I met her. But you know, John, I never was much for the 'society' page. I'm a man of mediocre means and never circulated in that part of Washington. It wouldn't surprise me, though, if she would have met him. Charity stuff, investment stuff. It's a bit out of my comfort zone."

Brannigan smiled. *I can believe that, James. A little too sophisticated for you,* he mused.

"Would you vouch for him personally? Not just professionally?"

The question surprised James. He needed to clarify it. "You mean for his character and reliability, not just skills?"

Brannigan nodded. "And for his being circumspect, tightlipped, trustworthy?"

"As I said, I'd want him to come for me." James looked at it a little more and added, "But, to answer your question directly, I would say, yes, I could. You don't run your own operation in that game without being trusted. He can't afford to 'burn' a client or informant. Not healthy."

"Bingo, James, bingo. It's the self-employed with happy customers who are the most reliable." Brannigan leaned back in his chair with an almost Cheshire grin on his face, finishing off his drink, as Vince returned to the table.

What happened next was totally unexpected. James didn't see it coming. Nor did Vince. Vince McCoy's question about how he could possibly get close to Brannigan was about to be answered.

"McCoy, this might be a bit presumptuous of me, given we just met. But…I have something I need some help with, and you might be the man. I assume you are not in the middle of some 'extraction' right now here in Washington."

"That's right," Vince snorted. "One of the drawbacks of being freelance is one isn't always working. I am not always needed."

"I may have a need for you. I'll need to check out a few things on you, of course, but there is someone I need surveilled, and I need it to be done by someone who would not be known by anyone in this town." He let that sink in a moment and then leaned in conspiratorially. "And I may need some protection myself."

"You?"

Brannigan was playing it close. He sighed. "Yeah, one of the drawbacks of becoming a celebrity, I'm afraid. Everyone knows what I look like now. I feel a little naked somehow."

Vince nodded that he understood. "There's paparazzi and there's *paparazzi*…"

"Exactly. The ones who might be tailing me or surveilling me aren't just looking for a photo for the tabloids."

"I completely understand. So, you want me to surveil any surveillance of you, and you also want me to surveil someone else?"

"That's about it."

"Body or electronic? Or both?"

"Hopefully, just body. But electronic, if necessary," Brannigan responded.

"How long are you thinking you might need me?"

"I am guessing a few months. We should have wrapped up the project that would put me into some crosshairs—if, in fact, that were to happen—in a few months."

"I gather the one you want surveilled will be for about the same amount of time?"

Brannigan knew Vince McCoy completely understood that whatever this "project" was he was referring to, the other party was part of it. *He's picked up that I smell a double-cross, and that's exactly where I want him. That's enough for now.* Brannigan's answer was a simple pat on Vince's arm.

James thought he'd better give himself an excuse to exit this negotiation if they needed him to. "Do you guys want me to make a restroom visit of my own? You know, not sit here and listen to this?"

"Nah," Brannigan responded. His arrogance combined with the two scotch and sodas he had consumed clouded his judgment slightly. Or perhaps it was the fact he had joined the inner circle of Ernst Schweiner and felt somehow bulletproof in that rare air. He was a man who made few mistakes. But he made one that day in the Mayflower Hotel.

Shortly thereafter, Vince had secured the pay needed, and expenses, and committed to the enterprise. Being somewhat circumspect still, Brannigan said he would lay out the details more the following morning when McCoy would arrive at his Georgetown home.

"I'll run a check on some things today, Vince, as I said. But if you are who James here says you are, this should work out very well."

"I understand. And you'll tell me tomorrow the name of the target?"

"Yes." Then Brannigan grinned. "You ever worked in Europe, young man?"

"No. Almost always Central America."

"Then, you won't know him. He owns a public relations firm in Paris and has been in Washington providing his services to some high-level people here."

Vince rose, shook hands with Brannigan, and took the note with Brannigan's address.

Suddenly, Brannigan realized he was leaving without paying and turned to handle it. "Well, this turned into a business lunch. So, I will handle the check for us, James. Thank you for a very illuminating and productive lunch."

After he exited the restaurant, Vince whispered, "Did what I think just happened happen?"

"Amazing, isn't it?" James knew Brannigan had to be referring to Peter Loren. "Seems we just caught two fish with one hook!"

Chapter Fifteen

*T*he next day, two men left their hotel around 7:30 AM. James walked to the Washington, D.C. metro and took a train out to Arlington in order to check his mailbox. Vince, dressed in business attire, but without a briefcase, took the metro in another direction to meet up with his new employer, John Brannigan, at his home in Georgetown. Each was in for some surprising revelations but, for the moment, were just enjoying the fragrant spring day in the capital city.

There was, in fact, a letter in the box for James. He'd checked every Friday, as he said he would, but for a couple of weeks, there had been nothing. Today, a letter from Carver & Weir, written in Andy's engineering block handwriting, was inside. For the past few weeks, James had been forwarding to Andy and Brian mail containing news clippings, some social media posts, tweets screen-captured, YouTube video clips, online magazine pages—a news bouillabaisse of things that had caught James' eye. His 30-plus years of not only being a field operative in Eastern Europe for the CIA, but especially his last few years where his analytical ability shone, had developed in him an ability to spot little things randomly appearing in the culture—things he called "little dots." And he had developed the talent for connecting those dots. Mostly, he trusted his power of observation and his ability to think like a bad guy—and his gut hunches.

That combination of skill and sheer perception and intuition had saved his country three times in the last 20 years and earned him his much-longed-for retirement. Deciding not to analyze just yet, he was simply sending the material to Andy, with some notes attached as to which dots might connect. It was his hope that Andy's grandmaster chess champion mind would not just connect the dots, but would identify who was orchestrating things and what they were planning—if anything. *I'd like to be wrong on this one,* he had told himself consistently. But James knew he was not. Too many things in terms of the United States and its institutions had turned vertically south, in his opinion, in the last few years for this to be just a coincidence.

What he needed to know was whether it was just a catastrophic conflation of societal changes or was it by design. His gut told him it was by design, and that the men on the list Ari had provided were the primary movers. That being the case, he was optimistic Andy could develop a strategy to get out in front of it and defang the attackers without them even knowing it. At least, that is what he hoped for. Did the dots connect? Was there a thread that could be pulled that would untangle these unholy alliances and evaporate their secret plot? Would it be possible to call off the dogs of war?

Andy's one-page note gave no comfort, however. It read merely: "We need to meet. Your 'Pal' and I are headed to Montana."

Brian and Andy both, huh. Folding the paper and sticking it in his windbreaker pocket, he knew that meant a trip west. So, without going back to the hotel, he rented a car and drove to the Manassas farm. Jessica was still there. The plane was still there.

"Jessica," James shouted as he strode into the farmhouse, "how fast can we get up to Montana? The boys want to talk."

"Are we staying?" she asked.

"Don't know. Hopefully not."

She rose, called out to the hangar, and said, "Then, let's roll right now. We are always fueled."

As they walked to the hangar, she turned to James and advised him, "James, just enjoy some of this fresh air. Breathe." She smiled. He took her advice. The last patches of frozen earth had surrendered to soft ground, and that smell of farms at the beginning of a season, ready for planting, was pervasive. The metaphor did not escape him.

Brannigan himself opened the door. *Apparently, he doesn't keep a staff here,* Vince noted.

"Good morning."

"Good morning, sir." Vince entered the vestibule of a very spacious brownstone. From the outside, these older homes were quite deceptive, presenting the appearance of narrowness and confining walls. Once you walked in, though, it usually was quite the opposite. Brownstones in Georgetown had high ceilings and equally tall windows, which did, in fact, allow in a great deal of light. And the sheer height of each room created the apparency of space.

Brannigan's home was easily a million-dollar-plus residence. The main floor had a front drawing room, a living space with fireplace, a formal dining room, and an older square kitchen, completely remodeled but consistent with the stately design of the original. There was a door leading to the lower level that one accessed from the hallway, and upstairs were bedrooms.

"Let's sit in the front room for a bit and discuss some things," Brannigan said, directing Vince to a leather-furniture-filled room. Everything was dark brown except for the bright colors of an original stain-glassed transom. "Take your pick." Brannigan gestured for Vince to sit.

Brannigan got straight to the point. Vince knew he would. "Vince, I had some people run checks on you yesterday. You know, to verify."

"Sure."

Keeping an eye on Vince, Brannigan said, "Basically, everything came back just as you said. Which is good. We even had a report out of Colombia that you and a bunch of, let's see, how did they refer to you? Oh yes, 'amateurs' is the word they used..." Brannigan chuckled at his own discovery. "That you, and these 'amateurs' had, in fact, rescued some women and, in the process, alerted authorities as to the location of a slave-trading operation across the border in Venezuela. Quite a cleanup, according to them."

Brannigan paused to see what Vince might have to say. "Well, we hoped they wouldn't drop the ball, sir. I was there to locate and extract— not to do what the Colombian army should have. We just got the hell outta Dodge, barely."

"I read that. Did you know that you killed a very high-level Al Qaeda there?" This was the part Brannigan had to reassure himself about. Was it just a bizarre coincidence, an act of fate, or something more sinister?

"Excuse me?" Vince was genuinely surprised by that statement.

"Hah!" Brannigan laughed. "You didn't know you killed the propaganda chief for Al Qaeda in that hut?"

"Sir, who are you talking about?" Vince asked with total sincerity.

"A man named Samir. Samir Taghavi."

Vince's mouth dropped. He knew who he was. *Is this for real?*

"I know that name, Mr. Brannigan, but what the hell was he doing there?"

"According to what I read, he was spearheading a new income stream for Al Qaeda, human trafficking, and he was handling the sex traffic part of it."

Brannigan could see Vince was trying to process this. Vince shook his head back and forth. "Jesus, what a waste of talent on their part. Thank God for us, though!"

Brannigan laughed. He, too, appreciated this irony. "Didn't you see him?"

"The man I saw—the man I killed—never saw me. If he did, sir, it was the instant he died. And I didn't have time to check him out. All I wanted were the women. Things were getting a bit hairy, and, as you know, I had a crew of 'amateurs.'" Vince was looking at a mental replay of that moment and seemed to appreciate the significance of having scored a big hit. "Wow. It's a good thing I didn't know who I was opposing there, sir, or I might have turned that job down." He chuckled.

"Understood. But the reason I brought it up, Vince, is that the man I want you to 'watch' for me is Peter Loren—a PR guy from Paris. His mentor was Samir Taghavi."

Vince McCoy was speechless. But he was also a seasoned operator, and he knew his reactions were genuine and that Brannigan was too sharp himself not to evaluate it as such. Brannigan said nothing. "So, is this Peter Loren Al Qaeda, do you think?"

"I don't know. He says he's not, says he never knew who Samir really was. Says he was running a very legitimate corporate PR firm and rarely spent time with a team within the firm that Taghavi was apparently ramrodding—deep PR, if you will."

"Do you believe him?" Vince asked. It was an honest question.

Brannigan gave him an honest answer. "I don't know. The Israelis gave him a pass, felt that he was an unwitting player in an information-laundering operation. On the surface, it appeared legit. That was the Loren part. Deeper, that was the Al Qaeda Black Propaganda team."

Vince sighed. "Well, I never was much into the intelligence analysis part, Mr. Brannigan. As you discovered, I am a snatch-and-rescue guy. Different game, you know."

Brannigan did know and, having watched what he believed to be genuine reactions by Vince McCoy, Brannigan concluded that the reports he had received on McCoy were accurate and that Vince McCoy was who he said he was. The interconnection of a number of people from a dark world did not, in and of itself, bother Brannigan. In truth, the community of intelligence operators was smaller than one might guess. Branch to branch, it could even be quite incestuous. So, he overlooked the intersection of James Mikolas, Vince McCoy, Jessica Ranger, and Samir Taghavi.

"Well, as long as this guy Loren never got a look at you, we should be fine. It's Loren I want you to keep an eye on. Your 'cover' is as my security. Everyone will buy that I now need a bodyguard."

"That should work well in settings where the two of you would likely meet and connect with one another..." Vince suggested. He was interrupted, however, by Brannigan.

"Right, now that's the wrinkle. You'd be expected to be there, if I am there. But we have to look at how you keep an 'eye'—and I mean that literally as well—when I am not there."

Vince nodded, waiting for Brannigan to elaborate. "If I remember, you said you do electronic surveillance as well, right?"

"Yes, sir. Necessary to not only locate, but to find out who is involved, who's paying, how...it's fairly involved."

"I know. And you use your own people, right?"

"Yes. Actually, it's one guy. I have more than one, but this one, in particular, is a brilliant hacker and also can do setup of undetectable electronic surveillance."

Brannigan hoped for something like this, so he leaned in toward Vince. "Where'd you recruit him? Defense Intelligence Agency? Because we will need him, and I'd have to check him out, too. Make certain his techniques aren't recognized by someone, you know, anything that could burn us."

"They won't be. He's a real independent—only worked for me. And he has no connection ever with any military, law enforcement, or intelligence communities."

"Jesus, you have my attention now," Brannigan said. "Where'd he get dropped down from? A cloud?"

Vince laughed. Grinning, he answered simply, "Better. From a Compton gang."

Brannigan chewed on that for a moment, then said, "A gang? In Los Angeles? Who were they hacking?"

"No one, sir. He just discovered these skill sets accidentally hanging around me and my crew. No one knows him. And no one knows his 'signature.'"

"Does he have one?" Brannigan asked.

"Not that I know. Probably why no one knows him…"

This is perfect, Brannigan reflected. *A stealth snatch-and-rescue guy—and an unknown hacker!*

Changing the subject altogether, Brannigan decided to give Vince a tour of the lower level, his personal office, which Vince knew would have encryption technology at every turn. Brannigan had his own "black world" inside his own home. Then, he led him upstairs to the bedroom area, though Vince had no idea why, until Brannigan opened a door off the central hallway that went up to an attic area. It had been completely refurnished, though, into a large bedroom, small kitchenette, and bath.

"Will this work for you, Vince?"

"You mean, you want me to live here?"

"Yeah. Someone coming for me, you know, would be a little too late to call you at some hotel." Brannigan shook his head, deciding not to invoke any of his usual sarcasm.

Vince agreed. "You're right. The hotel's not far, but you are absolutely right. I'm no good to you in that scenario unless I am right on the scene."

"Good. So, you check out of that place and move in here tomorrow." As they turned to go downstairs, Brannigan added, "And, your fellow… what did you say his name was?"

"I didn't. But it's Rodriguez. Hector Rodriguez."

"Well, what do we do with him?"

"I'll take care of him, sir. He's part of my 'expenses' we negotiated. And I don't think we want him to be visible around here." Vince reminded Brannigan of that obvious outpoint. "You wanted me to find out if someone is surveilling you, remember? Well, if they are, we don't want Hector suddenly showing up. Me, you can justify. Him, he'd raise a red flag."

"You're right. Good. Good."

Ten minutes later, Vince McCoy walked into his hotel, only to be told by the clerk that a message had been called in for him. The hotel operator had transcribed it. It read simply, "Had to fly out unexpectedly. Should be back in a few days. I'll check out then. Leave word for me where I can find you. Nice running into you again. Let's stay in touch. Regards, James"

Vince McCoy knew that was the signal something had changed, and the game had begun. *Quite a day!*

A few hours later, Jessica's jet landed on her ranch in Ovando, Montana. The SUV was waiting, and she and James made their way back to the sprawling ranch that had become her home after her marriage to Bud Walker. She didn't know if he was there, but she was pretty sure Andy and Brian would have arrived.

"The boys"—as James referred to them—were indeed at the house. Seeing the car, they leaped off the porch to greet James. "Geez, James," Brian joked, "we haven't seen you in almost 10 years and now twice in one month!"

"Yeah, I know. I know. Don't rag on me, Pal! I'm too tired for that tonight."

"Bro, I am not raggin' on you. Frankly, I've missed you."

Deciding to ignore that, James turned to Jessica. "Jessica, do you think there's anything in the kitchen?" he asked. "I'm really hungry."

She knew there would be. Her husband never failed to keep a stocked refrigerator these days. Their kitchen was large enough and equipped enough to entertain at professional venue standards. They were mostly homebodies now, and Jessica was a good cook, so—though she rarely challenged the capabilities of the appliances—she relished making her husband's favorite dishes. It had been a long life, a rich one, but a lonely one for her. And marrying Bud Walker at a time in his life when he was mellowing out had been a godsend.

It didn't take her long to whip up something for James. Oddly, all he really wanted was his perennial bacon and eggs. The others just sat at the table with him, not eating, waiting for him to be alert and on his game. The meal seemed to have perked him up, and he was ready now to find out why Andy felt they needed to meet. Andy wasted no time. "A couple of things, James."

"Yes?"

"Brian and I are going to be moving up here. We'll explain later, but we just felt we'd all be better off if we stuck together up here. California's not what it used to be, and we feel it's better for our girls."

James couldn't resist. "Which ones, the little ones or your wives?"

"All of them, James." Brian's tone was a little terse.

"Sorry, Brian, I didn't mean anything by that. I just thought the little ones might be pushing this more than your wives. Reagan and Alicia have always struck me as gals who like the city, like the action."

"True enough," Andy responded. "But they also want to be safe." That was all Andy said.

James dipped his chin and peered at Andy over his reading glasses. "I agree, if that makes any difference."

The boys grinned. It didn't really make a difference. They were grown, wealthy American businessmen, who could pretty much write their own ticket. What James didn't know was that day when he showed up at the birthday party, and they all realized everyone there was an orphan, had aroused something in Andy and Brian. They had all lost family in the years they had worked together, and they had truly grown to be each other's family. And given what Andy was trying to sort out for James, he had concluded it would be best for the family to get together, while they still could.

"Good. Glad we got that settled," Andy retorted.

He certainly seems perturbed about something, James thought. *He's usually the unflappable one of the bunch.*

Andy dove in, "James, we got the list of names you forwarded. That's a pretty formidable list of international players. This is the A team here on this planet."

James said nothing. He was listening, knowing that Andy would get to the point.

"The deputy director of the GWO made sense, but we were a little perplexed by the president of Decu-Hehiz." Andy paused. "Until that is, we dug into the company a bit more."

"They are a major psychiatric pharmaceutical manufacturer, if I remember," James said.

"Yeah, for sure, but there's more. They are currently working on development and manufacturing of manmade antibodies that can be inserted to fight against viruses, etc. The goal: to make it unnecessary for people to rely upon their own immune system, but rather to rely upon a synthetic immune system, created and injected."

James hadn't put it together, so Andy helped him. "That makes man part human with his own biological systems and defenses, but also part 'more than human'—for lack of better words. The objective is to make people more durable, more resilient."

"And is that bad, Andy?"

"Well, it depends. Like anything, it can cut both ways. Me and Brian concluded that it is likely bad, given the rest of the company this man is in. The question is, who decides? Who controls the timing and the impact of any 'insertion'? Who determines which is more powerful, the natural human body or a human body altered by the injection of 'solutions' more potent than that body could normally produce?"

It hung there in the air for a moment. To James, it was as if time stood still, for just a fraction of a second, giving him time to process the idea and calculate its future potential with regard to control. Once he grasped it, it was truly chilling. Whoever controlled the superior technologies could control the man if that man embraced the newest solutions to real-world existing problems.

"You are sure of this?" he asked. Andy nodded.

"How did you discover this?"

"Well…you remember my wife is a human rights activist. Notice I said 'is,' not 'was.' These people never turn off the antenna that seeks out and locates ways and means of violating a person's rights. She sniffed it out."

James leaned forward on the table, cupping his hands to his forehead, leaning into them. Andy then added something even worse. "That's not the main point. That's bad enough—given the rest of these folks and their power in their individual spheres of influence."

"What?" James snapped. He didn't even want to look up.

"You gave us seven. Three Americans, two Swiss, plus Schweiner and Schmidt. There's got to be one more—to level the playing field of these guys against the world."

Probably only a few people in the world would have understood what Andy had spotted. But that strategic gift—and extraordinary applications from chess that this whiz kid had done—had, in fact, allowed James to figure out what Al Qaeda had been doing to America, in time for America to adjust. So, James knew that if Andy said there was a player missing from the board, then there must be one. And he would have to find out who it was.

The air was heavy with worry—and something else. Fear. This unknown person might be the individual who could tip any game, any direction. James did not know if Andy's analysis was correct, but he was overcome by a memory from almost 20 years earlier when he had brought this whiz kid to Langley to test out a theory he had about an enemy who played chess. Andy was right that day and had been right all along the way.

"So, Schweiner is not the top guy?" James asked, disheartened.

"No. He's the top guy. But he's got a backup man—or group. There's someone providing him the certainty he could put this crew together and yet still maintain control of them. If this were chess, he's got a 'hidden queen.' That's all."

"Is there even such a thing?" James asked.

"Hell, no! Not in any legal game. But we are not dealing with a legal game here, James. Something's amiss with this bunch. Your theory is still holding."

In his usual cheerful way, Brian chimed in, "And you're going to have to figure out who that is, James. That's all."

James shrugged, sighed, and appeared to collapse a bit. Resigned to yet another mystery, he slowly commented, "So, you are saying there is another seat at the table."

"Yes, my man, that is what we are saying. And until you find out who or what that is, we are stuck."

"You got any ideas for me, at this point?" James asked hopefully, guessing Andy would not have insisted on an in-person meeting if he did not have some idea.

Andy smiled. "Well, you did tell me long ago that it's always about the money. I've got a gut hunch we have been down part of this road before. I asked myself, what entity with global impact is missing from this diverse group?"

No one else had anything to say. They sat quietly at the table. Though James knew Andy was speaking metaphorically, he had no idea at that moment that there was indeed an empty seat at the table in Dinkelsbühl, Germany. They were closer than they knew.

CHAPTER SIXTEEN

*J*ames had returned to Manassas solo. Needing to do some things at home on the ranch and having volunteered to help Brian and Andy find homes in Northwest Montana, Jessica had decided to remain behind. Neither man trusted themselves to pick for their wives. Jessica, on the other hand, had no compunction whatsoever about narrowing the search and giving Reagan and Alicia each some final choices before they would fly up to make decisions and offers.

The trip back was a sobering one for James. He knew that he and the boys had used the same research and evaluation tools and methods they had used for years to ferret out bad guys and defang their attacks. But to hear from Andy that there was a missing piece, and that the piece might be the linchpin on the whole cabal, was unnerving. James couldn't help but wish he had a colleague or two that he really trusted in the intelligence community, but the only one actually was Ari.

Fortunately, Ari Ben-Gurion had remained in the United States and was caught on camera frequently entering and exiting the Israeli embassy. He rarely carried anything in or out, and if he did, it was not electronic—strictly papers in envelopes. His insistence on going old school on communication delayed things quite a bit, but James knew it was wise. By the time he landed, he had decided to reach out to Ben-Gurion.

Getting back to his hotel, there was a note from Vince saying he had moved in to Brannigan's and that he expected he'd run into James at the restaurant, since Brannigan went there every Wednesday and Friday. *I'll deal with all this tomorrow,* he told himself, and immediately fell asleep. Crossing multiple time zones back and forth in just 24 hours was not something he handled as well as when he was young.

What day is it? James thought as he suddenly woke up, turning on like a light switch. The clock on the nightstand said it was Wednesday. James hurriedly showered and dressed to make his way to the restaurant for lunch. The Mayflower restaurant was renowned for great coffee, which attracted even more patrons, and James was grateful that morning for the brew.

Just as he was settling his bill, Vince and Brannigan walked in, coming directly to him. The three men greeted each other effusively. Brannigan was clearly in a good mood. James knew him well enough to know that when he got that Cheshire grin on his face, he was letting his ego get out in front of him a bit. Brannigan viewed himself as the smartest man in the world of intelligence, and for all James knew, he might be. But Brannigan had a killer instinct—one which he would often reveal like a poker player with a "tell." Whenever he felt he had just bested someone, he became more jovial. James had often wondered if it was fake or if Brannigan did truly relish the kill.

This morning, he was manifesting that exuberance. "James, I want to tell you I am grateful to have run into you the other day."

James seemed to have a question mark on his face, so Brannigan continued. "It just so happens that Vince here has the perfect requisites for what I need, and he agreed to come work for me for a while."

James smiled and nodded to Vince. "Yeah, that was a happy coincidence."

"What are your plans, James?" Brannigan asked. "Staying in D.C. long?"

"No, not too much longer, few days maybe."

"You know, I don't think I asked the other day, but what did bring you here?"

"Sightseeing."

"Sightseeing?" Brannigan seemed a little incredulous.

James laughed. "Yeah. All these years of coming and going from the D.C. area, and I never took the time to see the sights. I'd see some monuments now and again, but I always told myself that one day I'd tour the Smithsonian. You know, the National Archives, too."

"That's what you have been doing?"

"John, I had no idea how big the Smithsonian is! I mean, it is several Smithsonians, and they are constantly rotating displays in and out. Jesus, a person could live here their whole life and not see it all!"

Truth be told, Brannigan had never been either. His only interest really in history was current history and his ability to manipulate and influence it. Rummaging around in inauguration gowns of First Ladies held no appeal for him. Yet, he feigned interest.

James continued, "So, I'm giving up on that project and will take a couple more days to check out the National Archives. I'm ashamed to say I've never even seen the Declaration of Independence!" All three of them just took that comment in. No one spoke for a minute.

Finally, Vince broke the silence. "Where to after you check out? Home?"

"Yes, but not directly, I don't think. I have time, you know, now. So, I thought I'd pick up that old car of mine I parked out of the city, maybe head west a bit to check out some of the Civil War battlefields. Never been to them either. But I know Manassas is not too far."

"Fredericksburg, too," Brannigan added.

"Right, I'd forgotten. Thanks. I'll have the concierge set me up with an itinerary." Jokingly, he said, "Not that I'll stick to it, but what is that they say about good intentions…?"

"Beats me," Vince said.

"Anyway, I'm glad this worked out for both of you. Good luck. I'm headed out now for a bit, probably make my way to the World War II Memorial."

"Well, maybe I'll pass you on the Mall," Vince said. "I wanted to leave a tribute to a friend of mine at the Vietnam Wall."

"Yeah? You lost a friend?" Brannigan asked, noting mentally that Vince seemed a bit young for that.

"Several, John." Vince realized he needed to cover his tracks a bit, so he added, "My dad's friends actually, but one was real special to me. Almost like an uncle." He stopped to assess if Brannigan was accepting this. He seemed to be. That fortified Vince to add, "I think of him often. George Hamilton. Hell of a helicopter pilot. Killed early. I stop by there from time to time."

"Yeah, well, we've all lost someone along the way, I'm afraid," Brannigan commented, almost dismissively.

James had heard every word Vince said and made a mental note that he needed to look up the marble slab Hamilton's name would be etched in. More than 50,000 Americans had lost their lives in that conflict, and each was remembered by name on an inground sculpture. Most Americans James' age knew someone on that wall. The significance today for James, though, was that Vince had just hinted at the oldest—and actually, safest—surreptitious communication mechanism in the intelligence community: personal hand-off.

Fortunately, it went completely over Brannigan's head. For too many years now, he had been engaged in the nastiest of information warfare, and cyber warfare, and he was a little rusty at the old techniques he had been taught by his first handlers. That oversight would cost him—that and his arrogant assumption that he knew more than anyone else and that no one could best him at his own game.

Once James stepped out into the spring air, he grinned. "Gotcha!"

Later that afternoon, James did wander over to the Vietnam Veterans Memorial. Almost no one was in the mall these days, so he was able to search the large book of names immediately. Sure enough, there was a George Hamilton listed, along with the panel and line location of the dead man's name. Making his way to the slab, he located the name near the top.

Knowing Vince, he's probably stashed a note in one of the memorial notes, flowers, or flags that are left at the foot of each slab. Through the years, people had come to pay their respects to a family member who perished, and they would leave a remembrance. Most had no name on the token, but a few did. This was a shrine, and it was unlikely any sojourner would remove or vandalize a memento. So, James looked directly below the line for Hamilton, and sure enough, there was a flag at the base, with his name on it.

No one was around, so James fingered the flag and realized the small pole was hollow. Pulling it up, he extracted a note that had been rolled up and inserted. Replacing the flag into its established spot, he read the note. It said simply: "Have Hector give you an encrypted phone." That was all.

A few hours later, James checked out and headed for Manassas.

Schmidt had locked himself inside one of the glass phone booths in the New York City offices of the Global Commerce Forum. The Forum was housed on two floors of a New York high rise on Park Avenue. One floor looked like a space devoted to private conversation and private group meetings. The rooms were all glass, as were the phone booths.

That gave an elegant appearance of transparency to a casual observer. But in fact, each space was set up with encrypted communication capabilities and multiple screens in the conference room. Other than the fact the walls were glass panels, the larger spaces looked like situation rooms. Multiple people could be participating in the meeting, and they could be interacting with multiple locations on large screens.

All of the glass was tempered to be completely bullet proof, and each room was especially sound-proofed. The smaller glass phone booths had the same types of technology but were designed for just one person to be inside.

Earlier in the day, Schmidt had received an email from Schweiner, saying he needed to urgently speak with him. No other information was included except the time in Europe. Rutger made the connection and waited as Ernst Schweiner came onto the screen. Schweiner was clearly agitated about something.

"Rutger, I need you to get Brannigan and Loren up to your office by tomorrow. Our friend from Decu-Hehiz is ready to manufacture and distribute something that I feel we need to implement while attention is still on the pandemic. I'll have the GWO representative in on this as well. This is a big step forward, and I need to get Brannigan and Loren 'read in' and on board. I would rather have them with you than at their homes."

"Understood. I'll email them to get up here tomorrow afternoon."

"Sehr gut. Situations are escalating, but this part of the plan is ready."

Schweiner then disconnected, leaving Schmidt to wonder why the urgency and why Ernst had been abrupt and not very forthcoming with him. Dismissing it as just one of Schweiner's idiosyncrasies, he sent a private message to Brannigan and Loren, demanding their presence in NYC the following day. Within minutes, he received text acknowledgments from both men.

At his home in Georgetown, Brannigan simply turned to Vince McCoy and informed him to be ready to fly out of Reagan Airport in the morning and advised him that he would be meeting Peter Loren for the first time tomorrow.

Perfect. Brannigan smiled at the innocuous connection he was about to make. *Peter won't suspect anything.*

Perfect, McCoy thought. *This establishes my cover, for sure, and brings me in up close and personal.* Things were moving rapidly now, and he wondered what was up. *I sure hope James found my note!*

Chapter Seventeen

The presence of Vince McCoy didn't seem to phase Schmidt in the least. He expected someone like Brannigan to perhaps have his own private security. He, himself, did. Personally, he had never found a need for it much in Geneva, but New York City was another story. And the United States, at this time, was volatile and violent—in ways that were out of his control.

Though his machinations were contributing to a world of anarchy, he had never really imagined what that would look like, playing out on the streets where he lived. His own apartment was on Central Park East, and up to this point, there had not been much violence or destruction in his immediate neighborhood. But what had happened some months earlier down near Macy's had unnerved him.

I'll be glad to get back to Geneva, he told himself. *Even though I do feel safer with this guy McCoy around. He protects Brannigan, he protects me!*

And it was with that ease that the three conspirators accepted into their midst a spy. Brannigan trusted his own flawless instincts. Brannigan's recent string of successes had inflated his already gargantuan ego. Believing now that no one could outsmart him, given the hoaxes he had pulled off in the last five years, he just wasn't watching. Loren had always lived in the shadows, so he knew no one would be after him. That complacency on the part of these two allowed Vince to do what he did best—blend into the environment.

Today, as they came onto the 10th floor and headed into one of the glass conference rooms, Schmidt suggested Vince wait outside. "There are secure phone booths, if you need to make any calls."

"I'm fine. I'll just sit in that comfortable chair over there and handle some emails, read some news."

"Fine. You'll find coffee, water with gas or still, and croissants around the corner."

"Thank you," Vince said and sat down. The positioning of his chair enabled him to see into the room but left him unable to see the screen. He suspected that was intentional. He had no concerns about that, since his primary mission was to be introduced to, and accepted by, these other men. Gambling that they would be comfortable with his presence in the future, if need be, nothing in his behavior aroused suspicion. *First mission accomplished*, he thought.

What he could see, however, as the three men took seats at the table, was that Schmidt used a laptop of some kind to begin the virtual call. He had inserted a flash drive into it just before he logged in. *As long as Hector can hack into that laptop, we'll see what occurred, even without the flash drive*, he thought. *If I can get that wireless code, we can work backward from there.*

He had no idea whether this would work, but he used his phone and turned on a scan for any signals in the room he was in and, hopefully, inside the glass conference room. To him, it seemed like just a lot of noise, and he wondered if they were jamming somehow. But he sent what he had picked up through to Hector, all the while masking it by ANN news on his phone. The app he and Hector used to do this was buried beneath the app for ANN news. Using the camouflage of America's News Network, he could appear to watch the news, and anyone near him would think that is exactly what he was doing.

A moment or two later, a flicker on his screen alerted him that Hector was on, was surveilling the scene, trying to locate and record conversations. Or at the very least find transmissions he could hack into. Vince simply waited, having no idea whether they were successful or not.

He had not been, at least not totally. Back in Manassas, in the hangar at the back of the property, Hector Rodriguez turned to James Mikolas and said, "I've located where they are. And I don't think I have been detected. But we may need to get into that room. It's really firewalled. Or enter through one of the participants. Got to work on this."

"Brannigan, Loren, I need you to listen to some information we have for you. Then we'll discuss what you will do with it." Ernst Schweiner spoke in his usual professorial tone, with one exception. He was speaking faster than normal. Brannigan did not know the significance of that, but he made note of it.

Appearing on two additional screens flanking Ernst were Cedric Cornell of the GWO and Rudi Iseli, the president of Decu-Hehiz. Schweiner took the lead. "Gentlemen, we plan to execute the full plan all simultaneously, as I mentioned. But these two elements are especially important right now. They involve a breakthrough that will ensure that we are able to manage mass populations. What the American press, however, and what their leaders do with this will determine how effective it is."

"First, let us hear from the GWO." Cedric Cornell spoke and assumed prominence on the screen. "The Chinese have been very helpful to us. Whether they are doing it for their own political agenda, or whether they are actually following through with commitments they made to Ernst, the recent virus pandemic has set the stage for what will have to come next." He paused, took a sip of water, and held up a paper he was reading from. "This is confirmation that we have developed a Global Outbreak Report app. It will enable any person from any country who has the app to report if one of their fellow citizens seems ill, or sneezes, or coughs even. Once they report who it is, and where they are, we in the GWO will dispatch a response team to locate the individual and take them into isolation for observation."

"To many, that might seem like a wonderful tool for any future outbreaks or viruses that might surface—ostensibly to detect and prevent a pandemic such as the one in 2020," Ernst cheerfully chimed in. "But tell them the rest, Cedric."

"Yes, well, that is the obvious use of such a development, and with the right incentivization, I believe that every government can be persuaded to embrace the app and mass distribute it to their citizens. Then, the people themselves become our citizen spies, and we can then isolate as many people as we deem necessary." Cedric stopped for a moment and let that sink in. "Quite innocuous on the surface, isn't it?"

All of them concurred. Then he added, "Quite desirable. Follows so logically from the chaos and confusion about the earlier virus." He smiled. "But, for us, it provides a perfect way to locate anyone who is being turned in and decide if we have a bona fide dissident on our hands or just some hapless chap who happened to sneeze. Gentlemen, it puts us in complete control of who we incarcerate in internment areas and who we release. Right under their self-righteous noses!"

Ernst interrupted at this point. "Excellent, Cedric, excellent! But what must happen in the United States is for the media that you are running,

Peter, to embrace this with such enthusiasm and deadly earnest that their political leaders will follow. John, you will have to deepen their interest through your connections and your appearances on the air." Brannigan nodded. His acceptance as a totally credible expert by a fawning media had been a real serendipity—both for Branigan's bank account and for the disinformation he wanted to advance.

Peter responded first. "Ernst, I think you can be very confident that we are there on that—or almost there. I'll just keep punching that 'fear' button, and anxiety about another round of infections, and the networks and media outlets will embrace it—not as a dangerous tool, but as their savior. I can even see them now, congratulating themselves on their role in saving their fellow countrymen from fear and exposure like they lived through with the COVID-19 situation."

"But I want it to go even further, Peter," Ernst resumed. "John, listen, too. We need the Americans to choose, on their own, a vaccination certificate passport system that is mandatory for any American to travel inside the United States. We are going to need to stop their mobility and stop it in the very near future. To move around, they will need a vaccination passport, and we will control who gets the passports based upon the app."

Brannigan was tracking very well at this point. "You can count on the politicians to fall in lockstep with the media on this. I'll see they get 'intel' and data that confirms the need for all of this. For their own political futures, they will rush to the bandwagon." Despite the contempt with which Brannigan had just referred to the men and women of the swamp, this group laughed.

"Now, it gets even better, gentlemen. Let us have Decu-Hehiz explain what they have developed. Rudi, the floor is yours."

"Thank you, Ernst. I am proud to announce that we have successfully developed, tested, and are ready to deliver pharmaceutical antibodies for the viruses of the future. We all know people don't eat well enough to have the immune system they might need. We also know that traditional vaccines work, typically, to help the body's antibodies fight the infection. But...there are wild variables, and the outcome is very much at risk. We can't have that. We want the people to survive that we choose to survive, and the ones we want to go away, to go away."

He had said it so dispassionately that, for a moment, Loren almost missed it. *They're talking about selecting who will survive and who will not,* Peter thought.

"We need the media to embrace the idea of injectable, pharmaceutical antibodies—ones that are more powerful than naturally developed or triggered ones. Again, if the fear level remains high, we have concluded they will embrace this new development."

"Yes, but doesn't that mean that almost the whole world will want them? Doesn't that defeat the purpose of selection?" Peter asked.

Ernst interjected and took center screen. "I'll answer that. Yes, Peter, and that is exactly what we want for the long game. Of course— at the moment—*we* can control who gets the more exacting, effective synthetic antibodies to run around in their body. They will benefit. But for the long game, we want everyone remaining to have them. This will modify the human body over time. We are taking our first steps into the trans-human we desire in order to create the future world. Designed properly, we may be able to remotely dictate what those pharmaceutical antibodies can and cannot do. However, my friends, the human body will be morphing into a body that is more and more synthetic, and that is the man of tomorrow!" Ernst was tremoring with enthusiasm over that prospect and how close they were to implementing it.

Brannigan felt compelled to ask, "Why are we sure there will be another virus capable of creating a global pandemic?"

"Simple, John, simple," Ernst responded. "Because China will make sure of it."

Jesus, Brannigan almost exclaimed, *thank God we're in a secure room! The man just admitted the Chinese intentionally did it.* "So, are you saying you are sure the Chinese deliberately released the virus?"

"No. The GWO here tells me it could have been accidental, not deliberate. But what I can tell you is that it was a biological weapon. Whether it got out of control by carelessness, or by deliberation, our friends the Chinese have not told us."

"My intel does tell me it is a weapon and not just some random virus," Brannigan concurred. "Word is—and we have to make sure, Peter, that the public never gets wind of this—the U.S. was onto it and getting ready to put the screws to the Chinese on their long habit of suspicious virus outbreaks and their odd obsession with bats. Whatever the circumstances, it turned into a 'happy circumstance' for us."

"Agreed, John. The United States is ripe for the taking now. The people have chosen to imprison themselves, and if Peter keeps up his attack, they will continue to turn on themselves until it is too late to do otherwise."

Peter nodded his complete agreement.

"Ernst, what if the Chinese are satisfied that they have achieved their objective? And they don't plan on any more weapons development?" Brannigan continued to press.

"That's not likely."

He had said it with such authority and certainty that Brannigan was taken aback. "Why is that, if I may ask?

"Because they are working on population control. They've come very far economically in 30 years, but they still have a problem of too many people." Then Ernst laughed, relishing his next thought. "Someone may just have a different picture of who 'desirables' are."

"Who would that be?"

"Not anyone on this call. And not Serge. But one who already has a seat at the table. As I mentioned to you in Dinkelsbühl, there are others who appear at our GCF meetings, and discussions—some who are keynote speakers even. They hold a revered position, and they are very wealthy and powerful in their fields, and within their governments."

Brannigan said nothing. He expected Ernst to brag a little more about the team he had recruited over the years. His expectation was warranted. Ernst smiled again, pursed his lips, and looked down his nose into the camera once again. "This 'gentleman' feels that a planetary population of 8 billion is unsustainable and that it is time for true world leaders to depopulate the Earth, leaving room for those who warrant it. Thus, he has a keen interest in targeted viruses and targeted vaccines. The test run, in his mind, was COVID-19. It eliminated elderly and the sick. That is just common sense to me."

The two men flanking Ernst agreed wholeheartedly and applauded his last statement. Brannigan and Peter simply took it in.

"And what is our role, relevant to this new information?" Peter asked.

"Just keep the Americans afraid and divided. The more strident the voices, the deeper the divide, the easier it will be to conquer that thing Americans pride themselves in—their spirit. Surely, there are enough selfish, ambitious politicians who have already found ways to exploit Americans' fear of this first virus. And the more afraid people are, the more the robotic media can help us control them. I meant to congratulate you again, Peter, on your stellar work there."

"Absolutely," the others agreed almost in chorus.

"We just continue to persuade people to choose to do what we want them to do. Only faster, and more intensely now."

Propaganda warfare at its best, you sly old man! Brannigan thought admiringly. *Lies and truths so intertwined, and so indistinguishable, that the person goes insane trying to figure it out...that's the best of mind control. Long time since I've seen anybody this good.* John Brannigan stopped himself from reminiscing and said, "Understood. Consider it done, right, Peter?"

Peter nodded. "We'll need Pilaf, though. Are you going to talk to him, Ernst?"

"Yes. Well, gentlemen, that is all for today, I believe. Thank you, Rudi and Cedric, for the briefing." Then, he suddenly terminated the call.

And, all the while, outside in a comfortable chair sipping on a black coffee, Vince McCoy was watching ANN news on his phone.

CHAPTER EIGHTEEN

Vince was headed out to Manassas to meet up with Hector and, hopefully, James. He'd laid a good cover story with Brannigan when they returned from New York that he had to meet with Rodriguez and get the plan on how Hector wanted to set up surveillance of Loren. Pleading ignorance of things too technical, he expected Brannigan accepted that—given that Brannigan, though savvy on the basic elements of cyber warfare, was more the concept guy than the execution guy. He, too, needed his own special brand of "tech support."

Frankly, I'm glad to be out of that place, Vince thought. He had never actually spent much time in the District of Columbia, and he clearly sensed the murky swamp of deception, excessive ambition, and treachery. Even a few hours away was going to feel like a vacation to him. Brannigan wasn't expecting him back until the next day.

What Vince didn't know was that Brannigan planned to spend the day in his basement, connecting with his own team in order to plant some information about the unreliability of certain vaccines and the looming revelation that there was a more lethal strain of virus that appeared to have been spotted in Africa. All of it was disinformation, and it might or might not be needed. But Brannigan liked a wide variety of options when it came to leaking material to the DPP. Considering them intelligent enough, but amateurs in the intelligence game, and now completely manipulated by Loren, he liked to be able to turn in any direction in order to create more chaos and distractions.

The fact Brannigan called his own team on his encrypted phone from his home would prove providential in the weeks to come. But that day, he had no inkling of any danger. Any periodic feelings of suspicion he experienced were now directed squarely at Peter Loren, and his "gaze" never turned to Vince.

Vince arrived at the farm around noon and was greeted by James, who walked him back to the house.

"Did you get my message?" he asked James.

"Sure did!" James answered, grinning as he held up his new phone. "Gotta hand it to Hector. Same phone, same number. Just a new secret coding that encrypts selectively."

Vince nodded his approval. Knowing that James was more of an old-school warrior, he intended to have James remain at the farm, yet be equipped to receive and send communication to either him or Hector if he stumbled onto something or needed something. "Where's Hector?"

"He's out in the hangar. Spends most of his time there."

Vince and James walked back along the two-track path through the field that led to the hangar. He really wanted to know how Hector planned to play this.

"Hey, man," Hector grinned as the two walked in. "Good to see you! You been covering a lot of territory since you left me!"

The three sat down in some typical steel chairs and pulled them into a huddle at the back of the hangar, under the tail of the jet. "So, how do you want to play this?" Vince asked.

"The New York space is going to be tricky. That building is crawling with groups that have encrypted communications and high security. I've located lines to the Global Bank, some office at the United Nations, and some development group I haven't identified yet. That's just the in-country stuff. Obviously, there was an international call going on when you were there, and I haven't quite figured out yet how to get eyes and/or ears inside that. There are redundant firewalls and a lot of overlapping security. I just don't want to trigger an alarm on someone else's system. Makes you wonder if all these folks aren't collaborating with one another, given the interconnectivity." He let that sink in for a moment.

"They might all be using some form of Shadow IT, and it might be easier for me to hack into that cloud. You know, some form of cyber shadowing until I find an entry point." The look on James' face told Hector that James didn't understand any of this. Turning to Vince for moral support, Vince didn't seem any more enlightened than James. He tried once again. "My guess is that I can somehow shadow one of the other lines for data traveling there and slide in on that channel—if they are connected to communicate with one another. You understand?"

"Not really, Hector," James admitted. "Can you give it to me in layman's terms?"

"Sure, James, sure. Bottom line—it's tricky."

Vince could see Hector was turning ideas over in his mind—almost as if he could see the machinery working. Unconsciously, he laughed.

"What are you laughing at?" Hector challenged.

"Did I laugh? Sorry, it wasn't at you. Sometimes, I can almost see smoke coming out of your ears when you are working on a puzzle, that's all!" That seemed to handle it. Hector just rolled his eyes and offered them a candy bar from a large bag he kept on hand.

Moving on, Hector advised, "Now, we got James set up, and we three should all be able to communicate if need be. But I still want you to keep the flag at the Vietnam Memorial and, James, you keep that mail box." James nodded his agreement. He'd been around long enough to know that technology can get screwed up, and he had seen many a mission scrapped or fail due to it.

What Hector said next, however, surprised them both. "I think the easier part is going to be Brannigan's house, and Loren's—once I find him. He's got offices and presumably a home. I'll need to have Brannigan show me both."

"Well, you are assuming Brannigan knows those locations. What if he doesn't?" James asked.

"He'll find them, once I explain to him that I am going to need Loren's haunts in order to surveil him or have Vince surveil him."

Both men were surprised. Vince was the first to speak. "You said *you* are going to explain it to Brannigan? Really?"

Hector grinned again and said, "For sure. Vince, you are going to tell him I need to speak to him. Call me on your phone and put him on. I want to record a voice pattern on him as well. He won't be suspicious. Frankly, I think it's weirder if you don't have him at least talk to me."

This was Hector's wheelhouse, and James could not see any hesitancy whatsoever in Hector as he took command of this part of the mission. Vince then asked, "So, you talk to Brannigan…and what are you going to tell him to do?"

"I'm going to tell him I will need to do a more conventional surveillance of Loren electronically, but also will need to have his physical location in case you two need me to be eyes on. The man isn't going to do everything by computer or phone. That's what I'll explain to Brannigan."

"And…if Brannigan doesn't know?" Vince asked.

"I'm gambling he doesn't! That's the sweet part. He'll have to use his communication lines to have someone find Loren's various whereabouts. Whether he does it right then, or after our call, what I will have you set up in your room beforehand should enable us to begin monitoring his communications." He stopped, satisfied they both understood. But before Vince could ask, he added, "And if you are worried he'll try it right then, don't worry, we are covered as long as you leave your phone on. Simple. As I said, Brannigan is simple. I'll take him, one way or another."

Hector Rodriguez was 28 years old, had no schooling, and had grown up a thug in a gang in south Los Angeles. Yet, clearly, he had an intellect and aptitude for work far beyond his life's experiences. James was somewhat awestruck. *Not since Brian have I met someone like this,* James thought. And that was as high a compliment that this unsuspecting young man could have received.

Hector continued. "OK, then, you got that?" They both nodded. Neither one of them really did, but they knew they could at least execute his instructions. That was a good usage of their talents for the moment, they concluded.

Then, almost as an afterthought, Hector said, "Oh, and you should assume he has wired your room. Watch your conversations."

"Roger."

"Loren should be fairly simple to do electronically, even if I have to do something old school, since I won't have an invitation into his house. He's a PR and opposition research consultant. Not likely to be as suspicious as Brannigan. Physical contact will be between Brannigan, Vince, and Loren. I should be able to stay out of it. I'm your ace up your sleeve, if a need arises for someone to follow his car or watch the neighborhood."

Once it was decided how Hector might use physical surveillance, stealth phone conversation tapping, and cyber hacking, Vince felt comfortable returning to Georgetown and was prepared to let Brannigan know the strategy his colleague wanted to pursue. Hector stopped him. "No. Just tell him I have a good plan and am working out the details now. Tell him I will be calling to talk with him."

Vince understood and said, "Yeah, you call when you know he is there with me. Do you have a cover story for needing to talk with him?"

Hector shook his head, "Vince, Vince, when are you ever gonna learn? I'll just tell him the truth, that's all. I wanted to talk with him, get some info, and I expect he wanted to size me up as well."

After that simplicity, and since Brannigan wasn't expecting Vince back, the three decided to go into the town of Manassas to a barbecue place the farm hand had raved about to Hector. They took Jessica's pilot and the lucky farm hand with them to make it a day of relaxation. It would be the last one they would have for a very long time.

The following day, Vince was preparing to return to Brannigan's with a "special jar" of peanut butter and a box of saltines. The devices Hector wanted him to have were enclosed in the jar, and he had shown Vince what to do with them.

For some reason Hector and Vince did not understand, James found that ruse comical. They didn't know that the only things James knew how to cook were scrambled eggs and tuna fish sandwiches. *I wonder if one of the requisites for intelligence work is not being a cook,* James mused. *Geez, I thought I was bad about that. But peanut butter and crackers?!* He laughed.

Hector and Vince both turned to him with question marks on their faces. "Nothing," James said. "Don't mind me. Hector, after he leaves, you can fill me in on what *your* personal culinary preferences are."

James could see Hector was not tracking with this, so he just waived it off. "Forget it. I'm just a little punchy today is all."

CHAPTER NINETEEN

*I*t was an uncharacteristically warm spring day in Geneva. Schweiner was an avid skier and mountain walker, but in early spring, he enjoyed strolling along the shoreline of Lake Geneva. The bike and walking path clung to the shore, allowing pedestrians to enjoy not only the magnificent views, but the sound of the water lapping against the rock embankments. Today, he was working up an appetite and looking forward to sitting outside at his favorite restaurant overlooking the lake. Arriving ahead of his guest, the maître d greeted him effusively. "It is a pleasure to see you again, Herr Schweiner!"

"Likewise."

"Your usual table by the water?"

"Yes. It's a calm day on the water, and I think my guest will especially enjoy the view and privacy."

The maître d knew then to be expecting someone else, that this was one of those lunches where Schweiner was not to be disturbed and the waiter needed to be the most discreet. "Very well. And I will have Pierre serve you today, mein Herr."

Schweiner smiled. He had always loved it when people who served others for a living showed him the proper respect. "My guest will ask for me." The man nodded, knowing also never to ask the name of any of Schweiner's guests at this type of lunch.

Schweiner was facing the water, adding a bit more sugar to his latte when Serge Pilaf was ushered to the table. "Serge, so glad you could join me today. Come sit. I have saved the best view for you," Ernst said with a flourishing gesture toward the surrounding beauty. "Pleasant drive?" Schweiner knew Pilaf was not a great fan of flying—even though as one of the top 100 wealthiest men in the world, he had multiple private jets of his own, as well as corporate jets. He split his time between Silicon Valley and Amalfi, Italy. Schweiner supposed correctly that Serge would have chosen a lovely winding road through the Alps.

"Tell me, Serge, do you have aspirations of ever driving in the Grand Prix? I understand you have a zest for speed and a considerable driving skill?"

Shaking his head no, Pilaf smiled and said, "I am afraid I am more of a dilettante when it comes to racing. Would never have the nerve, actually."

"I understand. I feel the same about downhill skiing. Always been more of a cross-country man myself."

Pilaf laughed. "Well, as long as we each know our own limitations, we can't come to too much harm!"

"Precisely, my dear boy, precisely. And it is just something like that which I wish to discuss with you."

Serge Pilaf may have been one of the wealthiest men in the world, and certainly one of the most powerful, but he also knew the master of them all was Ernst Schweiner. Schweiner had set a vision before Pilaf was ever born and had painstakingly worked, maneuvered, and manipulated every sector of society for 40 years to bring that vision into reality. Pilaf knew he was a player in this master's game, but that Schweiner was boss. It had not escaped his notice that he had literally been summoned to this meeting. Knowing now that it was a private meeting, he knew Ernst had something on his mind.

Before he could say anything, Ernst mercifully smiled and said, "But first, let us enjoy our repast and this magnificent time on the water."

What happened next cemented in Serge's mind that he was not only a player, but certainly the most pivotal piece in this elaborate, breathtaking takeover of multiple countries and continents. Such a concept was not only brazen, but fraught with possible fissures and failures. He was about to get a personal briefing on his precise role.

"I was speaking a few days ago with Cedric Cornell and Rudi Iseli. Cedric is confident in his ability to keep the necessary global medical issues front and center for some time. The Chinese appear more than willing to participate. But the key thing is the continual reinforcement of fear and chaos by raising the specter of another pandemic, as well as still-hidden characteristics of this one, any time various populations get the idea they can return to life as normal."

Serge nodded. Ernst continued, "And deliciously, Brannigan and his still-existent agency cohorts can plant any intel necessary about secret viruses that one or another bad-actor government could unleash. Keep everybody guessing as to who is the real 'who' here…the real villain, if you will."

By then, Serge felt compelled to ask something that had concerned him from the beginning about biological warfare. "Ernst, my expertise is not in warfare, let alone biological warfare. Frankly, it has always horrified me. So, let me voice a concern of mine, if I may."

"Of course."

"What if one of the 'gain of function' viruses does escape, becoming more widespread than COVID-19 and more lethal? What happens to us?"

Schweiner couldn't help but notice that Serge's concern was not with any of the world's population, but himself. *Natural, I suppose,* he thought. Smiling, and adjusting his spectacles, he reassured his colleague. "My concern precisely. And I am assured by Rudi Iseli that Decu-Hehiz is ready with antibodies that are artificial and can be inserted into the body to destroy any more powerful attacker."

Pilaf was noticeably relieved by that. "That's amazing. Reassuring, too."

"Yes. I think perhaps our friend Rudi is salivating over widespread manufacture and use of this technology. He sees money, for sure. As for me, I am most pleased that it will keep *us* safe and that we could then select others who would receive it. Selective salvation, if you will." And with that simple statement, Serge fully understood that Ernst Schweiner was indeed planning to reset the world and the world's leadership—even if it meant unleashing population-control diseases on the world—as long as he could maintain control of his own safety and maintain control over who would be the ones to survive such a scourge, if it should unhappily develop at any given time.

"Well, that's comforting. Chilling but comforting."

"That is not what concerns me, Serge. What concerns me is that we have a very limited time to execute successfully this transfer of power. I think it is obvious to all of us that as the United States goes, so goes the world—more or less. And it is the United States that has me concerned."

"How so?" Pilaf inquired.

"At Dinkelsbühl, I explained to you all that those damned freedom-loving Americans, and their insistence on rule of law and their confounded Constitution, were a threat to our plans. The masses would never yield easily to the ruling elites." He stopped for a moment, took a sip of his dessert espresso, and continued, "I am afraid they are waking up. It seems the current regimes in American politics, education, medicine, media have pushed this 'woke culture' so far they have even agitated the French. Possibly even the Germans."

"Yes, I noticed the French president's comments on what he fears most. Frankly, I was startled about his concern over the 'woke cancel culture' in the United States and how destructive it would be for France. It was so unexpected, I didn't even have time to block it or take it down."

"Exactly," Ernst said. "That tells me there are more than 75 million Americans now who would oppose any of our intentions and certainly not yield to the reset. I am afraid their numbers are growing—especially if their geschrei is now even reaching the ears of European leaders who normally would have been sympathetic to the social justice causes, etc."

Continuing, Ernst elaborated a bit. "My mounting concern is this— and we must address it. I am afraid that if the Americans get to 100 million in their population who are not 'woke,' but rather 'awake' and taking action, they will overwhelm our plan and we could fail."

"Do you have a reason for selecting that particular number?"

"Yes. They almost fractured in the 2020 election, with all of the fighting over the 75 million voters and all the mystery surrounding that. Worked in our favor brilliantly. But if they get to 100 million, it would mean that they somehow have siphoned off millions who before opposed them and who now would stand with them. I am no political scientist, but I don't think American politicians could offset that many voters voting in a block. That creates a real problem for us. They could stop our progress. Discredit us. Even override our voices, perhaps."

Ernst paused once again. "And, again, those damned French seeming to be willing to join in makes the issue even worse. I know my history well enough to remember that the French Revolution was driven really by peasants. Bloody and unsuccessful as that was, ultimately, it certainly put an end to the ruling class. We cannot have that now. So, the possibility of a populist revolution in the United States and the UK spreading into Europe would be devastating."

Pilaf asked, "You said *we* must address this. Is that why you asked me here today?"

"Yes. If all goes well, your part in this will be more the vanguard, as you and the Big Tech companies, and the technology development companies, lead us into an exciting future. But if the number of Americans who embrace the populism ideals keeps rising, then your role is the safeguard. Meaning you will need to be ready to take down all communication except for the people on this list." He handed Serge a one-page typewritten document.

As Pilaf scanned the list, he found his own name there, as well as the names of the others who had met in Dinkelsbühl. But the rest of the names were what he would have referred to as the Davos Crowd—major players in the corporate world and in the political world.

Ernst then said, "The key is that the Americans have to choose all this, you understand?"

"Yes, Ernst, I most definitely do. Too much force or enforcement, and they instinctively resist. The average American must choose this himself."

"You've got it. All of your Big Tech devices must be happily accepted— no, not just accepted, rather *desired*—by the American consumer. They must want all your devices. And all those devices and apps must gradually make them more dependent on the device. And appreciative of the surveillance our technologies are now making possible."

"Agreed," Serge said. "You see how quickly the Americans—even their so-called populist leaders—embraced the smart glasses! I doubt any of them gave even a thought to the advancement of that into facial recognition, and the tracking and location of anyone at any time, no matter what disguise they might have attempted. Rebellion will not be possible."

"Amazing isn't it, Serge, how people only see the positive, fun, life-enhancing aspects of our breakthroughs, not the reverse usage that allows us to monitor and control them."

"Well, that's why you have Peter Loren on the team. He'll be the first one to help us with how to market all of our new technologies so that ordinary people never even suspect a Trojan Horse, let alone recognize that they chose it and brought it into their lives."

Ernst was very animated now. All of his life, he had been envisioning and planning for these next few years. And the prospect of seeing the world reset the way it should be, with the worthy and brightest of mankind running the show—evolving into a supreme human—made him cheerful and talkative. He felt a kindred spirit in Serge. The other members were exceptional tools to be used to achieve what was needed. Serge Pilaf, on the other hand, had such an eccentric appearance with his shock of hair and long, unruly beard, one wondered if he were high on peyote or just a mad visionary. Ernst believed the latter, and he sensed that Serge naturally saw the future world as he himself did.

For that reason, he embraced Serge a bit more intimately mentally by placing a huge responsibility on him. "Can you persuade what I call Big Tech—your software companies and all platform providers—to comply? We could need all social media and broadcast networks and all search engine networks to find only what we want people to find, to hear only what we want them to hear, and to see only what we want them to see. While the U.S. is distracted by this 'cancel culture,' we will set up to erase anything from the past and present that would be counterproductive in our new world."

Serge's response was immediate. He looked over his shoulder to reassure himself that no one, in fact, was eavesdropping. They were not, of course. "Yes. We can install brakes to slow down any communication through our media. We can install firewalls to prevent browsing and locating any source information we deem undesirable. And most definitely, we can black out any person or organization—all simultaneously, if need be. Frankly, we can do that now. We have just never been tasked to do so."

"My dear boy, I am tasking you to do so. To be ready, that is, in case such measures are needed." He gazed at Serge for a moment, as if debating whether or not to add this. Then, he decided to confide more in the man he felt was an odd-looking younger version of himself. "If all goes well—and that will depend a great deal on the other members of our team—you will architect the new communication channels in the new world. In the reset, there will be no competition. You will have control of it all. The ultimate monopoly, if you will. Unfettered, though, by disparate governments. The ultimate seat at the table."

Serge Pilaf understood perfectly where he was headed. And he also understood that Ernst Schweiner could not have entrusted that role to anyone more qualified than himself. What was enticing to him was the fact that many of the men he would end up dominating and dictating courses of action to were far wealthier than he. *You may have more money and more power than me,* he thought about them, *but, from here forward, you will need me in order to retain that wealth.* He sighed like a man who is happily full and content following a magnificent meal.

CHAPTER TWENTY

"*D*addy, Daddy!" Faith squealed as she pushed open the door into the home office Andy and Brian were working in. Reagan had tried to catch her, but when she got up a head of steam, the toddler was too quick for her mom.

The family had moved into their new home, set up high on a hill, just outside of Bigfork, Montana. The views in one direction looked down the length of Flathead Lake, presenting breathtaking vistas of the 35-mile-long lake. And in the other direction, views looked up into Glacier National Park and some of its majestic peaks. Unlike their Los Angeles home, with views out over the city lights, this home was a log structure and felt very peaceful and remote. In fact, it was just five minutes into the quaint town that housed more artists than people, it seemed. Yet, the house disappeared into the trees, making it virtually invisible to anyone scanning the hills around Bigfork.

Brian and Alicia's home was close by and equally secluded. Theirs, however, was a Usonian architectural feast, designed by a disciple of Frank Lloyd Wright. In the finest tradition of organic architecture, their home, too, blended into the environment, making it almost invisible. For both families, that gave them the privacy they needed, and each was enjoying being so close to the other.

Especially the two little girls, Faith and Hope. Almost inseparable, they played together and napped together every day, alternating between the two residences. Today, however, Hope was a little under the weather, and Faith had been left to entertain herself. Andy had often noticed that this little one was a bit of a tomboy, and he had finally persuaded Reagan to give up trying to keep her clean all the time. Not that she minded her bath. She loved it, in fact. But her philosophy seemed to be: arrive for the bath as dirty as possible, accumulate as many souvenirs of the day's explorations as possible, empty your pockets only if demanded, and be prepared to find almost anything in your shoes.

Today seemed to be a productive one for Faith. The twinkle in her eyes, and the fact she was jumping up and down, managing to release the knob and enter her father's office, signaled to Andy that she must have some fine prize to show him. "Look, look," she commanded him, not quite fully pronouncing the "k" yet.

"What have you got, Faith? Let me see." *As if she's not dying to show me her latest treasure!*

Coming close to him, she dug her little fists into the front pockets of her overalls and pulled out a green garden snake in her right hand and a large beetle in her left. Both critters seemed too terrified to even move. Just then, Reagan burst in, throwing her hands up apologetically for having interrupted Andy. She reached Faith just as she was holding up her trophies to her dad. Reagan hated snakes and most bugs. Her mouth flew open, but Andy signaled not to cry out.

"Well, aren't these lovely," he said, reaching for a cardboard box he kept nearby for just such occurrences. "Where did you find them?"

"In da yart." Faith answered that quite stoically and then lit up, "I too kick for dem, Daddy!"

"I see that you were too quick for them," he repeated back to her so she could hear the pronunciation of some words again. "Well, what do you want to do with them?"

Clearly, Faith had not thought that far ahead. She pouted and said, "Doe know."

"You don't know?" he articulated her answer back. She nodded. "Well, tell you what, sweetie. These are harmless little critters. What do you say we put them in this box, and you and mommy—he winked at Reagan as he said this—can take them outside and let them go?"

"But, I wan tem!"

"I know. But they will die if you keep them. They need to be outdoors where you found them."

"Die?" Faith looked up at him, as if she didn't quite know whether to believe him or not. Clearly, she wanted to keep her catch, but she was a gentle young girl, and Andy knew she would be heartbroken if her actions killed them.

Frankly, it's a miracle they survived being shoved into her pockets, he thought.

"Oh, otay," she sighed, surrendering the snake and bug into the box.

Reagan immediately sprang forward, took the box, and ushered her daughter out of the office. "Bye, Daddy! We doe wan tem to die, Mommy," she explained to her mother.

"Wow, I thought we might need an interpreter there for a minute!" Brian joked, admiring Andy's ability to understand what his daughter was saying and his patience in repeating it correctly for her to continue to learn. "I learned a lot, bro. Hope's still in the two-word sentences stage, and most of the time, I don't catch all of them." Andy chuckled at the changes two little girls had brought into their lives.

"Whew, that was close, though!" Brian continued. "I was afraid we might be in for a little drama there for a minute."

"Yeah. She's actually pretty good about that. She has her grandmother's disposition, thank God!"

Hearing Andy reference his late mother made Brian a bit nostalgic. Both of them had lost their mothers too young and too tragically. And Mrs. Weir had been the closest thing to a mother to him from his days in Arlington playing football with Andy, to the night she had to come to his dorm and told him his whole family had died in a murder/suicide incident, to the day she herself was killed in retribution for the work Andy and Brian had done that foiled a terrorist attack.

"You know, Andy, I am glad we moved here. Much less drama…"

Andy nodded, reflecting for a moment on their adventurous lives, then returning to the task at hand. "Well, now that the emergency is over, what do you say we get back to work?"

"All right, bro. Tell you the truth, I was grateful for the interruption. This has me stumped today. It's like walking in quicksand! If only things could be as simple as a child's viewpoint!"

Neither Andy nor Brian knew at that moment just how prophetic that statement would turn out to be.

———————————————————

Andy and Brian were standing in front of five Mylar sheets that Andy had hung from rails in the middle of the room. Hanging there, he could draw with a marker on either side and see things from either side. Each clear plate had a printed heading and a few dots located around the plate. "Well, this is going to give new meaning to the term 'connect the dots,'" Andy joked.

"Hmmm," Brian looked at this new contraption and asked, "Is there a reason we are doing this like a Chinese laundry, instead of on the computer?"

"Very funny! And what would you know about 'Chinese laundries'?" he ribbed his friend. Brian just rolled his eyes. "I think we might miss something doing it on a computer, even if we tried a three-dimensional plane. Better to plot this out here and feed it into the computer later."

"Well, you're the man at this stage of the game. As long as this gets us out of the quicksand..." Andy shot him a look. So, Brian obligingly sobered up and put his attention fully on the display.

"Each sheet is an institution James and *we* believe is under attack in the United States. The weakening of each institution weakens the whole. So, I am trying to plot what the attack tactics are and who is implementing what. Basically, just trying to disentangle a confused, seething pile of data."

Andy went on to explain that he couldn't decide whether there was a central point that should be on each sheet or whether the dots would connect on their own without having a source point for each of the attacks. He knew figuring that out would be key to solving the problem and helping James with the men he was tracking.

"Brian, I am going to say that since James brought this to us, he is pretty sure that all of these dangerous circumstances are emanating from one source, so we should start with that assumption for our first analysis."

"But, what if he's wrong on that, bro? His hypothesis could be wrong, you know."

"I suppose," Andy hedged. "But he never has been before. So, I am willing to start with that assumption and see if it proves out. If it doesn't, hopefully, something else will emerge here. Besides, you and I have a lot of backstory on some of these issues from all of our other games."

Grabbing a black Sharpie, Brian approached the first hanging Mylar. "True. We do. Which one do we start with?" It was only then he noticed that there were five different tracks on the ceiling, close together, and each Mylar was hanging on a separate track. That enabled Andy to change the sequence by simply moving the sheets on their respective tracks.

"Let's start with the family," Andy answered. "I'm no sociologist, but it seems to me that's the basic building block of a society." Andy had already put some dots on the sheet but had not labeled them, let alone connected any of them. Pondering it a bit, he concluded, "It doesn't matter. We just need to start. The rest will fall in line eventually. Kind of like my three-dimensional chess analysis I did for James many moons ago. Eventually, it sorted itself out."

"Yeah, but not until after you'd gotten so depressed about it that James had your mom invite me over to toss footballs with you in the street! First time I met James…" Brian's voice trailed off as he recalled that time in 2002. So much had happened since then. He smiled. "Well, if that happens to you again, we got plenty of space to toss some balls."

Andy laughed.

The first Mylar had proven the hardest and the one that required a lot of discipline. Andy began by having the two of them list the things that eroded the family unit, that seemed to have the greatest negative impact on a cohesive force. He decided to plot them in a circular shape, rather than just list them vertically. Once plotted, each dot was labeled. Almost immediately, they ran into some psychological barriers and reluctances—particularly on Brian's part.

"Brian, help me just brainstorm here, and list out the things that would undermine the traditional family," Andy coached with just a hint of annoyance. The list started with Divorce, then Weak, Irresponsible Men, TV Promoting Infidelity and Promiscuity—which they shortened to TV Morals—and Disrespect. When Andy called out Abortion, Brian protested and said, "Man, we are getting into some controversial stuff here, Andy. This is going to be hard to sell. I can hear it now!"

To Brian's surprise, Andy retorted quite firmly, "Brian, we are just making a list of things we know are topics related to families. This is not the time for any discussion, debate, or judgment. We are just listing, OK?"

Brian nodded, and they continued. "Single Mom Households, No Dads," Brian added.

"That's one, for sure." Andy said. The list continued, and they added Self-centeredness, Throwaway Relationships, Separate Careers, Money Trap, and No Marriage/Live-in Relationships. On the wheel shape Andy had created with the dots, Divorce was on the top in the 12 o'clock position, and Throwaway Relationships was in the 3 o'clock position, No Marriage/Live-in Relationships in the 6 o'clock, and Abortion in the 9 o'clock.

Andy held up his hand and said, "There's more, I am sure, but this is enough for me to see what connects. He then asked himself what could be connected with Weak, Irresponsible Men and drew a line to Money Trap. Abortion was connected to Single Mom Households, to Separate Careers, to Self-centeredness. TV Morals was connected to Throwaway Relationships and Divorce. Each time he drew a line from one dot to another, he could see Brian wince. "Remember, Brian, we are not debating this," he admonished. "I am trying to identify elements that undermine the family. Some of these may play in both directions, but I am looking for an enemy attack line here, that is all… a chink in the armor."

"I know, I know," Brian responded almost apologetically. "I just didn't realize how much I am emotionally impacted just by words—more than I would have thought. I don't know whether it's fear…or anger…" his voice trailed. "Wow, if I can't even face the words, I guess we do have something going on here that certainly doesn't add to calm, family environments."

Andy exhaled deeply, as he rubbed his chin and stared at the Mylar sheet. It was a mess of crisscrossed lines, but one thing did jump out. Almost all of them went through the center to an element opposite the point he had plotted. Not all did. But the ones that went, say, directly to Divorce bounced back to the center and on through to yet another dot.

"All right, you, I think I got this," Andy pronounced. This is an 'All Roads Lead to Rome' depiction. No matter where we start, and what we connect in any direction, eventually they cross or meet in the center. And center is?" He paused, thinking.

Brian helped him out. "Geez, bro. It's a Collapsed Cohesive Family. **No Family** would be a better way to put it. "

Andy slapped him on the back and yelled, "Now, you are talking! It's Ones and Zeroes—Dichotomies. The enemy is attacking along the lines of the 'Thing' and 'It's Opposite.' The enemy goal is the opposite of the institution we value. I can think with that."

Just then, there was a knock on the door and Reagan popped her head in. "Are you two going to get some dinner?" Their lack of response told her that was not likely. She'd been married to her geek long enough to know that when he was solving a puzzle, he lost track of time. "I'll just leave some sandwiches for you inside the door. Be back in a few minutes."

While she was gone, the boys moved onto the institution of Education. Brian seemed a little calmer now and was focused just on listing the elements, not on getting into discussions or debates about the elements or his personal opinion about them. It was on the second Mylar that Brian spotted something that reassured him. Brian was a marketing genius and, through the years, had come to understand the importance of marketing buttons—the words that symbolized something and drew an immediate response. Once he had spotted that, he was comfortable working in the realm with Andy.

The assault on Education as a foundational institution for a free people had an even longer list. Everything from Unions to No Choice, from Low Standards to Low Self-esteem, from "Wokeism" to Psychiatric Medications. The list continued with Enforced Thought, Altered History, Lack of Money, Critical Race Theory, and No Critical Thinking. And once again, as they began to connect the dots with the Sharpie, multiple dots connected with multiple other dots, creating a pattern of crisscrossing lines and also a circular perimeter. Just as in the Collapsed Family on the first Mylar, the dots not only connected to the next one near, forming a circle, but they went through the center on their way to another dot.

"OK, it appears they all go through the center here. So, the center is?" Andy asked himself.

"**Collapsed, Ignorant & Dependent Citizen—Fear**," Brian offered.

"That's a little wordy, don't you think?" Andy asked.

"Maybe, but it sure as hell is the result of all we listed and, I might add, what we are experiencing today!"

Before Andy could admonish him with a look, Brian threw up his hands and said, "Hey, bro, we done completed this one. I can have an opinion now!"

Andy laughed, and he accepted Brian's title. Then he pulled the third Mylar into place, and they began plotting the dots related to the institution of Religion. That one was a juicy one, and a painful one, but by the end, the dots connected in yet another circle with a center. They labeled that center **No Religion—Isolation, Hopelessness & Control.**

The work was going faster, now that they had the hang of it. Though they were prepared for different outcomes on the separate Mylars, this next one proved to provide an almost identical pattern. The fourth one was **Justice.** And the hub was **Injustice, No Law and Order—Hate.**

Standing back, Andy was looking at each of them separately, studying them. "Hmmm, each one a condition and an emotion. Especially if we add Loneliness to **No Family.** Interesting."

Brian squinted his eyes and looked at what they had concluded on each Mylar sheet, and he spotted also what Andy saw. "So, what we are looking at are actions, programs, propaganda that bring about a condition in the society, accompanied by a strong, virulent emotion."

What happened next would determine the outcome of this global attack. At the moment, though, it seemed innocuous enough. Andy decided to slide all the sheets together, one in front of the other, and what emerged was a circular pattern with complete chaos and confusion in the lines, making it almost impossible to see through the Mylar—but most definitely revealing the center as the stand-out point.

"Jesus, Andy," Brian exclaimed. "This reminds me of the movie *The Shining.*" Seeing that Andy did not have a clue what he was talking about, he explained, "You know, the Jack Nicholson film where you think he is writing a novel, and then you realize he has been writing hundreds of pages of the same sentence, day after day. Horrifying!"

"Oh yeah, I remember trying to watch that one with Reagan. When he chopped the ax through the bathroom door and said, 'Jack's back' or something like that, I lost her. She was gone. Never did see the end of it."

"Andy, looking at this is like looking at the inside of an insane person's mind. Complete confusion in all areas of life that matter. And complete collapse."

It seemed like an eternity to both men before Andy responded. "So, James was right. They are doing this in a coordinated attack to collapse us all into nothing. From there, we will have been prepared for a totalitarian state."

A terrible, paralyzing wave of fear ran up and down Andy's body. He could not look at Brian, fearing that Brian was probably in the same state. They just stood there, silent, looking at the Mylar sheets and the likely goal of the enemy. Andy and Brian were brave and brilliant men. They had faced a lot in their lives. But there was something about this that was far more sinister than any other treacherous villains they had tackled.

Still numb, Andy turned to Brian, and said, "What do you say we 'take a walk'?" That was Andy's way of decompressing whenever a problem started to overwhelm him.

"Only if we can toss some footballs, too," Brian responded. They both released a bit of tension with that idea and opened the door to head out.

Before they left the room, however, Andy stopped in his tracks in the door frame, looking into the great room where his daughter was standing beside the sofa, her arm draped up on it, watching on the big screen *The Wizard of Oz*. She was motionless, totally fixated on the movie. Andy motioned to Reagan to come over. "Hey, what's she doing?" he whispered.

"Watching *The Wizard of Oz*."

"Like that, just standing there?" Reagan nodded. "How long has she been standing there?"

"The whole movie," Reagan responded. "She hasn't moved."

"Amazing!" Andy looked at his little girl as she stood there with her panties hanging down a bit below her skirt.

"Yep, this is her third time through this today," Reagan commented.

"No!" Andy couldn't believe it. "She has watched this movie three times today?"

"Yes, Andy, she has—all the way through and standing like that the whole time. She stopped only for dinner and to pee." Andy just shook his head. As he did so, something seemed to shift in him, lightening his load somehow.

"Well, I'll be damned!" he said. "The Wizard, the invisible man behind the curtain. All illusion. Controlling through fear…" Reagan looked at him, wondering what on earth he was referring to. He seemed to be connecting the film character with something else.

Brian got it at the same instant Andy did. Looking over Andy's shoulder to Brian, Reagan asked, "Do you know what he's talking about?"

Brian started to almost bounce from one side to the other as he always did while playing football—the wide receiver to Andy as quarterback. That was a signal he was ready, excited, and going for the ball. "Yes, Reagan, I do. I *sure* do." Stepping out of the office, he turned to Andy. "So, you still need to take that walk? Or can we just toss some balls?"

"I think we can just toss some balls. Faith's binge-watching jerked me out of my funk. Don't take this wrong, but it was providential that Hope was sick today, or the two of them would have been playing. Instead, Faith got to learn about the Wizard."

The two men then dashed out the door, leaving Reagan wondering what on earth they were talking about.

Chapter Twenty-One

*R*utger was waiting in the glass conference room for a call from Ernst. It was 5 AM, and no one else was in the building. Though he normally might have enjoyed the view of the Manhattan towers around him, since their offices looked downtown, most of them were eerily dark. Given the near closure of New York City during the pandemic, the city was a virtual ghost of its former self.

He had no idea why Ernst had set the call so early. *Perhaps he lost track of the time zones!* he silently complained. In any case, Schweiner was his boss, and if Schweiner wanted an early-morning conference call, no matter what time zone, he would be there and be prepared.

It was a bit spooky coming onto the darkened floors of the Global Commerce Forum. There weren't even cleaning crews in the building, only the lone guard downstairs. Most other finance firms and businesses were still working remotely for business and safety reasons. The streets of Manhattan were no longer safe. The violent crime rate had soared, leaving most residents of Manhattan virtual prisoners in their own apartments. Schmidt was grateful to have superior quarters, and an office space that was impenetrable, but he, nonetheless, looked forward to the day he could return to Switzerland and Germany to continue his role from that continent.

Best not to think about that now, though, he coached himself. Just then, the screen came alive in front of him, and Ernst Schweiner appeared, looking rested and dapper as always.

"Good morning, Rutger."

"Good morning to you, Ernst."

"My apologies for rousting you out so early. It was not accidental, I am afraid."

"That's fine. I rather enjoy seeing the city wake up, as it will in about an hour. You know I am available when needed." He could see Schweiner nodding, as he reached for some documents he had placed in front of him.

Ernst looked directly into the camera now, straight at his friend. "There needs to be a greater urgency than we are exemplifying at the moment. In a few weeks, I will summon all of the men at the table for a global conference of our own."

Before he could explain, Rutger asked, "You mean all of the Davos players?"

"No. Oh my, no. Just those I assembled in Dinkelsbühl. They are the tip of the spear right now."

Schweiner explained he was not going to gather them all in Germany, but rather gather them in a conference. After some discussion, the two decided not to bring the Americans into the GCF offices either. His offices were so connected with the United Nations and the Global Bank that Ernst did not want to "compromise" any of the men. He was well aware that many governments—most especially Israel, as well as elements of the United States government—likely had all of those entities under surveillance. It was commonplace for a sovereign nation to keep tabs on what other countries and multinational organizations might be doing within their border.

It was a very lucky happenstance that the United Nations had been placed in New York City, as far as Schweiner was concerned. Though he personally believed the future seat of world government should be in Europe, along with the global finance enterprises that would control all economics worldwide, and also the world court, Schweiner recognized that the coming changes in regime and control of the population would likely be accepted more readily by Americans if the organization that would assume power at least was on their soil.

In his plan, if all went well, the Americans would yield power to the United Nations and allow themselves to gradually assimilate into the global governance, abandoning their more nationalistic approach. The Paris Climate Accords, and the rules and restrictions they were about to place on the Capitalist and Free Enterprise markets, were moving the project along nicely. But Schweiner knew time was growing short—and so did the men who had a seat at the table in Dinkelsbühl.

"Rutger, we will have each man join from his own secure location. But in advance of that, I want you to get Loren and Brannigan to step up a transition, move the timeline up and as fast as they can."

"All right. What is it that you need?"

"They need to persuade not just the U.S. government—and by *that*, I mean the executive branch, not that sideshow of a Congress they have going on over there now. That's a great distraction and tool for us and our purposes, but they can't even decide when to go to the bathroom at this point. And what I need requires immediate action. You can likely work through the State Department and Justice."

"Understood, Ernst, but I think I missed what you want our men to do."

"No." Ernst was somewhat short. "You did not miss it. I had not stated it." Then Ernst laughed, chuckling at the joke on him. "I distracted myself even. I want the U.S. government to begin to enforce more control over the citizens and for the people to accept it. It is key that they must accept it! We have a third of a billion people to subjugate."

Ernst paused for a few moments, taking a sip from the crystal water goblet he ubiquitously had with him. Looking up again, he continued the instruction. "They need to restrict the movements, the travel of Americans, and the congregation of Americans—right of assembly notwithstanding. *And* the Americans must desire it."

"Ernst," Rutger interjected, "that should be simple for those two at this point. Peter has educated us all, I believe, to the reality that, if you punch the "convenience button," he calls it, Americans will reach for or accept what you are offering because they do not like to be inconvenienced."

Ernst laughed. "And that is exactly why a global government could never emerge from America. Too impatient. We've painstakingly set this up. Only we Europeans could do this."

"Precisely."

"So, here is what is needed. Those two can figure out how to do it. I need the Americans to embrace the idea of a vaccine passport. The Israelis have already embraced it, so you should be able to get it done in the United States. It will make it so much more convenient for them to travel without hassle—or so they think. So much more convenient for them to enter buildings, attend events, etc. They will accept it as something that gives them greater freedom. Just the opposite will have occurred. Once done, they will not be allowed to travel, etc., unless vaccinated. Ironic, isn't it, that they lost their freedom, and now to get that freedom back, they have to give up even more freedom. What was once a 'right' is now a 'privilege' granted to them by someone else."

Schweiner paused to assure himself that Schmidt was tracking with him and appreciating the irony of what they had accomplished.

Satisfied, he continued, "Whoever controls the pandemic—now and in the future—controls who has to be vaccinated and who can assemble, travel, participate. After that, it is a short 'convenient' step to have them choose more attractive bracelets to store the medical information and then, from there, an even more convenient implant of a medical wellness chip. Saves all that paperwork, you know, and updates and renewals of cards and lost cards." He had said it very sincerely, but the underlying menace and disdain did not escape Schmidt.

"Rutger, the same thing that is driving them to embrace digital currency will drive them in this area. And you can count on the political class to go along with this. Their government has morphed into something that is just as much about power as any other government is. Make no mistake. We just need to be able to identify the ones that need to be culled out of the herd, the independent ones."

"Ernst, speaking of that, is everything on track with the move to a global, digital currency?"

"Yes." That was all he said. His failure to elaborate at all perplexed Rutger somewhat, as he was the liaison in the United States with so many banking communities. But he let it go, telling himself that Ernst would fill him in on that later.

Apparently, Ernst thought better of it right then because he suddenly added, "Yes, there is more, of course, and we don't need to get into that today. Brannigan and Loren need to give us a boost in the area I mentioned. But you can be assured, if the people accept control of their movements, and feel righteous even in having their movements curtailed, we are on the path. Once we have passports, wellness implants, smart glasses that enable them to 'conveniently' read, do business, play games—and, at the same time, allow us to do facial recognition on them—they will accept digital currency, too. Just think, Rutger, no more TSA lines. We just use the smart glasses, and they are good to go. And, of course, we will know where every citizen is at all times."

"What ensures us that they will all do this?"

"Oh, that is the beauty of this!" he exclaimed, clapping his hands, clasping them together in front of his chest. "Those who don't or won't wear the glasses are the ones we will be culling out. They are the rebellious ones. And if Peter does his part, they will be excoriated and ostracized by their own countrymen for spreading disease, not caring—you name it. I am sure the fear-driven American can come up with any number of reasons to persecute the noncompliant. I am counting on that. Peter and John simply have to short-circuit their reason. Well on their way, don't you think?"

Rutger chuckled. "Yes, Ernst, I do agree. I understand completely why they were chosen."

"So, *after* that comes embracing the 'digital currency' in all its various forms. It is the natural evolution in the world of money and finance. It makes exchange easier, more convenient transactions, you know…no more checks, credit cards, cash, all the things people lose or which expire. Pesky outdated technologies…" he joked. "From there, we wipe out any resistance to us manipulating bodies. Whoever elevated transgenderism into political legitimacy did us a huge favor. Discrediting the science of biology, and male and female, opens the door for our trans-human and all that we envision for the future of man." He stopped, looked at Rutger again, smiled, and asked, "Did that answer your question, Rutger?" There was a hint of sarcasm in the question. Schmidt could feel it even across the thousands of miles of separation.

He sighed, "Most definitely. I appreciate you taking that time with me though, Ernst," he said hoping to reassure Schweiner. "It's comforting actually to see how far we have come."

"Absolutely. That's why I just need these two to ratchet it up so that the acceptance level within the government—and the people—is high enough that if anyone balks, or resists, they will be put down by their own people, their fellow citizens. The citizen will control the citizen into conformity and compliance. Good form of 'enemy identification' we are supplying to the people of the United States, don't you think?"

With no reservation whatsoever, Rutger said, "I do indeed, sir. I do indeed. I will reach out to Brannigan and Loren and set them onto this immediately. More of the same…"

"Yes, more of the same, just much more, and much more rapidly."

With that, Ernst ended the call. Rutger was wide awake at this point, and it was still dark outside. Only thirty minutes on that call. 5:30 AM. *Too early to roust them, I think. I'll give them a couple of hours at least.*

The basement office in Georgetown appeared like any other office a retired bureaucrat might have set up to keep his hand in, write his memoirs, present consulting offers and the like. There was nothing out of the ordinary in the room, save for the fact that a highly secured communication line came into the room, and the room itself was soundproofed and wired. John Brannigan was taking no chances that any of his work would be located, hacked, or compromised in any way.

None of his former colleagues knew what level of depth he had gone to in order to bury "opposition research" against any political candidate he might need to injure. His files and activities were not just limited to the now colloquial term "opposition research." Over the last four years, enough classified documents had been unearthed and released to have revealed the whole Russia Collusion to, in fact, have been a hoax. Nonetheless, it had been a brilliant counterintelligence operation, a national disruption, and direct interference with the governing of the United States.

Brannigan was very proud of his work. Others might end up with criminal charges and the word "Disgraced" written after their name. But not him. His role in the conspiracy whirlwinds that had raged in Washington for five years would never be unearthed. Yet, he still held a couple of aces up his sleeve. If Russia did get out of line, he could make any criminal activity he chose appear to circle back to Russia. The cyber security team in the CIA was stellar, and it could make anything appear to originate from anywhere. Nor was that limited to Russia. It would be his way of compromising any nation or person who would not comply with his demands. Though "retired" from service, he—like most agency heads—had numerous subordinates loyal to them and their policies. Brannigan was no different.

Yet he, himself, remained invisible. Other former agency heads and prominent figures might have their fingerprints all over an operation to disrupt, but his would not be found. Coupled with that was the extensive collection of blackmail folders he possessed. These were not digitized. Brannigan knew all too well what murky type of things can be unearthed from servers and flash drives. *No, no,* he praised himself. *No one sees these unless I choose for them to be seen.* Standing in the corner near the small basement windows were several filing cabinets. Nothing was unique about them, save the contents. Each one held compromising folders on everyone John Brannigan had blackmailed, intended to blackmail, or considered he might need to blackmail, in order to keep them in line.

He was good at this, and after Rutger had called him and Peter to hasten their work, he gazed at the file cabinets this morning. *I will have to review what juicy material may be in there and assess relative merit for this escalation of speed that Ernst desires.*

But this morning, his attention was on his computer and some computer files he was looking over. All of them were on a flash drive, and that was secured in one of the locked file cabinets. Nothing was stored on his server just in case the server accidentally ended up in the wrong hands. One of the items stored on the flash drive caused him to laugh out loud. He couldn't help but think of the mischief he could create with this technology.

Time to ask Peter, he thought as he dialed Peter's number.

"Peter, you have a minute? I want to ask you something, and then perhaps, if you like the idea, get some additional information from you on future targets."

"I do. What's up? I am sitting here racking my brain to decide what will be the next 'crisis' I can promote."

"What do you know about deepfake video?" Brannigan asked rather nonchalantly.

"You got me stumped there, John. I am not sure I know what you are talking about."

That pleased Brannigan and confirmed that he and his information warfare team still lodged inside the Agency had a new tool—one that could be very helpful in speeding up the process and in destroying people who needed to be neutralized. "Well, it's an evolution of technology. Instead of having to rely upon the artistry of people who could alter photos and videos, re-edit seamlessly, or insert false content, this one makes it appear that someone is actively in present time doing something they are not. It can disperse attention immediately, create endless rabbit trails for the media and politicians to run down, cause lawsuits, and pretty much destroy any relationship that needs to be destroyed. We have successfully upended the rule of law in the United States. We've got guilt by association, guilt by accusation, guilty until proven innocent, no rule of law, no due process—all of these pretty well part of the normal operating procedure of the media, justice personnel, and the population at large."

"Yes. One of the things I am most proud of, John, is what the DPP and I have been able to do to totally control the news narrative. As we have discussed, a huge portion of the United States now operates on stimulus-response. Like one raw nerve, exposed, if you will. The quintessential lynch mob."

"Well, this is the next evolution, my friend. You are going to have a field day with this. All I will need to have is a list of people who we need to target and be prepared to knock out. Deepfake video is a computer-generated image—a person, let's say—who is actually artificial intelligence created to appear like an actual person. We can thank Hollywood for the inspiration here when they started to employ artificial intelligence and use computer-generated movie actors in the starring roles. They are getting so good that, in some cases, the audience cannot tell the difference between the computer-generated person and the actual actor."

Peter laughed loudly. "That's got to be a real FU to these bloated stars and the Screen Actors Guild. Let us create something fake that obviates the need for the real person. One way to handle temperamental prima donnas if you ask me!"

Brannigan, too, laughed at that. "I had not thought of it that way, but you are so right." Sobering a bit, he continued his explanation. "Well, these computer-generated 'people,' using AI to simulate the movements, gestures, attitudes, emotions of an actual person, are fake! But the face of the real person, and their body language, is superimposed on the fake person, and the ensuing video is such a copy of the original person that no one can tell the difference."

"Ever?"

"Eventually, they will figure it out, but you and I both know that once something has aired and the media has pushed it out, they never retract. And the person stands guilty as accused, and it is corroborated by their own video."

"I see...," Peter was clearly thinking with this. "So, you are telling me you can make it appear anyone has done anything? Not just report on their alleged wrongdoing, but actually show them doing it or talking about it?"

"That's pretty much it. With this tool I have, you can create any false narrative you want about someone. The culture is set up to accept it as true. They are, therefore, guilty simply by the accusation. Moreover, since it is backed up by this deepfake video, the person locks it in, saying to themselves, 'But I saw it.' They don't doubt it because they saw it."

"Jesus, that is a deadly tool. Do you have this now?"

"Oh, yes. That's why I called you. You can look up a recent video

of that action/adventure actor, whose name I have forgotten for the
moment. It was so real, I could not tell that it was not him."

"So, we don't 'hold patent' on this, it appears."

"Nah, you know these super bright techies—always playing with
creating some new thing and new applications of it. Me, I look for who
I can destroy with it, if need be." Brannigan said it with a sincerity and
simplicity that left Peter with no doubt as to why Brannigan could have
gotten away with what he had up to this point.

"Well, given that we need to speed things up, I guess it is great that you
brilliant Americans are constantly dreaming up new things—especially if we
can corrupt them to our purpose. Saves us time. Should make Ernst happy."

Brannigan laughed. "My thinking exactly."

"You said you had a question?"

"Yes, Peter, what I will need is a list of people that you have assessed
may need to be taken down in the future. If secret videos, recordings, and
testimony of witnesses have not done it, this tool will. I am making up a
film library, if you will, of the men and women we may need to control
or gain assistance from. And I thought I would get my files ready—
you know, words from their own mouth, hanging them, if you will. No
matter that it is not even them, let alone their face or their words, in the
mind of the public—with your assistance—it will be **true**."

Brannigan had emphasized that word. Loren understood the
implications. Peter was thinking out loud. "Yes. The lie told often
enough becomes the truth. Even faster, a lying image. And with social
media today, we can move much faster than the mainstream media. We'll
relegate them to second position—merely there to confirm what they
saw on the internet. Delicious!"

"Names?" Brannigan pressed again.

"I will give you a list. Some are current politicians, even if their
careers seem derailed at the moment. Some will be those whose ambition
will make them want to make a name for themselves. I have a couple of
corporate heads in the U.S. who may need to be taken down a notch
or two. A judge I can think of. And a few heads of state who might try
to assist the United States in the coming conflagration. We will need to
dead agent them, too."

"Good." Brannigan liked Peter's use of the term "dead agent." It was
a technique used in propaganda to discredit the opponent before the
opponent could knock you out.

"John, do you already have the insider law enforcement and intelligence list?"

"Yes, Peter, leave that one to me. I just want to deliver to you knockout material on anyone who gets in our way or gets up on some righteous horse."

"Understood. How do you want me to deliver the list?"

"Send it over in a document to me to this email. Encrypt it. But rest assured, it will come straight in here, where I will grab it and convert it to my own security system before I destroy it. Once I acknowledge receipt, you should destroy the list. I don't want this coming back to you."

"Will do. Thank you, John. This will help."

"Well, as I said while we were feeding the ducks, 'we are going to need each other.'"

That brief call cemented a relationship between John Brannigan and Peter Loren. It also, unbeknownst to them, opened the door for their adversary. They would never know it had started there, but they would know the consequences. And neither would know which one of them had done it, for neither of them knew that a cyber burglar was testing the "doors and windows," looking for a way in—a cracked window.

CHAPTER TWENTY-TWO

Vince was lying on his bed talking with Hector when Brannigan called up the stairs to the remodeled attic apartment. "Vince, can you come down here, please?"

"Sure thing. Be right there."

Well, that's fortuitous, he thought. "Hector, James, hang on, I'm going down to the boss right now."

The three of them were just talking about getting Brannigan on Vince's phone so Hector could explain to Brannigan what he needed. It had been on Hector's "to do" list for the day, and this seemed like the perfect time.

Coming downstairs with his phone on mute, Vince found Brannigan in the kitchen microwaving a cup of coffee. "Vince, good, I want to go over our schedule today." Noticing Vince's phone, he said, "Are you on a call? You can finish it, if you are."

"I'm on with my surveillance guy. I put him on mute. But he wants to talk with you."

"Me?"

"Yeah. He's about to set up the target, and he needs some info from you. Can you do that now?"

"Sure."

Vince unmuted the phone and spoke to Hector before he handed it to Brannigan. "Hector, we're just going out, so let's do this now. I am going to hand the phone to Brannigan. John, this is Hector Rodriguez."

From that point on, Vince could only hear Brannigan's half of the call. But it sounded like he was responding exactly as they had preplanned. Watching Brannigan's face for any signs of suspicion or displeasure, Vince brought Brannigan his coffee. Brannigan gave him a thumbs up and sat down at the banquette in the corner of the kitchen.

"I was wondering when I might get to meet you, Hector. Vince tells me you are a talented boy."

Hector laughed and responded, "Hah! He should tell me that some time!" He and Brannigan seemed to enjoy that little private joke for a moment. Then Hector said, "Sir, I know you checked me out before you put us on this case, so you know who I am and where I come from."

"Yes, I did. Your anonymity appealed to me for this part of Vince's assignment."

Hector was nodding vigorously, even though Brannigan, of course, could not see him. "Well, sir, that is why you and I are not likely to meet in person. Hopefully, we won't need to." He waited to see if Brannigan would engage and query him for more details.

"And why is that?" Brannigan asked with an edge of criticism in his voice.

"The primary reason is that the work I do to hack into something is typically done in the 'dark.' You know that, I am sure. I'm kind of a 'home body' that way," Hector joked. Brannigan was listening. "And more importantly, because there is a component of actual physical surveillance here, I don't want anyone to see us together—no matter how innocuous the environment—and put two and two together. That's to keep you out of the picture. In my book, you are a confidential client, and I am sure I am a confidential asset in yours."

"True, you are right about that," Brannigan said. "But do you want to come to the house, to visit Vince, let's say?"

Hector's response was planned and immediate. "No, sir, that would be the worst. That might compromise all three of us. I don't want you to think I am being disrespectful, sir, but I am sure you are being surveilled by any number of people, for any number of reasons, and that is why you have a 'bodyguard.'" They all knew that was just the cover for Vince McCoy being around, but Brannigan also knew that, given his former position, it was possible any number of people might be snooping around.

"Understood."

"Well, I have to protect Vince's anonymity, too, and whatever cover story he has going for any mission. Vince and me seen together...well that's a bit of an odd couple, if you understand me."

Again, Brannigan laughed and winked at Vince. "I do. At the risk of seeming xenophobic, I trust by your name that you don't look like someone who would be hanging around a preppy Irish guy...."

"Sí, señor. That is correct. But that allows me the freedom to move about as well. Vince told me you asked if he had worked in Europe. Since I have been with him, it's only Central and South America. But being Latino, I can fit into any part of the country where Hispanics have emigrated and are doing 'service jobs,' for lack of a better term. Let's just say I don't stand out in a crowd of landscapers, maintenance, road crews…"

"I understand." Brannigan interrupted. "I have run many a covert crew in my day, Hector. You don't need to educate me."

"That's exactly what I told Vince. A man with your credentials would understand all this just on surface conversation. But let me get to the point of what I do need." Hector then explained to Brannigan that he needed to know where Peter Loren lived, and where his offices were, so that he could begin to set up both physical surveillance and electronic or cyber surveillance. "My assessment is that he'll have some junior-level security protecting his propaganda pieces but that he is probably not that conscious of security risks and should be fairly easy to hack. Simple encryption, which I can break. That should put us in a good position."

Brannigan agreed with Hector's assessment and was comfortable talking with him. He explained that he could easily get the address of his office, but he would need to dig up the home address. The simplest way he could think of, without seeming to be encroaching on someone's private address, was to ask one of the men at the DPP. They were all cohorts of his in the disinformation campaigns he had masterminded over the last five years, and they were not likely to remember that he and Loren had not ever met before. Besides, he reasoned, they knew he was aware of the public relations firm that was guiding the use of the disinformation and all the dirty tricks that followed from its release.

He and Hector ended their conversation, and Brannigan handed off the phone to Vince. Vince ended the call. At that point, Brannigan said, "I'll get that information—perhaps even today. Hector wants me to give it to you." Vince nodded.

Seeing that Brannigan seemed to be chewing on something, Vince asked, "Something you have attention on, John?"

"Maybe. Why wouldn't he just have me give it directly to him—you know, call him or text him?"

"Well…he's really good at protecting the people he works with and for. And himself."

"Doesn't he trust you?"

Vince laughed. "Yeah, he does. Think of it this way, John. We're hired guns—like in the Old West—only we work in the cyber world. His job is to serve your needs. But also to live to fight another day, if anyone comes through another door at you."

"Jesus, that's the kind of talk you get from double agents," Brannigan retorted, getting a little red under the sometimes-too-tight collar of his heavy-starched shirt he wore to meetings.

"More like someone with 'swinish suspicion,' I would say. Look, you hired me to find out what, if anything, this guy Loren is doing. I don't know why you want him checked out. That's not for me to know, unless you tell me. You have your reasons, and given your past government responsibilities, if there is something you are working on, and you need to test the creds of someone, that's good enough for me. But this is a clandestine operation, and my man is the best I know at not only getting the information needed, but doing it in such a way as to save our asses."

"I hear you." Brannigan waived it off, putting his cup in the sink.

"We are going to make sure this guy isn't coming through any back doors at you, setting you up for something—or to cut you out of something. That's all." Brannigan seemed satisfied with that. Vince then joked. "Besides, he's from the gangs. He's a pretty rough character."

"Rougher than me?"

Vince cocked his head to one side and shrugged his shoulders. "What do you say we get on with today's schedule."

Brannigan agreed. "I'll brief you on the way. We are headed to the Mayflower. I have to see someone there."

What Brannigan did not tell Vince was that he was doing a near-final interview with a Special Counsel lead investigator to confirm the misconduct of one of his longtime colleagues. In truth, a cabal of about 10 men and women had participated in what would later be recorded as the dirtiest political trick in American history. It would take decades to really unravel the depths of the misuse of the United States intelligence and law enforcement agencies. Through the many months of the investigation, Brannigan had skillfully deflected innuendo and evidence to incriminate other cabal participants, at the same time making it appear he had nothing to do with it.

John Brannigan was a master at deception and self-preservation. The cabal's mission had likely failed, but there was no way he was going to be thrown under the bus. Others would be exposed, and possibly put on trial, but, if anything, he would be a government witness against them.

So, when he went into the meeting in a private suite at the hotel, he was confident yet wary. He had been assured he was not a target of the investigation. But that the information he possessed could either confirm the evidence against the others, or he might perhaps have exculpatory evidence about them.

He had enough manufactured or secreted emails and texts to "sink or swim" any of his former pals. But something was gnawing at him. John Brannigan knew full well that law enforcement lies regularly to people to get them to submit. He couldn't shake from his thoughts the possibility that he was, in fact, the target. Fortunately, his attorney was deft at fending off unnecessary and potentially incriminating answers, and they both left the meeting confident that the next few years might be hard for some of the executives in intelligence and law enforcement that were his peers, but he, himself, would skate on.

Since his attorney was one of the attorneys in the DPP, he seized upon the opportunity to secure Loren's home address and to confirm his office's location. The man never gave it a thought. In his mind, they were all part of the same team, and Loren's whereabouts were not a secret. Without thinking, he texted his client the address card for Peter Loren from his phone. The address cards had not only the addresses, but also phone numbers. "Are you going to have him help you spin this?"

"Yeah. I want the dogs called off my trail, no sniffing around. It's a sweet contract I have with the network, and I don't want this lingering witch hunt to spoil anything for me."

Picking Vince up in the lobby and signaling they could leave, Brannigan texted Vince the address card he had just received. Perhaps John Brannigan was tired that day, perhaps he was distracted and thrown off his pins by some question in the interview. Perhaps John Brannigan was not on his A game, or maybe he never had an A game. Whatever the reason, he passed that text without even looking at it. Even though he was prepared to provide this all to Hector, he made a mistake. He had texted the information to Vince from the encrypted phone he had been using with his attorney, not from his flip phone.

Vince smiled and nodded. He was stunned but not surprised. He had always known that eventually bad guys make mistakes, and they leave clues, for not only had Brannigan delivered what he promised to Hector Rodriguez, he had texted it to Vince. Vince McCoy now had a message from John Brannigan's personal, encrypted cellphone. By day's end, Hector Rodriguez had Peter Loren's home address and, very importantly, his cellphone. A records check revealed this was a special cellphone number whose user was redacted.

More important than that, however, was that he was able to hack into Brannigan's phone by way of McCoy's. A review of recent activities revealed a call from Brannigan's phone to Loren's phone. Hector called out to James to come into the hangar. He had been holed up in his "workshop" too long to contain this.

When James Mikolas came into the hangar, he found Hector looming in the doorway of the "workshop," grinning. "What's happened?"

"I got 'em!" Hector yelled, pumping his fist up and down.

"You got Loren?" James asked. His heart was pounding.

Hector just shook his head from side to side as if he were playing the shell game, keeping James in suspense. "I got 'em both!"

There was no one else around to hug. Had the farm hand been there, he would have been grabbed by James. Instead, James lurched forward, throwing his arms around the hulking young man and giving him a hug.

Pulling away after a bit, Hector recovered with, "Geez, man, that's awkward!"

James dutifully let go and shrugged.

"I got work to do, man! Now we're rollin'!" Hector then turned and went back into his "workshop." "Now don't you come huggin' me again, James," Hector said over his shoulder, disappearing into his own world.

CHAPTER TWENTY-THREE

*T*he last thing James expected was for Ari to message him that they needed to meet. Rather than risking meeting at the normal restaurant, Ari told James to meet him in the mall, near the Korean War Veterans Memorial. Though the capital city was still occupied by federal troops, giving the appearance of an occupied territory, the area near the Vietnam, Korean, Lincoln, and Jefferson memorials was relatively open. And the benches that lined the mall were still there, giving locals a place to rest as they explored not just the monuments, but the museums that lined the expanse. Few had any idea just how long this mall was. Benches, therefore, adorned the landscape, providing one the opportunity to catch one's breath and rest one's feet.

Ari had characteristically arrived first and was reading a newspaper when James sat down beside him. For a moment or two, neither spoke. Then Ari looked up from the paper, his gaze still ahead and asked, "Were you followed?"

"No. Were you?"

"That I am not sure of, my friend." Ari then folded the newspaper, pulled out his cellphone, and pretended to be reading emails on the phone. James, on the other hand, pulled out his phone and appeared to be listening to some podcast or another.

"Really, isn't this a little cloak and dagger, Ari?" James joked.

"Not when you hear what I have to tell you, no."

James knew that whatever he was about to hear was coming from Mossad. He believed Ari hung around the embassy not only to provide a safe haven for himself, but also to have a secure location to receive information or instructions from his colleagues in Israel. *I wonder if there is such a thing as "former Mossad"?* he asked himself. In the United States, James would not automatically be welcomed out at Langley. He knew he might be able to pull off a visitor's pass from one of his analyst buddies, if the need arose, but he certainly wouldn't have the run of the place.

"Let me ask you something, Ari," James said.

"Yeah?"

"Do you live at the embassy?"

Ari considered for a moment how best to answer that question. He and James were friends and counterparts, but there still were some lines that could not be crossed. His answer was honest but somewhat evasive. "Well, I don't have it listed as a mailing address!" He laughed at his own joke and then added, "But, there are a few rooms inside available for short-term visitors from Israel."

"I see."

"But my residence isn't really the issue, James. I have good cover in that respect. What is of issue for someone like me is the centralization of our classified communications."

That was all James needed to hear. Whether active or not, Ari obviously still had access to top secret information. "I am profoundly glad to hear that, Ari. And I want you to know I don't take our connection lightly."

"Of course, my friend, of course," Ari assured him. "This is just developing now, but my gut tells me there is a connection between this and what you are working on. So, I want to read you in on something. Frankly, if you unearth anything, I would hope you would graciously read my government in on it as well."

James nodded. Ari then said, "The Chinese are up to something."

"The Chinese are always up to something, Ari. They've hacked into, stolen in some way, or actually been hired to facilitate the stealing of most of the world's secrets. We're over here bitching and moaning about stolen intellectual property when, in reality, their intelligence operatives are plentiful and deeply imbedded in our systems. They've burrowed into all of our secrets!"

"Well, if you'll get off the soapbox a minute, I want to alert you to a new wrinkle."

James shook his head, totally accepting the admonishment. "All right, you're right. What's up with them now?"

"You and I know just how pervasive their espionage activities are. Not just government, but business espionage. Frankly, any rock we turn over may reveal a Chinese spy. It took me a while to adjust to the reality that they are, in fact, the Chinese Communist Party, run by a dictator, and not the warm, fuzzy, 'we need to be part of the WTO as a developing nation, and we just love all things American' residue from their earlier Communist iteration."

James nodded, turning slightly toward Ari.

"Our crew at the embassy were laughing our heads off at the pretended alarm of your government in finding that a Congressman had been compromised by a Chinese honey pot. Or that one of your most prominent Senators had a Chinese spy driving her around for 20 years. We were shaking our heads, frankly, at that feigned naivete."

"For sure. But we're not here to talk about James Bond-like activities, are we?"

"Nope. They are gifted at cyber warfare. That's why I mentioned it at all. But they are investing heavily now into space warfare. Seems they have a sort of hybrid attack line being developed."

He had James' total attention now. "I'm listening."

"In recent years, the Chinese have been launching a lot of satellites into space. They're pretty brazen, giving the U.S. the finger when they launch a 'weather satellite' into orbit, in the same orbit as U.S. satellites. Then they blow up their own weather satellite—all legal, of course. But the debris from the destroyed satellite, floating in that band, knocks out every satellite still moving in the orbit. Like hitting a shrapnel field."

"Did they actually do that?" James had never heard about that.

"Yep. They are quite the mischief makers. Very clever at preventing anyone from spying on them." Ari stopped, and the tone in his voice changed now to a steely delivery. "But they are far more menacing than that. Your government tends to think in cliches—or at least your media does—regarding terms like cyber warfare and space warfare. No doubt the Chinese are cooking up a host of grizzly weapons that can and will be in space, but there is another way they use their satellites."

"And that's why we are here?"

"Yes. Not too long ago, the CCP launched a satellite into a different orbit. It is sitting up there all alone—nothing else in that band. Real puzzle for our intel guys, to figure out why it is there."

James was very interested in this now, especially since cyber and space had never been areas of his expertise. He, too, was on a learning curve. Ari continued, "We've looked it over with our eyes in the skies, and it doesn't seem like a weapon. Looks more like a communication satellite. But the puzzle is that it is very rarely on. It just sits and rotates around the Earth. Doesn't seem to have active functionality most of the time."

James interjected. "You said 'most of the time'? But it does come on?"

"Yes. For a few short minutes. We've tracked it, and it seems to have only one purpose: to receive or send communication to and from a location in Beijing and one other location." Ari stopped, looking at the picture of a lone satellite in his mind.

"Ari, where is it sending a Beijing communication to? Is this a private industry satellite like some of our private space companies send up?"

"We asked the same question, James. Was this a private commercial satellite used as the relay between a business in Beijing and a U.S. commercial location?" He sighed and added, "But we concluded it was not."

"Why's that?"

"Because the satellite—what few times it is on—has only two points of communication. One is in Beijing, and the other is here in the Washington, D.C. area. The satellite triangulates only those two communication points with itself."

"Huh," James was looking at that. "Are you sure it's D.C.? Not a military base? Not Langley?"

"That's the tough part, James. We have identified it does not appear to be communicating with any channels linked to your intelligence community—at least not as far as we can tell. And the receipt point doesn't seem to be anywhere near a military installation."

The two sat silent for a moment. Both were trained analysts and were working through the problem Ari had decided to lay on James. James asked, "Do you know where, then?"

"Near as we can tell, the receiver is somewhere in or near Bethesda, Maryland. The transmissions are so infrequent, and so brief, it's been like trying to trace a phone call where the perp knows precisely the length of time needed for anyone to track and locate…and ends the transmission before we have any joy."

"Would the person transmitting on our end have to be an intel guy?"

"No, not likely. They'd just need to know the equipment and its limitations. That is part of the issue for us. It appears the first communication fires up the satellite, and it immediately relays to the other party. And then, it goes dark again. It's not like a conversation. We don't even get the alert until the satellite turns on. And then, it's gone again. Damned frustrating!"

"For sure…a real mystery, I can see." James paused and then asked, "But what makes you think this is related to the cabal in Dinkelsbühl?"

"Don't know for sure, James. May be nothing. I just have a feeling they are connected, and to be honest with you, I wanted your fine mind at work on this one, too."

"I appreciate that." James chuckled. "Is there anything else?"

"Yes. The satellite came on just a few days after the meeting in the house in Dinkelsbühl. If they are connected—and that's a big *if*, I realize—then someone at the meeting came back to the States and sent a message."

"Who came back?"

"There were four. John Brannigan, Peter Loren, Rutger Schmidt, and, a couple of days after that, Serge Pilaf."

James was thinking out loud. "So, if they are connected—and for the sake of argument right now and for reasons I can't tell you just yet, Ari—I am going to assume they are. So, if..." he was turning something over in his mind, "the Kid said there would be an eighth player."

"What are you mumbling about, James?"

"Suppose the Kid—you remember my boy, Andy?" Ari nodded he definitely remembered who James referred to as the Kid. "Suppose he nailed it again? That there was an eighth chair at the table, so to speak. Maybe with no one sitting in it. A 'kitchen cabinet-type player,' that even the others at the table weren't aware of yet." He chewed on that for a while. "Wow, that would certainly keep everyone slightly off balance, wouldn't it? Schweiner keeping the last man a secret. CCP? A Chinese Big Tech company?"

"You know, I've been at this game a long time, my friend, and I always have to remind myself that there is always a nest of rattlesnakes— that bad guys have an innate tendency to mistrust one another and keep a cheating hand somewhere up their sleeve, to ensure their own survival," Ari said.

"Ari, that is absolutely the truth of it," James said admiringly. "And, if that is the case, we may have ourselves a chink in the armor here. I can use any break I can get!"

Standing up to stretch his legs, and still staring straight out in front, Ari responded. "That's why I wanted to meet—even if I don't have the thing totally nailed down yet, I just feel better having read you in on it."

"I'm glad you did. Now, if you find out this is all much ado about nothing?" James asked.

"I'll let you know, for sure. No need to chase down fake distractions.

Because we think that is just what it is: a phony communication line set up to get people to feel there is a hidden communication between Washington and Beijing—a real propaganda ruse."

"That's what your government thinks?"

"At the moment, yes. We are used to the Chinese with their false flags and red herrings. They are masters of deception, for sure."

The two parted with an agreement that, if the thing turned out to just be some weird outlier holding no significance of merit, Ari would invite James for a drink at the Mayflower. That was an outcome that neither man expected, nor welcomed. For these two Cold War warriors, they preferred to be in the hunt and on the trail of dangerous men and plots. Both men left with a sort of calm about their temporary conclusion, albeit it unsubstantiated. They were closer than they knew.

CHAPTER TWENTY-FOUR

*E*rnst Schweiner's mood was as foul as the weather in Geneva. Looking out of the penthouse offices of the Global Commerce Forum, he could barely see the lake, which was shrouded in clouds and rain. All he could see was the surf lapping up on the boardwalk, driven by the winds on the lake. As far as he was concerned, he was as angry as the sea.

Reports had just come in that the Swiss people had rejected the idea of an "e-ID," which was a voluntary system to electronically ID everyone in order, ostensibly, to make transactions more efficient. It was clearly one of the programs Ernst Schweiner had a keen interest in. Whether the Swiss were rejecting the automaticity of their identities, or whether they simply feared privacy matters, their vote had startled Ernst. *How the hell can we imminently complete this reset if my own people are resisting electronic identification?!*

What further irritated him was the fact that the e-IDs had been set to be created by private corporations, and the Big Tech companies he was working with wanted the business. More than just the small number of Swiss citizens who would be affected was the precedent of a people choosing to put everything about their identity into electronic means.

Well, it's a small setback. We'll get past it, I am sure, he told himself. Then, just as his assistant brought in a cozy with tea and his favorite biscuits and jam, he settled down some. After all, the Americans were far more likely to reach for it, in their headlong race to identify and track everyone. *Theirs is the significant population,* he thought. *If we take them rapidly down this path, we take the rest of the world.*

Fortunately, the BBC was more concerned about the Burqa Ban— as the media referred to it—and had steered that narrative. Just as in the United States, all the British media parroted each other, and the news about the e-ID being rejected virtually vanished. It devolved into a throwaway story.

But that situation drove the point home to Ernst Schweiner as to how precarious the timeline was. Every one of this group had been used to working at a pace that slowly, over decades, had set the stage for the reset planetwide. Speed was not a challenge they had been given. But the rumblings in the U.S. were unnerving him now. Unlike many, he had not been alarmed by the former President of the United States. He was alarmed by the people who elected him. And he could almost feel something shifting in that country.

He remembered well what Admiral Yamamoto had said after Pearl Harbor. His family had impressed it upon him, as he lived through not the rise, but the fall of the Third Reich. Yamamoto had tried to warn his superiors that he feared they had awakened a sleeping giant. That had proven true. And he and others had just spent the last 75 years putting that giant back to sleep. At this age, and with victory in sight, Ernst Schweiner was not about to let it slip from his grasp, nor did he want to waste more precious time on a people he regarded as undisciplined, soft, conceited, and narcissistic. True, he had been impressed, though, with the courage and resolve the United States had demonstrated in its attacks upon Al Qaeda, Isis, and all global terror groups in general.

Their military leaders are not as easily fooled, he reminded himself. *But the American citizens, they are a different matter. If we act fast enough, they will never see this coming. No chance to jump out of the boiling water.*

And with that, he realized he needed to turn the heat up and get that water boiling before there was more action in America.

Returning to his desk, he hit the speed dial to Rutger. He had already dialed before he checked the time. He had done it again! It was 10 AM in Geneva, Switzerland, and 4 AM in New York City. *Well, it is a small price to pay for fame and fortune,* he joked to himself.

Without any kind of apology, he launched right into the conversation as soon as he heard Schmidt's uncharacteristically husky voice. *Woke him!* he reminded himself. "Rutger, I am not satisfied with the pace—at least I should say I am not satisfied with the results I see or read about. It seems as if the countries have settled into a rhythm in this global health crisis and are becoming somewhat complacent in their discomfort."

Recognizing that seemed like a conundrum, he had observed it happen in many endeavors. As an avid sports fan, he had seen champion athletes and teams lose their edge. But he had also seen champion fighters get defeated because they settled into a new routine that embraced, almost, their defeat. The actions that had made them successful were changed in some way, and that movement away from the successful actions led to their subsequent defeat. And Ernst Schweiner was going to make certain that did not happen to his team. Clearly, they had been winning globally in every arena they were sparring in. But as far as he was concerned, it was time for the knockout punch.

"I need to goose our colleagues a bit. And I need to have Peter educate every member how they—by themselves—can cause inversions and collapses in the institutions they are engaged with and undermining."

Rutger responded immediately, "I can set up whatever you need. How urgent? We had plans anyway to assemble the team, Ernst. I can just advance that timeline and bring them together sooner."

"I have an uneasiness that I have not been able to shake. But I am sure this next conference will handle it."

"Do you now want this to occur in Geneva?"

"No, no. As I said before, most definitely not. These men should not be seen together."

"Well, I could summon them to Dinkelsbühl rather quickly. That seemed a suitable environment for privacy."

Ernst responded. "No, my first instinct was correct. I would rather not pull these men too far from their work and projects. Let us do a video conference call like we spoke about. Each has indicated they are able to handle high-security video, so rather than bring the Americans to your offices, query them to verify they are capable of a video conference currently that protects all data and all personnel."

Rutger smiled. He knew their office on Park Avenue could certainly accommodate the call. But if each could stay in his own environment, that would be preferable. "And if someone is wobbly, we do it in New York?"

"Yes. So, listen intently to their answers, Rutger. Each of them, I am sure you have noticed, is very competitive and self-confident—perhaps even overly so. That is the liability, isn't it, my friend?"

"Agreed. The price of hiring the world's best in anything, I am afraid." At that, they both had a good laugh. Once Ernst hung up, Rutger began the calls. Ernst was wise to ask Rutger to pay close attention to each man's responses. One of them, in fact, was not as "secure" as he perceived himself to be. Rutger, unfortunately, was not as discerning as Schweiner and would miss it, and that oversight would prove to be very costly.

CHAPTER TWENTY-FIVE

"*T*he greatest dangers to liberty lurk in insidious encroachments by men of zeal, **well meaning**, but without understanding." Ernst opened without any fanfare, once all men were on the call. With the screen opened for all participants to see each other, one screen was there, but masked. No one, at that moment, knew who was behind that screen, except for Ernst and Rutger.

"Who knows who wrote that?"

"I believe that was Justice Brandeis of the United States Supreme Court," Peter responded without hesitation.

Ernst was not surprised that it was Peter Loren who would have that reference at his fingertips. "Correct. So, tell us, Peter, how it is you are so familiar with it?"

There was no delay whatsoever. "Because it is that which I have used as a strategy in order to bring about the PR victories we have achieved. It is also why no one knows my name, but they know the **well-meaning men of zeal** I have used." He had placed the same emphasis on those words as Ernst had. And that helped focus the discussion. "In order to implement a Trojan Horse strategy against the U.S. government, and to effectuate a Fifth Column, I had to find the men of zeal who would be well meaning but without understanding—and influence them to come to **my** understanding and begin to implement it."

Ernst could see the faces of the others. They all seemed in agreement with that. "Do you feel you have been instrumental in the embracing of censorship by United States leaders?"

Peter laughed, then said somewhat self-deprecatingly, "Well, I hope so, sir. I rather assumed it was part of why I am in the company of such prestigious men." Ernst gestured for him to elaborate. "One of my great recent accomplishments was to hear a man of the 'free press' justify blatant censorship as 'damage reduction.' Is he a man of good will? I think he thinks he is. That's why I targeted him. If I could get one of the five parts of the First Amendment to attack one of the other sacrilegious parts of the First Amendment—without any understanding of what he was doing or what his corporate masters were doing—then drip by drip, it would be parroted by the other networks and, eventually, the people themselves. We all know the power of repetition. The more something is repeated, the more real it becomes."

"There, now you have it, gentlemen!" Ernst dove in enthusiastically. "Peter has always understood that it is the American people who are the target, and he has to use tools in order to get those people under control. I myself am more of a cerebral fellow, more subdued, but the United States has always had that unseemly element of zeal. Witness their populist presidential choice. Rather than fight the man, we have chosen to undermine the people who sent the man. And in order to do that, they have to dismember the very document they have held as foundational and untouchable."

He paused and let that sink in. "You know, of course, that is their Constitution, and frankly, we all have made remarkable progress in knocking the American population off that base. It is almost as if they are no longer resting on the plinth of their Constitution—like the statues in the rotunda of their Capitol. Rather, they have been set off it and are now examining it, doubting it, or even disavowing it. They are accomplishing their own 'reset,' if you will—all done by men of zeal and without understanding."

He then pulled up three newspapers with highlighted paragraphs on the Politics and World Politics pages. "However, we have a problem, my friends. It is one we must solve at once. It is a matter of urgency and of speed. And I am afraid we are going to have to play more at the American pace—helter-skelter though it may be—and not so much as our more measured, refined pace."

Holding the papers up, he showed them the article where President Macron of France was lamenting the danger America's "woke cancel culture" posed to his country. Then German Chancellor Merkel's disagreement with the social media blocking, and subsequent cancellation of, an American president. She rightly had perceived that her own power structure could also be compromised or destroyed by such a move, and she had spoken out strongly and immediately—as a head of state. He touched also on the recent Swiss rejection of the e-ID, but Ernst's attention seemed to be homed in on the flare-ups of the heads of state of countries they were going to need to accomplish the reset.

"What I am trying to make clear is that there is a chink in the armor. Just little cracks here and there, but if we allow things to fester—unanswered—then it may prove much harder to accomplish our goals in Europe than we thought. The United Kingdom is won. With the change of regimes in the United States, Great Britain seems to have lost her verve for the Brexit plan. So, I don't want to end up playing that American game at carnivals..." he was searching for words. "Oh, dear, what is the word for the game where you knock one pop-up thing down, and another pop-up occurs somewhere else?"

"Whack-a-Mole," Brannigan answered. He smiled, as it was a strategy he had used to arouse and confuse the Washington media elites and government deep state bureaucrats. He had successfully caused the FBI to "whack" the CIA to "whack" the Russians to "whack" the media elites to "whack" lobby groups to "whack" ambitious politicians. It was a game he was good at. *An infuriating game, actually, for anyone trying to play to stop the pop-ups of disgusting and dangerous issues or people,* he thought. Brannigan was very confident now because he had successfully duped the American people—and almost all of its government, entertainment, and media establishment—into believing the completely false Russia Collusion hoax. *Had it not been for that damned Freedom of Information Act, the truth would never have surfaced.*

"Yes! Yes! That is it," Ernst responded. "So, given the chinks in the armor, and the restlessness I sense in some of the American population, we are going to speed up and intensify our activities. The target for the reset is now within the year, and we have sub-targets that must be met. Are you ready to discuss those?"

All of them nodded, relieved frankly to finally be getting some marching orders. Before Ernst could continue, Brannigan raised his hand. "May I ask who is behind the blank screen? Who else has a seat with us?"

"In good time, John. All in good time." Schweiner realized he didn't want to seem to be playing games with his entrusted team, so he added, "It is not so much a secret as it is the fact that our next conversation will determine when they come on and what they recommend. Perhaps the eighth seat will not be needed at all. But just in case, two are on standby."

"Like alternate jurors," Pilaf joked.

"Precisely," Ernst said. "In any case, I ask that you indulge the cerebral for the next several hours. Rather, I should say, that you indulge me. Let us challenge our minds some. I must confess that I am fascinated by this 'woke culture' that has emerged in the United States and is spreading. Despite France's position on this, I expect we can use it to our advantage as well. After all, every sword has two edges. It is only a matter of public relations on our part. We promote the side of our technologies that are innocuous, desirable, fun—or the reverse, which creates aversion. They will embrace the former willingly. With the latter, when they reject a technology, they walk right into us as their savior. The double-edged sword, it cuts both ways."

Signaling to Peter, Ernst asked, "Am I right?"

"Yes. Whatever the rest of you are working on, bring it to me, and we will package it for consumption in such a way that the people will 'digest' it, if you will. I personally believe, Ernst, that this inclusiveness phenomenon in the United States can only redound to a speedier journey for us. Frankly, I believe it has made a mess of the education system—at all levels—in the U.S. That's a serendipity to me. The French president may be alarmed, but he has no real weight when it comes to influencing the American media."

Ernst approved of Peter's contribution and then took the reins again. "Just to make clear my understanding of man as he was, and my desire of what he can be, I want to share with you some of my vision. This should help us keep our goal in front of us and in the forefront of our minds. To my mind, what we are embarking upon at all levels, and with each of you in your arenas, is simply a matter of evolution." He grinned and then continued. Schweiner had always relished the professorial role, and he was basking in it today.

"There was a time when we were all apes—religious theologies notwithstanding—but we evolved. It is time to evolve again into a greater intelligence. It took many millennia for apes to evolve to humans as we know them. But we have a greater intelligence now than at any point in our species' history. We can move exponentially now. It is time, as I mentioned when we first met, to evolve again into a greater intelligence. We—all of us in this conference—are in a position to help it along."

He paused, looked toward the window in his office, then back to them. "No, my friends, we will not have to wait millions of years for the structure to evolve like ape to man. We have learned to adapt to the environment and even to control the environment. Our sciences have assured us of that. But now is the time for a *higher man*. It is inevitable, and I would dare to use the term 'natural.'"

Brannigan could not even remotely relate to this. His interests were personal and political, and he was rooted firmly to the ground activities of manipulating the actions that were part of Schweiner's grand scheme. But he had learned in the last months that Schweiner was an intellectual who liked to listen to himself talk and that he valued people who would listen to him. *So that is what I am going to be, Ernst—a dutiful listener. Engage me really when we are ready to implement some of the dirty activities like Environment, Social Justice, Governance scores, and Deepfake videos. You know, the ones needed to accomplish your loftier goal. I remember the pictures on your wall at Dinkelsbühl. You don't fool me!*

Despite the fact the men were not even on the same continent, let alone in the same room, Ernst Schweiner could easily see and perceive what the men were doing. His eagle eye, which looked at people through the innocuous professorial glasses, did not miss much. And he recognized that Brannigan was dutifully listening but seemed to hold some heavier, darker thought. It was not the first time his attention had come around to the former CIA director. He decided to ignore it for now and discuss it with Rutger later.

"All right, gentlemen, we are going to go around the table and identify the strategies and tactics we will be using to bring the United States to her knees within six months and how we might handle any rebellion we encounter along the way. Each of you will learn your role in all of this or have your role be embellished upon. In other words, we are going a little deeper today than in our first meeting. Understood?"

Every man nodded. In fact, every man was eager for this.

"I learned long ago that one should begin with the end in mind. We have discussed what end we want in resetting the world to a type of government, and a level of appreciation for science, that will allow mankind to, in fact, evolve. For 70 years or more, we have laid pieces of the puzzle into place, laid the foundation. You use whatever metaphor best suits your psyche..." he paused to give them time to laugh at his little joke. They each did, for each one of them, in fact, did perceive war games differently based upon the business they were in.

Grabbing their attention once again, he said. "Succinctly stated, the end I have in mind for the United States—which is the first and most important target for us—is their willing surrender into a totalitarian government. Personally, I prefer fascism as a system because of the partnership between government and business, but for our purposes, the acceptance by the world of an authoritarian form of government of any kind is desirable. Regrettably, with the Americans, I don't believe it will be a benign one for them."

At that point, Ernst held up an almost ridiculously small white board, with four lines written on it. "Gentlemen, this is how you take a higher-level democracy or republican form of government—a rule of law type of society—and convert it into one of your making. Please look at this scale and commit it to memory. Peter, John, and Serge, you will be implementing a lot of the tactics for this. And before you try to say you already are, I acknowledge that you are. I merely want everyone to be on the same page with the same understanding and frame of reference."

Everyone nodded that they understood and agreed. "First, you encourage the idea of people breaking laws they do not like or agree with, rather than working to change the laws—little ones at first, with no repercussions. Then, more and more until it is an acceptable part of the culture for people to routinely break laws for their own purposes. That descends then in time to a level of lawlessness, which, in time, descends into anarchy. Your efforts, by the way, using ever-escalating riots have accomplished this in the United States already. The society then devolves from anarchy into totalitarianism because the living conditions in anarchy are so extreme, and the government so out of control, the people themselves will reach for and be grateful for a calm, certain, authoritarian figure or figures. In our case, of course, it will be figures!"

Placing the white board down, Ernst leaned forward, hands together, knuckles intertwined. "And this is where we have the double-edged sword. People want their freedom, but the freedom has led to anarchy, to fear and hatred. So, they take the sword that provides safety and rules but lacks freedom." He stopped, looked at each man separately, and then continued, "This is what I want each of you to know. Most often, when people have a problem, they create a solution that becomes a greater problem down the road. Now, I want you to burn that into your minds. We are helping the United States create a host of unanticipated problems, and we are offering solutions to those problems. Since the situation is severe, the solution is embraced without anyone looking to the long game—down the road, if you will. They cannot see the problems that portend, or if they do see them, they dismiss them and embrace the solution anyway. But…you must remember, it leads to a trap for them always."

"That is one of the truths we in information warfare operate on. In the chaos of the situation we are creating, the person reaches for the solution we are also offering, not knowing we have created an even greater problem for him to face." Brannigan interjected, unable to resist affirming the truth of Schweiner's statement.

For the moment, Ernst welcomed the interruption, acknowledging John's great background in this area. He added, "And this skill set, too, belongs with the propaganda people such as Peter. That is why these two, I believe, are a great pair."

Peter seemed fine with that statement, but Brannigan didn't know yet what Ernst Schweiner's true take on him was. *It's nothing serious, though,* he reassured himself. *I wouldn't be here otherwise. Besides, he doesn't know what I will be demonstrating when called upon.*

Unflustered, Ernst continued, "Therefore, the roles we are going to discuss—and you all will be privy to—and the tactics to be used have the goal in mind of driving the people of the United States downward through those four lines." He held up the board once again. "Downward through those four to the fourth one—a new, authoritarian government that the people accept and that their military will not interfere with. That, gentlemen, is the goal. And it must be attained within the year. We are ramping up the pressure to speed up the timeline. And all attacks will be simultaneous and designed to overwhelm the opponent. The time of the religiosity of man is at an end, and the linchpin that has held all that in place is the United States and its pesky First Amendment. The whole world has ridden on those coattails."

At that moment, Ernst Schweiner had exposed a level of venom he rarely let out. His personality belied his malevolence. Almost instantly, he recognized that a peek at his real emotions had been allowed, and he shut it down. "I want to take a break for lunch—or breakfast or dinner—depending upon where you all are. When we return, we launch into your 'role.'"

———————————————

Hector threw open the door to his "workshop" and yelled at the top of his lungs for James to come. He had feverishly tried texting, but James must have been somewhere without his phone. When Hector lurched out of the hangar door, he saw James sitting and reading on the wrap-around porch of the farmhouse. In fact, James *had* left his phone inside and did not see the repeated texts sent through.

James dropped the book and ran to the hangar, as the look on Hector's face told him something had happened—something of importance. "What is it?" he asked, out of breath. "You all right?"

"Oh yeah, man. Didn't you see my texts?" Realizing that was a futile question, he got over it and led James into the "workshop." "I have something to show you. You're not going to believe it. But…you are going to like it. Better be prepared to settle in out here today, James. This is big."

The suspense and Hector's wordiness were too much for James. "What the hell is it?!"

"You know I got in successfully to Loren and Brannigan?" James nodded enthusiastically but somewhat anxiously.

"Well, those two are on a video conference call."

"By themselves?" James interrupted.

"No. And they didn't call themselves. Someone called them." Words were pouring out of Hector now. "That guy Schmidt is on. I recognize him from the photo you showed me. There's a whole bunch of other people, too. But you know, I am not the best at current events. I don't know these men. You do, though. I think these are the men you are after—by the way they are talkin', man—the ones you hoped Brannigan would lead you to."

"Jesus!" James was speechless. "What did you get? Voice conversation so we can ID by voice recognition?"

"That, too." Hector smiled.

"Too?"

"Yeah, man, I got the whole thing—audio and video." He let that sink in for a minute.

James was having a hard time putting this together. "Are you telling me you have hacked into a video conference with a bunch of men you know are persons of interest to me?"

This time, Hector grinned. "That's exactly what I am telling you. It's all recorded. I am backing it up now. But there's more. They're on some kind of break, so I suggest you go get a blanket and some snacks or something because there is no tellin' how long we's going to be here!"

"You stay here. Don't miss anything," James directed.

"I'm not goin' anywhere until you get back. Then, man, you gotta spell me so I can pee."

James Mikolas was not a technology guy himself. All he could do was shake his head in disbelief—and relief. Then, a dark cloud crowded into his mind. "Do they know you're there?"

"No, man. That's my 'skill set,'" Hector teased him. "They don't know anybody's there. And if some bright eager beaver comes sniffing, I am rigged so that it loops back and forth from Brannigan to Loren. Real confusing. They won't spot me."

"Did you get anything incriminating, from my perspective?"

"Yeah. I think you could definitely say that. As I said, I'm not much for politics, current events, science, sci-fi..." he let the thought linger there.

"Sci-fi?"

Hector shrugged his shoulders. "Yep. You'll see. There's some weird shit goin' on here, James. It's above my IQ, but I can tell you this: There are some very bad gangs planning some very bad retaliation against some other gangs."

James knew not to waste time asking questions. He raced back to the house, grabbing his cellphone and charger and his little note pad—and all the snack goodies Hector seemed to thrive on. *This may be it,* he repeated over and over.

CHAPTER TWENTY-SIX

Vince McCoy had no idea what was transpiring, and he did not like that feeling of sensing something was developing and not knowing if his man was on top of it. Torn between leaving the house to place a message at the Vietnam Veterans Memorial, where he might run the risk of Brannigan becoming suspicious of his being AWOL, and staying there, hoping to gain some other type of intel, he went down the stairs and into the kitchen.

Just then, Brannigan came up from his downstairs "lair," as Vince mentally referred to it. "Oh, Vince, good, I thought you would be here."

"Yeah, I didn't want to interrupt you, and I assumed you were down in your office. Figured you would have told me if you were going out. What's the plan for today? Studio?"

"Nah," Brannigan brushed it aside. "It was, but something has come up. I notified the network to reschedule me."

Vince queried. "Got it. Then, what is the plan?"

"Well, I have a meeting that came up suddenly, and I am likely to be on a conference call the whole day." He looked at Vince a little sheepishly and said, "I know this is beneath your pay grade, Vince, and probably your status, but can I ask you to go get some groceries and dinner for us?"

Vince laughed and said reassuringly, "No problem, John. I'll be happy to do it. What do you want me to pick up, and on dinner, you want it delivered?"

"No. Definitely not!" Brannigan snapped. "I don't want anyone coming around here for any reason today."

"Understood. So, just add what you want to this list here," he pointed to the pad on the counter, "and I'll make a couple of trips out."

Brannigan jotted a few grocery items on the paper. He seemed distracted but not agitated. "Listen, I am going back down. There's something I want to prepare before we start back up. Just bring me a sandwich or something when you get back."

Vince nodded, picking up the list and keys, and headed for the front. Brannigan called after him. "Get whatever you like, too. It's on me. Get me some Cheetos, too. This is a Cheetos kind of meeting."

McCoy had no idea what that meant, but he was relieved to be out of the house with Brannigan's permission. Deciding to get groceries first and bring the man the lunch he needed, he gauged that he would have enough time later to get over to the memorial and then stop maybe at a Chinese restaurant Brannigan liked, without Brannigan feeling he'd been gone too long.

Whistling as he walked to the corner market, he almost forgot the rest of the city looked like a war zone and seemed under siege. To him, a ray of hope had sneaked in, even if shrouded in mystery for the moment.

—————————————

"All right, gentlemen, everyone refueled?" Ernst asked. "I am going to have each of you brief the others, and we may do some question and answer to make sure we are all coordinated on this. And I am going to start with the Americans first. Peter, you are up first. John, you will follow. Serge, you follow John."

Peter Loren thanked Schweiner and looked at each of his global colleagues. Graciously, he said, "I am honored to start first. And Ernst, feel free to interrupt me if you feel you need to. Much of what I have done and will be doing in the future is driven by the work John, Serge, and, frankly, all of you do. So, probably the simplest thing for me is to provide you with some foundational propaganda philosophy and strategies. That may help you determine what you will do, what you will emphasize, and how you emphasize it in the event I am not working directly with you. Fair enough?"

Peter then explained a fundamental aspect of information warfare and mind control that could cause people to doubt their own system and embrace another one. Breathtakingly simple, it, nonetheless, had wreaked havoc all over the world for a very long time. And it was coming home to roost in the United States.

"Just as Ernst diagrammed the descent to totalitarianism, here is how I—and you as well in your arenas—can move that along. First, remember always that our role is to make right wrong, and wrong right. Just flip it. This disorients the opponent and eventually turns the whole culture upside down. Once that has happened, their desire to be right forces them to defend the wrong, which they have now made right. They dig in, repeat it over and over, and eventually, it becomes the 'truth.' All right with you if I give you an example or two?"

All vigorously indicated yes. Peter continued. "The United States is built upon the foundational principle of the family unit, believing it is key to their rise in the world. So, the right thing in the American psyche up until now is that one should create a family—you know, husband, wife, children. That is *right* in their minds." He said, emphasizing the word *right*. "So, we work to disparage the old family concept, get them to relinquish adherence to it as a belief in the face of rising mockery and criticism. Now, gentlemen, there are many ways or elements that can be deployed to accomplish that. But for example, let's play upon the feminist movement in the United States and make it wrong for an American woman to want to be home, raise children, and nurture the family. Make it right for her to leave the children to the care of minimum wage people—or better yet, the centralized education system, which we can control—and wrong for her to be something as menial as just a mother or homemaker."

Ernst interjected, "Peter, that has been going on for some time, don't you think?"

"Oh, yes. I was merely using it as an illustration. The erosion, though, was to take living together without marriage and make it the norm—or, at the very least, acceptable. Then to erode family again by confusing genders in the family, with gay marriages, etc. You could make it babies without fathers. You could make it better for the state to pay for and raise the children than for a father to be involved. You could make aborting children the *right thing to do,* rather than something considered wrong. Frankly, there are endless examples here and in your own countries. The key is that whatever the social and moral issues are: **Make right wrong, and wrong right.**"

Looking at his notes, Peter continued. "Word of caution here. You have to do this on a gradient, and you must weight the two choices equally. Your goal is to drive the confusion right down the middle. If you have equal weight to each of the arguments for and against something, you create a massive schism. The parties are equally opposed, so there is a stalemate, and neither can conquer the other. You know, of course,

I mean that both figuratively and literally? That is where we are now, gentlemen. The U.S. is virtually locked up in a stalemate."

"You know, that's right." Rudi Iseli commented, shaking his head in recognition of the simplicity of it. "How did that come about?"

"My mentor was very instrumental in that," Peter responded. "He paved the way for me, and us, by persuading the media to embrace the idea of 'fair and balanced.' I don't think he cared if it was fair, but he made sure they tried to balance it. So, they had two opposing sides. And here's the kicker though…" he paused and leaned forward to make sure they appreciated this next part, which he relished. "My job has been to come in and relentlessly get the two equally opposed sides to have flipped on the right-wrong scale. Prior to my work, the person or issue that would have been considered 'right' by the American people is now being hounded as being wrong, undesirable. The person advocating for the 'right' is excoriated or punished, and eventually, they themselves switch and embrace the 'wrong' and abandon their resistance." He stopped to let his colleagues absorb that and then continued, "You see then a great deal of capitulation and attrition. The ones still trying to cling to their honor quit, and you get the attrition. Either way, we win. They can continue in a submissive mode, or they can quit. But they have left the battlefield, so to speak."

Ernst enthusiastically interjected, "Outstanding!"

Peter continued, "Take belief in God. That is certainly one of the things Americans have embraced as something that is right. They have carried that all over the world, and they refer to it regularly when they discuss the founding of their country. Secular belief in man as the superior being was considered wrong, if considered at all. But…I think we can all agree that we are making headway at taking what was formerly considered wrong about the secular viewpoint and making it right. Churches, religion, and religious or moral teaching are condemned and made wrong now. Again, right made wrong and wrong made right."

"But doesn't that idea of right or wrong vary from culture to culture?" Cedric Cornell asked. "Surely, there is not universal agreement even on these examples you have given."

Peter looked at Ernst, as if to get permission to respond. "Go on, my boy, you have the floor."

"Your perception is accurate in the current world, and you, of course, are a global player in that world. But that is not my understanding of what we are doing. *We* are deciding what is right—even if the culture of the United States, let's say, says it is wrong. It is our job to force them to accept our idea of what is right, and we do that by continually expounding upon the value and benefits of whatever thing we are promoting. It is my job to help you all change peoples' perceptions and flip their moral compasses—lest we be in an enforcement situation from here forward. Control their mind, we control their emotions. Control those, we control their actions—all the while they think they are doing what is right." He sat back, looking at Cornell.

Ernst pondered the two men for a moment and turned to Cornell. "Let me ask you, Cedric—since this is certainly in your purview—do you believe the COVID-19 virus was a biological weapon? Don't think, just respond." It was an order.

"I do. But…" Cedric tried to qualify his answer but was cut off.

"No. I simply asked you for that answer only. So, to tell the world that it was naturally occurring in a cave with a bat, and did not escape or was not let loose by a person, is 'wrong,' isn't it?"

The man sighed and answered. "Yes, it is. But it is necessary for our purposes, Ernst. You know that."

"Absolutely I know it. But it is, nonetheless, still false information, and it is information that our American colleagues here have worked hard to 'make right.' I mean by that the American people have accepted your lie. It is now 'right' what you did."

Suddenly laugher interrupted the meeting. Everyone looked up at their screen to see who seemed to be on a giggle spree. It was Rudi Iseli.

"Forgive me." He stopped, again surrendering to the laughter, trying in vain to rein in his unexpected hysteria. "Forgive me."

Blessedly, all the others smiled and waited for it to subside, at which point, Ernst asked, "Do you want to elaborate on that outburst, Rudi?"

Not daring to look at them for fear of bursting into laughter again, Iseli said, "It's enough to make your head spin. No wonder the mind guys are in control. Very disorienting."

"Yes, I agree, wholeheartedly, Rudi," Peter affirmed. "That's why you practice in order to figure out how to get others to view their right thing as a wrong thing and to view their wrong thing as a right thing. Bottom line: In everything within your jurisdiction that involves explanation, or necessitates agreement, look for what you can make wrong in the other's viewpoint or actions or habits, and look for what you can make right in your viewpoint, actions or habits. Rule of thumb. That is all."

"Hey, Rudi," Brannigan interjected jovially, "Think of it like a diabolical debate where the goal is not to seek *truth*, but to seek the opposite. Pretend you're a defense attorney or something trying to make your pig look like a choir boy! Trying to get some granny to let loose of her idea of what a crime is and feel sorry for your guy who just killed three people. Turn her into the holdout in the jury room!" There was silence in the room until he said, "How's that for an analogy?!"

"Crude, but excellent." Peter winked and upheld his colleague.

They spent the next few hours hashing out all the destructive things they needed to accomplish and how they might sell them to the authorities, who otherwise would have rejected them with disgust. At first, it was like pulling teeth, but Peter kept at it, and eventually every man at the table was becoming quite deft at that element of propaganda."

After some hours, Cedric said, "My brain hurts!"

"Are you OK?" Peter asked.

Acting as if he was being addressed instead of Cornell, Brannigan responded. "Yeah, sure. I do this for a living. Spent a lifetime creating salacious counterintelligence operations, recruiting double agents. This is like child's play to me now. But I'll tell you what does hurt on me."

"What's that?"

"My butt. My shorter leg acts up on me if I sit too long."

Ernst looked at the clock and realized they did need to take a break. "Good point, John. I don't even have a sensitive leg, but my mind is swimming with ideas after Peter's tutorial. Let us stretch for a few minutes, and when we come back, we'll move over to you, John."

Facing each of the others, he explained, "I have asked John to cover disinformation and deception. John creates the stuff Peter has been teaching you to 'sell.'"

Apparently, it wasn't just John Brannigan who was tired of sitting. Every man over 50 jumped up and was on the move before Ernst even finished his sentence. Agreeing to 15 minutes, Brannigan opened the office door, eager to get into natural light and clear his head. He was ready with his presentation and the effect he was about to produce. *This will let them know just how much in charge I can be, if need be,* he thought.

John Brannigan was about to make a move guaranteed to elevate his position on this team and serve them notice that he would be a force to be reckoned with if anyone crossed him. He smiled. He just needed to make certain they didn't relegate him to low man on the totem pole, or try to edge him out, now that so much of his propaganda tactics had already been deployed to devastating consequences in the last few years. Always alert to being thrown under the bus and shoved aside once his purpose had been served—as if he had outlived his usefulness—he had a surprise for Ernst. What was an expected occupational hazard for someone in his line of work was not going to happen to him this time.

No, sir. John Brannigan worked hard to get here. And I am staying, now that I am here. These other fellows outrank me in wealth, but I have something none of them have. A great equalizer!

James Mikolas had done stealth work all his life, either as an operative in the field or as an analyst, figuring out what bad guys might do next and why. But nothing had prepared him for what he had just watched on the screen. He didn't know what he had expected really. Maybe a recorded conversation where he was listening in, maybe a transcript. But to be "watching" the actual meeting as if he were a participant in it was very disorienting at first.

He kept shushing Hector, trying to silence the noise of Hector's candy wrappers. *Honestly, I don't know how many of those miniature Milky Ways he had! He and Ari would sure get along,* he joked with himself. Finally, Hector had turned to him and said, "Man, they can't hear us. They have no idea we are listening or watching. Just chill. Everything is OK."

When the parties in the conference stood up to take a short break, James said, "Do you think we should find out where Vince is and let him know?"

"No way, man. No comms with him—NONE!" Hector was especially assertive on that. "We just have to wait it out now, or we could blow his cover. Besides, there is nothing he needs to know now. This part of the operation is mine, and I am in charge."

It was said so authoritatively that James nodded that he totally got it. Even saluted.

Hector surprised him, though, with what he said next. "Are you a praying man, James?"

"What?"

"Do you believe in God? Do you pray?"

James stumbled on this, appearing a bit tongue-tied for a moment. Hector was staring at him, clearly expecting an answer. "I hadn't thought about that much, Hector, but yes. Yes, I do believe in God. And I sure as hell pray every time I blurt out something like, 'Jesus, help me!' if you want to call it that." James thought that was humorous, but Hector apparently did not seem satisfied with that answer or levity. More solemnly, James said, "Why do you ask, Hector?"

"Because we are going to need a power greater than us, James, to get out of this. Vince and I have come up against some real scum—some real bad hombres—in the last few years, but at least those bastards looked like scum. This crew…" His voice trailed off as he gestured toward the blank screen, and he gave up even searching for words.

Sliding his chair a little closer to Hector, James patted him on the shoulder. "I understand, Pal. This is some dark shit. But I can tell you one thing, for sure. I am grateful you are here, Hector. And I am *real* grateful that you possess the talents that you do."

"You called me 'Pal.'"

James must have had a question mark on his face because Hector added, "That's what you call Brian. You call him 'Pal.' You never had no nickname for me."

For a moment, James didn't know whether to cry or laugh. How much these young, troubled men had changed his life. Instead, he said, "Well, you remind me of him. And I trust you like I trust him."

Hector tried to conceal his misty eyes, sniffled a bit and turned his head away. Standing up, he crumpled up the candy wrappers, walked over to the trash can with his back to James, and dropped them in. He still had his back to James when he said quietly, resolutely, "This is a hill worth dying on, you know."

"I know." It was a dangerous time and a dangerous mission—for these three, and for the country they were trying to save.

What neither of them could know was what was coming in the second act of this reality TV show they were surreptitiously watching. There was one good thing they were unaware of, though. John Brannigan's only interest in Peter Loren was to find out who he really was—and to see who he really was connected to. He had no doubts as to Peter's part in the plans being laid out by Schweiner. For that reason, he had no attention on surveillance of Peter that day. As far as he was concerned, if Peter were with him all day, he couldn't be with anyone else. He had no intentions of checking with Vince to see if Vince's "partner" had observed any unusual activity. It was a blind spot he would later come to regret—and have to deal with.

But, for now, all three were safe.

"They're sitting back down," Hector called to James.

James had taken a short walk, during which time he called Jessica to tell her he would likely be flying back to the ranch within a few days, and he asked her to tell the boys to be ready to meet with him. He had information.

"John, given that we need to speed up the timeline and intensify the emotional response of the public, what do you have to offer?" Ernst opened the meeting, setting down the crystal goblet.

Brannigan decided to reassert some basic principles he was working with and then deliver the shocking tool he now had in his arsenal. "Gentlemen, you all know that war is deception—at least from the standpoint of the information warrior." Indicating Peter and Serge, he continued, "We three deliver the information and control its distribution. My part is to create disinformation so plausible that the people—over time—come to accept it as truth. My primary target has been to sabotage any credible threats to our plan of getting the people of the United States to abandon the idea of a constitutional republic and to help them get mentally ready for the advisability of a more authoritarian, centrally planned, and centrally controlled government. Basically, get the people to doubt the people. And to doubt their heritage."

"It's a matter of relentless misinformation now, Ernst. More, faster, more diverse, and more shocking."

Ernst leaned in a little as if discussing a philosophical point with a student. "So, you feel the Americans are nearly ready to devalue their Constitution?"

"No doubt. The D.C. establishment has already been compromised to the point they will trot out their Constitution as a tool when it serves their ends. That's the key. Rather than a foundation to anchor on, and measure against, they now just view it as a handy crutch—to quote or lean on when they want compliance. Frankly, the U.S. government is almost on autopilot regarding that. It's a mere tool now. Use/don't use? Embrace/don't embrace? That's pretty much where they are at. Very easy position for us to manipulate."

Though the men in this meeting were scattered on two continents, there was a palpable air of agreement. Brannigan was assured now that he had their attention.

"We can make anything look like it came from anywhere. So, if you need to deflect attention away from you, we can make the source appear to be someone else. We can make it look like any nation we choose has exercised some horrible action against the U.S., and even the best of our forensic cyber guys will fall for it. Moreover, my job is the manufacturing of false data so authentic it is accepted—even by our intelligence community. For years now, I have had inside people I can feed false data to. The key is it seems credible to them, and they run with it. That distances it from me or my team and makes it almost impossible for anyone to trace back."

Gesturing to Peter, he continued. "That's the beauty of what Peter has done. I provide what is fake, and he gets it out so that it is now coming from the media or from a trusted government source. No one has any reason to suspect it is fake. They just accept it. And then the person's instinctive need to be right takes over, and they become an unwitting accomplice in the spread of disinformation."

Rutger interrupted him. "Well, how do we even know what is true? What is happening then?"

"You won't. If I have done my job, you, too, would not be able to tell the difference."

"Then, what's to keep you from playing us as well?" Rutger added. The challenge was said conservatively, but Brannigan recognized the flicker of doubt it represented.

Before Brannigan could answer, Ernst slid into the discussion. "Because he has a seat at the table, Rutger. Trust is the one thing we have with one another." Brannigan nodded. "John, would it be fair to say that if someone is accepting the propaganda themselves, or can't seem to sort it out, that they should come to me and you, and we will lay it out for them?"

"Absolutely, Ernst. That's the point, I think, Rutger. If the disinformation is so compelling and plausible that you cannot even discern the falsity of it, then you certainly could not be accused of having a hand in it. My job is to surprise even you." Brannigan smiled, knowing that last statement would produce a bit of uneasiness in more than one man at the table. *That's knocked them off their pins for a moment,* he thought.

Ernst appeared to be looking at Brannigan over the top of his wire-rims. Always the gentleman, always the professor in charge, it was almost never possible to know what his true thoughts were. Brannigan decided to reveal the tool he knew would keep him at the table—forever.

"In the event that any individual or organization gains enough steam and following to disrupt any of your work, or any of our plans, we have a new tool that will stop them in their tracks. All I have to do is unleash it and, given the people's degraded adherence to the rule of law, they will operate on the 'guilt by accusation' mode—almost like the lynch mobs of yesteryear in America. Let me show it to you. That is, if it is all right with Ernst." He leaned back, waiting for the man in the hot seat to decide.

Ernst never flinched, never hesitated. "By all means, John. That is the purpose of our meeting. For all of us to know what the others are working on that may become part of our simultaneous attack. Do you need anything special for this demonstration?"

"No. I'll just play a short video for you, just to illustrate something the CIA is currently very concerned about." At that point, Brannigan brought up on the screen what appeared to be an amateur video shot from someone's cellphone. The picture was clear, but the angle was slightly off and occasionally unsteady. It was a video of Ernst Schweiner standing in front of what appeared to be a young man on his knees. Schweiner was visible from the waist up and was looking down at the young man, smiling. "There you are. That's it. Accept this, my young friend. Let this be a part of your life now." The apparency of a pornographic display of pedophilia perpetrated by Ernst Schweiner on an unknown boy was so shocking Schweiner himself stood up, flushed red, angered to the point a vein in his neck bulged and pulsed.

"That is not me! What in hell are you doing, John? That is fake." Realizing all his players were at the table, he recovered himself and looked at each one of them, pleading. "Surely, you know that is not me. I am not capable of such a thing."

Brannigan waited, watching each man. Clearly, he had rocked them, and he could see each struggling inwardly to either accept this video— and reject Ernst—or reject the video. What made it so difficult was it was Ernst's voice, and clearly, it was Ernst. Schweiner just sank into his chair, regaining his composure somewhat. Taking the challenge on now, he demanded, "All right, John. You said this was a demonstration. Would you care to explain what this is and what the meaning of it is?"

"This is deepfake video." Turning to Peter, he said, "A devastating tool for us to use with the DPP, right?" Peter nodded, still shaken by this unexpected blindsiding. "It makes it appear anyone has done anything. A completely false narrative depicted in a fake video—a video so convincing that people believe it. And once they have seen it with their own 'lying eyes,' they cling to it. No matter a later retraction by some news agency. No matter it is established later to be a false narrative. They 'saw it,' and that is what they cling to, what lingers." Turning to look at Ernst, he lowered his head somewhat, shook it back and forth, and said, "My apologies for having used you as the model, Ernst. But I felt it was the most effective way of demonstrating it. To have shown you a deepfake video of just some celebrity, or anyone, frankly, that you don't care about, would not have made the impact, stirred the emotions we all experienced just now."

No one wanted to admit that the video had, in fact, cast doubt upon the man who was leading this. There was an awkward silence in the meeting. "You can see why the intelligence communities are concerned about this, right?"

Each man nodded, wondering what could surface about them.

Brannigan continued, knowing he had the upper hand now, that each of them had been warned. "We all know this is preposterous, but we also know there are conspiracy theories out there—gaining momentum potentially—that the whole world is being run by a gang of pedophiles. Something like this, if released into the wrong hands, adds fuel to the fire at the very minimum."

"At a minimum is an understatement, John," Ernst said simply, unemotionally.

"So, how is this done? It seemed so real. Can it be proven to be false?" The questions came from Cedric Cornell.

"Oh yes, Cedric, experts can do a forensic examination, and they will discover that it is fake, but the damage has been done, as I mentioned. People remember their first impression—if the impression is emotional and not intellectual. It's the emotional response that lingers, almost hypnotically. Am I right, Peter?"

"Yes, that is one of the essential ingredients of mind control. Emotion. Emotion accompanied by a command."

"That command, gentlemen, will universally be applied by the media. Whoever takes a deepfake video and uses it has an ax to grind. The video makes that person's point. And I might add it makes it in such a salacious way that the person nearly salivates over the victory."

A long silence followed as the various men looked over this concept and realized that, in their own way, they were all deploying it—just not with manipulated videos. Brannigan continued, "As for how it is done, one does a computer-generated image of the scene they want to display, and then they overlay the likeness of the person they want to replicate. Like I said, anyone can appear to be doing anything. Let me show you what I did here."

Brannigan then showed the initial computer-generated image of a young boy kneeling in front of an altar—his back to the camera. A priest stood in front of the boy, evidently offering him a wafer of Christ. He nodded, then smiled. The boy looked up at the priest for encouragement, then looked down at the likely wafer, leaning forward for it. Or for something. The priest appeared to insert something into the boy's mouth. The scene was an ordinary scene of a boy's First Communion. Then, Brannigan laid in the image of Ernst Schweiner where the priest was, leaving the young boy in place. This gave the appearance immediately that the boy was on his knees in front of Schweiner and was being encouraged into a lewd act by Schweiner. As a propaganda and career-destroyer video, all in the meeting had experienced emotions from loathing, to titillation, to fear, to anger. Ernst broke the silence.

"But, my voice, John? Did you just record me speaking and then manipulate it to have my sounds spliced into the sentence?"

"No. I could have done that. But that would have been easier to spot as a fake. Instead, I used your actual words. Do you remember ever saying that, Ernst?"

Clearly Schweiner had no recollection, but he was sincerely searching his mind. A memory seemed to be surfacing. It was slow in coming, but it surfaced enough to cause Ernst to smile. "Yes, I think I do remember." Ernst looked at Brannigan. John just waited. He wanted Ernst to experience the full sense eventually of the invasion of privacy this also represented. It was a dark and threatening technology, and Brannigan needed Ernst to fully comprehend it.

"There it is. I see it now. It is Bruno! Ha!" The laugh was unexpected, but it was clear Ernst had found what Brannigan had unearthed somehow in archive videos. Turning to everyone with a grin on his face now, Ernst said, "I own a Rottweiler named Bruno. He was born with a weak kidney, but he is very dear to me, and the veterinarian had just provided me with a medication that Bruno takes daily by syringe. I was training him that day to take the medicine, encouraging him to accept it easily. Telling him it would be part of his life now." Schweiner stopped for a moment. "I wanted him to know that he is to lean forward and open his mouth, and I squirt the medicine in from the syringe. That is all."

Though the memory had surfaced, Ernst had no recollection of anyone else being there, let alone recording. Ernst Schweiner lived alone, save for servants who might have been about their duties that day. A chill went down his spine when he realized that he had been recorded. By whom? Why? Deciding not to explore that, he made a note that this John Brannigan was indeed a dangerous man. The others might not have concluded this yet. But Schweiner knew he was the one man—along with perhaps Peter Loren—who could unseat him at the head of the table. Today, however, he had to move on.

"John, that is remarkable. Something so innocent turned into something so appalling. Both for the boy and the priest, and for me and Bruno. And you say the CIA is concerned about this?"

"Yes. My buddies in the agency let me know this particular technology has the capability of creating havoc. It makes their job infinitely more complicated."

"Do you plan to deploy this?"

"Ernst, if anyone gets too close or is too threatening to any of your plans, or to the plans of anyone at this table, something like this can be created. You need just contact me, and I can create it. Peter then can get it into the hands of appropriate law enforcement, media, government people—you name it. And quiet Serge over there knows that he can get the gossip repeated virally through social media. Serge can make it unretractable, spreading out of control. Right?"

Serge Pilaf, characteristically, said nothing, but his subtle smile and gentle nod spoke volumes.

Peter looked up. He seemed to be distracted by something on his phone, but he had been listening to Brannigan and quickly affirmed that he would have the easier part. "Disseminating it is simple. John's the load bearer on that one." Then, almost apologetically, he added, "Ernst, I am very sorry, but I just received an urgent text. The Washington Post has confessed to lying about something in the last election, and it just blew up in their face. Bit of a flap, I am afraid. May I take a few minutes to settle these people down and give them a diversionary story to push out? That should handle it. U.S. media are like dogs chasing squirrels. I just need to give them a juicy squirrel to chase now to take the heat off all of them."

"My boy, let's all take a break. Ten minutes. I would like to finish our roundtable planning today. Workable?"

Everyone nodded, and Ernst texted Rutger on the encrypted line that he definitely needed to talk with him later about the morning's developments.

"Ten minutes, then." Smiling, he rose from his table and left the frame.

CHAPTER TWENTY-SEVEN

*R*utger left the conference room and went immediately to one of the smaller privacy rooms. Just as he closed the door, the screen indicated an incoming video call from Ernst Schweiner.

"So, Rutger, was that last demonstration a warning shot across my bow, do you think?" Ernst's tone showed no signs of alarm. Rather, he sounded exactly like he would if he were evaluating an international business deal where someone had changed the terms. Calm, assessing. Only the fact that he had immediately dialed Rutger belied true calm.

"It certainly felt that way."

"Why, though? What is his motive?"

Rutger paused for a moment, seeking the right words, then looked at Ernst. "Perhaps to unseat you?" He had said it as a question because he himself couldn't really assess the motive with certainty.

"No, no. There is nothing in Brannigan's background that suggests to me he deludes himself into thinking he is an international-level player in business or government. He's an espionage warrior, a troublemaker, not senior executive on a world stage." Schweiner squinted a bit, pursed his lips as he pondered his own statement, then added, "No. Now that I examine it a bit more, I think he just wanted to let me know that he has a seat at the table—permanently. A preemptive strike, if you will."

Rutger had worked with Ernst for many years and knew his position was often to be a sounding board and loyal partner who could be counted on to execute flawlessly. He considered his role also to be that of a sympathetic ear. Today was no different. "Are you all right with that, Ernst?"

That seemed to solidify Schweiner's assessment of the situation. "Yes. John is rough. He is coarse. Frankly, he is a ruffian. But he is so talented. And he is also ruthless and *fearless*. Now that I run that over in my mind, it took some—how is it the Americans say it—'guts' to try that in a meeting at this level."

"Well, that's one way to describe it!" Rutger scoffed.

Ernst laughed, looked at his friend reassuringly, and said, "No doubt it was very indiscreet. But we may need that ruthless streak at some point in the future. After all, what is a reset without at least one thug, heh?"

Schmidt, too, laughed at his senior's joke. "I believe the Americans call that person 'the enforcer.'"

They both laughed about that irony and the fact that this man was on their side—something they were grateful for at the moment. A few minutes later, they took their seat once again in the conference.

Peter's first call during the break had been to the head of the DPP. He had some feathers to smooth out, once he learned the DPP had given the press an anonymous report of someone who had overheard a significant call in the last election. What he knew now was that the content of the report was false. The recorded conversation did not include the remarks that were alleged against the former president. But the city's major newspaper executives either lacked the curiosity or were just too lazy to listen to the call themselves. Once Peter confirmed to the founder and director of the DPP that the recording was authentic and accurate, that just the summary and spin were mischaracterized, the man settled down. The paper's management might be furious with the DPP at the moment, but the DPP had, in fact, forwarded the accurate audio. Given the paper's attitude at the time, everyone *knew* the journalist would not even bother to listen to it. They went full steam ahead.

The liability then PR-wise was on the paper. And that is all Peter had to reassure his client of. "It's just a flap is all. They screwed up. You did not. Brannigan provided the tape. You forwarded it to the appropriate people who had a vested interest in its content. It is not your problem that they were so obsessed they didn't even listen to it. Anyway, just ride it out with the paper. They need you, remember that."

The man had asked what else could be done, and Peter very quickly suggested they simply feed the paper another juicy tidbit—also true—as a diversion. "They are like children over there. You know that. When you take something away from a child, you need to give him a piece of candy in his other hand. He stops bawling as soon as you divert his attention to the newest 'gift.'"

Before Peter hung up, he decided to play another hand in the game. He continued. "Frankly, I would have expected Brannigan to have pulled off one of his technical miracles and to have altered the tape, just in case the journalist did listen to it. But he appears to hold the same opinion of those editors that I do. Anyway, it's just another screwed-up story by a media that doesn't really care about cleaning up its own messes. Our hands are clean. In three days, if not sooner, it will be over with."

His certainty had calmed his employer down sufficiently enough that the man was already thinking about which of the basketful of titillating morsels he could offer up now to the unwitting press. Once they hung up, Peter called Brannigan directly, catching him just as he returned, sandwich in hand along with a second bag of Cheetos. He was trying to scarf down what Vince had brought him before he had to appear on camera again.

"Yeah, Peter, what's up?"

"I'm going to need to talk with you later about the flap. For now, it is handled, but it does involve one of your 'particles.'" That was the term Peter used to reference any moving piece of information, activity, documents, etc., that were being deployed in an operation.

"All right. As long as you are satisfied it is handled, I won't have any attention on it when we resume with Ernst."

"Speaking of that, John, what the hell were you thinking presenting that deepfake video of Ernst?!" His tone was challenging but not angry.

"I know. It was risky. But…I needed to demonstrate to all of them just how powerful and valuable our tools are. I needed it to be real to them— not just some cute rhetoric—that we can literally make anything look like anything and make anything look like it originated from any source we choose. In other words, Peter, I wanted them to really understand that you and I create reality by what we do. Reality is perception. And you and I control the perceptions. That's all."

Peter Loren was satisfied with the validity of Brannigan's statement but not with the motive behind it. He was suspicious that Brannigan was using the word *we*, which would tie the two of them together in the minds of the others. It was bad enough to be tethered to a man like Brannigan, even worse in his mind to be entangled with him. Like his mentor, Samir Taghavi, he preferred to be free to disengage at any moment and to do his stealthy work solo. Peter Loren trusted himself and no one else.

But, for now, he decided not to challenge Brannigan on it. *One snafu isn't too bad, given the amount of disinformation we have deployed. I can live with that.* Truth be told, Peter Loren was already salivating over some of the future deepfake videos he might have Brannigan concoct in order for them to render opponents impotent, if not knock them out of the arena altogether. "Point taken. See you in the meeting."

"Serge, everyone here is familiar with the scope of all your operations and all the tentacles you have connected to any, and all, Big Tech-related companies. You all seem to have a symbiotic relationship, and many of your CEOs are already part of the GCF. Please let these men in on some of what you and I addressed and what we can look for and count on from you."

"I think I can keep this simple. Keep it at a strategic level," he said, stroking his long beard. "We pretty much control and drive the censorship activities of the platforms—the distribution of all information, if you will—and the cancel culture aspect of the platforms. Not just the social media companies who are the front lines on interfering with communication, but also the companies that create the social media software and the platforms that make it possible for any in the technology industry to do business. You said *symbiotic.* Actually, to me, it is more incestuous. Rather like having sex with your sister or parent."

Judging by the sighs of disapproval he heard from his European counterparts, he laughed. "Gentlemen, after what we witnessed in John's arsenal, my little comment isn't even PG rated, right?" When truth is spoken, there is often a discharge of laughter as the person realizes the truth of the matter. That happened right then. Every man at the table instantly laughed. And in one comment, Serge Pilaf had not only placed perspective on Brannigan's role but had also illustrated the playing field they were all operating on.

"So, keep in mind that all warfare begins—if it is to be successful—with cutting or disrupting dramatically the enemy's communication lines. There is no exception. If your enemy cannot communicate with its commanders and forces, they together cannot organize or execute sufficiently to bring about a serious defense, let alone a victory. Just watch a few war movies, and you will see the attacker begins always with a team that cuts the communication lines, rendering the enemy informationless."

Again, they all laughed. Given they were all from different countries, and in not too many decades past had fought opposite each other, this clearly was a common denominator for all their personal realities. "This is the age of information and all the technologies related to it—the Fourth Industrial Revolution, right? Simple. Whoever controls the information controls the world. My role will be to cut all communication lines you deem necessary so that no one can resist us successfully. They will be unable to get education or information and, therefore, will also be unable to coordinate. My American countrymen may arrogantly think their short-wave radios could save them, but they have no idea how we can track and interfere with any type of sound wave, for lack of a better term. If they create a communication line, I can find it and knock it out. It's just a question of severity."

"Meaning?" Cedric asked.

"Meaning it is possible today to take the entire world—or portion of it—back into the stone age, Cedric. That's not our goal, and frankly, I would hope it never comes to that, but we can do it. Especially with the help of the Chinese." Serge could see by Ernst's expression that this was a rabbit trail he did not want to lead the men down.

"But more likely relevant is our ability to spot any solutions our opponents are starting to create for the issues they see and for us to delete them or block them. Our algorithms do the work, once we set the parameters. So, it is simple for us to monitor for the thought process and subsequent communications that get created. Once spotted, they are blocked, deleted, or, if necessary, de-platformed altogether."

John spoke up. "Playing devil's advocate here, what if your algorithms miss enough that they mount a significant 'resistance'? Ernst, I believe, has informed all of us already that he senses the American people are on the move somehow and that we have to stop their numbers from reaching 100 million or more. Can you do that?"

"In a word, yes. Without getting too technical, John, the United States is the target. The people of the United States have been programmed for several decades now to become not just dependent upon their technology tools, and the information they provide, but they are, in fact, addicted. We have known, for some time now, that the social media sites are a form of addiction—cutting into production and into sanity. We know that. But…we also know they are addicted—using absolutely no critical thinking, I might add—to the *information* they receive when they do their so-called research online. We change the information, and emotionally charge it, and they never know it. One of the 'victories,' if you want to call it that, of this age is that it has rendered whole populations addicted and dependent upon us for the data they need to make decisions. We control the data and, of course, its veracity. We control who has access. And now, we control any content deemed by the men in this room to be counter to our mission and victory."

There was silence in the room. Cedric, who was the least technical person at the table, had a tendency to engage in stream of consciousness information processing. Without even realizing it, he said, "So, basically, you could cancel all of us, too…"

As his voice trailed off, Serge said simply, "Yes. Yes, I could."

Hearing the deep intakes of breath by these men as that sobering thought sunk in, Ernst jumped in—always the discussion monitor, the moderator of the GCF. "Serge, explain please why you won't do that, even though you have the capability."

"Most assuredly, Ernst. For the same reason the United States and the Soviet Union never launched into a nuclear war. Mutually assured destruction. That's all. If Big Tech canceled you all, there would be no commerce, no investment, no money, no power. Canceling you cancels us. As I said, mutually assured destruction."

The tension eased, and he continued, "If I may add one last thing. We can also delay the timing on the communication to the point it is almost worthless. We did that on Jan. 6—successfully, for the first time, interfered with, by *delaying*, the communication of the President of the United States, the leader of the free world, who was trying to communicate with the American people. This is not politics, my friends. This is power. We did it. Nice test run, eh?" Answering his own rhetorical question, he concluded, "But that's not the real victory that day. The real victory is that our algorithms did it. We had clean hands—you know, plausible deniability. Even if there is a backlash, we blame it on our algorithm and the fool who set that up. Disposable people, not people like us."

"Understood, gentlemen?" Ernst asked. It was. "The only thing I would add is that you all bring to me what you feel needs to be 'disappeared' or silenced. We coordinate that through me, so that we can attack simultaneously—or at least on the sequence I determine. Here's why. You may not know, but the U.S. military is contracting for Cloud services now. See how vulnerable they are in doing so? We control the company that creates the Cloud for them. If we want to stop them, we can. That's why I need to be the central point here in order to coordinate. Agreed?"

It was. To the man. Turning to Cornell, Ernst moved on. "Cedric, you have had the most questions along the way. I understand them, my friend, as these tech wizards are way out in front of us. I call them all as a group the 'garage kids.' Seems to me, in the United States, to succeed in pioneering a technology business, you need to start your business in your garage." He stopped, expecting them to appreciate his joke. Obligingly, they did.

"At least I know Serge will be able to get us, in the future, to the point where we won't even have to speak words into the implanted ears and artificial intelligence we have provided the eager customers. We will simply think it, and the thought will be transmitted to them—and they will perceive it as their own idea. Our thought, their perceived idea. Now, that is mind and population control at its highest. Befitting the trans-human, don't you think?" Ernst did not expect a response. He wanted merely to plant a seed of future existence and to affirm in the minds of the men at the table that Serge Pilaf and the "garage kids" were the nexus—the team that could bridge the human and the technology in all areas of existence. Right now, their task was simpler. It was merely to stop any communication that interfered with their goal or its timeline.

"But, my friends, Cedric here has another pivotal role in the blocking of communication and beyond. He controls disease. The tools he uses can cause the American—on his own—to back away from in-person communication, to shy away from human contact and toward embracing technology more and more. In short, even if the person is awake but afraid to leave his house for fear of running into a ubiquitous and ever-changing, life-threatening disease, he is cut off by default. Hard to amass an army, or mount a counterattack, with everyone hunkered down. They can't coordinate, especially if Serge does his job. The American has no communication channels. And by himself, the lone individual has no power. He has to coalesce and coordinate in order to push back. Afraid and alone, he will succumb."

Pausing to fill his goblet once again from the sparkling water bottle, he added, "You see, gentlemen, how each of you by yourselves could bring about the Great Reset we dream of. Each of you. Together, if one line fails, the other lines hold. Striking in a coordinated attack from all directions, simultaneously, leaves the reluctant American with nowhere to go except to submit."

Emboldened now by Ernst's introduction, Cedric chimed in, "Voluntarily, the American will have given up his right to assembly. If the rest of you propaganda/tech types—that I must confess talk a bit over my head from time to time—do your job, that same American will fight anyone who tries to exercise that First Amendment right. They will wipe out their own First Amendment, right, Peter?"

"Exactly. What Cedric just said is a perfect example of the principle we addressed this morning. It is a 'wrong' called 'no assembly' made 'right' by 'disease' and a 'right' called 'assembly' made wrong by those who are governed by 'fear.'"

Peter could see these men seemed clear on the mechanics of that, so he added, "Moreover, it is an example of a strength turned into a weakness—and that is one of the basic strategies we have been deploying against the American citizen for years. Further, and even more delicious, is the serendipity of righteousness turned into self-righteousness. The American people have been more than annoying in their righteousness for two centuries. In this century, we have converted them to self-righteousness. To me, though comical to watch, self-righteousness is deliriously effective in getting them to do your bidding and then refusing to back off from it."

Turning the conversation back over to Cedric after his soapbox-like commentary, Peter shut up and sat back. Cedric eagerly resumed in his most assuring voice, "We work closely with the Chinese on this. No doubt a physical disease can be a pandemic. We have just been experiencing a test run, if you will. And we have unlimited 'variants,' which, by the way, is our new word in the vernacular. Call it mutations or variants, we can string this out, if need be, or resurrect it at any time. But one can also create a pandemic of fear and withdrawal. Of anxiety. In short, a pandemic of mental illness, which, of course, Rudi here is prepared to handle with cocktails of medications—all of which render the people more pliable, more sedated."

"And more controllable!" Ernst said, clapping his hands, pressing his fingers in almost prayer position against his lips. "I am not interested in just controlling the person's actions, but also selecting out of the world's population those who are best suited for the future. Society can advance, but not with billions acting as a dead weight."

Serge Pilaf was younger than most of the other men, and his understanding of world history was lacking. He was a victim of the very educational system he created that recharacterized—if it covered at all—the history of man. His reflexive response was indicative of the blissful ignorance of the intellectual elites from time to time. "You are way beyond just making people compliant and conforming. This sounds like you are talking about the elimination of sections of the population. Am I hearing you right?"

"Of course, Serge. Of course. The climate change crisis demands that we reduce the Earth's population. Indeed, one of the most prominent members of the GCF recently said that the world cannot sustain eight billion people."

"You're not talking about gas chambers, are you?" He said it as if he had bile in his mouth, almost causing him to heave. "We're not going down that path, are we?"

"I see our young friend has a righteous indignation at the reminder of times past. Very appropriate, I think. But let me assure you, Serge, we will visit this again. For today, let us just look at the simple fact that all people die eventually. It is part of life. We want to make sure that those capable of transcending this existing body survive and create a future world—and, hopefully, one without constant violent wars, my friend."

This is such bullshit! Brannigan thought. It had not escaped him that Ernst had sidestepped giving an answer to Serge's direct question. Knowing that he had to play along, though, he sat quietly while Ernst assumed his professorial role.

"The Chinese unleased a virus, Serge. Intentionally or unintentionally, they did it. And Cedric here covered for them so the whole world would not treat them like a pariah. Right or wrong, the Chinese did it. But Cedric never failed to hold his post as one of the key directors of the organization that studies disease and wellness. What did you learn, Cedric?"

"We learned very early on that the disease attacks the elderly and the chronically sick. Knowing the Chinese have voiced and executed a reduction of their population by means of abortion, and strict family planning, my team concluded this was a weapon created to eliminate the people who were the greatest drain on the society. It was not a race thing or a religion thing—not like that fool Hitler and his hatred of an entire people. No, it appears to be the Chinese reducing the 'dead weight.'"

Even Peter rolled his eyes at that analogy, a fact not unnoticed by Ernst. "Something to say, Peter?"

Peter laughed. "Well, I can certainly understand why you need a spin doctor like me! I'll even have to put my thinking cap on to make that sound palatable!" Again, he laughed, and that allowed the others to see the humor in the dispassionate scientist's description of a discovered phenomenon.

"That is so true, Peter," Cedric affirmed. "None of us could feasibly discuss this with the world's press without sounding like a remake of an old World War II film. We were fortunate the political climate in the United States made this something their media wanted to bludgeon the President with—and we skated without having to answer up. But...and I cannot stress this enough...we found if the Chinese could do that for that reason, we could engineer a biologic for another reason. I personally don't believe we are trying to kill off a lot of people here. We are trying to be ready—if need be—to frighten people so much that they burrow in, stop communicating. At least with that strategy and tactic, I fully tracked with you all today."

Before Ernst could turn to someone else, and getting his second wind, Cedric raised his hand as if to ask for permission and wagged his finger. "Moreover, it is the China model of how they get around people naturally wanting to assemble. They control all communication in and out of China, obviously. But they can use a disease to control the motion of all Chinese, and they can do it selectively by province or in the whole of China. We saw that with the virus."

"Can you do that, Cedric? Can you create a disease—targeted—to effect desired control?" Rutger's baritone voice interrupted. He already knew the answer, but he wanted to keep the discussion on track.

"Yes. Yes, we can. Especially with China's help. The U.S. could help us, but I think that is a 'bridge too far' at the moment. Many countries have secret military biological labs, but we would need one that operates in complete secrecy and without any apparent coordination with other countries. U.S. and Europe—too much cooperation or duplicate research. It would not be stealth. But the Chinese are stealth masters."

Brannigan and Peter both looked at the empty chair in the meeting. That mystery was part of any conference they had with Ernst—either in person or in video. The empty chair was always there. Brannigan decided to broach it now. "So, is that the empty chair, Ernst? Is that what gives China a seat at the table?"

For Ernst, it was important for each man to know as much as possible. Some things were still being withheld by him, so he assessed very carefully how to handle his response. Leaning forward, he laced his fingers together in front of his chest and said, "The Global Commerce Forum has always had a vision of blending business and governments into a global scene more productive and streamlined than all the decentralized efforts of individual states. The epitome of centralized planning and governance. It is cooperation and exchange that can take economics, enterprise, and forms of government to higher levels than ever imagined. You know this.

"To accomplish the even higher goals that we have laid out here together in our meetings, we may need a nation state to facilitate our end objectives. That is pure business. Pure pragmatics. It should be obvious to all of you…I am sure it is…that we cannot have a nation state partner that is a democracy or even higher on a scale of governments. Nothing where the government is dictated to by the people. The people are not qualified. They have never been, and they never will be. Therefore, we would need to select a nation state that is already authoritarian in nature and which has demonstrably proven themselves to be a proper fit at the table. Meaning? They must bring something to the rest in terms of economics, prosperity, business, technology—all of it. And they must also have no qualms about a select group ruling."

He stopped for all of that to sink in. Smiling, he added, "That, John, limits our choices. I agree. And China would be one of those choices. But there are a few other entities—for lack of a better word—that might fit the bill. That is why that chair," he pointed in the direction of the still-empty seat at the table, "has not been revealed to you."

"But have you chosen, Ernst?"

"Yes. I have chosen. But I am in the process of putting in place some leverage over that country, since they, by definition, have 'tools' we would not possess individually. Again, I apologize, gentlemen, for the mystery. It is not that I do not trust you. My goodness, I think you know that by now. We have laid ourselves very bare in our discussions, have we not?"

They all nodded. "Rather, it is that I do not trust the invisible occupant of the chair until I have the leverage in place we might need to discipline them. At that time, I will happily reveal to you the eighth seat."

Brannigan wouldn't be dismissed immediately. "Do you know when that might be, Ernst? It seems that with the urgency you have impressed upon the rest of us to be ready and able to fire all weapons simultaneously and with an impending deadline, you would need that seat filled. That's all. I am not challenging you, just inquiring."

"That is understood. I did not take it as a challenge. And to answer your question, I expect in a few days to convene again, with a representative in that chair. If you remember, when this subject came up before, I said someone was watching, though not participating."

"Ah, yes, the alternate juror!" Brannigan joked.

"Exactly. Well, they have heard all of our plans. They are up to speed. And when we end this meeting, I will be meeting with them in person to get the assurances I need that the back-up leverage we might need for the actual occupant of the eighth seat is in place. Until then, I request your patience and that you indulge me. Good enough for now, John?"

John Brannigan did not like at all that there seemed to be two mysteries now—one regarding who would occupy the eighth seat and one regarding who was actually giving the "green light" to Schweiner. Dutifully, however, he said, "Yes. Most definitely. Hell, guys, you're looking at a guy who can't stand to read mysteries. I read the last page first. Can't stand the suspense!" That irony caused everyone to laugh and any residual tension to evaporate.

"No way. You're in intelligence/counterintelligence! How can you not stand suspense?!" Peter jabbed in fun.

Sheepishly, Brannigan just threw his hands up in a gesture of surrender and smiled.

CHAPTER TWENTY-EIGHT

While the members of the cabal left the meeting, focused and determined to line up all resources in their respective wheelhouses, Rutger had set up a follow-up call with the "mystery" participant Ernst had alluded to.

As she came on the screen, the chief economist for the International Currency Fund, Ernst could not help but wish the woman was headquartered in Europe where he might see her more frequently. Given that he rarely traveled to the United States, and those trips were for paid speaking engagements and symposiums, it would have been easier to have created the kind of collegial friendship he enjoyed with other female members of the economic and financial elites in the world. But her offices were in Washington, D.C.

Ernst Schweiner knew that was an ideal place for a key partner to be operating. As a foreign citizen, Svetlana Carolina could come and go and hold a diplomatic immunity that would be necessary for someone who came from Europe, but who was employed by an international organization housed in the United States. In fact, her proximity to the United Nations as well could prove pivotal if the worst-case scenarios he had not yet discussed with his colleagues ever materialized. She was an elegant, poised, middle-aged woman with a charming eastern European accent. And she was highly respected in all international financial seats of power.

It was his intention that Svetlana never have to show her face or officially take a seat at the table. Rutger Schmidt was like an executive producer who set up all the players. He had arranged, on Ernst's behalf, for Carolina to attend, without anyone else knowing she was monitoring the meetings. Ernst had allowed her to observe all his plans. Why a Princeton-educated, beautiful, and brilliant woman—whose rise in financial circles had been meteoric—would entertain the type of coup they envisioned was a bit of a mystery.

Perhaps she does want a seat at the table, after all, he thought. *Her charming dimples and gracious smile belie, I fear, the ambition she appears to have.* Despite his graciousness toward women, Schweiner's personal philosophy was rather disparaging of them. He saw their rise into power and influence as something inevitable but something to be wary of. *I have never met a power-driven woman who was not calculating and capable of betrayal at the most profound levels.* Yet, his breathtaking recruiting of her when they were both at a meeting in Chicago some years earlier had been a calculated gamble on his part that he should keep his enemies close. Though she did not know it, Ernst Schweiner viewed her as a potential enemy, not just a competitor. If she had guessed it, she showed no sign of it.

"Ernst, all of those meetings have been very illuminating. It is clear to me you are very far along the path. And I relish the day when I can return to life in Europe and when all the global governance organizations are in one location," Svetlana gushed.

"Why, my dear, I had no idea you were not enamored of your life in Washington, D.C., and New York City."

"Really, Ernst, you jest," she flirted. "The Americans are extremely hard to deal with. You warned me they knew less about monetary policy than they crowed about. I trusted you, and that was when I felt perhaps someone like me, at my age, could rise."

"Yes. I am glad you and I see things the same way along those lines," he said. "Regrettably, we can't meet for dinner and discuss all this over a lovely Champagne." He noted she had smiled. "So, my dear, can you handle the Chinese Communist Party if they decide to balk or blackmail us?"

Svetlana Carolina did not hesitate even a fraction of a second. "Yes, most definitely. Frankly, the world will embrace the digital currency of the Central Banks in the very near future. We at the ICF will push them in that direction. China has its own, and as we both have witnessed, it provides them a breathtaking means of surveillance of all their citizens—all transactions, all communications, all locations. And most interesting to me is the reality that since they control the currency by digits, they can control the behavior of any person. It is a very simple matter to get a man to submit if you starve him, and they can starve the entire population in one 'press of a button,' as the Americans say."

"Understood. But if this reset occurs with the CCP at the table with us, and if they refuse to yield to *our* digital currency—meaning a global digital currency—and maintain their own, can you handle them? I don't want any damned competition after we have taken all this trouble to bring the world together."

She cocked her head to one side and leaned into the camera. "That is decidedly simple. Legitimately under the function of our organization, we control the flow of money and the coordination of countries in their trade deals. We are monitoring constantly for the fair and steady flow of commerce and money, and the stability of it, as you know."

He nodded. "And therein lies their vulnerability, Ernst. If the CCP does not follow through with promises made, or threatens you in any way, we may not control their currency, but we control—or could control— all future Chinese business and trade expansion. They are too deep into, not just the United States any longer, but into many other nations. Their greed and desire to co-own international businesses, and to even invest in land and U.S. companies, have entangled them and their entire economy into the financial and monetary practices of those very companies and countries. Simple. If we need to collapse their digital currency and get them to play like good little boys and girls with the rest of you, we simply block all trade and business they have or attempt to create."

"Do you care to elaborate how you could do that?" Ernst asked.

"Ironically, just as they have their own digital currency, they also created their own Environmental Social Justice and Governance score. Their ESG is yet another one of the tools to get the citizenry and businesses to submit. If the score is not high enough, no matter the credit score, a business or entity cannot get a loan." With a somewhat menacing smile, she continued, "Well, they unwittingly gave us a good idea. We will develop and use our own ESG score. Not just as a means of controlling the actions of nations relevant to political, environmental, and sociological factors, but also corporations and even individuals, if we choose. China will need loans to expand the country's economy. They will have to come to the ICF for that money. We naturally will run not only their credit scores as an applying nation, but we will also run their ESG score. It should be obvious to anyone that China will have a very low ESG score, and we can hold that over them like the Sword of Damocles. They will fail on the ESG, and therefore, no money will be granted."

Now it was Ernst's turn to smile. Turning to Rutger, he said, "There, didn't I tell you, Rutger, that Svetlana would perceive this to be a simple issue?"

"Indeed you did. Will the rest of the world agree with you, Svetlana?"

"That is a moot point, is it not, Rutger? Ernst?" Looking from one to the other, she added, "It will appear complicated, painful, and appallingly fraught with tension, but the United States will be under your control by then, so to speak. There will be global governance, and for the sake of all other countries in our global alliance, each one will accept your solutions and participate. We exercise our authority to keep those countries, and their monopolistic businesses, stable. We will issue whatever money *they* need, and we crash the Chinese economy. No one but the Chinese will care if China's digital currency implodes and their economy comes crashing. The CCP will yield." She stopped and chuckled, seeming to look at something. "The rest of the world, by then, will have a formidable military consortium, easily capable of defeating any war machine China might possess. And the ICF can prevent any further buildup." Again, she laughed.

"I must say I find your laughter a bit disarming, Svetlana. Do you want to let us in on the joke?"

"No joke, Ernst. I was just reflecting on how the former U.S. president used to tell everyone how he was going to apply leverage to encourage compliance from some country like Iran, or whoever, and how certain he was that after a particularly nasty period of U.S. bullying, the first call they would make would be to him to submit."

"Please, please, don't remind me!" Ernst threw up his hands. "His viewpoint was just the rigorous view we exemplify, but his goals were the antithesis of ours. He had to go. Someone like that is a menace to the entire world. No. NO. The days of U.S. dominance are over. We can't have anyone like that rise again, ever!"

Noticing that Ernst had heated himself up on that exchange to the degree his face was flushed red, and he was pursing his lips back and forth in disgust, she chuckled once again. Before he could inquire, and before she would risk his temper flaring in her direction, she cajoled, "Now, Ernst, take a deep breath. That is never going to happen. You won, and given what I have watched auditing your meetings, you won't have to deal with that rugged individualism in the name of populism ever again."

Now it was Rutger's turn to laugh and weigh in. "She's right, Ernst. That's a hill we have taken and will not have to take again. Now, back to China…"

Svetlana took the hint. "As I said, before I accidentally triggered a little diversion of attention there, China is simple. We will take them. And I believe they know that."

Ernst's color returned to normal as he surveyed the landscape of his machinations mentally. Turning to his cohorts, he took a deep breath, grinned that cherubic grin he could turn on, and said, "That is precisely what I had concluded. But I value your talents, my dear, and I really wanted your views before I seat them at the table." Knowing she might be curious about this, he added, "And, Svetlana, I want you there—in the cloaked chair, invisible but auditing it all. Should we need to handle them, you will be brought forward, I assure you. You have a seat already, whether the others know your name or not."

He could not tell whether Svetlana needed any reassurance or even if she were grateful. His experience with these women, whom he really considered to be barracudas—if not vipers—caused him to maintain grace but always be aware they could turn. He liked Svetlana more than most, and he hoped in the future they could enjoy a truly open relationship. *She is a most interesting dinner companion, after all.*

After a pause and acknowledgment, she said, "Of course. I'm the alternate juror, am I not?"

"No, my dear, you are not an alternate. That person mischaracterized your role. You? You are the member of the 'Kitchen Cabinet.'" Svetlana was infinitely satisfied with that final clarification. A Kitchen Cabinet member may be anonymous, ruling from the kitchen and not the main dining table. But it is their secret identity and, therefore, candid and unfettered advice that is the value such a member brings to any endeavor. It was precisely the role she hoped to play. Hearing Ernst express it that way reassured her totally that she was secure.

"James, how many lines can you have in that note?" Hector asked as James was penning a hasty note for Vince. No one had been able to communicate with him since the start of this top-level strategy meeting, and James insisted that they let Vince know things were fine—just breaking very fast.

He planned to drive into the city quickly, deposit the note in the flag stick, and then return in time to have the pilot take him to Walker's ranch in Montana. Intending to use only the copious notes he had taken for Andy, he, nonetheless, planned to take a video copy of the entire day's meetings. James expected that by the time he got back from the mall, Hector would have copied and secured the whole session they had miraculously witnessed. He wanted it converted to a flash drive, which he expected to secure in a safe deposit box in Montana. All he felt he needed to brief Andy, Brian, and the others would be his notes and his memory. Yet, another voice within him was still equivocating on the best way to reveal this. Fortunately, James Mikolas, in the end, would listen to that voice.

Hoping that Hector had not noticed James was shaken by what he witnessed, he kept his head down as he responded. "Just a few. Do you have something you need to tell him?"

"Yeah, bro. Write it this way: 'You need to watch ANN for breaking news over the next few days.'"

"Watch ANN? What the hell?"

"Don't worry, James, he'll know what that means. We can't just keep leavin' notes. I may need to reach him, or warn him, and he knows what 'watch ANN Breaking News' means."

James shook his head vigorously, indicating he understood. After he had written the short sentence or two to alert Vince and reassure him that things were afoot and all was well, he wrote, "And Hector says, you need to watch ANN for breaking news over the next few days."

Before rolling it up, he passed it to Hector for his review. Getting the thumbs up, he took off in the Mustang. Hector waved, then made the call to Jessica to say James would be coming in. Her pilot seemed to always be ready for anything, so Hector returned to copying the hours-long meeting, storing it, and getting it onto the flash drive. James was right in his time estimate. Just as the last bit was transferring, the sound of that old Mustang could be heard turning onto the farm driveway.

"James, we're ready here. Just one thing…" Hector explained.

"Yeah, what's that?"

"They are likely to go back into a meeting today or tomorrow, don't you think? You know, the mystery chair?"

"Ahh, yes. Yeah, I think you may be right. Brannigan opened up a challenge there, and I think Schweiner will have to make a move. The longer he delays, the more suspicious it looks. He's got to keep that nefarious bunch of reprobates all in line. Must be like herding cats," James scoffed. "So, you are going to be here, business as usual."

"For sure. I just want you to keep that encrypted phone with you. Use your flip phone for normal stuff, but keep that other one handy. Understand, James?" He did. "Because I want you to have Jessica confirm they can receive the next installment of this reality TV show we are previewing." He forced a grin.

"Atta boy. Keep your spirits up! I wouldn't want any of this to drag you down." James ribbed him.

"I'm just focused on the task at hand right now, James. I figure, if we win, I'll have the rest of my life to ponder the content. Right now, it's the job at hand…" His voiced trailed off, and then he added humbly, "You know, Vince was a SEAL. I think I understand him now. It's the mission. You stay focused. You can't think about the evil or the emotion. You just do the job. Yep, I understand him now."

Slapping Hector on the back, James said, "Well, you can tell him that when you see him. Whenever the hell that will be. See you, Pal!"

CHAPTER TWENTY-NINE

*H*ector was right. Before James' plane had landed in Ovando, Montana, Rutger Schmidt had called everyone back into what he and Ernst hoped would be their final confab for a while. Hector had had time to shower, heat up some pizza, and get set with his bag of chocolates, even taking a half-hour nap, when his screens lit up that a call was commencing.

One of the things Hector had learned from Vince in their three years of surveillance, mostly in Central America, was how to take a power nap. His life in Compton had actually been far more predictable than now, given that those you are pursuing do not necessarily behave as you would expect. They keep their own clock, and Hector had learned to run his body in such a way as to be able to be awake, alert, and observant. Today was no different.

He popped the top of his favorite orange soda and settled in. Deciding not to signal Vince yet, he sensed that Vince and Brannigan were together, or at the very least in the same location, and Vince would already have eyes on. He had assumed Brannigan would not go anywhere without Vince. That, however, proved to be an erroneous assumption and a potentially costly one in the days ahead.

Vince had made his second trip out that day. Finding the message James had left at the Vietnam Veterans Memorial, he then stopped at a Korean barbecue place in the Georgetown neighborhood. He was just coming in when Brannigan appeared from upstairs.

"Oh good, Vince. I was just looking for you. What's that?" he asked.

"That, John, is **dinner!**"

Brannigan laughed at Vince's exuberance over his find. "Ahh, you found one of my favorite places!" The two scarfed down the fresh meal—Vince because he always ate like that and Brannigan because he expected to have one final session. His years of experience in intelligence and psychological warfare told him that his nudge to Ernst would not go unnoticed. And he especially wanted that eighth chair filled. It was time for the whole team to be assembled and coordinated. There was only so much mystery he would tolerate. In his mind, that was in his purview.

He didn't have to wait long. A text came in shortly after he ate, asking all players to resume. As the call began, Ernst appeared immediately and, with no delay whatsoever, informed the men that he felt it was now time to bring the member who would occupy the eighth chair into their discussions. "Rutger, will you bring our friend in from the 'Green Room'?" The reference to the waiting area for performers before they make their entrance onto the stage or in front of the cameras was a fitting description. In the Green Room, actors could relax and, at the same time, potentially observe whatever was occurring during the performance. Kept separate, yet involved, they could easily rise and enter the stage.

As the man appeared, conservatively dressed in Western attire, it was presumed he was Chinese. No one at the table had the same racial self-righteousness they had implanted into the "woke" culture. They did not hesitate whatsoever to judge a person by his appearance. And no one at that table could overlook the fact the man was from East Asia—and they each knew it would be preposterous to think it would be Taiwan, Japan, or South Korea.

"Gentlemen, may I introduce Mr. Xiang Koo, from the People's Republic of China, the eighth man at the table." Koo was a cool character who clearly could interact with any major leader globally. He smiled graciously to each one individually, with a forward nod resembling a slight bow. "He is coming to us from Beijing and represents the Chinese Communist Party, so he is quite familiar with all of your work."

No one at the table seemed to take special interest in him, except Brannigan. Knowing the Chinese, he knew that no matter what background the man espoused, he, in fact, would be with Chinese intelligence, and someone at the highest level in his own government if he had been delegated to commit his leaders to any future course of action.

Ernst took the lead. "I do not wish this meeting to be long. Mr. Koo has been kept apprised of all that we have discussed. But it is time to engage the entire team. Cedric," he said, turning to the GWO leader, "I believe you two have worked together before, is that right?"

"Yes." Cedric was clearly caught off guard by that statement and the admission it forced from him. He had to remind himself that he was at this table now and shouldn't fear any reprisals. He had made it. He could be candid. At least, that is what he told himself.

Schweiner then laid out the relationship between the GWO and Decu-Hehiz Pharmaceuticals and, by implication, the Chinese. "Cedric, you artfully managed to keep lockdowns in place—albeit shifting locations at times—during this pandemic. Those lockdowns afforded opportunity for us to break the solidarity of groups and to prevent communications and human interaction. Basically, you put the entire world—nation by nation—in solitary confinement."

"Yes, that was the strategy. Once the disease appeared, I saw it as an opportunity to further our objectives. And Rudi here has not only developed these super antibodies that portend so very well for all of us, but he has kept the increasingly anxious populations of the countries affected subdued through the powerful anti-anxiety and anti-depressants his company has become renowned for."

"Cedric, be candid here to reassure our other colleagues. Is this pandemic going away soon?"

His answer confirmed what only maligned conspiracy theorists in the United States had dared utter. "This pandemic will last as long as we need it to last."

"Meaning?" Ernst asked, leading this interview.

"Even with the Operation Warp Speed the United States launched, even if the virus is revealed to be highly contagious but not very lethal, and even if all the therapeutics and vaccines prove relatively effective, I can keep the fear going. We simply—with the help of our American colleagues in the room—plant the seeds of doubt and fear of mutations and, the new term to scare people, variants. I control the words and their definitions and can keep people so fearful of what might yet come that they won't take any comfort in the fact that this particular virus has been defeated."

Peter interjected at that point. "Cedric, that is true to a point. But I can tell you that, at some point, the emotional hysteria settles down and one returns to his native sense of reality. What do you do when that happens?"

With no hesitation, and with the same stoic statements that were characteristic of Schweiner, Ernst said, "We create Pandemic 2." He laughed at his own joke. "After all, the Americans have a propensity for nauseatingly extending a film or game with sequels upon sequels upon sequels."

"Can you be sure of that?" Peter again pressed.

"Most definitely. We will proffer the Chinese model of assembly. Basically, there is no assembly without the permission of the government. The Americans will willingly strip themselves of their own freedom of assembly and grow accustomed to that freedom only being given to them with the permission of the government."

It was a moment before the men at the table realized this soft answer had come—not from Cedric—but from the representative of the CCP. Quiet hung over the meeting until Ernst said, "That, gentlemen, is what is known as a 'pregnant pause.'"

Brannigan had had enough of these theatrical references and felt that if he had earlier been forced to reveal some very incriminating behind-the-scenes material relevant to his activities, so should Mr. Koo. "That would mean you have other viruses, then?"

Ernst considered interrupting, but, looking at Rutger, he decided to let this play out.

"Yes."

"Was this COVID-19 a biological weapon, Mr. Koo?"

"Mr. Pilaf, Mr. Loren, no matter how you control the information in the United States, I believe it is obvious, is it not, that the Americans do not believe my country's propaganda assertion that this virus was naturally occurring in a cave from a bat? And that somehow the bat managed to infect the world?"

Both men nodded. In fact, it had become increasingly challenging for Loren and Brannigan to get government investigators, law enforcement, and the media to accept it without help from them in the spin. Koo then stated what the GWO already knew but was keeping silent about. "The virus came from a bat. Yes. But...you also know it appears to have 'escaped' from a lab. And your government, Mr. Brannigan, I am sure you can confirm, knows that this particular lab is a bio lab working on bio warfare."

"We do. Or at least my CIA contacts tell me so."

At that point, Peter Loren's frustration boiled over. He was tired of playing from behind and wanted to make sure he understood not just what had been done, but what they contemplated, so that he could prepare his PR lines to promote what this group needed. "Did you release this virus into the world?"

Mr. Xiang Koo knew that it served no purpose to withhold from these men. Ernst Schweiner had offered him and the CCP a seat at the table in the entire global reset. China was about to fulfill its destiny, and obviously this group needed what his country could bring to the table. "Yes."

"Deliberately?" Peter asked.

"No. It was accidental. Carelessness on the part of one of our scientists, who is no longer on the project. But it opened up a unique opportunity to us politically, and I can see to you all, as well, in *your* revolution."

Rutger Schmidt was watching Xiang Koo very closely, noting his choice of words. It was a great reset they were creating. Yet, Koo had called it a revolution. He needed more time to reflect on that and talk with Ernst. He made a note of that on the tablet in front of him.

"So, in other words, you can accommodate Cedric here if he needs a Pandemic 2?" Brannigan asked.

"Yes. But in that case, the sequel would be deliberate." Koo was a man of few words, very characteristic of his government and its private and secret ways. Deciding to expound a bit more, he simply added, "You see, if we all are going to create the world we envision and maintain control over the people of this planet, we will need natural ways of selecting out where the planet's resources should appropriately be directed."

"And if the people resist?" Brannigan queried, trying to ascertain China's view on this.

"That will be more your concern than ours, I believe. Listening to you all these past few meetings, I believe you can handle the repercussions of any future devastating diseases. In fact, it seems to me that, in the future, our colleague here, Rudi Iseli, will be pivotal. Not only can he subdue, with medication, entire populations, but he can keep them in permanent submission if need be. Am I right, Mr. Iseli?"

"Yes. If people are persuaded their mental health depends upon medication, we can subdue them. Our drugs are designed to addict them as well. Only the people we choose will be weaned off if they desire. Any others will go through a catastrophic and violent withdrawal." Rudi let that sink in for a moment, knowing that each man's thoughts would land on the dramatic increase in suicide and homicides connected to those medications. "You can congratulate Loren, and likely Pilaf, on squelching anyone discovering the truth on that. Nice diversion, gentlemen, to the subject of 'guns.' And whoever convinced the Americans to embrace marijuana did us all a huge favor. The bottom line is this: If you get anyone hooked on anything, you can control them. And the beauty of it is they will willingly choose their 'controllers'—not the men necessarily, but the instrument."

Wanting a more positive note injected, Ernst interrupted. "But your more important work is on the super antibodies that will protect **us**— and others we choose—from whatever may be unleashed in the future." Rudi nodded.

"I find it comforting to know that, with this team, whatever hardships await us in the coming months, we have the capability of closing all countries and, with Pilaf's power, shutting down all communication, except the most primitive, if need be." Not wanting this to continue interminably, Ernst then said, "That is all I wanted for Mr. Koo today. It was important for you to meet him and for him to actually meet you from the point of view of insider, not spectator. I know it is a very awkward time of day for you, so we will let you get back to your official duties. We are comforted by your presence and what you personally bring to the table."

Taking his cue, Xiang Koo politely said goodbye to each of the members. Once he was no longer at the table, Schmidt confirmed the Green Room was empty. Koo had departed.

"Before we adjourn, Ernst, I have one question, if I may," Peter said.

Schweiner shifted a bit in his seat, revealing just a hint of pique. Desiring to keep the esprit de corps, he yielded.

"How do we know the Chinese, with the power they have not just in biological warfare, but economically and militarily, won't betray us and attempt to wrest the planetary control away from us? After all, they have the military, they have industry, commerce, communications, their own currency, and clearly a cold-blooded ambition. Have we not, perhaps, just let the fox into the hen house?"

Ernst lowered his chin, chuckled, and assumed again his superior scholarly role. After all, his wheelhouse was economics and commerce. "I have a plan for that, gentlemen. If they attempt to blackmail any of us to expose our activities, or threaten us with biological weapons, we have a way to not only stop it, but bring them to their knees, if need be."

"And how is that?" Peter asked.

"You forget that the International Currency Fund, though not at this table, is already a part of our reset. That fund's new ESG scores control who gets money. China's score will, of course, be low. Gentlemen, we control the currencies of the planet, the flow of money, the exchange of that money, international trade, monetary cooperation, and the rise or fall of the economies that depend upon that interchange. And notwithstanding that debacle about 10 years ago with the insurrection at the Repository of International Transactions, and the disastrous attempted takeover of Central Banks by Sir Harley Grantham-Jones, we still retain the power."

Everyone listening remembered the attempt by a cabal of Central Bankers to do a power grab of their own. It failed when a computer game from some upstart gaming company in the United States had outfoxed Grantham-Jones, causing his plot to collapse. Schweiner was relieved at the time, and the name of the gaming company had long been buried in the recesses of his mind. As long as he could deal with the likes of Serge Pilaf, a small private company like that wasn't even worth remembering.

What was the name of that company? Serge Pilaf asked himself, making a note to locate it. *I remember those boys were really smart. Outfoxed me on some games even.*

Pilaf did not remember the name, nor did he voice the question. For the moment, Andy Weir and Brian Washington Carver were not on the radar screen of the GCF. And, for the moment, no one knew the connection between Vince McCoy, James Mikolas, and Andy Weir. For the moment.

"Peter, I don't want you to fret yourself. Not only can we stop them, even if they have their own digital currency and fancy themselves the top global player, becoming the world's reserve currency. The Chinese have made a fatal mistake. In their haste and hubris, in their attempt to spread their influence across the globe, they are entangled inextricably in all their trade deals with other countries. No matter how smugly they sit with their presumed currency independence, we can stop all trade, blow up all flow of commerce, and their economy will implode. They can neither buy nor sell—once we have the power. China will help us achieve that power. They have a seat at the table, for now."

Brannigan's eyes turned sharply toward Ernst. Without changing his body position in the slightest, he asked, "Are you planning a double cross, Ernst? Rutger?" Neither man answered immediately, but Schweiner knew that the other players would need to be read in on this fallback plan at some point, and to thwart any festering suspicions or divisions in the group, he decided to be done with the issue.

"Your choice of words is a bit challenging, John, but I would say that, in the long run, we all know the Chinese would not just settle for a seat at the table. Left on their own, and empowered by the global reset, we all know they would want the *whole* table." He could see the others were listening, filtering that statement through their own biases about the Chinese. "Am I right? Of course, I am. Do you really see yourselves in the future being governed by the CCP? Hmmm?" He let the silence stand. "No, of course, you do not. They are not *our kind*, after all. And once they have served their purposes, we will end our relationship."

It was not that every individual at that table was not capable of perfidy, of betrayal, of self-service. They were. But each man had candied up his own justifications for the various power plays and alliances that had brought them to this point in history. No, it was not that. It was the simple, unadulterated candor of Ernst Schweiner at that moment that struck them. And psychologically, they all fell in line. No one there wanted Schweiner to "end the relationship" on them. His simple statement had not exposed an intention as much as it had exposed a capability. And that was humbling.

It was also exactly what Ernst Schweiner wanted to accomplish.

Chapter Thirty

*N*ot long after, Brannigan emerged from his basement "war room," as he thought of it. Vince heard him pacing in the downstairs area, so he descended to the first level to see what was up. As he turned the corner at the foot of the stairs, it was obvious Brannigan was distressed about something. Brannigan's face, at rest, had an almost horse-like appearance, without any emotion. When he was putting something over on someone, he had that shit-eating grin Vince deplored.

But this look was neither. Emotion poured out of Brannigan, but Vince could not tell whether it was anger, or frustration, or what. *Clearly, something went wrong in that meeting,* he thought.

Catching sight of Vince standing at the foot of the stairs, Brannigan pulled himself together. He didn't speak, but he raised his hand and waved an acknowledgment that he had seen Vince.

"Where are we going?"

"Not you, me!" Brannigan retorted. Breezing past Vince to head upstairs, he tossed over his shoulder, "I'm going to take a nap, and then I'm going out for a few hours." Vince nodded, and Brannigan added, "I won't need you at all tonight. Not going to the studio, just going to see a friend. You're free for the evening, Vince."

"OK." Vince smiled and said, "Well, I don't know as I earned my 'keep' today, John…" Brannigan waived it off as if it were nothing. Vince tried to be very casual in his next statement. "I may follow your lead on that nap. Then, I think I'll just catch up on some news. Got a new app I want to try."

Brannigan grunted, and Vince could tell he was obviously distracted and probably hadn't even heard Vince's cover story about the app. *He's off his pins, for sure!* "Just holler if you change your mind. I'll be here," he called after Brannigan. who was lumbering up the stairs with the same heavy peg-leg thumping he had been pacing the living area with.

"Thanks." The gruff voice rolled down the stairs.

As soon as he heard Brannigan's door close, Vince returned to his attic quarters, grabbed his cell from its charger and opened the ANN app. Buried in it was the encrypted communication link to Hector. For years, people had used pictures to hide secret pictures in, using the technology of steganography. One had to decode the first picture to extract the hidden picture. It had graduated up now into the cyber world with cyber attackers using it as a means of sending a secret message within something that is not secret.

Impossible to see by anyone looking at the phone or snooping in its contents, it would take a very skilled cyber forensic auditor to locate the communication app inside the news app that allowed Vince and Hector to send secret messages to one another. Buried inside America's News Network's "Breaking News" section was the secret app. The "hidden text" would be encrypted before being incorporated into the innocuous-looking "cover text" or data stream. Vince knew that even if someone did stumble onto it, the likelihood of them figuring out what it was, where it came from, and who it led to was not great. They'd more likely think they had stumbled onto some link to a YouTube video or something.

"Get here ASAP. Need covert physical surveillance of #1." That was all that was in the message. He and Hector had preset that #1 was Brannigan and #2 was Loren. Hoping that Hector had received the message and could depart immediately for the Georgetown home, and that Brannigan's nap would be long enough, there was no doubt in Vince's mind that Brannigan was going to meet with someone or going to some location where he did not want a bodyguard—or thought he didn't even need one.

During the few weeks that he had worked with Brannigan, the man never seemed to lose his cool. The daily routines seemed rote and very much under Brannigan's control. Even his meetings downstairs seemed to have gone as planned—or at least Vince figured it that way. Excursions to the network's studio for his appearances were ordinary, except for his celebrity status and the need for Vince to play the role of bodyguard in earnest. Smiling, he reminded himself that he would never have to justify to Brannigan the fact he was carrying a concealed weapon. After all, Brannigan had hired him for a covert mission.

But today was different. Brannigan did not want anyone to know where he was going—not even his bodyguard. Not even the men he had hired to spy on a colleague. Vince had a nervous feeling in his stomach and began to make plans on how he could follow Brannigan, in the event Hector didn't make it on time.

It's risky, but I think I need to try it. Vince couldn't shake his sense that whatever was about to happen, it had a huge significance of some kind. Removing the bug from the peanut butter jar, he decided to place it on Brannigan's car, rather than try to use the time he had been given by Brannigan to surreptitiously stash it in the basement. *Damn, I wish I knew what Hector and James had accomplished!*

Knowing that his was a true undercover assignment, Vince McCoy was not accustomed to being in that position. He was usually in the God seat, exercising overview. But today, it was time for electronic surveillance. A few minutes later, he had placed the bug on the car, securely enough that it would not shake loose but available enough that he could retrieve it in a minute, if need be.

A while later, Brannigan emerged from upstairs, grabbed his coat and keys, and headed for the back door. Stopping, he jerked around and asked, "Vince, what do you hear from your man on Peter Loren? Anything?" Vince had to be careful here not to give away that Hector had hacked in. Brannigan might put two and two together and realize that if he had hacked into Loren, he might be picking up the communications between Loren and himself. Deciding to ignore that for the moment, he tossed the dog a bone. "I believe he has set up physical surveillance and possibly electronic surveillance. Both locations. Home and office. We should probably know something fairly soon."

That seemed to satisfy Brannigan's appetite. "Good. Good. I want to know who he meets with physically. All his computer stuff, it will be business related and non-incriminating. My take on Peter Loren is that if he is not on the up and up, he will transact by phone call, but more likely by personal meeting. It's his associates who may open up some info for me."

"Understood. I'll make a point of getting to Hector later tonight. See what he has observed so far."

As Brannigan started to leave, Vince added, "Do you know when you will be home?"

"What the hell are you, my mother?" Brannigan grinned and left. For whatever reason, that last comment had shaken his gloom a bit. It also put Vince in his place. And it left Vince on shaky ground not knowing what Brannigan's real thoughts were.

"He's a cool character, a real enigma, that one," Vince said under his breath, as he let out a long whistle. Opening up his app, he texted Hector: "Don't know if you made it here, but I bugged his car. You can find him, at least. We will call you later tonight."

Hector was, in fact, within blocks of the Georgetown address, and turning on his tracker, he located Brannigan's vehicle. He was relieved that he would not have to follow closely. Vince had warned him that Brannigan would be extremely savvy and perceptive when it comes to tails. And with three years in the jungles of Central and South America with Vince, GPS was Hector's tracker of choice. Hector Rodriguez knew he could locate anyone, even if he was hiding under a rock somewhere. It was another of his skill sets.

CHAPTER THIRTY-ONE

*B*rannigan drove north on Wisconsin Avenue, careful to observe the speed limits as he crossed from the District into Maryland. He was grateful for the time to collect his thoughts. This message had to be concise but revealing. A few minutes later, he pulled into a public storage facility in Bethesda. He was about to enter his code when the manager waved him through. Brannigan had been a customer for years, and the man recognized him and his car.

Pulling around, he parked in front of a first-floor unit that had a garage door. He, however, walked into the building through a common entry door, disappearing inside. A moment or two after Brannigan went inside, Hector Rodriguez pulled into the storage facility. This presented an issue for him regarding surveillance, but he slowly pulled forward, as if looking for a parking place outside of the gates, near the manager's office.

He had visual eyes on Brannigan's car, and presumed unit, but could not see whether the door was up or not. Exiting his car, he entered the manager's office and approached the desk. The man came out of the living quarters behind the office and asked what he needed. Hector turned to point through the window to the buildings behind him. This time, he could see the garage door and that it was down. Wherever Brannigan had gone, Hector concluded, he must have closed the door or entered another way.

"I'd like to rent a unit," Hector said.

"What size, sir?"

"Well, judging by the looks of it, I would think about the size of the one where that car is parked. What size is that?"

"10 x 15, and the prices vary."

Hector said, "I'd prefer a ground floor like that. I presume you enter with a garage opener of some kind?"

"No. No. Those doors only open from the inside. Everything here is by digital code. You enter through the regular door and access it from inside the building."

Hector pretended to be mulling that over in his mind. "Oh, that's a good idea actually. So, I can load in and out but don't have to be concerned about the large opening. I like that idea."

"Me, too," the manager said. "Better for security, too. You lock from the inside, both entrances."

"Good. Do you have something, say, down there?" he asked, pointing toward Brannigan's unit.

Checking in the computer, the manager said he had one about three units away from there. "Do you want to see it?"

"Yes, please."

Entry into the building was indeed secure, just beyond Brannigan's car. Hector knew he could figure it out from there. A cursory look at the available unit was satisfactory for him, and he said he'd take it. The manager quoted him $350/month, with one month in advance.

Back in the office, Hector was just finishing paperwork and putting his photo ID away when Brannigan appeared from the building and got into his car. All told, he had been in the unit about 30 minutes. Hector wanted to finish up as quickly as he could but did not want to attract any unnecessary attention. Fortunately, he had his receipt in hand, and the manager took him out to the gate to show him how to use his access code to enter the facility, just as Brannigan pulled up to exit. Once again, the manager entered a code and waved Brannigan through. Brannigan courteously smiled an acknowledgment to the manager but paid little attention to what seemed to be a new customer of the facility.

Now back in his car and ready to follow Brannigan, there was a sudden interruption in the GPS, as if it had been offline and was rebooting. *Odd,* he thought. *Wonder what that was all about.* Nonetheless, he could see it was still working and Brannigan appeared to be heading back down Wisconsin Avenue toward home.

Ari Ben-Gurion got the flash traffic alert a few minutes later. He had hoped to have a quiet Shabbat, but any urgent intel coming in demanded his attention. The decoded message coming into the office in the embassy said only, "Satellite X fired up at 6 PM ET. Duration 30 seconds. Download to Beijing, People's Republic of China. Ten minutes later, satellite fired up again. Duration 2 seconds. Download to Bethesda, Md. Unable to identify location."

Disappointed as Ari was to still be no closer to identifying the purpose of this odd satellite, let alone the two terminals who might be communicating, he felt somewhat reassured that the transmitter was, in fact, in Bethesda, Md. Short as it had been, Israel's intelligence apparatus was homing in, a little at a time.

I'll have to see if James has turned up any leads for us on this, he reminded himself. Before calling it a day, he texted James innocuously, "Where are you tonight? Available to meet tomorrow?"

James, however, was already on the ground in Montana. He responded immediately, "No. In Montana for a few days. Fishing. Why?"

"Just got another satellite burst. Short, but Bethesda. Do you have anything for us?"

"No, sorry."

"10-4. Let me know when you get back. We'll have dinner or something."

"Will do."

That was all. And for the moment, James did not put much attention on this text. It seemed to him like some unrelated particle that he would help his counterpart with, if he could. But tonight, his mind was on the dilemma of how he was going to reveal the content of what he had just experienced during the surveillance. James knew it was too big for him. And almost too much to even contemplate. But he had watched it in real time. *Frankly, I need some time with the boys. If nothing else, it will settle me down. Need a game plan!*

Just as he was coming out of the bunk house Jessica had put him up in, Bud drove up in the ATV, shouting that Andy and Brian needed them in Bigfork ASAP. *I'll deal with that other thing when I get back,* he told himself. With that, he compartmentalized what would turn out to be a critical piece in this global puzzle he was attempting to solve.

Before Brannigan could get home, Hector alerted Vince to check ANN. The message was simple. "Storage facility in Bethesda. I rented a unit close by. He's on his way back. No additional stops."

A few minutes later, Brannigan pulled down the narrow driveway to the rear where what had been a carriage house years ago was now a garage—just big enough for one car. Brannigan had a habit of pulling in head-first, preferring to back out for some reason. Vince had been looking out for him, garbage bag in hand, intending to intercept Brannigan on a faux "take the garbage out" mission. It worked.

"Jesus, Vince, you must really be bored!"

Vince just laughed and headed to the back of the garage. An alley behind the row of brownstones allowed the garbage trucks and other service vehicles to move in what otherwise would have been narrow, congested streets. Fortunately, Brannigan didn't stop to help or talk. He just entered the kitchen without looking back. And that provided just enough cover for Vince to snag the GPS tracker so that it would not be detected, stuff the garbage bags in their containers, and return. Brannigan exited the main-floor powder room, thankfully being too preoccupied with his pitstop to have even checked on Vince.

"You want to watch a game?" Brannigan asked.

"Sure."

During the half-time, Brannigan called to Vince that he wanted to check in with Hector Rodriguez to see what he had learned. Vince called from his own phone, and Hector answered immediately. He had not had enough time to get back to Manassas, so he pulled over onto a quiet country lane to answer.

"Hector…"

"Yeah, bro, what's up?"

"Brannigan wants to talk with you. Can you talk?"

Handing Brannigan the phone, Vince stepped back a bit, once again able to hear only Brannigan's side of the conversation. "Hector, I need to know what you've got on the man I asked you to watch. Anything unusual?"

Hector knew to immediately take control of this interview. "Mr. Brannigan, I am glad you called. Before I get to that, I realized today myself that we need to set up some routine between us so that I can get you timely updates. You pick it. And how you want me to communicate."

Brannigan seemed to chew on that for a moment. It was not that he did not want regular intel; he just had to figure out what was the easiest, and the most secure, way. His natural swinish suspicion might have caused him to doubt Vince and Hector, but it was more a matter of who else might decide they wanted to hack him. To date, he had kept his communications battened down and avoided a whole host of adversaries, both foreign and domestic, who would have wanted to know what he was doing. After a moment, he said, "Good idea. Once a week—unless something out of the ordinary occurs. Then immediately. Text Vince with 'Target update' and we'll get back to you."

"Works for me, sir." Hector responded.

"So far, I have electronic surveillance on his office, but frankly, the traffic there is clearly about public relations. No one in there seems to be doing anything but servicing clients. Every morning, though, he does call a number at the Democracy Preservation Project."

Brannigan knew exactly what that was about since he did the same on a daily basis. It was those two calls that were driving the narrative and divisiveness in the United States. But Brannigan did not show even an inkling of interest. "What else?"

"I'm into his cell, but so far, he is a guy who doesn't use it that much. Mostly calendar and some notes. Few calls."

"That's odd," Brannigan commented.

"I agree, sir. That's what made me conclude he does any activities you might be looking for in person. Since I don't know exactly what those things might be, that's when I realized I may need to communicate with you more often, so that you can assess the significance of what I observe."

Brannigan nodded. "Has he been feeding any ducks lately?" Brannigan joked. Realizing Hector would have no idea what he meant by that, he added hastily, "Just a joke, Hector, just an inside joke." He winked at Vince.

Hector chuckled and then said, "He's a real keep-to-himself-type guy. No bars, no restaurants. In the last couple of weeks, he has had four visitors a week. Three women…"

"On the same night?"

"No, sir. One on Monday, one on Wednesday, and one on Friday. Each arrives around 10 PM, stays about two hours, and leaves. Each arrives with a car service."

That stopped Brannigan for a moment. *Regular meetings, with a paid car service, a different woman each time.* "Is this an escort service, do you think?"

"Could be. I thought I'd follow one of them the next time a woman shows up, you know, see where it goes."

Brannigan clapped his hands together. "Yes! Good idea. We may be onto something here."

As Vince watched Brannigan's enthusiasm climb, he could not help but surmise Brannigan was hoping for a lascivious purpose behind the late-night visits. *I can just imagine what his blackmail folders must be like! In this town! I doubt juicy would be descriptive enough,* Vince thought.

"And one delivery guy from Petra 2001. That's a local Middle Eastern food place. He does that on Saturdays. Like I said, not a real social butterfly. Anyway, that's it so far."

John Brannigan's mindset for years had been geared to salacious sexual content when it came to dealing with government and business types. And he'd been exceptional in finding, or creating, blackmail material—as he had in the case of the Russia Dossier and other files he had used over the years to force the resignation of people who needed to be moved aside. It did not matter in his world whether the information was true or fabricated. What mattered to John Brannigan was the takedown of any target he or his superiors felt was in the way.

Given how prissy and skittish Ernst Schweiner had been about the shocking deepfake video he had tested on them all, he knew that if he had opposition research of a sexual nature on anyone at "the table," he would have leverage at any time.

And for that reason, he paid almost no attention to the report that, weekly, a delivery came from a Middle Eastern restaurant with Halal Lebanese and Egyptian food. That oversight would cost him.

CHAPTER THIRTY-TWO

*T*he drive up "the Swan" took them through a 90-mile-long valley embraced by the Swan Range and the Mission Mountains and adorned by a string of lakes that ran the length of the valley like a string of pearls. The space and views served to calm James, and he understood totally why Bud and Jessica were so entrenched in this part of "the last best place." Though he longed for the quiet of Cape Fear, he somehow felt that it was so distant from him now that he might never be able to get back. Surprisingly, he knew as a long career operative in the field, whose whole purpose had been to protect the people of the United States, that what you cannot face will take you down. But what you do face, you have a chance of defeating. There was some solace there.

Fingering the flash drive he had carried with him, he knew this was going to be a hard day for his friends. No one would want to think that the lovely lives they had created, and the families they were enjoying in a free country, could be taken from them. Thinking of Abe, he thought, *Not on my watch!* It was at that moment he decided he would show them the entirety of it, rather than try to talk them through its indescribable content.

Everyone convened at Andy's home. It was early in the day, and after some coffee and cinnamon buns from a local bakery, Andy said he had a lot to show James and that he needed help. James, however, knew that it was more important for them all to see what was on the flash drive and that perhaps that might clear some hurdles for Andy. Hopefully, it would not sink him further into a quagmire.

Andy and Reagan had a large and comfortable movie room, and all adjourned there, except Faith and Hope. They were down for their morning nap when James brought up the content of his last day's viewing. "This is going to take a while." Turning to Reagan and Jessica, he said, "When you want us to break for lunch, let me know."

And so, Andy and Reagan, Brian and Alicia, and Bud and Jessica braced themselves. "This is what Hector has captured so far. Because these men decided to do a video conference call at their 'table,' once Hector got in, he was able to see what was on their screens."

Many hours later, they all had viewed the conference and the two add-on conferences Schweiner had conducted later that day and which Hector had forwarded. No one had said a word. Each had varying expressions as they watched. Each experienced a range of emotions. But they were seasoned fighters in their own arenas, and this was their first encounter with the foe they were going to have to defeat. Whatever it took for them to remain stoic and to dispassionately watch and listen probably would be discussed between husbands and wives privately.

Even after the video was finished, there was total silence in the room. The only sound was the projector itself shutting off and cooling down. It was almost as if they were not even breathing. No one was looking at any of the others. In their own worlds, comparing what these men had just discussed with the world all Americans were living in now, it was obvious to them they were already in a battle—and losing. They looked down at the floor or just straight ahead.

"Well, I am certainly proud of Vince and Hector," Jessica commented. "I didn't know this type of thing was possible."

"Yeah. We don't know where Vince is, but Hector has delivered the part I needed you to see, Andy, before we got into what you brought us over here for."

Andy was silent, staring at the floor, frowning. Still, no one else spoke. After a minute or two, Andy rose, nodded his head in the direction of the back of the house, and said, "James, let me show you the results of the 'work' of these men. What they have produced."

Rising, James said, "All right. These people are real. What they are doing is real. All these strategies you just witnessed will have been deployed through tactics in real life and in real time. And there will have been consequences to us already."

Brian stood, slapped James on the back, and said, trying to force a grin, "You could say that, bro, you could say that!" Pushing both Andy and James through the door, he turned to the others and said, "I'd rather you not see this next part. We need the time with James. And he can decide what to do with it later."

They nodded agreement and seemed relieved not to have to endure any more. Once Andy, James, and Brian had left, Jessica turned to her husband with an inquiring look. "What do you think?"

"I think I have never been more frightened in my whole life than I am right now."

"But something can be done about it, I am sure," said Reagan, always the optimist. "Surely, Andy and Brian can figure something out here. Something can always be done about it…" her voice trailed off and, with it, her conviction. Braving it through, she said, "It's almost sunset now. Let's turn the light on the flag out front. We can do that, at least…keep it illuminated."

"Sorry I took so long with that, Kid, but I sensed it might provide a frame of reference, something."

Andy waived it off as if to say it was fine. Pushing the door into their work room, he turned on the light and beckoned James and Brian to come in. "Brian, do you want to do the honors?"

"Not me, man, no way. This is your briefing."

Andy nodded, took a deep breath, and said, "All right, James, let me show you what we put together based upon your theory in that first note, and whatever materials you mailed, and what we already know from our experiences in the United States over the last 20 years." He could see that James was a little distracted by the curtains of Mylars with wheels, lines, and scribbling on them. To prevent him from jumping ahead, Andy said, "Not yet, James. I'll explain these in a moment, but I want you to know this 'analysis' has been done using not just the data, but it was extrapolated out against the three-dimensional chess model you and I used years ago to figure out who was doing what and what the Al Qaeda mastermind, Al-Zawahiri, would do next."

"Meaning?" James didn't fully get it.

"Meaning, each of these was filtered through all eight layers of that chess game I created. To reveal and connect all dots possible. Kind of like to the eighth power, if you will. It's like every dot can be multiplied by eight." Seeing nothing but a question mark on James' face, he said, "Never mind, that's too hard to tell. Easier if I just show you."

"Please."

"Now the first Mylar up front, which I will slide to the side just for us to reference, are the eight games in the order we discovered the enemy was attacking along, with the most important one, from Al Qaeda's leader's perspective, on the top. Let's start at the bottom. The first driving motivation was Religion. Next up was Military. Then Intelligence. Then a breakthrough one labeled Public Relations instead of Propaganda."

"I remember." James was starting to engage. "That was a real corker of a breakthrough there. Most study propaganda. But they need to study how the enemy morphed into using public relations to implement transforming people's mindsets. I remember."

"Right. Good. Do you remember what came after Public Relations?"

"Weapons." James was quite certain of that.

Andy smiled. "Then Sociology, where we looked at the impact of the weapon 'fear' on a population. How would it manifest in the society and culture if the bad guys were implementing a form of mind control using fear as the weapon? They were engaged in psychological warfare, using emotions, and, most especially, the emotion of fear."

"Well, this is like a walk down memory lane. It's all coming back to me!" James said sarcastically.

"Then Medical, where we looked at the ways one could use medicine—anything related to that field. And at the top was Money. We realized Al-Zawahiri was driven by that, and all the others were linked to it. But money—and power—were the top."

Letting that sink in for a moment, Andy continued, "So, what you are about to see is our analysis of the four critical foundational institutions in the United States that are imploding, under a Fifth Column attack from within. Likely implanted by a Trojan Horse in each of the four areas. But…and this is *really important*, James…each has been examined through the lens of each of the eight games. In other words, what Weapons may have been used. What Medical, what Sociological change, what Public Relations, what Intelligence, what Military, what Religious, and what Money elements may have been introduced—if any?"

"I get it. You filtered each of the categories eight times. Smart. Did you find the attack was multi-directional?"

Andy looked to Brian first. The two partners were ready to give James the news they brought him out to discuss. "Yes, James, we did. It is all in play in our current world, and your 'home movie' today shows the Who and the How." Letting that register, and perhaps realizing for the first time himself how connected this all was, he said, "OK, then. Let's start with the first institution to be destroyed if all the money and all the power is to be transferred to whomever."

"Didn't I just show you the 'whomever'?" James challenged.

"Probably, but what you gave us today, shocking as it is, has not gone through our usual thought process. Don't worry, it will. But first, I need to show you this. Please, James."

James yielded the field. "For sure. This is your party, Andy." Andy shot a glance at him over that seeming wisecrack.

Sliding the Mylar with the eight-game list off to the side of the first rail, Andy had James look at the first one on the left—Family. It was a mass of crisscrossing lines, presenting one with the snap reaction of confusion. And disorientation and a myriad of emotions. Then, he walked James to the right to show him the one for Education. Then Religion, then Justice. If that were not sobering enough, Andy then closed the gap in the room by having the first Mylar's almost circular web design touch the second one. The second touched the third and, finally, the fourth. Strung out like that, it was like a satanic rosary of interconnecting dots that tied all of them together. Clearly, they were not separate and isolated. The world might have geniuses working valiantly to fight the adversary in each of those four arenas, but in fact, they were all connected. It did not matter whether one started on the left or the right, as each led to the other. That was almost identical to what Andy had discovered years earlier with the eight games. No matter where you started, one led to the other. The enemy then, and the enemy now, had a plan—a blueprint.

"Wow. This is giving me a headache just looking at it," James commented.

"Right. Us, too. Unfortunately, our country is living this right now."

For the first time, James really understood the pain, the fear, and anxiety Americans were experiencing. He could see it in this horrible set of diagrams. Each dot, however, was an actual battle area, with real human suffering. Words did not come. He simply looked at it.

Andy waited for a bit and let James think with this. After all, it was James' analyses that had complemented anything he and Brian had done. In the shadows from the past, it was James' external eye combined with the altitude of his life's experiences that had connected dots. Reluctantly, Andy now had to show him why he himself was in a quandary.

"James, brace yourself. That was the rehearsal. All laid out in linear fashion. Here's the play." With that, he pushed the Mylars that were on separate tracks, each track behind the other, all into the center so they overlaid one another. The effect was staggering. It was like an impenetrable spider web, or layers of spider webs, one on top of the other—so dense with the connecting lines that you could almost see no daylight. And the center, where everything did cross, was like a black hole.

"My God," escaped James' lips.

Neither Andy nor Brian spoke. Brian came up to James and put his hand on his shoulder. The three of them stood there, staring at the snarled mess they would have to untangle. Not only was it daunting, it looked impossible.

Finally, James broke the silence. "Is it possible to unravel this?"

Andy looked off to his left and smiled. Turning back to James, he simply said, "Until today, I wasn't sure. The only consistency with what we handled before was the fact that Al Qaeda under Al-Zawahiri operated on the basis of independent cells, with no cell knowing what the others were working on. That provided security in case one cell was compromised or captured. They possessed no information to cough up regarding other cells. Central vision and deployment of cells came from the top man himself. Each of these areas here are under attack from different directions, by different people, for different reasons. A real mess. The black hole you are looking at told Brian and me there had to be a source point and a likely strategy. But James, we did not know where or who…until today."

"Schweiner and the 'Kitchen Cabinet' in his GCF and the Great Reset." James almost whispered it. Now James was smiling. "You know, I wonder how many regular members of the Global Commerce Forum have any idea how this is all being manipulated and what Schweiner's real intentions are." The statement really had no answer that James could discern. But he expected that there was a "witting" list of conspirators and an "unwitting" list of conspirators. In his mind, that provided some hope.

"I don't see how we could conclude anything other than that, given that horror show we just watched." Suddenly, Andy laughed. "You know, my wife won't let me watch horror movies. She hates them. If I even try, she gets up and leaves with a real attitude." Again, he laughed at his own private joke. "Did you notice, today, she sat through it all, though?"

Not knowing what to make of this outburst, Brian said solicitously, "I did notice that."

"Well, I am going to get an earful tonight, I can tell *you.*"

"I think our boy's a little punch drunk, James, what do you think?" Brian winked at James.

"But I saw that telltale smile of his, Brian. That means there is some hope, right?"

Nodding his head in the direction of Andy, Brian said, "I think we'd better have him tell us."

That brought Andy around long enough for him to say, "There is hope, James. Always hope."

"You can create a game to disentangle this whole mess, help us set our course straight again, right?"

"I can try." It was said simply and softly. "I can try."

The next morning after Faith took James on an obligatory tour of her doll's house and introduced him to all the critters she had made from yarn, James, Bud, and Jessica were ready to head back to the ranch. Bud had asked when and how James was going to get this video out for the people to see. James very quickly responded that he could not do that first. As far as James reasoned, a principle that Hitler and Stalin espoused, and had mastered, was in play here. In propaganda strategies, just as important as a lie told often enough becoming the "truth," a "truth" can be so outrageous it will be dismissed as a lie. Hitler wrote in his book what he believed and intended, but it was dismissed, ignored. "No, we have to prepare the ground for this one, lay a foundation that people can anchor on so they can actually see what we see."

Taking Andy and Brian aside to make sure they agreed, he said, "The game has to come first. You *have* to create a game, and we *have* to carpet-bomb the entire area so effectively that the people are ready to see and believe what's on this flash drive. Soften the target, Andy. Soften the target, Brian."

Turning to leave, he stopped himself and turned back, "But you have to do this fast—faster than any game you've done before. Time is short, as you can tell by what I played for you. These guys are attacking from all directions. They are creating redundancy, and they are shortening their timeline. They intend this war to be over before we even know we were attacked."

Andy was quite somber as he nodded that he fully understood. Almost wistfully, he said, "Well, we are long past the simmering frog now, aren't we? The water's boiling, and if we don't jump now, we are cooked." James couldn't remember if he had ever used that metaphor with Andy or not, but it was one of his favorites. Mentally, it had kept him in the game during the Cold War and during the attacks against the American people in the last 20 years. He did not respond except to give his young friends another handshake and hug. "Good luck, boys. Keep in touch."

CHAPTER THIRTY-THREE

*M*ikolas was bone-tired when he exited the plane and headed to his room in the Manassas farmhouse. *I'm too old for all these day cross-country trips and different mattresses.* He told himself that, but even as he thought it, he knew he would not change any of his habits. He had always gone where the data led him, and he wasn't going to change now. Right then, however, what he wanted was just a bed. Flopping down, having taken off only his shoes, James was fading into sleep when he heard the outside screen door on the porch bang. Next thing he knew, there was a lot of commotion in the kitchen. James thought he was alone here, except for Hector. But Hector moved about like a predatory cat, despite his large frame. If he didn't want you to hear him, you would not.

Curiosity was just too much for James, so he pulled himself up and padded into the kitchen to see what the farmhand, who was also their de facto caretaker, might be up to. Instead, he found Hector rummaging around in cabinets, looking for something.

"What's up, Pal? You're waking the dead with all that racket."

"Whoa, sorry, James! I don't think I noticed you come in."

"You didn't hear the plane land?"

"No. I been a bit distracted. Must have had my earphones on." Hector didn't seem the least bit apologetic for all the racket he had created and went on banging cookware around until he found what appeared to be an omelet pan. Holding it up, he asked, "What the hell is this? Pretty flimsy, if you ask me."

James needed some levity, and whether Hector had intended it or not, James found that Hector's complete lack of awareness of ordinary cookware struck James as funny—incongruous, but still funny. "Sorry, man, I'm just a little punch drunk from all this travel."

"I'm trying to scramble some eggs. Can I use this?" he asked, holding the folding omelet pan up again.

"Yep. Even if you tried to use it for its intended purpose, Hector, I think there is no way you won't be making scrambled eggs." James grinned.

About half an hour later, Hector had indeed had his scrambled eggs, and the two of them sat at the kitchen table, while Hector finished off his 16-ounce glass of milk. "Did you show them the 'movie'?" That was Hector's nickname for the horrific conspiracy on that stick.

"Yeah. It was sobering, for sure."

"I bet."

"Anything new happen while I was gone?" James inquired, not really expecting much.

"I don't know yet. I have a new wrinkle in the surveillance." James looked up but didn't speak. "Vince had me haul ass into the city to tail Brannigan. Seems he was behaving oddly, and Vince needed an eyes-on."

"Oh?"

"Yeah, I barely got there. But I tailed him and spent the rest of that night, and the next day, setting up the location in case he goes out there again. We're just covering our bases, that's all."

James sighed, letting out as much exhaustion as he could, not really registering what Hector was talking about.

"Anyway, I got us a unit in the storage facility almost next to Brannigan's. Good cover in the event I need to do a genuine 'out in plain sight' surveillance. Like I said…bases."

"A storage unit? That's where he went?" James asked offhandedly, placing the dishes in the sink and heading for the door back to bed.

"Yep. Didn't stay long. A helluva long drive back from Bethesda, though."

James froze in the doorway. Not knowing whether he had heard Hector correctly, he asked sharply, "Bethesda? Brannigan went to Bethesda?"

"Yeah, man. Don't have a clue *why* yet. But Vince had a bug up his rear about somethin'."

James' heart was racing more than normal. He couldn't tell whether that was the usual propitious signal that he was right on top of some significant piece of data or whether the possibility of the former director of the CIA being the person Ari was looking for—the missing link with Beijing—was just too dizzying to grasp. Whatever it was, it left James Mikolas speechless—and afraid.

He walked slowly back to his room, hoping sleep would mercifully overtake him.

He was startled awake as if being shaken by someone. Yet his body seemed immobilized, as if a heavy weight was pushing it down, making it impossible to rise. It took James a minute or two to orient himself and to shake the oppressive weight, which now just seemed focused on his chest. Once his breathing returned to normal, he pushed himself up and sat on the end of the bed.

Dismissing outright the possibility of a medical situation, he brushed it off as intense jet lag and the oppressive data on global subterfuge he was trying to process and solve with a handful of patriots. Each had power in his or her own right, but he didn't know if there was a way to pull it all together and reach the American people in time.

What distressed him the most was that he had no one he could talk to right now. He couldn't talk his theories through with Hector. Even though Hector had witnessed the seditious conference, Hector was a hacker and a surveillance guy, not an analyst. Turning to Vince, he knew Vince could provide some background and instinct perhaps, but he, too, was not an analyst.

Ari Ben-Gurion would be a trustworthy counterpart, but he knew he could not expose that video to the Israelis. At least not yet. *I just don't know what the Israelis know. Why did Ari decide to tell me about Brannigan and his suspicions in the first place? Are they using me, too?* James winced, unable to shake off a self-doubt he was experiencing. *Divide and conquer,* he told himself. Shouting to his nagging inner voice, he yelled, "Shut up. I am not listening to you. The way out is the way forward. You can come along, but I am moving forward!"

Grateful that no one was in the farmhouse to hear that outburst, it somehow made him feel better to take dominion over his own emotions. Taking a deep breath, James Mikolas stood up and did what he had done thousands of times over the course of his career. He picked up his small notebook and posed a question to himself in the small book. That question led to a cascade of questions. Is John Brannigan a Chinese spy? Is he a double agent? Was he a double agent even when he headed the CIA? Is it possible no one with a "seat at the table" knows it?

Just the aspect of writing down the questions seemed to move the thoughts from the swirling, crushing position they had in his mind to a draining of the emotional energy they possessed and exerted over him. He could almost feel a discharge as the thought was brought into words on paper.

James had no way of knowing it then, but the answer to that last question would change the outcome for everyone—forever. Right now, all he knew was that he felt vigor returning, and he was ready to face whatever was to come.

CHAPTER THIRTY-FOUR

*A*ndy had been struggling for days, trying to figure out a way to disentangle the web of destructive factors that seemed all interconnected. To design a game, he needed to pull the elements apart, but there were so many dots, and so many interconnections, that it seemed impossible.

Knowing the urgency, and the magnitude, his mood was sinking. Today, he simply stood in front of the transparent Mylars, almost idly shuffling the positions to see if changing their sequence would somehow change the morass or open up some daylight. It did not. And for some reason, Andy could not begin to create in his mind a game this complex.

His head was bowed, and his shoulders slumped, when Brian entered their workplace. "Well, I have to say, bro, that you—from the rear—look like the picture of dejection!" Andy did not respond to Brian's attempt at humor. And that told Brian that this was serious. Coming close, he stood beside his partner and said, "What's the problem?"

"The problem is the **problem**!" Andy barked, indicating the screens in front of them. Sighing, he added, "Brian, here's what I have tried so far. I tried disconnecting each of the institutions, hoping the dots that connected one to the other might disconnect. I was trying to see if making it sequential was more workable than the overlaid version, which is so dense."

"I take it that did not work?"

Andy nodded. "Stand-alone attacks, or coordinated, it is still impossible to separate the interconnection of the cultural dots from the demise of the institution. All roads still lead to Rome—our center point and presumed goal of the enemy."

"Humph!" Brian stared at it for a moment, knowing that his expertise was the marketing, not the design, of the game. At least looking at the problem in front of the two of them bought him some time.

Andy then said, "They are like spider webs, Brian. Not the shape, although that shows up, too, as one dot connects with dots on the opposite side. But it's like they are gossamer. I thought maybe if they are that tenuous, I could just yank them apart and scuttle the whole thing..." his voiced trailed.

"Wrecking ball approach, I gather."

Andy laughed at that. "Yeah! I knew it wouldn't work." He laughed again.

"Why not?"

"Because, like any good spider web, even if you break it up, the spider puts it back, and you have the same web there the next day."

As Brian looked at that, the imagery of it worked for him. An idea was germinating, but it was not to a point he was even aware of it yet. "So, can you delicately, like a surgeon, maybe pull one layer off of the others?"

"Nope. Tried that. The thing breaks apart. The lines drop away, and I'm left with nothing, until the damned spider creates the threads again, and the dots reconnect."

"Huh."

Brian was scrunching his face, as if squinting somehow might help, when the door burst open and Reagan stormed in. She was fuming mad, and Brian—who had never seen her display any kind of temper—could almost see smoke coming out of her head. Oh, boy! he thought.

"Andy, you have got to do something about this! I have never been this angry in my life!" As she said that, Andy could see Faith, looking terrified, peer in for a moment and then dash off, wailing.

"What on earth?' Andy asked, as he went over to see if he could stop Reagan's display. "What's happened? My God, Reagan, calm down. What did she do?"

"She did not do anything!" Reagan said, bursting into tears.

"Then, why is she crying? And why are you yelling? I don't understand, sweetie, what has happened?"

"Taking a deep breath might help," Brian interjected.

"Oh, shut up, Brian! We are not the three of us advising each other like years ago," Reagan yelled.

Andy shot Brian a look that warned him to just step back. Brian sheepishly yielded. "Yeah, I know, Reagan. You know me. I was always listening to you two and butting in. You're right. I'm zippin' my mouth right now," he said, using his thumb and forefinger to mimic him zipping his lips shut.

Reagan saw that comical gesture and surrendered as well. "Oh, Brian, I am so sorry. It's just…" she had a hard time trying to get her thoughts into words. "Andy, I went to pick Faith up from the preschool, and on the way home, she told me joyfully that she was going to be a boy."

Not knowing where Reagan was going with this, he just stood, calmly listening. Reagan continued, "I explained to her that she was a little girl—which she nodded she knew—and that she could do things like a boy—you know, like wear overalls, collect her snakes and bugs, and go fishing with Bud. You know." Andy nodded that he was following her. "She can do things that boys do, but she is a girl."

Reagan stopped for a moment to take a deep breath. "Andy, I thought maybe somebody made fun of her or something for the pretty little dress she wore today, the one Brian and Alicia gave her for her birthday. But she told me, in no uncertain words, that she was going to **be** a boy and then she could do what boys do. And she was mad at me for making her a girl!"

Brian and Andy looked at each other, aware now that their mouths were open, looking totally confused.

"When I insisted she was a girl, but it was fine for her to like boys' things, she pitched a fit. And she's been like that since."

"Where did this come from, do you know?"

"I'm getting to that!" Reagan raised her voice, and her eyes flashed again. "She told me the woman at school told her she could become a boy if she didn't want to be a girl, and—I swear to God, Andy, I could kill this woman—they could give her some kind of medicine, and you and I wouldn't have any say about it."

At that moment, Andy understood that the first Mylar of the Destruction of the Family game had just come crashing into his own home. "Are you trying to tell me that a preschool in Montana is promoting those—what are they called?"

"Puberty blockers?"

"Yeah, that's what I read about." Turning to Brian, he said, "I thought it was so insane, I didn't even put it up there as a dot."

"Yes, Andy. In Montana. The teacher's from California, though. I should have known!"

"Reagan, Reagan, stay with me on this. I need to understand. Someone thinks they can turn a 3-year-old into a different sex?"

"Yes. Or start the process. But Andy, my fury is they apparently can do this to children without parental consent. And what parent is going to consent to confusing the hell out of a child, and maybe destroy their entire life, maybe even kill them?!"

At that point, Brian decided to risk it. Stepping forward, thinking of his own daughter, he asked quietly, "Does Alicia know about this?"

"You bet she does!" Reagan snarled. Again, Brian stepped back. "And she's as mad about this as I am."

"Okay. Okay. What are you going to do?" Andy asked.

"Alicia and I didn't risk our lives in human rights activism for nothing, Andy. This is the last place I thought anyone would try to harm women and children. Apparently…it is not. So, Alicia and I are going over to that school and have a **real serious** talk with the principal and teacher."

Though that seemed to calm Reagan down, knowing that she had action she could take, it terrified Brian. "Oh, man, a hot-tempered Latina and a hot-tempered Irishwoman ganging up on the local school…"

He didn't even complete the sentence before Reagan interrupted, her green eyes piercing him. "We are not ganging up, Brian. We are standing up for our rights, and we are protecting our daughters—and I might add, your daughters, too, you two!" she said, jabbing a finger in Andy's chest.

Brian knew exactly what to do. "Andy, you need to go, too. You go." And before Andy could even protest about the work they needed to do and that the two gals could probably handle it, Brian sealed the deal. "You need to go, Andy. I have no doubt listening to Reagan right now that she and Alicia can 'handle' it. You need to go, if for no other reason than to protect the teacher."

Reagan shot him a look, moved past Andy, and had her finger waving up into Brian's face, when Andy got what Brian was hinting at. No telling whether these two women had been seduced by tales of the Old West and had turned into the fierce pioneering women who, centuries earlier, had had to fight to save their families. Andy loved this passion in Reagan, but he did realize that with Reagan and Alicia both on a tear, he might end up having to bail someone out of jail or something.

Hands up in surrender position, he said, "All right! I'll go, too. I think maybe having a dad there as well might help in some way. You know, parental unity, solidarity…"

"Okay then. Let's go right now. Alicia's waiting."

Andy turned to look back at Brian, as if to ask if he wanted to come, too. "No, bro, I'll stay here. You don't want that southeast Washington, D.C. kid to come out of me. I trust you three to protect my little girl as well. I'll stay here, work on this a bit. You know, see if an idea comes to me."

That relieved Andy of some angst over the conflict of life colliding with this crisis of a game design. Before, when he, Brian, and James had tackled awful problems, he had been single. Today, he was not only a husband, but more importantly, he was a dad. And his family needed him.

"Thanks, Brian. Take a look. See if your eyes catch something."

After they left, Brian pulled up a card table chair in front of the Mylar screens, sat down, and stared at the spider's web of American decay. Years ago, he had solved a problem by accidentally bringing it down to one word. Softly, he prayed to a God he hoped was there to help him and Andy.

It was already dusk when he heard the front door open. He had split his time between the workplace and Faith's bedroom. She had worn herself out, crying, but she loved her "Unka Bian," as she called him. Seeing him come in with a peanut butter sandwich and orange juice made her light up. She gobbled it down, thanked him, and snuggled into his lap. After she had fallen asleep, he went back to his chair in front of the problem.

That's where Andy found him. Reagan stuck her head in, and, without turning, Brian said, "She's napping in her room. I fed her."

"So, how did it go?"

"Fine," Andy said returning to the work area.

"Care to elaborate on that?"

"Well, the principal had no idea his teacher had told that to Faith or even discussed gender or sex with a 3-year-old, let alone offered this radical idea to the little girl. Turns out the teacher is from California…"

"That figures," Brian interrupted.

"Yeah. Exactly what the girls said. You should have heard them, Brian. They were like a duet or something. Said the same things at almost the same time. It was like listening to them in stereo."

Brian laughed, still eyes forward.

"Anyway, he brought the teacher in. Asked her to confirm what Faith told Reagan. She did. He fired her on the spot. Warned her there was no point in protesting or involving lawyers. Said something about 'child abuse' charges and suggested she return to the state that was so enamored of what he called 'insanity.'"

"Yay for our team! Anything else?"

Andy chuckled a bit. "Matter of fact, yes. He told all three of us that other foolish people and state education systems might be toying with this insanity, but Montana was not one of them. There never will be an education-system enforcement or promotion of any such thing. Montana would see that however far this insanity went, it would be a family matter, and no parents would ever be left out, or left to find out like Reagan had."

"You believe him?" Brian sounded tired now.

"I believe he believes it. I believe he handled this situation with integrity and firmness."

"Well, that's good enough for now, I guess." Brian looked over his shoulder and grinned at Andy. "That sure was some fireworks with Reagan, and I can just imagine the two of them."

Andy grinned. "Yeah, those two sure know how to defend their young. Just like the old days. Defend women everywhere." For a moment, the two friends were silent, remembering how they had met their wives and how dedicated those women had been to the cause of rescuing women from slave trafficking. Both were smart. Both were brave. And both were fierce.

Breaking the reverie, Andy said, "So, how about you? Have any breakthroughs while I was gone?"

He was not prepared for what happened next. Brian rose, grabbed another card table chair, and brought it beside his own. Motioning for Andy to sit, he said, "As a matter of fact, I did."

Instantly, Andy put on his 'hat' of game designer and master player. He just let Brian talk because he could see in Brian's demeanor that something significant had happened.

"Well, first, I just sat here staring at this self-restoring spider web of entanglements you described. There didn't seem to me to be any way to break apart these institutional collapses and their sub-elements—you know, our dots—or you would have found them. You're the chess genius."

Brian stopped long enough to take a sip from his water bottle. And then, I don't know, suddenly I got the idea we were approaching this from the wrong angle. What if we didn't try to break it apart? You said it was like a gossamer web that, even if you broke through it, and the thin, clingy threads broke and went away, they would reappear again the next day. Like the spider came back and put it all back together." He stopped again, as if framing the description in his mind before he spoke. Brian wanted Andy to see what he had seen. So, he took his time.

"With spider webs, the spider is what binds the anchor points and connecting threads together. If they get damaged, he restores them all. The spider is the common binder. So, I got to thinking instead of worrying about destroying, and re-destroying these elements, we should see what it is that binds them all together, gives them sustainability, keeps this wicked game going forever."

Andy leaned forward in his chair. Something was starting to shift mentally, and he was hanging on every word now. "Andy, I realized we have been thinking it is a person or persons who would cause the implosion of the institution. They are, but that is not what binds this. It has to be an emotion, not a person. Only an emotion transcends the players. People can come and go. God knows we watched a bunch of them with James. They are playing the game, but they are anchoring it all on an emotion. It is that *emotion* that is carrying through and connecting all the dots and connecting all the games."

"An emotion…" Andy repeated.

"Andy, it's simple, actually. Right in front of us. I remembered something James said way back. And I got to thinking that one emotion is common to every horrible thing that is happening in our country today. And we can't heal or solve anything as long as that emotion is the binding emotion. Smart, actually, on their part. But here's the thing. If an emotion is binding people to **do** things, they can **undo** them just as easily. We just need to dissolve the emotion, and the whole damned game collapses. So, I looked at each of these separately, as well as sliding them all together, from the point of view that it was all driven by one emotion. I asked myself—dot by dot—what happens to the dot if the underlying emotion goes away?"

"The dot goes away?"

"Um huh, or at least the lines do, and—here's the kicker—there's no emotion left to put it back together. No spider to make it again, don't you see?"

Andy did see, and he could feel emotionally something rocking in him. He couldn't stand the suspense, but before he asked Brian what the emotion was, he asked, "How did you spot it?"

"Sheer luck. We may owe a lot to that fool teacher and what she did to Faith."

Andy had a questioning look on his face. "When I saw that look on Reagan's face, and knew what Alicia would look like as well, I realized something had triggered in Reagan that I had not ever seen in her."

"What?"

"Hate." Brian stopped, looked at his friend, and said, "The emotion that binds, Andy, is *hate*. We solve that, the rest winds down."

Andy Weir looked off into the distance, thought for a moment, and smiled. And Brian knew that was the signal that Andy had a solution. Turning to Brian, Andy put his hand on his lifelong friend's knee and said simply, "You know, Brian, in all the years I've known you, there was never a time when I tossed you the ball that you didn't catch it. Today's no different."

"Good. Now, all we have to do is figure out how to dissolve hate in the minds of the American people. That's all. Piece of cake, that!"

"That's not as daunting as it might seem, my friend." Andy reassured Brian. "I have an idea. I think I can design this one."

Rising, he pushed his chair back, slapped Brian on the shoulder, and said, "You'd better alert the team in Los Angeles that we are going to do another game. Get production geared up. Maybe move it out of California, up here. We're going to ambush those folks along the very line they have attacked us. We are going to receive their blow and turn it back at them." And for the first time in a long time, hope returned.

CHAPTER THIRTY-FIVE

*B*rannigan closed his review of the latest false stories his still-loyal team inside the CIA had been concocting in order to bludgeon targets into submission. He had decided to have the DOJ carry the water for a while, have someone there do some leaking, if need be. This latest material was juicy, and he expected to hand it off to the Democracy Preservation Project on Monday. That would allow the DPP to select what they leaked to the press and what they handed off personally to legislators and D.C. buzzards. It was the material he would provide the DOJ that created the best loop of all, though. If a leak came from the DOJ, the "media pygmies," as he referred to them, would snatch it up.

It didn't matter whether it was true or not. As far as they were concerned, if it came from DOJ, it must be true. So, he would create something and pass it in both directions, and if both used it, each would corroborate the other. It was just one big circle. And he had been doing this successfully for years. Making it even more delicious in recent years was the fact he was a hired expert for ANN and got to provide expert analysis and opinion about the fake stories he himself had fabricated and disseminated. A sweet gig!

But today, he still had attention on Peter Loren. *I don't want to pay a surveillance team forever,* he thought. He had an idea of something he might be able to do to speed up the process or, at the very least, shed some light on whether Peter Loren could be trusted or not. Calling out to Vince, he said he wanted to go over an idea.

"Hey, Vince, anything further from your man Hector?"

"Not that I am aware of, John. Like he said yesterday, the conversations seem normal. Nothing that flags our attention. What's on your mind?"

"Well, I was thinking we need someone *inside* the house, you know. Eyes on the scene to see if there is something inside that would give him away."

"If indeed there is actually anything wrong," Vince reminded him.

"He may be clean."

Realizing he had overstepped a bit, and demonstrated a pre-conclusion of guilt, without any evidence even, John covered his tracks. "You're right. That's what I was thinking…that there may be nothing there, and it's not fair to keep digging into a guy if he's clean."

"Agreed." Vince didn't know where this was going. "What do you have in mind?"

"Well, I thought I'd invite Peter out to dinner. See what he does with that. My bet is that he will suggest I come to him, given what Hector has observed. It is Saturday, after all."

They discussed it a bit and decided it was worth a try. Frankly, Vince reassured Brannigan that he was the client, and if he wanted to add a new wrinkle, it was totally his call. That was enough for Brannigan. He called Peter, hoping to catch him. It was Saturday afternoon. And when Peter Loren answered the phone, he was surprised that Brannigan was calling him on a Saturday but did not sound the least bit alarmed.

"What's up, John? Something happen?"

"No, no." Brannigan assured him. "It's Saturday. I thought you might want to have dinner together. That is, if you don't have plans this evening. I don't know about you, but sometimes, I just want to kick back a little bit. Not all work, you know."

Peter said he certainly did know and usually spent a quiet Saturday. Graciously, he offered, "Tell you what. Why don't you come here, and we'll order some food in—maybe watch a movie? Do you like Middle Eastern food, John?"

Brannigan broke into a grin, winking at Vince. "I like just about anything, Peter, but yes, I do. I gather you know someplace special?"

"Yes. Close by. Exceptional food."

"Sounds great. What time do you want me there? And remind me of your address, please."

Brannigan clapped his hands together and said, "Well, that was simple. Looks like I'll get a chance to see what I can see—and even get a good meal out of it!"

"Do you need me for anything?"

"Nah, take the night off, too." Brannigan was feeling magnanimous. Then, as an afterthought, he said, "You might have Hector standing by, though. Who knows if Peter might actually call someone after I leave?" Again, he winked.

"Understood."

Once in his room, Vince called Hector to alert him and then asked if James was there.

"James, are you up for a walk in the park? I've got the whole evening off. The boss is having dinner with the target and doesn't need me. I really need to be read in on what the hell has been going on since I went into this 'black world' situation I live in."

James laughed at the reference to top secret work environments known as the "black world." Somehow, he had never pictured a Georgetown brownstone as a black world but, given that CIA safe houses came in all shapes and sizes, in all kinds of neighborhoods, he reminded himself it shouldn't surprise him. "Sure. We might even have a drink at the Mayflower. Who knows who we might run into?"

Peter greeted John effusively and escorted him into what appeared to be a nice townhome in the area near Dupont Circle. It was almost Danish modern in its interior décor, which was a nice contrast to the more Victorian architecture and appearance of the exterior. The living room was sparse, decorated entirely in white, and accented by a 70-inch TV.

"Wow, I guess you do like to catch a movie," Brannigan said. "This is better than the theaters. Thanks for inviting me."

"You are welcome. Dinner should be here in a few minutes. Want a drink while we are waiting?"

"Sure. You have whiskey and soda?"

"I do." Making himself a Cosmopolitan, which struck Brannigan as odd, Peter handed Brannigan his drink, and the two went to a brick patio in the rear of the house. A stone wall that likely dated around the Civil War, judging by the ivy on it and the age of the bricks, surrounded the back yard, providing privacy and security.

"Nice place, Peter."

"Cheers."

The two conversed lightly about their backgrounds, sports, avoiding subjects of work. Each seemed to welcome a night off. Joking about the koi pond that nestled against the back wall, Brannigan said, "Too small, though, for ducks."

Peter laughed and said, "I can see that is going to be a running joke between us!"

Just then the food arrived. Following Peter in, the delivery man—who looked like hundreds of other young Muslim men who had emigrated to the United States from Lebanon, Syria, you name it—started to enter the vestibule but stopped when he spotted another person in the house. Peter nodded in the direction of his guest and said, "That's why I ordered so much tonight. Not eating alone."

The young man smiled but said nothing. He accepted the generous tip, dipped his head in acknowledgment, and handed Peter his receipt. Peter had handed the large brown bag to Brannigan, who turned away for just a moment, looking for a place to set it. That moment was just sufficient for the delivery man to palm a note to Peter. Without looking at it, Peter slipped it into his pocket. Brannigan missed the exchange altogether.

It was warm enough for a street vendor to venture into the National Mall near the Lincoln Memorial, hoping to sell some last-minute Italian ice to passersby. It was tough going for all street entrepreneurs, given the state of crime in the city and the fact that people just didn't dare come out anymore—especially at night. James bought Vince an ice, doing his best to help the vendor, who likely had a family to support. The two walked in the direction of the Thomas Jefferson Memorial. These days, it was not even lit and had a fence surrounding it, which blocked the entrance.

That was disheartening to James, but it also provided a degree of privacy they might not otherwise have had. They located a bench.

James gave Vince the CliffsNotes version of the meetings that had transpired online in Brannigan's basement while Vince was upstairs "cooking." They both found that amusing. Somehow, the idea that an elite group of globalist insurgents was planning the final takeover of the governments and economies of the world literally under Vince's feet, with his having absolutely no awareness of it, was comical to them—humbling, but comical.

"Jesus, I had no idea," Vince lamented. "This makes it very real to me now that villains can get away with the most nefarious acts right under the noses of their families, work colleagues, neighbors. I'm a bachelor. But if I had been his wife, I would have had no idea what was occurring down in that basement office."

"I understand. What's he like when he's not destroying things surreptitiously?"

"Just another guy, James. That's the thing. He's just another guy. He does ordinary things."

James snorted. "Except when he isn't!"

Vince nodded, still reflecting on the magnitude of what James had described to him. After a while, he said, "Here's the thing, though. He may not need my services much longer, given that we haven't surfaced anything apparently that bothers Brannigan. And it's only his ego that makes him think he needs a bodyguard."

"Really?" James doubted somehow that a former head of a major intelligence agency would not need some security.

"No. The places he visits are secure, in and of themselves. And from what I see, he doesn't associate with anyone who isn't in on this deep state nonsense and now this…this…disgusting revolution. My guess…he'll play it pretty close to home until they do whatever it is you have heard them say they will do."

James looked at that for a moment and said, "Well, if you are right, then you may soon be free to join me at the farm." Then, he added, "Actually, I hope so. That would leave us free to surveil both of these characters without the risks you have been taking in the house."

"So, you think there is more to Peter Loren than we have unearthed so far?"

"I do. I don't know what yet. But Brannigan clearly has, or at least had, a gut feeling about him. This may give us the opportunity to hunt him on our own." James felt Vince wince a bit and jokingly said, "Forgive the metaphor there, Vince. But you got to admit, these guys are like a nest of vipers—any one of them capable of biting the other, taking him out."

"No problem, man. It's the same no matter the villain. Drug cartels we tangled with in Mexico, Venezuela. We wouldn't have gotten anything done if it hadn't been for the 'vipers,' like you just called them, turning on their own boss. Deception and betrayal are part and parcel of it all."

"Yep. Organized crime, too," James said. "I remember one of my first mentors in the Agency taught me that bad guys always leave the trail to themselves. They leave the means to bring them down, and without that, we would never find them."

Vince nodded aggressively in agreement on that. He couldn't help but remind himself that this was a different class of criminal, however. There had been absolutely not one clue in the lifestyle of John Brannigan that would have caused anyone to turn attention to him, let alone conclude he was anything other than an honest, dedicated servant of the people of the United States.

And he recognized now that if Brannigan was world class, so, too, must Peter Loren be. Standing, he shook off the oppressive sense of dread he had experienced during James' briefing and dove into the game once again. "So, let's go catch these bastards."

A few days later, Brannigan informed Vince he felt his services weren't needed anymore and assured him he was free to take another assignment. As Vince was packing to leave, Brannigan came upstairs to the attic and amended that a bit to make certain he could call Vince, if circumstances changed.

"Absolutely. And if you need Hector for anything—provided we are still in the area—just holler."

They started downstairs when Brannigan noticed the peanut butter jar on the nightstand, picked it up, and said to Vince, "Hey, you forgot your peanut butter. Somehow, I might have guessed you would be a snack in bed guy. But peanut butter?! Come on, man." He grinned.

Vince laughed, and Brannigan started to toss it into the trash when Vince said, "Hey, glad you caught that. That's my 'special brand,' and I almost forgot it. Thanks for the save."

Brannigan handed it over, thinking, *Christ, he's even more pedestrian than I am! A favorite peanut butter?*

Once Vince was safely out of the house, had turned the corner, and descended into the subway entrance, he let out a long, slow breath. *That was close! All he needed was to find that bug in the jar…wake up, man!*

CHAPTER THIRTY-SIX

"You wanna take a walk?" Andy asked, as he walked out onto the porch, where Brian was playing with Faith and Hope.

"Sure. How far you got in mind?"

"Calgary, maybe."

"That bad, huh?" Brian knew that whenever Andy got stuck on a problem, or too overwhelmed, he had learned to just take a walk. Suggesting they walk from Bigfork, Montana, to Calgary, Canada, was a real clue as to the severity of the problem.

Andy looked out over the lake and just nodded. "Well, let's go in and take a look. You can explain it to me," Brian offered. Andy and Brian walked to the back, and into their workspace, with two little girls in tow. This time, attention was on the computer screen, as Andy explained what he had done with the game so far. Faith and Hope occupied themselves running in between the Mylar sheets and sliding them back and forth. Neither Andy nor Brian had any intention of distracting them.

"This is how far I got." Andy opened the screen, revealing the title page for the game. The game was called "Hate." Brian was hoping he'd gotten a bit farther than just the title, when Andy caught the look on his face and said, "Don't worry. That's just the title. I think it's the right one because, with all the hate flowing from all our connecting dots on those Mylars, I figure everyone would be caught by the title and want to see what this particular *hate* was about."

"I agree. Good title. Sad, but good."

Andy then described the first level of the game, whereby the players self-identified which team they would be on, based upon how they felt about various elements that Andy had placed on the Mylars in the form of dots. Every societal aspect in the institutions they felt were under attack was included in an almost "questionnaire" format. Depending on their responses as they navigated through the "dots," at the end, their responses indicated what color jersey they would wear. The game placed the appropriate jersey on them. Each player was choosing the elements they felt the strongest about, what point of view they valued, or what point of view they hated.

Looking at the players in their jerseys, Andy explained that he had settled on sports jerseys because he felt that would be the least divisive. He wanted the hate to be created by the game elements, not the jersey or team identification. One player was wearing a blue and white jersey, and the other a red and white jersey.

"You sure you want red and blue, Andy?"

"Yep. Other colors are just colors. Subliminally, and philosophically, each player has a bent toward red and blue in our country. So much politics. All referred to in red and blue."

Brian said he got that and wondered if they would change colors for the international games. Andy liked that idea and made a note for later. Then, the game continued with each player trying to recruit other players to his side by getting the next set of players in the game to agree with his attack on the opponent. The goal was to amass as big a team as one could, using hate as the common denominator. Players would gravitate toward the other players who hated what they did and who would be willing to do battle for that "dot."

Brian could see that the recruiting was done through rhetoric, demagoguery, and ridicule, but once the players were chosen, it was clear that the game would be played violently—using guns, knives, Molotov cocktails, tear gas, bricks, and an assortment of other weapons used by actual contemporary citizens. How they used those weapons was being decided by what jersey they wore.

Then, they got to the spot where Andy was stuck. "I just don't see how to solve it, Brian. I can easily have these ever-larger teams keep bashing at each other verbally and physically, each trying to get the upper hand and level up, but by the top of the game, hate has to have been dissolved. And...I just can't get there by layer after layer of people outdoing each other on hate."

"I see."

Brian did see. "I do like, though, that you are allowing each player to pick out of his quiver what weapon he wants to use to browbeat the opponent into submission or retreat. The players themselves are also picking their verbal arguments and creating make-shift weapons in the game, is that right?" Andy nodded. Brian continued, "Well, that's good. Keeps them creative and engaged. It is their game, not one manufactured by us. They choose."

"For sure. That is signature of all our games. The player gets to put himself literally into the game. Did you notice that at the beginning the player sets up what he hates and what he loves? So, each player has things he will try to destroy and things he will try to save."

Brian agreed with that and also agreed with Andy's choice that when a player or his team lost a round, it meant they had not destroyed what the opponent had brought into that round, or they had what *they* brought into that particular round destroyed. Then, all of the failures had to go back a level. Each level was a surprise because neither player knew what the other player was going to select to bring into that level. Each choice, however, was connected into one or more of the dots on the Mylars, and all, hopefully, would be selected naturally by individual players when they entered the game. If not, they could select from a pre-chosen list of all the dots that had merged together in the real-world spider's web Andy and Brian were trying to disentangle.

"Andy, if that mess on those Mylars is right, if your analysis of the attacks upon our foundational institutions that are plotted there is correct—and it is these things people are fighting about, engaging in hate about—then all those dots should show up here in the game, somewhere. Of course, if we mis-evaluated the intensity and the hate it engenders…"

Before he finished the sentence, Andy interrupted. "We haven't. I think between you, me, and James, we got enough here to make everybody fighting mad who even starts this game, let alone continues it. At least, I hope so. And I think leaving it up to them to randomly insert something else they feel is taking down the family, or education, or religion, or justice, I think empowers them."

Brian looked that over in his mind, then winced a bit as he said, "So, what is it again you are stuck on?"

"Brian, I can get the players to hate. That's simple, and the rewards and penalties are simple. What I don't know how to do is to get them to change sufficiently that they cease hating, and then they themselves change the game to one of solutions, rather than just ridges of opposition and stalemate."

Looking at Andy, Brian held back a smile. Personally, he felt Andy had already laid into the design beautiful elements, and he looked forward to testing it. But he, too, felt the weight of how to create a design solution that actually stops the hate that had been so thoroughly programmed into the United States that the country was tearing itself apart.

"You see?" Andy asked, his voice pained. "If I don't get that right, Brian, nothing works. We fail. We just can't fail!"

"I do see, bro." Checking the time, he added, "So, we do need to take a walk. Not sure we have time enough to walk to Calgary..." he joked. Andy did not respond to the joke, so Brian pushed him toward the door. "What do you say we go up to Glacier National Park and take a long walk up there?"

Andy was compliant. And he was distracted. Not even thinking, he left the game open. Motioning to the two girls to follow them, he, Brian, and Hope left the room. Taking Hope over to her mom, who was in Reagan's office, where the two moms had their heads together on some serious project, Andy didn't notice that Faith was still in the room.

While her dad was getting organized, explaining to Reagan and Alicia that he and Brian were going up to the park for a little breather, Faith climbed up on the chair and started to fondle the keyboard. Seeing that the screen changed when she poked a key on the keyboard, she giggled and explored more. The program screen started to scroll quite erratically, as repetitive symbols that were code for something in the game, appeared and then disappeared. When a big error warning box came up, she, not being able to read, pressed Accept. That seemed to stop it all, and the screen went black.

Just then, she heard Andy calling for her. "Faith, come here, sweetie. Your mom wants to see you."

Scrambling off the chair as fast as she could, she flew out the door. "Here I come, Daddy. Here I come." The little 3-year-old, curly-haired redhead with the green eyes had no idea that she had just set in motion a chain of events that would alter the outcome of Ernst Schweiner's global reset.

A couple of hours later, Andy and Brian found themselves sitting on a rocky beach near Lake McDonald Lodge in Glacier National Park. Not realizing that Going-to-the-Sun Road, which goes from the west side of the park to the east side, is generally closed until July due to the snow and elevation, they had walked along a creek and hiking trail called Avalanche Creek. Despite it being a beautiful late-spring day, there were not too many people on the trail.

Andy, nonetheless, wanted to find some pristine place where there would be no one else. And this rocky beach fit the bill. Brian was a few yards away, skipping flat multicolored rocks over the water. Andy sat on a log that had drifted in some time in the past. The breeze off the lake, the quiet sound of the monstrously large park seemed to calm him. What helped the most was the clarity of the water. Montana rivers and lakes were pure, allowing the boater or spectator on the sidelines to see deep into the water, if not to the bottom. Lake McDonald was too deep and cold at this point to see bottom, but the area along the shore was so clear, Andy could see all the colors of the bottom rocks shimmering below the surface like a kaleidoscope. *I'm glad we moved here,* he told himself. Knowing that this area would be safer for his family than Southern California, and knowing that most of the people he regarded as family were all in this area as well, gave him a sense of belonging.

The only one missing today was James. Bucking up, he suggested to Brian that they head back and see if the time of peace and exercise had jogged any ideas into action.

Faith scampered out on the porch, enthusiastically greeting them both, and, grabbing her father's hand, she walked with him into the workspace. Brian went off to see what their wives were up to, hoping they were close to dinner. Andy sat down at the computer, preparing to work. Realizing he had left the game up, he expected to just restart where he had left it. Clicking to bring the screen up on the last level he was designing, he expected to see his players in their blue and red jerseys. Instead, all the color was gone, leaving only white jerseys. Worse yet, any of the features he had designed facially or physically had disappeared.

Frustrated, he looked for the source of the problem when Faith tugged at his pant leg. "Daddy, Daddy," she said, trying to get his attention.

"Not now, Faith," he brushed her little hand aside. "Daddy's got a problem here."

She tugged again, more insistently. "What?!" he snapped.

Startled but undaunted, she grinned, pointed to the screen, and said, "I fitz it." It took Andy a moment to realize that Faith had done something to the game, somehow.

"What the hell? What did you do?" he yelled at her, as if she would have any idea what she had done.

"I fitz it," she said proudly.

Andy was more frantic now, trying to recover the level of the game, the identity of the players, and the colors. But it would not come back up. Any gain he had from his walk vanished, as the prospect of game elements being wrecked angered him.

Faith tried to climb up in his lap, but he pushed her away, saying, "Get out of here, Faith. I don't want you in here!" The tone and volume of his voice now registered, and the little girl became scared and upset. She ran crying from the room, seeking out her mother for comfort and protection. Reagan was indeed in the kitchen, frying some chicken when Faith ran in screaming, running behind Reagan's long western skirt, clinging to her leg.

Before she could ask what had happened, Andy ran into the kitchen. "I'm sorry, Faith." But before he could say anything else, just the speed of his entry made Faith scream again and burrow deeper into her mom's skirt. Andy looked pleadingly at Reagan as if to say, "help me." But Reagan was too startled herself to do anything but stare. She shot him a look, though, that told Andy they would have a conversation about this later.

"Faith, sweetie, I'm sorry. Daddy's sorry. I didn't mean to yell at you."

"I wooned it." The muffled cry floated up from where Faith was hiding and cowering. "I wooned it. I sowy, Daddy. I sowy." For a moment, Andy didn't understand what she had said. He needed a translator. Suddenly, he realized she thought she had ruined something and was so frightened of what the penalty might be. Reagan just stood there, as Andy dropped to his knees and peered at his daughter.

Softly, he said, "It's all right, Faith. You didn't ruin it. You hurt it a bit, but I can fix it. It's OK."

"Otay?" she asked in a tiny, uncertain voice.

"Yes, it's OK."

Faith stopped crying, hiccupped a couple of times as she gulped in air, and then dried her eyes with her fists. Suddenly, she sprang into her daddy's arms. The squall had passed. There had been some thunder and fury, but it had passed, and she was once again safe with her daddy.

Andy pulled her away from her mother, lifted her up, kissed her, and asked if she would like to help him make it 'Otay.'" Faith grinned and nodded vigorously. Somehow, she knew that if she could help fix it, it made the damage less. Sometimes life's lessons are spoken to us, and some we just discern. Faith Weir was young, but she possessed an intelligence and awareness that were truly special.

Reagan still stood there—her eyes steely. Seeing Andy angry was a rare occurrence. In fact, she couldn't remember a time when he let emotions run away with him like that. *I hope he can handle this pressure,* she thought.

Just then, Brian, who had witnessed the whole little drama from a distance, spoke up. "What happened?"

Andy jerked his head toward the back of the house, inviting Brian to join him. "I'll show you."

How long the two of them had stood there, staring at the screen, had escaped them. Faith had long tired of trying to fix it. She, Hope, Reagan, and Alicia all had supper outside.

"Can't you reverse engineer it?" Brian asked. "I don't know what you call it, but, you know, find it again somewhere and restore it?"

"I would have thought so. But…it didn't restore. I just can't figure out yet what the hell she did that wiped out this particular data."

Brian was as curious as Andy. "No backup, huh?"

"Nope. I forgot. Careless." He wrinkled his face, as if squinting would help him find where it had vanished. "It's so strange, Brian, the rest of the game is there, the work done up to this level. But without the colored jerseys and facial distinctions, I don't know who is who. The players won't know whose team they are on, and the leader won't know who he had chosen for his team. Without that, I can't go forward. Damn!"

He sat down and just stared at the computer. "I just have never run into something just plain vanishing, without a trace. You can always forensically analyze and locate when something has been deleted or altered." Shaking his head from side to side, he sighed.

"So, if you can't recover it—for whatever reason—what are you going to do?" Brian asked.

Andy thumped his right hand on the table for a minute and sighed once again, as if giving up. "Well, the only thing I can think of is to just start over again. I can go back to the layer where each player identified himself with a jersey—where the game chose sides for him. Then, start applying those answers, so to speak, to these white figures. Eventually, I should have everyone with the right jersey."

"Man, that's a lot of work."

"Yep, because many of these 'characters' had gone through transitions, so I will have to find the spots where they changed and make sure I get that assigned properly in this level of the game. Let that be a lesson to you, my friend."

"Yeah, what?" Brian could see Andy was coming out of his funk. Andy was sane enough to always play the hand he was dealt. There had been a flurry of emotion, but once Andy realized he had spat his emotion out at his little girl, he pulled himself up and became the Andy Weir who had faced bigger stuff than this before.

"Never let your little girl write code." They both laughed. "At least not when she's three."

Suddenly, Andy pushed his chair back, stood up, raising both hands to the sides of his head. "Oh, man, wait a minute. Wait a minute!" he said, drawing out the pronunciation of the word *minute*. Brian had seen Andy call audibles before when they played football together. His trust in Andy's instincts had earned Brian a football scholarship at one of the most prestigious universities in the nation and put him into the NFL draft. So, he knew to pay attention when Andy changed a play.

Further, he guessed that is how Andy's extraordinary natural chess genius—which made him the most famous chess champion of his generation—had allowed him to outsmart in a real-world chess game the brightest and most feared man in terrorism—Ayman Al-Zawahiri. So, Brian Washington Carver just stood there, waiting for the next play.

"Oh, my God, I'm no longer stuck. I'm delayed, but not stuck," Andy exclaimed.

"You want to let me in on this, bro?"

"Yeah. Brian, Faith's little escapade has set me back timewise, but she unstuck the project. I see what to do now, to dissolve the hate, to raise the players up to the highest level." Sitting down, he pulled up a chair for Brian. "So simple. The only way for me to fix what she did would have been to go back to the beginning and 'ask' each of the players the questions to discern where they stood—you know, which jersey, which hate. Then, as they progressed, I would have to 'ask' again—and you understand I am using that term figuratively…" Brian nodded that he did. "Well, it's a reconstruct. But…what if I don't do that? What if I leave this layer of game just like *this*. Each layer has a surprise."

"Yeah, true. What?"

"Well, suppose the surprise of this level is that when the players level up, they arrive to a field where they are all alike—no jerseys, no facial recognition, no mannerisms, no race, no ethnicities. Nothing. No player can tell who the opponent is. It should shock them out of the automatic hate they have going on, blue against red."

"Then what?" Brian didn't know if Andy could answer that yet, but he did answer.

"The only way they can find the members of their own team is to begin to talk with players. You know, find out what they like and what they value. But this time, they can't ask any questions that bring them along a path to hate, none of the questions they used at the beginning of the game. If they do, they are sent back to the beginning. *Communicate*, in other words. So, by communicating and asking questions about what the other person values, they come along a path to understanding. They have to listen to see what that person really thinks, not just skate with their snap judgment based upon the Pavlovian response to the 'color of a jersey.'"

"They become individuals again." Brian was just thinking out loud.

"Yeah. So, they have to talk, listen, ask more questions, if in doubt, to find out which 'side' the other player is really on. If they can't figure a way to find out, they go back down the game. They go all around, and then they pick which team they individually think they were on and choose which team leader they think they were playing with. When the players are satisfied that they have chosen up sides again properly, and the team leader feels he has reassembled his team, every player has the computer put back on them the jersey they individually knew they had been playing with before. And the computer also puts the color back into their skin. Puts back any religious insignia—whatever had come up before." Andy stopped. Turning something over in his mind, he said, "Just spitballing here.

"Thinking on it some more, each player and leader is expecting that the team will restore to its original configuration—you know, the same guys he had before. Blue and white will expect the team to be blue and white players, with maybe one random red and white person. And the red and white will expect the players to be red and white, with also a random blue or two.

"But…what they find is, it is 50-50. Half blue, half red on each team."

Getting it, Brian leaned toward Andy. "In other words, they are all more alike than different…and talking and listening sorted it out on its own."

"Yep. It bypassed the stalemate of hatred and the fixed ideas—phrases and words that incite. They actually have to talk and listen and choose for themselves who they would want to associate with. And they realize that ridge of hatred that stood between them and the opponent had blinded them before to who was *actually* an ally, potentially. They won't destroy someone they like. They will only destroy someone they have been taught to hate."

"Oh, wow!" Brian exclaimed.

"What?"

"Andy, you remember my great-grandfather, Pappy, my touchstone in life?"

Andy smiled, remembering the kind old Black man whose wisdom was undeniable. He had been the bedrock of Brian's family and had died tragically when his own son, who had been on a cocktail of psychiatric meds for PTSD from Vietnam, succumbed to those drugs and murdered the whole family before killing himself. Though that was a common occurrence for those who took those drugs, the night that Kelly Weir had come to tell him of the death of his whole family had changed his life. His decision to find out why his grandfather had done it, and to save others from suffering as he had, led to the end of a diabolical and deadly plot by the mastermind of Al Qaeda to murder 35 million Americans.

"I do, Brian."

"Well, Pappy mostly read. But he liked musicals. He took me once to see 'South Pacific.' Think he didn't want me to turn into a bigoted Black man. And I remember just one song in that musical." Brian was clearly resting in the palm of a happy memory, a seminal moment of some kind. Andy just waited. "Hmmm, 'you've got to be carefully taught.'"

"What was that?" Andy asked.

"That might not be the title, but the song was about hatred, racial hatred. I remember the words: 'You've got to be carefully taught.'"

"I understand," Andy said softly. "We are pretty lucky guys, Brian."

"Yep. Yep, we are."

"What do you say we help 100 million Americans 'unlearn' some things? Huh?"

Brian had tears in his eyes when he high-fived his lifelong friend. It was a good night for these two partners and the daunting task they had assumed. And…it was a bad night for a group of men who plotted against those very same 100 million Americans.

That high five laid the foundation of what would later be known as the most brilliant, innovative, challenging, and interactive game ever created.

CHAPTER THIRTY-SEVEN

*A*ndy's eyes were a bit blurry, after almost 23 hours straight of writing code. He had refined the game elements several times over the last few days and had to just build it now. Reagan had allowed him to just hole up in his office. Mercifully, Andy had taken down the Mylars, and the space now looked more like a workspace. He had a modest desk in there, and a couple of chairs, and kept the drapes closed so as not to get distracted.

Hearing a knock on the door, he said, "Come in."

Brian peeked in, asking if he could interrupt for a few minutes. Andy welcomed it and suggested they adjourn into the great room, have a coffee, and take in the view. Seeing that Brian was bouncing from his right to his left foot in the dance from his football days, Andy asked, "OK, what is it?"

"Well, I have solved the production issues. There's an empty building south of Kalispell on U.S. 93, and I am moving all the guys up here to set up the production lines. There is plenty of space for me and the advertising and marketing people. In fact, I'll be drafting the first press releases probably this afternoon."

"Whoa, whoa," Andy put the brakes on. "Aren't you getting ahead of yourself? I haven't even finished building the game yet, let alone tested it."

"Bro, I know that! The first release is to let people know Carver & Weir are about to release a new game and are looking for gamers to test and possibly even provide content." Seeing that Andy looked somewhat dubious about that, he said, "We don't have to use any of the volunteers if we don't want, nor any ideas, but I thought this would test the waters a bit on who is reaching the most, you know, what sector is interested."

Getting it now, Andy joked, "Well, that is why you are the marketing director, and I am just the designer. Good idea, actually." A giant rainbow suddenly appeared over the lake and Andy digressed. "Geez, will you look at that!" He hadn't lived in that area long enough to have gotten over the sight of rainbows and double rainbows and the sudden appearances of the glorious arches that would hang for an hour or so. *I'll get an earful from Faith on that one,* he thought before returning his attention to Brian's plan.

"So, we'll have two production areas. One is for the physical product for everyone who wants it in their hands. The rest will be the digital version of the game, the registration of the players, and the distribution of it. So, one side will be the manufacturing, the other will be office and all things managerial. Then, when you are ready to test, we can decide who else we are going to test this on."

"And you are personally going to handle the releases and marketing, right?"

"For sure, bro. I can't farm this out to anyone else. The team knows that."

"How are they handling being moved from Los Angeles to Kalispell, Montana?" Andy asked.

"Great! Just great! Are you kidding me? They think they've died and gone to heaven. My biggest problem right now is keeping their attention off the mountain and the lake views and on the construction of the interior of the building." Brian explained he had contracted a local company for the inside work, but each team member was laying out how he wanted *his* section to work. That little gesture of respect was signature for Brian. But this time, he knew Carver & Weir was probably making a permanent move. Depending on how things worked out with this game called "Hate," they might not be welcome anywhere else. There had been a few days when he had thought of calling Elon Musk to inquire what it would take to get a ride on one of his space flights. Then, he would tell himself, *Just kidding,* and that flight of fancy would end.

Daring to broach the subject, he asked Andy, "So, do you have an ETA on when we will have a prototype to test out?" He held his breath.

"Pretty soon, I'd say about three days."

"That fast?!"

Andy nodded. "Yeah. I would have had it already, but I made some design changes, and I think they will work. Hope so, anyway."

"Like what?"

Andy then talked Brian through the new game design. This game was a team game, designed for multiple players, so initially the two teams would select their captain fairly early on. But what had changed at the beginning was that Andy had each player, as they entered, choose what they hated from the list he had culled from the Mylar morass. It could be people, groups, organizations, ideas. They could also choose what they valued, but given the name of the game, he knew most players would choose to select out who or what they hated. The answers there determined the blue and white team and the red and white team. The game chose that for them.

The first player to move to the next level became the team captain, and the teams continued to fight against the things they hated. But the major change was still at the point that little Faith had created with her mysterious computer programming stunt. "Brian, hatred stops looking. When people hate, they no longer look. And when you don't look, you can make some really bad choices."

"I agree with that. Where do you get these ideas?"

Andy demurred a bit. "Honestly, this one came to me watching Faith standing there watching 'The Wizard of Oz' for the third time. It's all illusion. Nobody could see the truth, and they submitted, because they bought into the illusion of the wizard. I figure that is what public relations is in the game of war."

"So," Andy continued, "in order to dissolve this hate impasse, and get them to look, that's why I kept the team captains shooting blind, not knowing who is who. They don't know which players belong on their team, and the players also can't tell whose team they were on—let alone their former playmates from the lower levels. I fleshed that out from what I was spitballing the other day. Here's the fun one: If the player starts to ask the questions he remembers being asked and having answered at the beginning of the game—meaning looking for what he hates—he is kicked back down to the beginning."

Brian was tracking with that. "Yeah, you were leaning toward that the other day. Creates a real change of mindset and direction…and it's a nice penalty for being a jerk!"

"I thought so," Andy joked. "But if he asks for what the other person values—you see, that opens the door to new communication, new content, new emotions, new feelings, new agreements. Then, when each had looked and talked with the others, they have in mind who their team captain must have been, and who their teammates were, before they lost all jersey colors, skin colors, genders, etc. The captain asks everyone to don their original jersey—they know that, of course. Each player knows his original choice. Others just can't see it yet. So, the computer allows them to do just that. And then we are back to the point in the game where both captains end up with a totally mixed team. In fact, the two teams are indistinguishable almost. Red and white and blue and white are all mixed together."

"Wow. I like that, Andy. I like that."

"Now, here's what I am still designing, but I think I have it. Since they are no longer divided by blue versus red, but rather all appear like one big team, the first player who turns his attention away from each of the elements they had hated, and turns instead to play the game of taking something they valued and seeing how they can advance that, levels up. The next one who also turns his attention to reinforcing something he valued, and looking for ways to enhance that person, group, or idea, also levels up. Bottom line, they are rewarded if—and only if—they play to build on what they like and value and not to destroy what they hate."

Brian was silent, looking at the picture Andy had painted. Andy broke the silence. "Anyway, that's my hope. The game dissolves hate, but it raises core values, using the individual's creativity and input. They have to get off their duff and solve something." Just then, he and Brian saw Faith rolling into the room as if she were a log. She seemed completely oblivious of the two men, not to mention the desk she was on a trajectory for. Knowing she would soon run into that piece of furniture, he paused. "Excuse me, bro, I need to confer with my game consultant."

Less than a day later, Andy walked into Brian and Alicia's home and turned over the programmed game to Brian. The star quarterback had just thrown the ball to his wide receiver. And both knew it was a Hail Mary pass for a world on the brink.

CHAPTER THIRTY-EIGHT

*T*he design of the game had been challenging enough and had carried a suspense of its own. Was the concept even plausible? Would it work? Those were the questions that had turned Andy into a recluse in his own home, focused on the task.

An even greater suspense awaited them now. With the game ready for testing, Andy and Brian were about to discover whether people would play the game, would win at the game, and, most important, experience a change in their emotional tone sufficient to cause them to advocate for the game and perhaps participate in solutions. What they needed was a great result, but also a massive penetration into the marketplace. This one had to take market share instantly.

Brian knew that was a tall order. He also knew the key would be to test it, and test it in true target markets, so he could survey the players and results and determine exactly how to promote it. Providing the game proved worthy of releasing, he was listing out his marketing ideas already. If it did not test well, Andy would have to go back to square one.

Alicia Quixote had been in many a tough situation herself during her career as a journalist and, later, a human rights advocate. She and Brian had each grown up with loving families, and yet each had experienced the tribulations that their own ethnic and racial communities manifested. Each had risen up out of their more-humble circumstances and succeeded. Today, Alicia knew that Brian was fully capable of delivering a best-selling game. And she knew he valued her insight as to who might make a good "guinea pig," as he referred to the testers.

"Hey, Babe," she shouted to him as she breezed in from the carport. "I took Hope over to Reagan, so I would be free to help you."

"Thanks." He barely nodded and went back to his list.

"Have you played the game, Brian?"

"Oh yeah, I played it as soon as Andy dropped it off."

"And?"

"Well, the game works—at least, it worked for me."

"What does that mean?" she asked. Brian explained to her quickly that Andy didn't feel testing this on himself, Brian, or Alicia would be productive because they were all so much alike, and since they were not all ensnared in the crippling insanity of the hate that had engulfed the American culture, they would not represent the true resistance points and potential victories.

Just then Andy pulled up, and the three of them adjourned to the outdoors, hoping the space and freedom they experienced sitting on their infinity patio would get the creative juices flowing. The sweet smell of summer peonies—resplendent with bright pink orbs—was refreshing and offered a wonderful color contrast to the shimmering blue pool and the inimitable blue Montana sky.

"What about Hector?" Brian offered. "After all, he was the first one we took 'White King Rising' to. One of the best, after all."

Andy shook his head no, as did Alicia. "Too much like us."

"And besides, he's busy," she reminded them. Somehow the understatement of that struck Andy and Brian as funny, and the three enjoyed a releasing few minutes of laughter.

Once they got control of themselves again, and parked the giddiness, Andy suggested, "Start with hate groups. We have to see if we can hook them, hold them, and change them positively. The others will be too easy and will skew the true stats."

Somewhat reluctantly, they added Bud Walker to the top of the list—not because they viewed him as hateful, but because he was a media mogul whose career had clearly put him in adversarial positions often. Plus, they knew he would not want to be left out. So, he was on the list but in a category of people whose response would not really affect the decisions Brian had to make. "What I'd like to see is for Bud to pick one of his own network journalists who he knows is a bit stimulus-response and have that person play the game," Alicia offered.

"Yes! Great idea!" Andy confirmed. "The trick is for him to pick someone who won't spill the beans and get us de-platformed before we even have a platform."

"I think we need Planned Parenthood to have a shot at this," Alicia said. Andy and Brian both looked at her skeptically. She stood her ground. "Not that they are a hate group. But they sure are in the midst of the controversy in all areas related to women and family." Andy reflected on that for a moment, and all the connecting dots from that entry point on the Mylar, and conceded it was a good choice. Alicia said she could go to a woman she knew from El Paso who was a real diehard on these issues, but who also was a gamer. "I can get her to do it. I know I can."

"Just don't be too persuasive, Alicia," Brian admonished. "One of the things we are looking at is whether people will pick it up and want to play it just by its title. Will 'Hate' attract attention and follow-through?"

All three concurred that the game should be taken to college campuses, particularly those with active political groups. The plan was to introduce themselves and say they were testing a new game. Would they like to try it? Andy and Brian were pretty confident that both ends of that spectrum would reach for it. They selected Berkeley, University of Montana-Missoula, University of Chicago, Harvard, George Mason University, Wellesley College, and Los Angeles Western, Brian's alma mater. Brian decided he would personally go to each of these campuses in the next three days and generate the invitation. He felt this would be very fertile territory.

An obvious choice was to call their friend, DeShawn Williams and see if any former gang members would like to play. His answer was typically DeShawn—"Hell, no! We is all 'Weirized' around here," he joked, referring to having fallen under the influence of Andy Weir. "In case you brothers have forgotten, I don't lead a gang anymore. I am a respectable businessman, you know that, Brian! Plus, all my boys work for me. They can't give you what you want."

Brian knew DeShawn was right, but he was disappointed, nonetheless. That Compton gang had opened the door years earlier to the stunning first game, "White King Rising." Memories of that night, and the dangers they experienced even going into that territory, still haunted some of Brian's dreams. But it had all worked out for each of them. Many a wasted life had set foot on a new path that night. And it was that gang that Hector Rodriguez had emerged from.

"Any ideas, bro?" Brian asked.

DeShawn thought for a moment, deciding whether this would be a good idea or a suicide mission. After a long pause, he offered, "Yeah. LA's a bad scene again now. But to really test it, you are gonna need the generals of three different gangs. Asian, Hispanic, Black—male and female. All the hell we got goin' on down here comes from them."

"Perfect!" Brian exclaimed.

"Well, maybe for you, bro, maybe for you."

"Do you know how to reach any of them? How I could reach them maybe?"

"Jesus, bro, you are outta touch!" DeShawn scolded loudly. "You're the last one who can come down here. It will have to be me." He stopped for a moment. "I don't think the Asians and the Hispanics will care about me, but the Blacks might. I'm a...whatchacallit?" Finding the term, he added, "An Uncle Tom to them. Once they saw me with that skinny Irishman you hang around with!" He laughed and then said, "Come to think of it, I am no friend of the Hispanics either. Those guys didn't know what to do once I took my men out of commission. Made a void, if you get my drift."

They did. "So, what can you do, do you think? We don't want you getting hurt, DeShawn," Andy said.

"There's a Baptist minister and a Muslim brother who have been doing some good work in the Inglewood area. Seems like they had some kind of convention where all the gangs showed up."

"Recently?" Andy asked hopefully.

"Nah. A few years back. But...the Generals were there. Made a difference, I think. At least, for a while."

"Do you think you could maybe go through one of them?"

"I do. The more I think of it, I do. If they will get me a meeting with those dudes, we could be onto something here. After all, they were supposed to all be seeking peace. A game called 'Hate' could just be the item." He had said it as a joke, but Brian and Andy knew that was DeShawn's style. Long ago, they realized that when one lived on the streets of South-Central LA, you had to have a sense of humor about your mortality. DeShawn knew he could have been killed many times over, so he had developed a rather flippant attitude toward danger.

"You sure, bro?" Brian checked again.

"Just get the game to me, and I will have it in the hands of some really bad guys. Give me extras for some ministers, too."

After they hung up, Brian and Andy felt better about the different markets and volunteers they had so far. But they wanted to try it on someone who might be accused or guilty of violence on the other side. City gangs were almost cliched. But white supremacists were another category altogether.

Unfortunately, that stumped them. They didn't know any of the groups and clearly had no connection to them. Brian got the bright idea of calling James.

"What is it again you are asking me for?" James asked, a little taken aback.

"Well, we were hoping you might be able to connect us to some white supremacy guy, you know. One of those guys who puts on white sheets maybe."

"Brian, is this a joke?"

"No, sir! We are serious. We want somebody to test this with us."

"Well, first of all, what makes you think I would know any Klansmen—or whatever they call themselves these days?"

"Not you personally, James. But you know, you being from the South," Andy chimed in.

This was going from bad to worse. "That's a little stereotyped, don't you think, boys? The South? And that somehow they'd be fishing on my river?"

Brian and Andy couldn't tell whether James was kidding or not, but the irony didn't escape them that they had just chosen a divisive identity for an area of the country. "You're right, James. We know you personally wouldn't be a game candidate, but we were hoping you might have run into some redneck somewhere who might want to take up the challenge."

"Sorry, boys, I can't help you," James calmly said, smiling, though he would not let them off the hook just yet. "Alicia, they have rednecks in Montana and Idaho, I hear—secretive types who meet in the forest, target practicing and picnicking…"

Not knowing whether James was getting back at them for the stereotype, Brian and Andy just sat and looked puzzled. But Alicia got it. "You know what, James? You are right. Bud can help us. He'll know if there's someone. Thanks."

"You are welcome." That was all he said before he hung up.

A short call with Bud Walker did indeed produce what they needed. Walker did not know anyone who fit the typical description of a redneck racist. But he did know a few really fine dudes who he suspected had another, darker side. All of them businessmen, he knew how to reach them and who to reach.

Within an hour, Bud informed the threesome of the name of a contact in Coeur d'Alene, Idaho. They had their test market set up. It would take them just three days to have players across the United States testing secretly a game called "Hate." Each player had eagerly agreed and started into the game within minutes of receiving it. Brian was confident that his password-protected game, delivered electronically, would make it simple for the gamer to engage. And it would make it simple for Andy to track exactly what the player was doing, where he went, how long it took him, when he stopped, and how he fared. In real time, they would be able to see what the gamers were experiencing. Any delay, or disparity, would come in the hoped-for positive outcome of the player getting high enough in the game that he or she started to select areas that engendered hate and conflict, but where they would now start to introduce solutions to those areas.

Assisting them was the natural tendency of superior gamers to enjoy being the tester, almost like a ghost writer. It gave them importance, and first shot at a challenge, especially a game from Carver & Weir. The honor of having been chosen, and the pledge to secrecy each had eagerly embraced, ensured that the game would not leak.

The test was real. And it was flying under the radar.

CHAPTER THIRTY-NINE

James was on pins and needles, waiting for the outcome on the game tests, and didn't like the fact there was nothing he could do at this point except wait. Reminding himself daily, though, that Andy had always delivered, and been able to perceive, analyze, and outsmart the enemy in the past, he calmed down.

Frankly, he knew they were going to have to find a way to release what they had uncovered in the hacking of the Schweiner meetings very soon. Conditions in the United States were worsening by the day, and the summer heat and potential of another year of "America Burning," as James referred to it, loomed on the horizon.

Vince, too, was betwixt and between, not being at the epicenter of Brannigan's world. Hector had insisted, however, that they keep full surveillance on Loren. There was just something unsettling about that man's lifestyle that kept grabbing Hector's attention. Today, though, they were debating what to do about the storage facility in Bethesda. It was entirely conceivable and plausible that Brannigan would have a storage facility. Many people did. It could be full of nothing but furniture, files, materials from his years of service.

But the unnerving coincidence of the mysterious satellite firing up while Brannigan was at the Bethesda facility—and not having come on since, according to Ari—just kept pushing itself to the forefront. All three operatives felt in their gut that this was not coincidence. And that put an urgency on that issue as well. "It's enough that we have to deal with Schweiner and his cabal—and their horrific plot. But to have something else going on with Brannigan makes me feel like I'm fighting a war on two fronts." James complained.

"Don't forget, Loren, too!" Hector shouted. He had a tendency to get very vocal when he felt anyone was overlooking or minimizing something in his purview.

"All right. All right," James demurred. "So that means possibly three fronts."

They sat for a while, and then James decided that since they had to wait on Andy and Brian anyway, and since Loren was under surveillance, they could perhaps take a chance on finding out what was in that storage unit.

"Well, it has to be me," Hector said. "I am going to drive over there. Put something in my own storage unit, and break into Brannigan's space."

"That simple?" Vince asked.

"Should be, bro. The interior door operates on a code. Each tenant sets the code, so he's the only one who can enter. Then, once inside, they can open the outer garage door or just come and go from the interior hallways. I can probably figure out his code in a minute or two. So, it will look like somebody legally entered it. That is, assuming anybody is monitoring, which I doubt."

That caught James by surprise. "Why do you think that, Hector?"

"I just get the feeling that whatever he is doing there, he's confident nobody knows about that location. He has used it for years, judging by how palsy-walsy he is with the manager. To me, he's gotten a little careless about the security. Or—just operating hiding in plain sight."

"That's more like it, I think," James concluded. "Something easy to access—and easy to clear out of if the location is 'blown.'"

Shortly after, Hector took off for Bethesda. He had taken a couple of chairs and boxes of photos from inside the farmhouse. One of the boxes contained his equipment, hidden under some of Jessica's family photo albums. It was mid-afternoon when he pulled up, entered his code, and drove into the facility.

Parking, he first entered the building using his own code, opened up his unit, and opened up the exterior garage door. Then, in plain sight, he unloaded the furniture and boxes into his unit, parked his car directly in front of the door, went back, and closed up. Withdrawing the nap sack containing his tools, he took what he needed and went a few doors down to Brannigan's unit. Hector was indeed correct in his estimation of effort to crack Brannigan's code. Two minutes later, he was inside.

At first, he was surprised, and he prepared himself to be disappointed. The unit did have some furniture pieces. There was a dining table and some chairs that looked like they had seen a few decades' use. A couple of lamps and an old leather chair were nearby. *I guess when he started making the big bucks on the news, he outfitted his house a little more befitting the big shot he is,* Hector mused.

The row of boxes—carefully sealed, labeled, and stacked—caught his attention. The boxes were behind the furniture, and the neatness almost suggested a wall. Careful not to touch anything, Hector made his way around them and hit pay dirt. There was a small fold-up table one might use for picnics, with a chair, and on top of it a type of black box receiver of some kind. Next to it, Hector recognized a transmitter, much like equipment he and Vince had come upon during some of their missions. This one seemed more advanced than anything he had seen, however. *Both of them,* in fact, he thought.

But very familiar was a computer. Donning gloves, he explored it a bit and realized that, although it was small enough to fit on the tabletop, it was very powerful. Rather than spend time in that vulnerable a location, Hector got to work and started to copy the hard drive. He had guessed correctly that the other two pieces were necessary, but the information that would reveal what Brannigan had been doing in that space, for however long, was on the hard drive.

Regrettably, since Vince was no longer employed as Brannigan's bodyguard, and not living with him at the moment, neither Vince nor Hector were aware that John Brannigan was driving north on Wisconsin Avenue, headed to Bethesda. There was no one to alert Hector.

Inside the unit, impatiently waiting for the voluminous content of the hard drive to be copied, Hector took photos of the rest of the equipment and the area in general. Just as the project completed, Hector heard a car pull up and park in front of the garage door to the unit.

Oh man, this is going to be close!

He had just escaped from Brannigan's unit, assuring that the door was closed and locked, when he realized he still had his gloves on. Knowing there was not a second to lose, he darted down the hall, pulling them off with his teeth while entering his own code. The door released, and Hector walked inside just as John Brannigan cleared the front entrance and approached his unit.

Hector heard Brannigan's garage door open and knew Brannigan would likely be at his car. He decided to take a chance. Leaving the furniture and all but one box behind, he carried the box with his gear inside and exited the building normally. Sure enough, Brannigan was loading something into his car.

As Hector passed him, he tipped his cap and said politely, "Afternoon."

"Afternoon," Brannigan responded, barely looking at Hector. As Hector walked around and got into his own car, Brannigan stood up, gazing at the vehicle as it exited the facility. Something about Hector's face was familiar to him. It clearly bothered him, so he racked his brain trying to remember where he had seen him before. Finally, it came to him. *I remember. He was with the manager renting a unit the last time I was here.*

Pleased that his powers of observation and memory were still sharp, he dropped any thoughts about the young man and finished what he had come for.

Three hours later, Hector was back at the Manassas farm. He was reviewing the content of the hard drive, with James looming over his shoulder and looking at everything Hector opened up. What they discovered was profound and incriminating at the highest level, but it further complicated the issue for the three of them.

"Who the hell do I take this to?" James asked himself. "Who can I trust?"

CHAPTER FORTY

*E*rnst Schweiner had a dilemma of his own. His recent meetings with the wealthiest businessmen and women in the world, and confirmations he had received from the GWO about governments yielding in fear to any threat of a flare-up of the China virus, reassured him that the United States was close to ripe for the taking. Knowing that if the United States toppled from its position as the world's super country, surrendering its wealth and its culture to the collectivist culture he envisioned, then the time was truly at hand for there to be a global government and a global economy.

He doubted that the members of the GCF really understood that he truly meant one government for the world and not just even playing fields for the various governments—where weak nations would be enhanced by lowering the dominance of larger nations; where wealthier nations and their people would have a reduced standard of living in order to elevate the standards of other nations; where everyone would be equal. That may have been their vision, but he meant something far more totalitarian than that. And the word "equity" was one he used to entrap and manipulate. He had zero interest in equal outcome, only interest in the outcome for him and for those he had chosen.

Ernst Schweiner had a fundamental mistrust and contempt for the wishes and ambitions of the men and women he considered weak. One government, one currency, one economy, one global defense system, one health organization for all the peoples of earth were his personal ambition. So, he knew he had the players at the table who could ruthlessly deliver that and who would have no qualms about taking their monopolies to new heights. But if they tipped their hand too soon, the others at the Global Commerce Forum might rebel and slow down the project.

So, the United States had to fall, and fall quickly, giving no time for a resistance or counterattack to be launched. And that was his dilemma.

Sitting in his sparsely furnished office at the family home in Dinkelsbühl, he always felt he had a better perspective from this remote location in Bavaria. And he knew he and Rutger could talk without any interruptions or sightings by any of his own special brand of "fans."

Not long after, Rutger Schmidt pulled his car into the arch and entered the home. Despite the fact that Ernst was the only one there, other than a cook, the medieval home was very brightly lit. *I hope that's reflective of his mood,* Rutger thought as he placed his attaché on a chair and entered the kitchen.

"Rutger, my friend, I am so glad you were able to come in person to talk with me," Ernst gushed. "I hope your flight was satisfactory…"

Before he finished, Rutger signaled it indeed was. "Private jets are so preferable, Ernst. I doubt I could get used to a world without one at my disposal."

"Well, you and I are not going to have to make any such adjustments, Rutger. People who do not have any real significance will have some initial shock adapting, of course. But us? We will use any service tool necessary to continue to create the new world."

Once the two had completed their dinner, they took the stairs to the top of the attached tower and sat comfortably in a rooftop garden that was invisible from the street, even from the ramparts. Letting down his hair a bit, Ernst asked, "Are we ready?"

"Yes, I believe so, Ernst. Every day, the division within the United States deepens, and the hatred mounts. The word 'anti' is descriptive of almost every citizen. It's religion against nonreligion, race against race, class against class, ethnic group against ethnic group, educated against uneducated, virus promoters against virus deniers, media networks against media networks. It's a pretty hostile place."

"Can we count on their choices, though?"

"Yes, Ernst. I believe the Americans are on the edge of choosing disorder instead of order, of choosing disobedience and criminality over the law. The rule of law is barely understood. It is underappreciated by the young generations we have cultivated, and rarely followed now." He stopped long enough to watch a hawk fly overhead and settle into a tree, evidently looking for food along the moat.

"So, that will be our window of opportunity. I have just one or two things nagging at me, and that is why I wanted to just sit in your company and plan," Ernst said.

Rutger leaned back, prepared to listen.

"When we make our move to take over and establish a global government, the first country has to be the United States." Rutger frowned, not knowing where this was going, as it had long been decided. He wondered what the doubt could be.

Ernst continued. "My question is, what commences the final attack, and if there is resistance, are we prepared to quash it immediately?"

Smiling, Rutger reassured him, "If they resist, or are slowing down in their descent into anarchy, we are prepared to trigger violent riots in every major city simultaneously. The money has already been provided, and the professionals who can agitate it are in place. That will force the deployment of National Guard everywhere, straining their resources."

"I expect it has softened them somewhat to have had their Capitol under a brief siege that led to martial law and the presence of military in their own streets," Ernst reflected.

"'Accepting' would be the word I would use, Ernst. The Americans are accepting martial law. They are accepting restricted movement. Their own politicians and media—under the magnificent guidance of Brannigan and Loren—have allowed the people to virtually erase each of those precious freedoms. Bottom line, politically, they are rudderless and drifting. They will welcome the restoration of order by the military."

"Will their military comply with a governing force from outside the United States stepping into their capital in the wake of the anarchy?"

"Yes, I believe so. Many are already hoping for a seat at the global military table. The idea of space warfare and defense, cyber warfare and defense has many of the new senior officers willing to turn. We divided them, too, you know. I believe some view it as more of a global issue. I am counting on personal ambition. That and the United Nations forces."

"We need it to be at the highest level of their military, you understand?" Again, Ernst's voice revealed an element of doubt.

"It will be." It was said with such certainty that Ernst smiled, shaking off any gloom he might have been experiencing.

At that point, the two discussed the fact that since the United Nations was in the United States, Americans would not balk so much if that body took over government and military, or at least assumed the lead in a time of crisis. It would seem like less of an invasion, especially since Americans had often asked UN Peacekeeping Forces to assist in the various past conflicts they had become embroiled in.

"Ernst, this is where Serge Pilaf will be pivotal. Once this commences and their government starts to implode, he will black out entirely any resistance pockets. Controlling all platforms, he will make sure no one in the United States is going to get any news of what is happening—if we decide they are to remain in the dark. Loren and Brannigan will debunk any leaks that surface about the changeover, further blinding the citizenry. The goal is to keep the Americans so shocked and afraid of each other, and the disintegration of their orderliness, that they will welcome anything they are told."

Ernst totally concurred and said simply, "The key is keeping the population in the dark while they helplessly struggle with unimaginable violence. Whoever hacked that oil pipeline also did us a favor. Replicating that can stop all movement by the citizenry. Once help arrives—even if it is the United Nations coming to the rescue—they will embrace it."

"The key, Ernst, is speed. A blitz…" Rutger offered.

Pausing for a moment, Schweiner asked, "Do we have enough instigators of the violence—you know, enough trigger points to enrage the populace?"

"Yes. And if there isn't some shooting of a Black man, or if there isn't some bombing of a school or church, or some neighbor shooting his neighbor, Peter and John will manufacture it, and Serge will see that it reaches the right people and that it inflames them. Once again, all others will be kept in the dark. You remember his briefing to us, right?"

Schweiner nodded. "One last question? Does something precede this?"

"Shutting down oil pipelines is a fallback plan. The primary plan is that the GWO and China will assure that something terrifying is promoted to force the 'dedicated' politicians in the country to stop the movement of their people. When movement is stopped, people eventually go mad. Decu-Hehiz is prepared to deliver hundreds of millions of sedatives and antidepressants to keep the people subdued."

"So, the attack line is to stop freedom of movement and sedate the angst and resistance, as we unleash anarchy to the degree that the mentally weakened American submits to a new authority that promises safety, security, and equity?" Ernst asked.

Rutger simply nodded.

Ernst continued, "As far as I can see, once the rioting and violence calm down under martial law, and once the GWO announces the virus is under control, and the displaced have shelter and food, they will settle for their new life—in harmony with all the world, not just their other selfish American neighbors."

Sipping their premier, barrel-aged cognac, contemplating their plot and its imminent victory, two men whose roots came out of a similar dream, decades earlier, enjoyed each other and the beautiful summer evening. Ernst Schweiner was confident that Rutger Schmidt was the rightful heir to the outcome of this Great Reset. Young enough to carry forward, diplomatic enough to deal with the brightest men on the planet, and ruthless enough to eliminate anyone capable of usurping the authority of the Great Reset, Schmidt alone enjoyed Schweiner's complete confidence.

Ernst rose, walked over, and patted his friend on the shoulder. "Thank you, my friend. I feel much better having had this time with you in person and this most reassuring chat. I think I might have been suffering a bit of stage fright there, like an actor just before the curtain goes up."

Ernst held up his glass, "Curtain's up!"

———————————————

More than 5,000 miles away, it was just mid-afternoon. Andy Weir was reviewing with Brian Washington Carver the initial test results of the game. Andy frowned and looked a bit perplexed. "A high number of the players who aggressively started the game were being kicked back down to the beginning at the pivotal point in the game.

"Is that bad, Andy?"

"It could be," Andy said stoically. "But how many started up again? How many quit?"

The percentage of failures was higher than Andy expected, and a review of the demographics of the players showed the bulk of the failures were with the blue and white jerseys. The red and white had failures, but not as disproportionately as the blue and white. Interestingly enough, as Andy looked closer, the blue and white players tried again, and again, if necessary.

He was shaking his head up and down, which Brian took to be a positive sign. He, himself, was on pins and needles waiting for the verdict. After a few minutes, Andy said, "The stats show that each of the 'markets' we tested reached for the game. They began, and most did not quit when they hit challenging resistance. Were all of these experienced gamers, Brian?"

"Yeah, bro. At my level of skill anyway."

"Forgive me, but I didn't even ask if DeShawn had had a hard time of it with the gangs…" Andy's voice trailed off, revealing that gentle level of concern he had for everyone he met and every problem he had approached in his life.

"All he said was he went in unarmed."

"Was that smart?" Andy winced.

"Apparently. They decided to play," Brian joked.

"And how about you—the colleges?"

Brian scrunched up his face and snorted, "Let's just say I'm glad I'm not attending any of those schools. Got out just in time, Andy, just in time." Then he grinned and added, "Great choice, though. Those campuses reek of pathology and hate. It was like walking through quicksand. But…now I understand how we got people making the insane decisions they are. So much emotion!"

"Pavlov's dogs." That was all Andy said, walking away.

Reviewing the percentages of players who eventually made it through the level of the game where they had to settle down and communicate, and those who made it to the top levels, the percentages were encouraging. "Big number failing, good percentage trying again, expected decent percentage making it to the top," Andy calculated. "The key is what did they do after they finished? Do we know that?"

"Yes. They had been told to play the game just on their own, that they were *especially selected*. No one else." Brian smiled.

"What?"

"Shortly after the finishers ended, someone else started into the game—you know, was given access."

"Are you telling me they didn't follow the rules we laid out?"

Brian slapped Andy playfully on the back. "What did you expect, bro? Half these people were criminals and the other half known haters! I didn't expect them to listen to us, really."

It took Andy a moment to realize what that might mean. "Wait a minute. Turning quickly through the printout, he said, "Is this right? Everyone who finished the game brought someone else surreptitiously to it? Turned it over to someone else?"

"That's what I'm saying. Of course, we have no idea who they were, or why, so we couldn't really evaluate their performance. But that number right there," he said, pointing to a number circled on the page, "that number is the real deal."

Andy dropped his head. Brian knew his friend's eyes were likely "sweating" a bit, so he gave him some space. Looking up and to the left, Andy smiled. At that moment, Brian knew they had it. They had a game that people would play, would struggle with, and, once victorious with it, would take to others.

"Ball's over to you, Brian."

"Yup. I expected that," he said, waving the stat sheets in the air. "And you threw a perfect pass, Andy. Let's get this game released!"

CHAPTER FORTY-ONE

*T*he game "Hate" hit the market two weeks later. Fortunately for the United States, the fans of Carver & Weir were broad spectrum. The players of their games spanned generations but especially embodied the troubled youth of America who found gaming more interesting than life itself. Many a young man or woman had been rescued from the clutches of the pharmaceutical cartels, and many a smart American had met the challenge years earlier to defeat a global financial cartel that was hell-bent on creating a financial Armageddon for its own gain.

Their audience was large—numbering in the millions, if not tens of millions—and it was enthusiastic, for characteristic of anything Carver & Weir produced was difficulty, challenges, and life-changing perspectives. And follow-through. Carver & Weir seemed to expect the person to not just win the game, but to learn something and then to carry that forward into society. Their years of speaking engagements and appearances had made these two trusted and very popular.

This time was different, however. As Brian released the game, mostly in hard copy, the publicists were almost universally unsuccessful in booking the creative team into anything on radio or television. Fear prevailed and overrode even economic interest. The game was destined to make money—a lot of money. It was a brilliant game, and it embodied the signature of the two men who had earned the respect of the nation from the mid-2000s to the present. Yet, no one in the business media wanted to know what Carver & Weir had to say.

"This was not unexpected, Andy," Brian explained at his home. "If these people can block out a coup, and overthrow of a government, and all attempts to bring truth to daylight, they can block us out."

There was nothing in Brian's tone, however, that depicted despair or loss. Quite the opposite. Brian Washington Carver and Andy Weir had risen through challenges most never face—at least not the elites. But they had risen through challenges ordinary Americans had faced. And they were an example that people from all backgrounds and all generations found common ground with.

"What do you think?" Andy asked.

"Ah," Brian said. "We knew where the enemy was. We move through our own channels, off the radar screen."

"Meaning?" Andy had complete trust in Brian's marketing instincts.

"We drop all conventional PR channels, and we go grassroots. Our central file of former purchasers is huge. We start with them. And we incentivize all the test markets to do what they appear to be doing anyway."

Andy didn't quite track with that, so Brian elaborated that the test gamers seemed to have started promoting it to their peers. And that group was a powerful, if not dangerous, segment of the American population. Brian had no fear of this.

"Andy, we chose to create a game where those who arrive at the highest levels are interacting with one another and choosing their own projects and solutions to further the things they value. Let's reward that behavior and continue to reward those who advance workable solutions. We adapt the game, and we credit them, and we provide financial incentive. Bottom line, we make them partners, or 'fellows' of some kind in the Carver & Weir Gaming Foundation." He laughed at the idiocy of his own off-the-cuff statement, but the idea was, nonetheless, viable.

"That's some really unlikely bedfellows, bro," Andy said.

'I know. But this will work because they have to get to those top levels to participate, and by then, they understand their countrymen better."

It was agreed. The only question Andy had was related to orders of magnitude. "How many game players did we reach with 'White King and the Battle of America'?"

"Close to 15 million."

Andy whistled. Then, he braced himself for the answer to the next question. "How many do we need to reach and impact now?"

"James says we've got to salvage 100 million or more. Half the electorate, more or less."

Andy walked over to Brian's coat closet, which was camouflaged in the wall of his organic architecture home. Opening it with a touch, rather than a pull, he reached in and pulled out a football.

Brian burst out laughing. "OK, OK. I know it's daunting. Almost 10 times our best. I know." He stopped for a moment, then started dancing from left to right, which was his decades-long signal he was ready to roll. "What have we got to lose?"

"Just the whole world, Brian. Just the whole country. Just freedom for our daughters, Brian!"

"So, I guess we'd better toss some balls then."

They were headed out when Reagan and Alicia returned. Seeing the ball in Andy's clutches, Reagan knew not to interfere. She simply said, "Alicia and I played the game."

Lending some moral support, Alicia smiled gently and said, "Yes. And we've been working on a project." She winked, and the two girls disappeared into the kitchen.

Before they left the room, Reagan teased, "We'll fill you in after you two get done playing." Tossing her long red hair over her shoulder, she followed Alicia.

The tone in Schmidt's voice signaled to both Loren and Brannigan that something was amiss. Normally a stoic and consummately professional colleague, today Rutger was tense and very edgy. "Ernst and I are reading some disturbing things in the news. And what we are seeing in television images on the networks is not what we expected. The clowns who run those networks may not have noticed, but we have."

Brannigan was in his basement office on the video call. Loren was supposedly secure as well, although Brannigan could not place where Peter actually was—even though he had been in the man's house. Brannigan was the first to speak. "What specifically are you referring to, Rutger?"

"We are attacking from all angles simultaneously and have been for some months. The U.S. government seems to be in shambles—that's the one bright spot. Individually, the gender issue in education, the racial component in education, for example. They seem to have impacted. Preachers propagandizing seems to be happening. The court system seems constricted and afraid. God knows the wild distortions in the reality on the virus, the vaccines, the mutations are apparent. Watching that, one could get whiplash!" He stopped long enough to credit the GWO and Cedric Cornell's efforts in that arena. "The morality issues seem to be upside down every time a parent or spouse brings things up. Individually, all of the areas that we have invested so much into in order to bring about escalating lawlessness and fear seem to be working. But something is not right, and Ernst is deeply concerned."

This time, Peter asked, "I am sorry, Rutger, but I still don't fully understand what the issue is that Ernst is concerned about."

"We expected that this relentless pounding from all directions, in all layers of their lives, would have ground the Americans down by now. You know, they would have just succumbed by now and given up any argument. Basically, be exhausted."

"Right. Are you seeing something else?" Peter asked.

"Yes. We are seeing pushback starting, and it is rising."

"Well, there has always been the expected pushback of the random radio talk or cable talk guys, but they are outnumbered. We made sure of that," Peter said.

"That's what we thought, too. And listening just to ANN—and anyone like them—you'd think that. But we are picking up stuff from the BBC, from Australia, from Europe, too, that the Americans are asking *more* questions, not fewer. They are slower to enrage. And when they do respond, they're not like Pavlov's dogs anymore. They are thinking. They are talking."

"Yes, that is a problem. We need to keep them listening just to us, not to each other," Brannigan commented. "Nature of propaganda war. You've got to maintain the narrative and control the direction." He looked at that for a moment. Clearly, he had more bile he could insert into the dialogue, more misdirection. But Brannigan now wanted to know what Ernst had in mind. "Peter, I am sure you will agree that it would help us to know what Ernst wants to do next."

Peter nodded.

"He plans to unleash the agitators he and some wealthy planners have amassed, and he intends to trigger massive riots all over the U.S., simultaneously. Basically, a shock and awe blitz designed to overwhelm the Americans and the Administration. They are weak anyway, and we expect—as long as they continue to enjoy the favor of the GCF—they will welcome the reset."

"And if they don't?" Brannigan challenged.

"Then, they lose the favor of the Global Commerce Forum and all that means. Your job, however, is to turn every incident anywhere in the

Lee Kessler

United States into a reason for violence and rioting—not just the race stuff, but guns, equity issues, sex issues, corporate greed issues, union issues. Anything. The 'evidence,' John, that you provide must incite violence, not a slow burn." Looking to see if Brannigan understood the implications there, he continued. "Your job is to keep citizens locked down, either hunkered down and immobile out of fear or out of orders by the government. Pilaf will be prepared to sever all communications at a certain point. The fact is you are going to be very busy. A lot is going to hit all at once. And Peter, there will be an avalanche of breaking news to disinform and create distrust."

Peter bristled a bit. "We have been doing that."

"Yes, and superbly. My point is the tempo is going to pick up. We have to outrun reason. We can't let sanity drive a wedge in. So, perpetual fear. Perpetual hatred. Perpetual suspicion. Freeze them up."

"I got it. If they don't know where to turn, or who to trust, they will turn to you."

Rutger smiled, indicating they understood. "The other members of the group will see that martial law becomes necessary and that it is accomplished. When that happens, your job is to get the people to accept it as the best solution—you know, to embrace their controllers as saviors."

Each knew this had been discussed before. It had been planned. Brannigan and Loren did not know the exact mechanism Schweiner would use—or get the American government to use—to impose the game-changing martial law that would open the door for an entirely new form of government. Weakened and controlled, the United States would just be another country struggling with bad leadership. U.S. supremacy in the global picture would vanish. And its priceless Supreme Court would cower.

"The last thing I want to say is this," Rutger said. "It's not your abilities that give us any concern. It's the timing. We are having to do this before all of the pieces are in place or, rather, all of the players. Something has changed. And we are moving more prematurely on this than anticipated."

"Can you put your finger yet, Rutger, on what it is that changed recently? I don't mean the results you are seeing, but what emboldened the people. Can other countries spot it?" Brannigan asked.

Rutger shook his head. "Regrettably. Something has caused the people to talk to one another, and they are asking too many questions.

We don't know why. And that, my friends, is disconcerting to our friend in Geneva."

Then, Rutger changed gears. "John, if you could stay on with me. Peter, you may go." It was said as an order, not a request, and Peter exited the call.

"John, I want *you* to find out who is causing this."

"I doubt that it lies in the disinformation I have given the group to use. And I doubt it lies in who Peter has directed to receive that disinformation. He knows who can be counted on to further the Black Propaganda and distortions. He knows by now who the reliable media are."

Pausing, deciding whether to add anything else, Rutger said, "That may be true—in which case, we have an enemy on the field. And he snuck in. That's your turf, Mr. Brannigan. That is your turf." Then Rutger abruptly ended the call.

CHAPTER FORTY-TWO

*T*he contrast could not have been more stark. On a quiet summer eve, Reagan, Alicia, Andy, and Brian sat on the Weirs' deck, overlooking the lake. Enjoying a barbecue, and the fragrance of the dozen or more species of pine trees that surrounded their property, they looked like any two couples who would be enjoying some time together.

But the conversation today was linked to a strategic planning session.

"Andy, I know James said we wouldn't be involved in this caper, but Alicia and I have been talking," Reagan said. Andy could see over her shoulder and observed Brian almost wince. Andy laughed. "Did I say something funny?"

"No, Reagan. I just took it humorously. The picture of you and Alicia working on something brought back some harrowing memories, that's all. Hope we are not in for a repeat."

Alicia couldn't stand it any longer and jumped in. "We are not! But Reagan and I are going to take the reputation and creds we do have and do something about education in our schools." Seeing that met with the agreement of both husbands, she continued, "We are going to tackle this Critical Race Theory head on."

"Andy, we had no idea this was pervasive in our education system, let alone spreading like a wildfire," Reagan said.

Brian nodded, and as he served the burgers to the group, he joked, "We need our *game* to spread like a wildfire." Alicia shot him a look, and he immediately said, "So, what is your plan?"

The two women laid out a plan to form a women's organization for the express purpose of retaking the school boards in every city and school district that had succumbed to what Alicia called "this withering version of history." Alicia had a recognizable face, and voice, from her years as the main anchor on WNG. That had earned her the respect, and the trust, of many Latino women.

Reagan's human rights activities had kept her out of the spotlight, so her face was nowhere near as recognizable as Alicia's, but her reputation as an effective human rights advocate would open many doors.

Their plan was simple. They would speak to every parent in the various religious organizations, business service organizations, and women's groups in the areas where the education had been taken over by a one-track indoctrination. The objective was to empower those who agreed with the mission to attend PTA and school board meetings and to speak up. Further, they would find and help train men and women to run for their school boards, thereby bringing the curriculum back to the people. And they had decided to do this by becoming a clearinghouse of resources for all the various groups and parental counterattacks. That way, each citizen could fight back in his own way, but he would have a place to go to get resources and get connected with others to determine what the successful actions were.

Eloquently stated by Reagan, the women had concluded this would strengthen families at the same time it would help reverse the descent into the abyss of self-loathing the United States was experiencing. Trying to avoid putting America on a perpetual amends project to the rest of the world, they felt education was the entry point. And they had concluded they needed to reach the women and, most especially, Latinas in order to elicit help. They knew men would follow along in likely agreement.

"My people are family people, Andy. And for those who emigrated here, the American dream includes family and freedom—not more dictatorial supervision. You can count on the Hispanic moms. I am sure of it."

"So, I guess this means this might be our last supper together for a while?" Brian asked. She knew that question was his tacit way of endorsing the project.

Alicia stroked his back, smiled, and said, "When we get back, I'll make the tamales."

———————————

A few days later, Alicia and Reagan departed on a speaking circuit around the perimeter of the United States. They began in Washington state and headed south along the coast. At the same time, Carver & Weir dropped all conventional advertising except on Walker News Group and spread—through their network—the criteria for becoming a stakeholder in the game "Hate."

"Kill the story." With that terse command, Peter ended his third call of the day from news producers whose on-the-ground journalists were reporting some unexpected and undesirable interactions occurring on the streets of Los Angeles and Portland.

This should not be happening, he told himself. *With more money and manpower, there should have been another riot. Something has changed.*

What was perplexing him was the report of yet another police shooting of an unarmed Black man in the Compton area of Los Angeles. Immediately, the anarchist leaders Schmidt and Schweiner had been funding indirectly through a squad of billionaire investors had deployed more belligerent agitators to turn the ensuing protest into a full-blown riot. This was a perfect opportunity for them to escalate violence and destruction and drive fear into even more of the Los Angeles population.

The protesters arrived, angry and hurt. Their numbers grew. The agitators were there with ample weaponry and incendiary verbal pitches to get this crowd roaring and rampaging. But it had not happened. Instead, the mob had taken to the streets, marching—but nonviolently. The police were ready. But the crowd remained nonconfrontational except for some angry voices and loud shouting.

Peter Loren had no way of knowing yet that DeShawn Williams had already texted Brian Washington Carver about the incident, saying that the crowd materialized but did not seem to be listening to the anarchists. Instead, the crowd seemed to be listening to some gang leaders, and ministers, who encouraged a massive protest but not violence.

It would take Loren some time to identify who was dissuading the crowd from violence and who was influencing them. But in his gut, he knew something had changed on the playing field.

To make matters worse, the situation in Portland was downright catastrophic and could not have reflected a greater propaganda failure. The anarchists had been deployed to simply burn, harass, and assault the federal courthouse once again. For over a year, the mob had had its way with city government and with law enforcement. They no longer needed a justification for it. No one waited for a shooting or an injustice. The mob simply deployed violently and mindlessly as if the whole system was unjust and they had a right as anarchists to tear it all down and burn it.

So, when they amassed and armed themselves—with deadly fireworks, Molotov cocktails, water bottle ice bricks, bats with nails in them, and gasoline-filled water bottles to be tossed in behind an incendiary device— the anarchistic mob expected to be met by the usual police defense lines, chain link fences, and officers inside the courthouse.

What happened there this time should have drawn the attention of every American citizen. But Peter Loren had skillfully made sure that more than half of the United States would never even see it. It represented a defeat for their strategies and tactics and was a harbinger of more devastating things to come.

The mob arrived. But what they encountered had been an unarmed group of Portland citizens—black and white, young and old, male and female, standing together in a formidable line of intransigence. They had decided to take their city back but not by engaging in tit for tat rioting. No one had come to rumble. Instead, they had come to deploy the tactics of giants from the past—Martin Luther King and Ghandi. Today, if someone wanted to burn down the city of Portland, they would have to first destroy a line of truly peaceful, unarmed Portland citizens.

No one knew how to handle it, not even the anarchists. At first a few thugs thumped on members of the thin line, but realizing that no one was fighting back, they scrambled back to their leaders to get a new play from the playbook. Somehow, even they recognized that with so many cameras running, it would not go over well for America to see thugs beating up on a truly "melting pot" group of unarmed American citizens.

Peter Loren had just stopped that from happening. No cable news or newspaper would report these anomalies. Loren hoped they were just outliers and not something more significant. He was wrong.

Before bringing this to Ernst's attention, Loren and Brannigan had appealed to Serge Pilaf to see if he could identify anything of coordinated magnitude that might have caused this unexpectedly civil behavior among the citizens of previously volatile cities and districts. The people were not behaving like the animals their propaganda teams had turned them into. Instead, they were just behaving like people.

"We're looking at all social media. All platforms. Nothing in particular jumps out, I am afraid," Serge explained to them on the three-way call. "Except…" his voiced trailed.

"What?" Brannigan demanded.

"It's not political. Wouldn't ordinarily be picked up by my algorithms that are set to monitor for dissent or any kind of disagreement you can then label as racist, or insurrectionist, treasonous—whatever you mind guys like to label things."

Brannigan's Irish temper was starting to flare. He knew he needed to handle this wunderkind with kid gloves, but he was impatient, and his tone of voice showed it, "Serge, for Christ's sake, what is it?"

Serge wanted to cover his own ass on this, so he hedged a bit. "Well, it may be nothing, and not related, but when the algorithms searched for key words, what surfaced was a lot of chat and chatter about a new computer game. Some game came out a week or so ago, and it seems to be raising an awful lot of excitement and enthusiasm."

Before he could finish, Peter cut in, "How is it being distributed?"

"Digitally and in stores. Checking the big online retailers, most sales appear to be coming from online platforms."

"Who made the game?" Peter continued.

"Some outfit called Carver & Weir. They've been game manufacturers for over a decade. Pretty successful. Kind of a niche group, I would figure. Never really came onto my radar."

"What's the name of the game, Serge?" Brannigan asked, trying to discover the information he would need.

"'Hate,' the game is called 'Hate.' That's the word the algorithm picked up."

Serge's seat at the table had been earned because of his ability to control the distribution of all information in the world. It had not been earned for propaganda. But—though they were each at their own homes—both Peter and John Brannigan experienced a sinking feeling in their stomachs. Peter more than John.

For Peter Loren knew in his gut that there could very well be a connection between a new game dropped into the American culture and an incipient but significant shift in the emotional tone of the American targets they were trying to take down. He had succeeded in controlling the minds and emotions of hundreds of millions of Americans by using brilliant Black Propaganda. *Is it possible someone is challenging us? Has someone found a covert way to flood the area with truth?*

He must have fallen silent in contemplation because Serge asked, "Are you guys still there?"

Peter Loren had used the emotion of hate to set a people up to be enslaved. Was it possible an opponent had decided to use hate in another form to free them? Finally, he responded, "Yeah, I'm here. John, your thoughts?"

Brannigan, too, had to be shaken out of a reverie. He was stuck on the name Carver & Weir. He knew he had come across this before, perhaps discussed them with someone before. But he could not remember who. Instinct told him he would need to remember where he had come across those names. At the moment, however, he answered, "I think we had better get our best gamers to play this game. See what's in it. May be nothing, you know, just a welcome distraction from the boredom people have experienced in their lockdowns. I'd like to rule it out."

"And if the game could have produced these anomalies?" Serge asked.

"Then, we will need to shut it down before this little blip turns into a tidal wave of reversals."

Peter agreed with that. "Yes. First, we investigate. Meanwhile, we impose a media blackout on the networks. I doubt WNG will comply. Its management has never been on board, but we have persistently sullied its reputation and discredited its journalism. It should be OK."

"And, as much as this pains me, I think we had better notify Ernst," Serge said.

"You mean Rutger, right?" Brannigan challenged.

"Him, too, but Ernst would expect to hear directly from me on this…if it, in fact, is something significant. So, how long will it take for you to find out if Carver & Weir have thrown a monkey wrench into our wheels?"

"A few days, at most," Brannigan reassured. "I'll call in a favor or two over at the Agency. They've got some pretty bright gamers over there that can be trusted."

It was agreed, and Brannigan immediately rounded up several gamers he knew would be secure and likely sympathetic to his mission were they ever to be read in. After all, he was compiling his own list of people to reward once the power on Earth had been reset. This would be a good way for them to stay in his favor, he reasoned.

Three days later, the threesome was back on the call. "Well, what do you have?" Serge asked.

Peter could feel it already. He had a sick feeling he had encountered this crew somehow in the past, but he tried to push that suspicion out of his mind. Brannigan opened, almost too cocky. "Well, two of the three guys played the game but found it repetitive and cliched and bailed about halfway through. They reported it just seemed like a game version of a lot of the news of the day. You know, people beating up on people, riots, hateful attacks, choosing teams of like mind to attack the other team. They felt it had some interesting leadership stuff in it, but when the violent activity settled down about midway through, and turned more to thought and speech, they got bored."

"And the third?" Peter asked.

"Well, sadly, that's the kicker. He did not bail. He forced himself to make it all the way through, even though he had to swallow some viewpoints along the way to make it to each level. He leveled up to the point where the game dissolved hate and the players started to seek solutions and ways of cooperating. They started to communicate with each other."

"Did you say, he reported the game dissolved **hate**? It dissolves **hate**?" Loren knew even before hearing the answer that this was not a coincidence, and Los Angeles and Portland were not just outliers. They were a counterattack. Someone had figured out how he had manipulated an entire population into a violent and irreversible divisiveness, making them ripe for authoritarian control. And they were reversing it. "Serge, you have to get this to Ernst. And tell him I am telling you to stop this at all costs. Someone is in the position of reversing our tactics. They know what we are doing. Stop their voice!"

Loren's passion was stunning. Brannigan kept his cool, after years of dealing with intelligence and counterintelligence. He knew the seriousness. But somehow, hearing the fear in the voice of the colleague he felt was the best propaganda expert in the world put an urgency into the scene.

"I agree totally," Brannigan said. "Get to Ernst. And Rutger. Tell them we will work on our end to identify for sure the source, but in the meantime, we want you, Serge, to stop any further spread of this cancer."

"Understood." That was all Pilaf said before he hung up, thinking, *Wow! Well, big games always encounter big challenges.*

CHAPTER FORTY-THREE

*F*or the next few weeks, Brannigan made a point of watching the one network that had proven to be a thorn all along the way, WNG. Consistently, for five years, it had its bloodhound investigative journalists ferreting out the true backstory of a lot of Brannigan's disinformation campaigns. But he and Peter had successfully minimized the network's impact with the viewers he wanted to retain for his purposes and had degraded utterly the significance of any of the other viewers. The competitive networks were eager to denigrate and ridicule the news empire that had, at one time, been number one in the United States. Recently, it had become a punching bag for any journalist and comedian who wanted to take a cheap shot.

That's the way Brannigan wanted it. He guessed, however, that he might get a clue about any possible counter actions some group might be engaged in by watching WNG. July in Washington, D.C. is notorious for its hellacious heat and humidity, so he was content to stay in his office, seeking answers.

Knowing that if WNG was found to be part of this, Serge would have to persuade the cable platform providers to remove the network. Failing that, he would have to persuade the advertisers on their key shows to stop advertising, thereby plunging the network and its subsidiaries into financial and customer emergencies. No advertising, no broadcast. That was the preferred "weapon of choice" against private corporations.

It was that consideration that caused John Brannigan to start to conceive a plan of attack—if it became needed. After all, he had successfully kept a President of the United States under siege for four years. Handling an old network, headed by a man who seemed distant and disinterested, should be simple. So, he started to break down the key actors who might be involved.

He began with Bud Walker, whom he had met on occasion, and

found to be an old-fashioned journalist and business leader. Assuming there would be nothing "woke" about Walker or any of his enterprises, he decided to probe the personnel and connections. First was his wife, Jessica Ranger. The first red flag came up on her name. Jessica Ranger was a wealthy and shadowy investor from Los Angeles. All of it seemed legitimate, but not even the CIA could figure out where her money came from or where it went. Someone that good at protecting her assets and connections always made spooks nervous.

And here she is married to Bud Walker. At that moment, Brannigan's attention froze on Ranger. *Who was I talking to not too long ago about her?* A memory was trying to surface—or a picture, at least, was. But he couldn't quite get it. He had had so many conversations in this last year relevant to his commentary on the network, his continuing disinformation campaigns, and his selection to Schweiner's elite team that he couldn't place things quite as quickly or as precisely as he used to.

As he walked into the kitchen to make himself an espresso, something about that room brought the memory closer to the surface. Why? He was the only one who had been in his kitchen. No. Vince had been here. *What's the connection?*

Like an itch you can't locate, he picked at it, with growing agitation. Suddenly, John Brannigan remembered that Vince McCoy and Hector Rodriguez were connected to Jessica Ranger. The memory was gushing now. "I remember now!" he shouted to no one. "It was Mikolas who said he knew Ranger when Mikolas was trying to help a friend." He was thinking it through out loud now, as if speaking it would lend greater weight and accuracy. "Ranger sent him to McCoy for the extraction. Saved his friend's fiancé."

He stopped. Setting his cup down, he asked himself, "Who was the friend?" And there it was. "Does this have to do with Carver & Weir? Is one of them the friend?" He almost whispered it.

Downstairs in his office once again, he texted Peter to see what he had found that was causing pushback from parents and citizens related to the education and indoctrination program Schweiner had been influential in. The answer was almost immediate: "A lot of independent organizations and groups forming. Common denominator seems to be a resource hub. Serge confirms that resource clearinghouse's social media connects to two women, Alicia Quixote Carver and Reagan Lynch Weir." Then, a second text came in from Peter. "What's up?"

"I'll get back to you later. Just connecting some dots."

The next hour was spent tapping into his elaborate data base on American citizens. Compiled initially by his surreptitious peeks into the unmasked American citizens from FISA warrants, he had painstakingly added to it any information on prominent people that might prove useful in a blackmail effort to ensure their compliance.

Though there was nothing of that nature on the two women, he found the decade-old story of Alicia Quixote's romantic connection to Samir Taghavi, Al Qaeda's propaganda chief. That scandal had nearly brought down WNG and destroyed her career. Further examination of her bio showed she had teamed up with one Reagan Lynch, a human rights activist, and they and another older woman had launched a campaign to rescue women kidnapped for sex trafficking. It was two of those women who had themselves been kidnapped and rescued. Quixote later married Brian Washington Carver, and Lynch later married Andy Weir.

Brannigan's stomach was starting to act up. He was experiencing almost an acid reflux. Knowing it was not from the espresso, but rather from the dots that were now bombarding him, he raced for an antacid tablet. That panacea worked for a minute. Then, the anxiety returned, and he knew he was now onto something.

"So, Carver & Weir has a game out called 'Hate.' Their wives are spearheading a nationwide network of parents in rebellion to school boards and curricula. Ranger is married to Bud Walker of WNG. Ranger financed Carver & Weir in its first game. Mikolas went to Ranger to get help when a friend's fiancé was kidnapped. Mikolas hired McCoy to locate and extract. Was that friend Weir?" Brannigan had always liked to talk through a puzzle out loud, as if hearing his own voice added a solidity to what he was examining.

He paused as a wave of nausea came over him. Flashing back to the meeting at the Mayflower where he had met and interviewed McCoy, he remembered now that Mikolas and McCoy were together that day, having lunch. Dismissing for the moment rising suspicions about McCoy, he simply said, "Carver, Weir, Walker, Quixote, Lynch, Ranger, McCoy, and Mikolas—all connected."

John Brannigan may have been overtaken in recent months with an exaggerated sense of self-importance following his invitation to a seat at the table. He may have been lulled a bit on the heels of clearly overwhelming victories in the field of deception and disinformation. He may have congratulated himself too often for his juicy and lucrative contract with the network. He may have fantasized too often of what his future power situation might be with Ernst Schweiner. He may have been off his pins.

But he still was John Brannigan, the most feared former head of the CIA. He had not lost his craft. And John Brannigan knew one thing. There were a lot of dots. Asking himself, *Could it all just be coincidence— my knowing or running into all of them, one way or another, at this time? Them all being connected possibly?* Brannigan knew that in the world of intelligence, there are no coincidences. He knew the answer.

He knew now he may have been played. But by whom? Now, the name Samir Taghavi had come up as well. *Was Peter Loren part of this?*

Calling in some favors at the Agency, he asked someone to run a check on him to make sure no one had hacked into any of his communications, that no one was cyber shadowing him. There were a few guys left from his reign who were willing to take a look. The world of cyber warfare was a new one to Brannigan, but he never underestimated the talents of these "flat food people." His pal Brendan was his link to them and had taught Brannigan what a "flat food person" was.

A few years earlier, Brendan stopped Brannigan from ordering a steak and salad bar luncheon for some guys who were trying to trace some Al Qaeda money-laundering operation in Liechtenstein. "No. No. John, these guys don't eat that. These super geeks live in their subterranean offices, or garages, or basements. They never come out. Even their moms know to just feed them food that can slide under the door. Flat food." Seeing that Brannigan had no clue what he meant, he explained, "You know, pizza, grilled cheese sandwiches, pop tarts, stuff like that."

"Are you serious? Flat food?"

"Yep. I'm not one of them, of course, because you suits make me put on a tie to deliver the results to the other suits in the Agency." Brendan had said it as if that part of his job was a true disappointment, as if he preferred to be with the "flat food people."

Whatever, Brannigan had changed his delivery order that day and ordered in the best pizza he could locate. Apparently, he had scored big on that one because, even now, years after he had left the Agency, these guys were willing to do him extra favors.

It took about a day, but Brendan called him and said they needed to talk. Sitting in a park down the block from Brannigan's home, Brendan pulled out a manila folder and handed it to him. "They found someone had hacked into your phone and computer, John. Skillfully. My guys almost missed it. They were able to identify who had done it. One Peter Loren from some PR firm in D.C. Do you know him?"

Trying not to reveal any emotional reaction, Brannigan nodded.

"All right. Well, for some reason, he appeared to be monitoring your communications."

"Appeared, you said?" That puzzled Brannigan.

Brendan cleared his throat, scratching below his well-groomed beard, and ventured further. "Yeah. That's the issue. They also found you had set up monitoring of him? Did you do that?" Brannigan hesitated, not knowing how much to reveal. Brendan helped him past that. "Hell, man, it's no concern of mine if you did. That's what we do. We spy. I just wanted you to know that if you are looking for who might have targeted you, you find *him*. If he goes looking for someone who may have targeted him, he finds *you*. That's all."

This made Brannigan's head hurt and his gimp leg ache. He stood up to shake it off. "So, what are you saying here? We are spying on each other?"

"All I know is it looks like you are. So, look at the last paragraph where my guys gave their conclusion."

As John was reading it, Brendan elaborated. "They concluded someone had set up a loop, and that's why, if you were looking for something, you found him. If he looks for something, he finds you."

"But who set up the loop?"

"That's the last couple of sentences. We don't know. It's a simple thing to do, but we weren't able to locate the source. There are no 'fingerprints' on this, no tell-tale signature moves."

He stopped, letting Brannigan absorb the data. "Anyway, if you find out who that is, you might want to recruit them, John. They're damned good."

"So, it's a person?"

Brendan snorted, "Of course, it's a person, but it could be the personnel of a state actor. Who the hell knows! You were the head of the CIA, remember, and you carry a pretty high profile, you know. Anyone could have decided they wanted to know just what you might still be monkeying with."

Brannigan shot him a look of warning as if to say Brendan was treading on thin ice. Getting it, Brendan finished, "Hey, man, that's all I am saying. Someone's got you, and we don't know who or why. Sorry, man."

Brannigan nodded. He had hoped for more. Unfortunately, although Hector and Vince might be part of this, the field had broadened considerably, given that both he and Peter were new members of the Great Reset. Frustratingly, now, Brannigan wondered if Schmidt himself was monitoring the American colleagues. Or was Serge monitoring Loren and Brannigan? If so, for whom?

Shaking out his leg one last time, Brannigan thanked Brendan and turned to head home, when Brendan added, "You might want to get a new phone, though. Just saying. Might help you narrow the search."

Again, Brannigan nodded. That was a simple first step, but it would narrow the field if he used the phone to selectively rule people out. Like a doctor ruling out one allergen after another until they home in on the patient's exact allergy, he realized that might be his only route.

Hector didn't recognize the phone number but answered anyway. "Yeah."

"Hector, it's Brannigan. Got a question for you. Any answer is fine. I'm just running something down."

Sitting back down, Hector hit record on the device he had connected to his phone. That way, he could capture both sides of a conversation without being on speaker phone, and the other party never knew he was being recorded.

"Sure. Shoot."

"Have you been monitoring my phone and emails as well as Peter's?"

Without any hesitancy, Hector's response was, "No, man. You asked me to monitor Loren electronically and physically. That was the assignment. Do you want me to monitor you, too?"

"No. No."

"Well, that's good. Because that wasn't part of the job. You're the boss. Never had a boss want me to spy on *them*," Hector said, with a slight chuckle.

"Agreed." Brannigan paused to reassure Rodriguez. "Just running something down, as I said."

"OK. I didn't recognize the number when you called. Should I use this one for you?"

"Yeah, I found the other had been compromised. It's still active, but you can use this one."

"Will do. But Vince said our assignment was wrapped with you. Maybe I misunderstood. Do you still need eyes-on surveillance of Loren?"

"No. Everything is fine. Thanks for the info."

After they both hung up, Hector took James and Vince out into the pasture and explained what had just transpired. Not knowing how much Brannigan had discovered, or if he was just fishing, they concluded that, whether they had been compromised or not, it was time to fold up surveillance, leaving the loop Brannigan had likely uncovered in place.

"I've got to get a message to the boys that our timeline has been bumped up. Whether we softened the target or not, we are going to need to strike soon," James shouted over his shoulder as he got into his Mustang and headed for the mailbox in Arlington. "No comms to one another other than normal traffic between Vince and Hector. No calls to the boys. We go old school now."

"Hey, Bud, I just got a message on the sports desk intended for you." Walker's sports editor had called him directly. "Do you want me to read it to you?"

"Sure."

"Fishing trip canceled. James."

Bud Walker did not respond immediately. He'd been caught off guard by the message that had been preset to indicate the mission was in jeopardy. Regaining his composure, he said, "Oh, that's too bad. I was looking forward to it. Send the email on over to me. I'll reach out to him."

"Great. I didn't know why this ended up on my desk."

"Me either," Walker assured him. "He's kind of a quirky guy. Probably lost his cellphone or something." He laughed, as did his editor.

Oh man, this is not good, he thought.

"Peter, I need to meet you at your office. Meet me in the lobby. 30 minutes." That was all the text said.

Peter Loren had no idea what the text was about, but just the fact he got one from Brannigan made him wrap up what he was doing and head down to the lobby. He had just exited the elevator when he saw Brannigan enter the office building. The guard saw Loren wave to the visitor and prepared to buzz him through. But Peter signaled it wasn't necessary and, instead, stepped out into the lobby, and the two men went outside.

Wasting no time, Brannigan said, "Peter, we have been hacked."

"What?" Loren was startled by this and had no idea really what Brannigan was talking about.

"Too long a story for full details, but my team runs a periodic sweep, you know, to make sure nobody is getting into any of my sensitive material." Loren indicated he understood. "Well, they discovered someone had hacked my phone and computer."

"Jesus!"

"It's routine for them to trace it back. It came back to you." Brannigan had already concluded the hack was not coming from Peter, but he wanted to test his reaction.

"What?" Loren was truly taken off guard and sincerely denying. "That's not possible. I never hacked you—or anyone, for that matter. Why the hell would I do that?!"

"Calm down, Peter. I know. You wouldn't." Seeing that Loren was less tense now after his reassurance, Brannigan continued, "But they found something else. They found you were hacked as well, and it traced back to me."

"Is this a joke, John? Because I don't follow..." his voice trailed off.

"Nope. Somebody set a loop. They were obviously looking for some type of information, and they set it that if I discovered it, it would look like you did it. And if you discovered it, it would look like I did it."

Suddenly, Peter laughed. "Somebody took a page out of our own playbook, John! Neat propaganda loop. We make something up to incriminate someone, send it out through a credible source to the media, and they send it out to the public and also back to the FBI, who believes it's a credible story and begins an investigation on our own lie."

Getting serious once again, Peter said malevolently, "I don't like that, John. I don't like that."

"I understand. I don't like it either."

"Do you know who?" Peter asked.

"No. But I ruled you out. Someone, though, has an interest in our connection to each other, I'm thinking."

"So, what do we do?"

"Well, intel is my game. Let me ferret it out. Meanwhile, get a new cell and number, and use it exclusively with me. Use your other as normal. I'm leaving the monitoring in place. Don't want whoever it is to think we are on to them. At least for now."

Offering Peter his new cell number, Brannigan coached him to make sure Peter's new phone was encrypted and asked if he still knew how to get one of those without attracting attention. Peter said he did. Then, he asked, "Should we tell Rutger?"

"Eventually. But I don't want to alarm him or Ernst if this has nothing to do with our 'project.' There may be someone who has interest in just you and me—or no interest but wanted to use you as a diversion for me. You know, my work with the network could be in play here. One thing I've learned about the news business, it is slimier even than politics."

Loren laughed. "Yeah, I discovered that, too, when I started applying what my mentor taught me. Viciously lazy, that bunch. Real parasites."

"And if they weren't, we wouldn't have been able to do what we did, and we wouldn't have been invited to Dinkelsbühl." Both men smiled, appreciating the irony of that statement. Brannigan ended with, "Anyway, when the time comes—if it comes—we'll fly to New York and tell him in person."

Neither man knew that the delay in that communication would allow an enemy a vital window for a counterattack.

Chapter Forty-four

James Mikolas was literally red-eyed when Jessica's plane landed in Ovando. Bud had assembled the team at his house. Urgently summoning Brian, Andy, and their wives, he had arranged for a Native American traditional dance show to entertain the two little girls. Both were adventurous, and he knew they would appreciate—even at their young age—pony rides, Sioux children's clothes, and helping the women make dinner before the traditional dances would begin. Guessing that would last several hours, and that the girls would be exhausted and ready for bed by the end, he calculated that their parents would have a window of time without interruption.

Something in his gut told him they would all need to be at the top of their game. The message from James confirmed something had gone wrong. And the overnight letter from an Arlington postal service had alerted Brian and Andy that all parties were going to need to meet.

Before anyone could even ask, James launched in. "Something's changed. I need information first, and then I'll fill you in."

"Shoot, James. The floor is yours," Andy said.

"Andy, Brian, your assignment was to create the game, release it, and soften the target so we could reveal what we have before those bastards accomplish their long-dreamed-of reset. I need to know what the progress is there."

"Well, it's going well. But we need more money if we are going to penetrate quick enough. An 800 to 1,000-percent increase in players is a tall order, and we don't have the capital to blitz everywhere, if need be. Frankly, Bud," he sheepishly said as he turned to Bud, "we were about to come to you and Jessica for help in that arena."

"What I need to know, Andy, is not so much about the money. I need to know the effectiveness of the game. I see the anecdotal material related to Portland and Compton. All good. But let me ask, "How many of the players were people who themselves were consumed with hate? Could you tell that from their responses on the first layers of the game?"

"Gotcha," Brian spoke up. He was running the marketing campaign and more likely to know that since he would be compiling information on who purchased the game, as well as what teams they ended up on and how they fared in the game. "About 80 percent. It seems we hit the right demographic with the game's title. People obsessed with topics involving that emotion seem drawn to it. That and where we tested and launched first were key."

James chewed on that for a moment. "Good. Now, how many of the players bailed on the game? Did not reach a level of change?"

"Fifty percent."

Andy didn't know whether to be alarmed by that or not. He had hoped a miracle would occur and all players would play on and win. Turning to Brian as if to get a read, Brian did not seem phased by that. He was merely reporting stats.

"Good," James said. "What percentage of those who played the game to the end changed course and started to build solutions, dropping the emotion-driven reactions they entered with?"

Brian smiled. "Again, 50 percent."

"So, about one quarter of people starting the game experienced a transformation and became positively and creatively constructive?"

Reagan chimed in, optimistic as always. "Alicia and me, too. That's when we got the idea of our clearinghouse."

"Bud, how about you?"

"I played. I stayed. But I ended up one of the team leaders who led the others."

Everyone laughed. "Figures!" James joked.

"One last question. What percentage of the players who completed it brought someone else to the game?"

"One hundred percent." Brian grinned. "That's why we've got to push the game out faster in order to carpet-bomb the gaming community, you know."

"Yeah, I do know," James responded, "but we have a bigger issue." That statement was sobering to all of them. "You do what you can, the best that you can, to keep pushing the game out. Continue to prepare the American people to be receptive to the 'truth so outrageous' that we are about to drop on them. You are the foundation. But…" he gave the bad news to them. "We are going to have to drop the video immediately."

"Define immediately," Andy asked.

"We are in a race now, Andy. I believe that Brannigan has figured out someone is onto him and his cohorts. Whether he has figured out it is us, I don't know. I am assuming so. But I also don't know whether he has realized we might have hacked into the encrypted video conferencing from Schweiner. I have to assume he will, if he hasn't already. He's a smart bastard. And he is not going to give up that seat at the table without a fight."

Seeing the stunned look on all of their faces, he knew he had to provide some optimistic way forward. "But, Brian, I am gratified with those numbers."

"How so?" Brian asked.

"Well, we already know that 70 to 75 million people may be shocked by the video, but they won't reject it out of hand as a lie. If anything, it may affirm for them some of their suspicions through the years. It was the next 25 million we needed to reach, to plant the seed. We need to get them to not necessarily embrace it, but to not reject it. They need to let it marinate. They need time to really see some of the societal debates and changes that are starting to occur as individual Americans fight back. In time, they will join. But for now, just allowing the truth in that video to continue to be exposed will slow Schweiner and the other slime down. A spotlight will be on them. Hot enough to destroy their plans? I don't know. But I believe it will be hot enough to give the people time to put a stop to their plans a little bit at a time."

"All right. We've got our marching orders. More of the same. Faster." Brian assessed.

James nodded.

"Now for the real mission. How do we drop this onto 331 million Americans so that at least 100 million of them take a real hard look at the enemy within? And do it *now*?"

Bud Walker broke the silence. "We can't do this using social media of any kind or mainstream media. Obviously, Pilaf and Loren will stop it. Block it. Ban it. Cancel it. And Brannigan will be peacocking it on every TV network to explain that this is just a…what was it he called it?" Bud was searching for a term. "Ah, yes, a deepfake video."

"We are going to have to reach the people, all simultaneously, and bypass all current methods of viral information distribution." Though Andy spoke the truth, somehow that succinct statement of the problem made it loom almost insurmountably.

The room fell ominously silent. "Well, I'd hoped for a more conventional ending to this *game*," Andy said, "but it looks now like we are going to need a true 'Hail Mary' pass of some kind."

"Personally, I'm going to turn to prayer, if you don't mind." Reagan's normally calm voice quivered.

Bud Walker was sitting by himself. His wife was to his right, some feet away. He was looking down at the floor. Only he seemed to be breathing deeply. After several minutes, he looked up at James and smiled. "Do you remember, James, that we met right here in this room? I was sprawled out where you are now sitting."

"I do."

"We've come a long way." He paused. Turning to Jessica, he again smiled and said, "Everyone, let's take a break. I need to talk with my wife."

Abrupt as that was, each person knew something was afoot. Since Alicia had worked directly with Walker at WNG years earlier, she was the most attuned to Bud, and she picked up immediately on that look he had when he was scheming up something, turning it over in his mind. "Yes, by all means, let's." she said. "We can play with the girls—and maybe even dance a bit."

Chapter Forty-five

Jessica Ranger waited until the others had left the great room that looked out into the Bob Marshall Wilderness. The room was their favorite spot in the house, and the wilderness always seemed to stand there as a perpetual challenge to rise to greater heights. Hard to conquer, only the brave, skilled, and trained dared venture into it.

Perhaps the fact that she and Bud both seemed to have a spiritual connection to the mysterious place allowed her to know something precipitous was about to occur.

Quietly, she sat down beside him. "So, Bud, what do you want to tell me?"

He stroked her hair. They were older now. It had taken them decades to come together. But they were a good team, and his affection was genuine and profound. "We've got a good life, don't we, Jessica?"

"Yes, most assuredly."

"We've done well, and we've stewarded our money well, right?"

"Yes." Jessica knew him enough to know not to interject. He was leading her somewhere, and she needed to just listen and acknowledge.

"It's quite an accomplishment, you know, to be a multibillionaire."

"Indeed."

"We have, between us, built many successful business enterprises. Employed many people." He stopped there. Wincing slightly, he seemed hung up a bit on the subject of their employees. Then, he pushed past it. "So, what I want to ask is this. Could you be happy if we didn't have that wealth anymore? If all that we ended up with was this ranch? You know, live out our lives quietly here? Maybe no employees even? Just us?"

Jessica patted his knee. "I could. But why are you asking, Bud?"

"I have an idea, Jessica. It could work. But it could cost us everything. And I don't want to do that to my bride, who I promised to provide for and care for until death do us part, without your willingness and agreement. I love you. And I want the best for you."

Jessica Ranger had climbed pinnacles on her own as a single financier—no husband, no children. She brought to their marriage her own power and income. She had, however, learned along the way something no one at Ernst Schweiner's "table" had ever learned, nor were likely capable of even understanding.

Leaning back and resting her head on her husband's shoulder, she said, "Yes, we have many things. We have the symbols of success. But we do not take them with us when we leave this Earth, do we, Bud? The only thing we carry into eternity is our character."

Bud Walker had his answer.

CHAPTER FORTY-SIX

A few minutes later, Bud called the group together. To his surprise, the first two to enter were Hope and Faith, who squirted through the door, super excited about something. Grinning, giggling, and jumping in front of him, each girl held up her index finger. The fingers appeared to have blood on them, and Bud wondered why they were giggling if they had been hurt during his little diversionary presentation.

"Look, Gampa Bud!" Faith said, proudly presenting her finger to him. She didn't quite have the pronunciation of his name, but he thoroughly enjoyed the term of endearment. "See?"

Right behind her, and not to be outdone, Hope plowed forward. "Thee?"

"We bud sistas now!" With that, Faith turned to Hope and they pushed their two bloody fingers together, joining them. It must have stung because each girl winced a bit, but they were too excited about the honor given to them that they blew right past the discomfort.

"I see," Bud said. "You are blood sisters in the Sioux Nation. What an honor!" Looking up to their mothers, he gestured to see if this was OK with them. The moms seemed to be relishing this moment, too, and Reagan had the presence of mind to snap a picture of Bud and the two little girls who had adopted him as their grandpa, since neither had any of their own.

He swooped both girls up in his arms, kissing each on the cheek, and said, "Now, will you girls lie down for a nap? I need to talk with your parents about something important."

"Weally impotent?" Faith asked.

"Yes. Weally."

"Otay. We go now. Come, Hope." With that, the two girls wiggled out of his arms and scampered into the bedroom they used for naps when they came to visit. Faith, walking out of the great room but before closing the door, turned and said, "Nappy now. Shush."

The brevity of the interaction with the generation they were trying to save steeled everyone for their next meeting. They all found seats, including Bud, who sat in the same spot James had found him—drunk and driven by self-pity—more than 10 years earlier.

"Jessica and I have talked. We both are on board with this. You need to know that."

Each nodded. He calmly continued as if conducting a meeting with his editors and department chiefs in his media empire. "I've got a plan. It's in two phases, and it's risky. But if James is correct, and the hammer is coming down on this country in the next short time, this just might work."

He laid out a plan where the first phase involved his canceling all advertisers to WNG's cable news shows. Knowing that Pilaf, Loren, and Brannigan would attack with the "opposition-type research" they had deployed in the political arena to get people discredited and terminated, he knew they would go after his advertisers in order to bring him down. So, he intended to do a preemptive strike on his own network to disarm and confuse them in that arena.

Further, all ads would be placed by Carver & Weir, promoting their new game nonstop, 24/7. "With no competition for the advertising slots, you should have an open shot at reaching millions over a shorter time. It will be clear to every audience member of our network that we want them to see and play this game."

Andy was speechless at first. Then he turned to Brian and asked, "Can we afford that kind of airtime, Brian?"

"No way." He tilted his head and looked to Bud. "You know we don't have that kind of money, Bud."

"Yep. I know. But...I am personally going to spot you for it. Carver & Weir will have a benefactor who is funding the advertising."

"An 'angel,'" Jessica interjected.

"What?" Brian's face showed he had never heard that term.

"In the theater world, Brian, wealthy supporters of the arts contribute great amounts to make it possible for a show to be created. They do it for the love of the theater, and they are not traditional corporate investors. Bud and I will be your 'angels.'"

Alicia slid her hand into her husband's, hoping no one had noticed. Emotion was rising in her, and she hoped squeezing his hand would help her control it.

Bud just rolled on, laying out instructions to Andy to purchase whatever size server farm he would need to handle the traffic they would have. "These have to be our servers, our platform. Secure. None of the Big Tech guys can have a part in this or access to it. None."

Andy understood and knew he could build a bulletproof platform, and with Bud paying for it, they should be able to acquire the servers and the talent they would need. It was agreed they would push the game out only digitally from here forward. They would avoid retail gaming outlets. There would not be enough time anyway to manufacture and produce, let alone ship, the quantities they would need.

Brian's idea of providing a stake in the game to the avid gamers led to the decision to allow the players themselves to sell a game and take the profits for themselves—as long as it remained feasible financially. The gamble was that the players themselves would do what they had done in the test markets by getting friends to play it, especially if there was a financial incentive to do so. Notwithstanding the fact nothing of this magnitude had ever been attempted, let alone accomplished, and driven by an insane timeline to boot, Andy and Brian appeared to be on board.

"Everybody agreed?" Bud asked. Authoritatively, he was not expecting any debate. "All right then. Good luck, boys. Good hunting." Taking a deep and determined breath, he said, "Now, is everyone ready for phase two?"

The question was rhetorical, given that everyone was hanging on his every word. Turning toward Andy, he asked one question. "Can you make a QR code for that video—one that can be printed in a pamphlet?"

Andy paused for a moment, then asked, "The link needs to go to the whole video, not an edited version, right?"

"Absolutely. This *has to be the truth* as we recorded it. No edits. The QR code needs to link to the whole video."

"It will be challenging, for sure, for our platform to play the video, given the size of it. But yes, I can create the QR code link. That is not hard. Advertisers and marketing people have been doing stuff like that for some time now."

"Good. Then create that QR code. That's the top priority for *you*, Andy. Now, here's the plan." Bud Walker was determined now. "These haters hold us in contempt. They despise the American people. And they have spewed that hate for many years now, ridiculing us and debasing our heritage. Recently, they seem determined to force us backward down a time track. They may intend to push us all the way to the Stone

Age. But right now, they have pushed us backward through the 1800s, through the Revolutionary War period, and are trying to stick everyone in a period of time 150 years before our revolution.

"So, we are going to stop that erosion right now, stop their insane time travel. If they are going to force America to time travel into the past, in hopes of us coming to a self-loathing that weakens us and causes us to hate like they do, we are going to do some time travel ourselves. We will take a page out of our own history—our Revolutionary War history."

Bud rose and walked over to the wall area just to the right of the large stone fireplace. "You may not have noticed this, but it is a portrait of Thomas Paine. Most people like portraits of George Washington. Me, I like Paine. Talk about a journalist! He's my inspiration."

Grinning, he returned to his seat. "We are going to take a play out of Thomas Paine's time-honored playbook. I will write the pamphlet we are going to get into the hands of all Americans who want it. It will set their level of expectation and arouse their desire to read the four pages. Because, inside our pamphlet, Andy, will be your QR code. Once opened, they can watch these esteemed world leaders plot the end of freedom as we know it."

James leaned in slightly. He was beginning to see the picture Bud was painting. Continuing, Bud laid out the strategy of distribution. "We are going to have to go old school on this, everyone. No technology. No arena where Pilaf could marshal forces and stop us. That's why the sequence will become so critical. This will surprise our adversary and leave them with no good moves. We'll let Andy weigh in on that when I am finished. The sequence of preparation is this.

"First, WNG will buy up every printing press available that can produce a four- to five-page pamphlet. Right now, I wish I'd stayed in the print news business, but what the hell...Anyway, lots of presses, positioned around the country, in every state—especially the states where our people are under siege with riots and lawlessness. Andy, your code will need to be ready to insert as soon as we have the presses."

Andy nodded his agreement. Only Reagan noticed that her husband seemed to have turned a bit pale. She hung in there with him.

"Next, we rent every delivery van available in the areas where violence and rioting are or have been occurring as well as in calm areas where we know the reader will immediately open the QR code. Brian, tell your players that, in addition to whatever you are giving them for promoting the game, those who want a real-life, real-time adventure are to meet us at the van locations around the country."

Alicia dipped her head and smiled. She told herself, *This is the old Bud I know!* She was used to the bold, colorful leader instructing his editors and anchors, setting a vision. *He's back!* And as she had done so many times before in the golden age of WNG, she stepped up.

"Bud, I can handle the logistics on that," Alicia blurted out, completely oblivious to the fact she had raised her hand as if to be recognized to speak. Noticing that, she dropped her hand. "I can do that. I can map it out, so Brian knows exactly where to send them."

"Piece of cake, Bud." Brian grinned. "The folks have been playing virtual games where they go chasing some virtual character out into a mapped-out, real-world environment. That's easy for us to replicate with vans and cities. Hah!"

"Good. But the vans—all at once, in the night, and at exactly the same time—will distribute the pamphlets. Dropping them off by the tens of thousands at every campus, every business complex, every church, every state capital, every family health center, every courthouse, we will instruct them as to what is legal and where they can deposit pamphlets. Jessica, that is in your wheelhouse. Get your legal team on that." Then, as an afterthought, he said to her, "And check out the legality of compensation to these gamers Brian wants to pay to distribute the game."

Getting back to the distribution of the pamphlets, he was getting creative now. "And every apartment building. Moving on, the goal is that as Americans wake up, the pamphlet is there. Many will discard it as junk promotion, but many will open the code. Now, in order to inspire people to open it, we are going to rent every plane—you know the ones that fly low, dragging banners behind them with a message on the banner like 'Sally, will you marry me?' or 'Opening day, get tickets at…!' We are going to launch them to fly all day over the areas where we have deposited the pamphlets, and the banner will say 'Open the QR code' and have a picture of the pamphlet."

"That's ambitious. But I like this," James commented.

Suddenly Bud laughed heartily. "Me, too. We are bypassing the Big Tech/media route altogether. We are using their knowledge of technology to defeat them by going old school. They will not be able to stop it."

"Bud," Andy said, "you asked me to weigh in. Well, that leaves them with no good move because if they try to cover it in the news to disparage us and say it isn't true, that causes people to go find a pamphlet and open the code. If they ignore it, you can have WNG hammering all day with this amazing phenomenon in the skies and on the streets of the country—the Thomas Paine of the 21st century. Even if people had thrown it away, they can go retrieve it. Pilaf can cut the feed on a network or social media attempt to share the code, but he can't stop the planes. He can't gather up all the pamphlets either. This is a 'check' move. Not 'checkmate,' but 'check.'"

"What would it take to make it checkmate?" James asked.

"The people have to watch it, believe it, and demand change. They can't take us down in any of the areas we witnessed on that deplorable video unless we give them permission. Our goal is to get the American people to withdraw permission. That's your best shot, James."

Bud resumed. "Got it. In the pamphlet, for sure, I will take the reader down the path of the multilevel marketing mindset. They watch it. Then, they each get 10 friends or family to watch it. They can simply take the pamphlet to them. Then, each of those gets 10 more. Let the people do what we can't. Let *them* saturate the marketplace. They are to stay off any technology platform—no video conferencing, no social media, nothing. I will make that clear in the pamphlet. The only thing will be the pressure on our server. I'm an ignoramus on that part. Andy?"

"It's a big task, Bud. The traffic coming through the front door to watch this could spiral out of control really fast. Whew. Daunting."

"So, what fixes that?" Bud challenged.

"Money. It comes down to money. And redundancy. We are not talking one server here. Many servers. We will need our own server farm. Yep, money."

"You will have the money, Andy. Jessica and I will immediately start liquidating assets that we will need for this. We start now, even before you have the QR code ready. I know they will pull banking stuff on us, try to delay or block transactions, so I want to do those under the radar. Jessica and I know we are in for a rough ride. But we have one advantage here. WNG is the only major news empire that is not owned by other big corporations. It is privately held, and I own it. I own everything, frankly. Never trusted banks."

For some reason, Andy laughed, remembering how close citizens had come to losing all their wealth during the attack by the Repository of International Transactions almost a decade earlier. Looking at this current cabal, however, that crew of renegade Central Bankers looked like pikers.

"Last best place, right, Bud?" Andy joked, referring to the name Montanans used to describe their state.

"Right. And a rich Sioux heritage on money. Saved my ass, for sure, on many a deal."

The group was digesting all this. They did not look at, or speak to, one another. They were preparing to meet the challenge. Bud understood their silence and wrapped up his strategic planning session by saying, "The days of Big Media laughing at and ridiculing WNG are over. On the day of the video drop, and as long as we are still on radio and TV, there will be wall-to-wall coverage of our reporters out in the field getting the candid, in-real-time reaction of the people to the QR code video as they watch it. We will deploy everyone. Wherever the vans go, our crews go. This may be our last hurrah, but WNG will go out swinging."

Jessica looked away briefly. Though she had tears in her eyes, she had never been more proud of this man. He ended with this: "Code name for our counterattack is Stone Age Viral."

Chapter Forty-seven

*T*here was a palpable emotion in the great room. It felt like a combination of exhilaration and fear—exhilaration that they had a plan and a fighting chance and fear that it was only that, a fighting chance. The outcome was, by no means, certain. Millions more needed to play the game successfully in order to be in a position to receive some truth and to act upon it justly. And the video delivery itself had to work without any failures. For every person in the room, the consequences would be enormous. They knew they would all be attacked. They might all lose what they had built. It would be in the hands of the American people.

Despite his awareness of everything that could go wrong, Andy Weir stood looking out the window toward the Bob Marshall Wilderness. Looking to his left, he smiled yet again. Through all the years, Andy had never lost sight of something his father and mother had imbued in him—an abiding faith in the people. He was going to lean on that now.

Just then, James got a call. It was John Brannigan. Pausing for a moment to decide whether or not to let it go to voicemail, he decided to just square up and find out what Brannigan wanted. *Hopefully, I can figure out what he has learned,* he thought.

Mikolas mouthed that the call was from Brannigan. Everyone froze for a moment, not knowing what that might portend. Motioning for the others to be quiet, or to leave the room, James took the call.

"Mikolas here," James answered.

"James. It's John Brannigan. You got a minute?"

"Sure. Let me get to a better reception area." James walked out onto the patio and sat near the cigar humidifier built into the stone wall. "There, that's better."

Brannigan wasted no time. "I'd like to meet with you in person, James. There's something I would like to go over with you. I'd value your opinion about it."

"Well, sure. But I'm not in the D.C. area right now," James answered honestly. "When were you thinking?"

"Are you at your Cape Fear place?"

"No. Still wandering, exploring. I'm out in the country. Might take me a day or so to get back in town. Can it wait until then? If not, I could probably do a web call with you."

"It can wait. Today's Sunday. How about Thursday lunch? The Mayflower?" Brannigan offered casually.

"That works. Time?"

"11. I'll make the reservation."

"Roger."

The call ended. Andy had been standing just outside the door, giving James room, yet blocking anyone from interrupting. Putting his phone back in his pocket, James joked, "Well, at least he didn't call on my encrypted phone. That would have been really bad."

Seeing the call had ended, everyone else exploded onto the patio, eager to know what had transpired.

"He wants to meet me for lunch. Thursday, 11 AM, the Mayflower."

"Is that good or bad?" Bud asked.

James shook his head. "I don't know for sure. Could be either. But Brannigan has not called me since I hooked him up with Vince and Hector. So, something's up, Bud. Knowing him, he's uncovered something, and he's covertly fishing to identify the source. He's a brilliant dissembler."

Mulling it over for a moment, he turned to Jessica. "I am going to need to fly back to Manassas right away, Jessica. Can you handle that?"

She knew her pilot was on standby, out at the bunk house. "You sure you want to go?"

"Oh, yeah. I don't have a choice. But I've got to get back to Vince and Hector and brief them, set up another cover story for all of us. And that has to be done—at the risk of overusing the term—old school."

Given the magnitude of the parts of Bud's plan, James had hoped to be able to remain where all the players were and where all the moving parts would be assembled. This need to be plausibly in the D.C. area, and very likely under some kind of surveillance, was adding an unpredictable and undesirable wrinkle. Communication between all the elements of Stone Age Viral would be critical, and this would put James nearly in the dark.

Andy spotted that right away and said what no one else wanted to. "James, if you can't be here and can't be seen getting on a plane, how are we going to coordinate with you?"

Bud responded even before James did. "First, James, use my sports editor's desk like you just did. I will give him a message for you when we are ready to launch. 'Fishing trip back on. Looking forward to it.' He'll call you from the WNG line you have used. Nothing out of the ordinary there. Anyone would know you have a relationship with me and with Jessica from the past."

James nodded, and Bud added, "Now, you are not going to be needed for much of anything, James, except to keep your head down. Vince or Hector either. This is all coming from WNG and Carver & Weir. We'll also send a letter to your Arlington box when we are ready. The day we do the pamphlet drop is the day you three will need to take real cover."

"Why is that?" Reagan asked.

James snorted and answered her. "That's the day Brannigan and Loren realize they were not only spied on but that the spy got everything. It's said in mythology that when a dragon is mortally wounded, he is most dangerous. His tail is flailing, and he can do a lot of damage in his death throes." Nodding vigorously to confirm his own conclusion, he said, "We'll lay low and clear out of the way."

"James, in the event of a worst-case scenario, something catastrophically wrong, my sports editor will call you on your encrypted phone. He would need to take the risk."

"All right, Bud. I got it. A call on the encrypted phone means a world of hurt."

"Yeah, that says it."

Suddenly, James sighed. "Actually, that's a relief. Once you launch, there is one more thing I will need to do. I need to involve the Israelis in something. Timing is tricky. It has to appear like they came upon this honestly and that they are assisting the U.S. government—you know, stumbled on it while surveilling Ernst Schweiner and his European crew. I just need to get this out of our borders." He laughed again, "Maybe having to hunker down will be a good thing. It will help me to figure the best plan and the sequence on it. For that, I do need to be in Washington…" his voice tapered off as he was mulling an idea over in his mind.

Like the breathtakingly simple plan Bud had concocted, even with its intricate components fraught with risk, James Mikolas was going to have to invent an equally simple plan, albeit fraught with its own dangerous components. He knew he had his work cut out for him. But he also knew he was a fine analyst and an even better field operative. He regretted what he was going to have to do and hoped Ari Ben-Gurion would understand. But an interesting diversion was germinating in his mind, and he shook his head up and down.

Less than 30 minutes later, he was wheels up to Manassas. He had quite a surprise in store for Vince and Hector.

CHAPTER FORTY-EIGHT

S miling, Brannigan decided to test the waters further and see what else might surface before his meeting with Mikolas. As soon as he hung up the phone with James, he called Vince McCoy. Hoping to lay some bait that Vince would fall for—if he were an adversary and not an ally—he eagerly waited.

Vince saw the call come in. Given that he had not heard from James since he took off for Montana, McCoy was suspicious. Years of doing extractions had put him in relationships with people who would betray their own mother, if need be, for money. Brannigan was his client, and he had done his job. The fact he had done two jobs—one for Brannigan and one for Mikolas—was an aspect he had to juggle. He knew not to do anything now that might connect some dots.

So, Vince McCoy just sat there and let it go to voicemail. *I'll have to get back to him at some point. James, hurry up, man. I need to know where you are!*

He didn't have to wait long. A transmission came in that the jet was approaching, and the farm hand went out to meet it and secure it. Once he deplaned, James suggested to Vince and Hector that they sit on the porch because he had news. Each listened intently to the plan James had received from Bud and Andy and what their own parts would be.

"Doesn't seem to me we are in any of the action," Hector observed somewhat morosely.

"That's correct. We are a decoy—if that," Mikolas responded.

"James," Vince interrupted, "I don't mean to rain on anyone's parade or anything, but that is the most outlandish plan I have ever heard. Almost defies imagination. Reeks of peril."

James was too tired to discern whether Vince was sincere or just being sarcastic. So, he hedged his response. "Yeah, exactly why you should be glad to be sitting this out on the ground." Hector winked at that response, and James knew he was in safe territory. "But, given that you told me Brannigan called, thank God you didn't answer. I need you to call him back, but be on guard. He may be looking to set us up. Don't let on I am here. Once you are done, we'll decide what to do."

Vince took a long deep breath, picked up his phone, and started to do the callback. Before he did, though, he turned to James once again. "You are meeting with him on Thursday. He, for sure, is planning to do something with, or to, you, James!"

"I know. I can handle it. Just do your job, Vince, as you have been these past months."

Brannigan immediately answered, and he and Vince dispatched with the polite amenities quickly. "Vince, something's come up relevant to the surveillance Hector did. I need to ask a question. Is he there?"

With no hesitation whatsoever, Vince responded, "He is. He's just finishing something right now on our current assignment. Let me…" Vince feigned checking with Hector and added, "He's coming right out."

While they waited for Hector to "become available," Brannigan asked if they were still in the country. Clearly, he was probing, hoping for some inconsistency. "For a couple of days anyway. You're lucky you caught me, though. We do as much prep as possible, but once we roll to the target area, I'm impossible to reach."

Brannigan said only, "Hmmm. So, you got somebody to rescue?"

"Well, that is my wheelhouse, John. You know that. Anyway, here's Hector."

"Mr. Brannigan, sorry, I had to finish an instruction on something."

Wasting no time and knowing that the speed of questions often trapped people into giving wrong or revealing information that could be used later against them, Brannigan jumped right to the point. "Hector, when you set up surveillance so that I could find out what Peter Loren was doing, did you set up two? I mean, did you set it up so that he could surveil me?"

"Jesus, no. My job was to do electronic surveillance and physical surveillance on him, not on you. Why the hell would I set it up for him to monitor you? What have you stumbled onto?"

Brannigan truly did not know at this juncture whether to trust the team he had hired or trust Loren. Assuming that he would ferret that out in the next few days, he played along, "Well, that's what I thought. But…here's the situation. Some buddies of mine at the Agency said they found I was monitoring Loren from my phone, but they found he was also monitoring me. They wanted to know if I knew that. Of course, I didn't know that. And I told it to them damned straight. Long story short, Hector, they explained there was a loop. Someone was monitoring both of us, and if either of us caught it, it would loop back to the other."

"Well, I'm no spook, Mr. Brannigan, but somebody wants you and Loren to doubt each other, I would guess—or just throw either of you off track in the event you stumbled on it."

"Exactly. That's what I am thinking." Brannigan paused only a fraction of a second and then said, "That's why I called you. Did you not see this loop?"

Hector's responses stunned James. It was still strange for him to see this street kid in this role, but the years he had worked with Vince undercover and stealth had certainly developed Hector Rodriguez into one smooth operative. "I did not. But then I wasn't lookin' for it, to be honest with you."

"You weren't? Why not?"

"You wanted surveillance on Loren, sir. Once I had the way into him, I was watching only his electronic communications, his visitors, and physical activities, as you probably remember. I had no reason to be looking around at your communications." He let that sink in, then he added, "But, from what you have described, someone hacked into you to get to Loren. And they hacked into Loren to get to you. That's two different transactions, looped to mask who did it. That wouldn't be me. I'm invisible in this. Can't your agency people locate the source?"

"I haven't asked them. No need to involve a whole lot of people. So, what you are saying is someone else is here and they, too, are invisible?"

"That's what I am saying, Mr. Brannigan."

Brannigan's stomach started to turn a bit. He had his sights and his expectations set on James Mikolas and this collection of unlikely bedfellows that James just coincidentally knew. He knew that was still a plausible scenario and one he would run down when he met Mikolas at lunch. But he also knew Hector could be right. There could be a third party in here that neither Peter nor he were aware of. Question was, who? And who hired them?

He didn't have time to analyze that on this call, though, so he simply said, "Well, Loren and I discussed it, and not knowing who did this, we each switched our encrypted phones."

"Good idea. Start fresh."

The line fell silent for a moment, and Hector decided to risk it. "I took down the surveillance, Mr. Brannigan. because Vince said our assignment was over with you. Do you want me to reinstate it?"

"No. But I would like you—if you can—to check me out and see if you see the loop I have been talking about. "

"If you can stay on the line, I can probably maneuver something. Give me a minute." Hector walked away from the phone to create some authenticity.

"Vince?" Brannigan yelled into the phone.

"Yeah, I'm here. He's working on it."

"Did you hear that?"

"Sure, most of it." He finished that sentence and feigned surprise at what Hector started to report.

"Mr. Brannigan," Hector said, leaning directly over the phone. "I don't see the loop. Whoever did this is good! But it would take a lot of work for me to try to figure that out."

Brannigan jumped in. "Don't bother, Hector. These Agency boys found it, lit a fire under me, and I'm going to toss this grenade back to them to figure out. Isn't that what our taxpayer dollars go for with these geniuses?!"

Hector laughed. "Si! I never thought of it that way. But yeah, you give it back to them." He laughed again.

"Well, thanks. That was helpful. Anyway, Vince, you need to take down my new number in case I need to reach you."

Once they had his new encrypted cell, they ended the call. No one said a word, making sure the call had, in fact, disconnected.

All three knew it was a trap. If they attempted to surveil Brannigan now, using his new phone, he would know it had been them. Assuming only Brannigan and Loren had the new numbers, those two were trying to narrow down who had done it. Only someone given the new number would be able to do a new hack.

"OK. So, you know to answer that line if he calls, but you know to do absolutely nothing with it, right?" James asked.

"Yep. Clean as a whistle on our side, James," Vince responded. "He won't see any suspicious activity on our part. Matter of fact, after you have your meeting with him, and then brief us, I'll act like Hector and I have left the country. If he calls, all he will get is a special outbound message alerting people that I am unavailable until…some date I will put in. I just need to hear from you after your lunch. Need to know what conniving new thing you are putting into motion."

James laughed and nodded. "Now, do you have anything other than 'flat food' in this house? I need a real meal."

CHAPTER FORTY-NINE

"*G*ood to see you again, Mr. Mikolas," the maître d greeted James as he entered the familiar restaurant at the Mayflower. "Mr. Brannigan is waiting for you."

I'll bet he is, James mused, as he was escorted to Brannigan's table. He had a plan, and he knew Brannigan did, too. Feeling like he was entering into a boxing arena to do battle, James squared his shoulders and, as he arrived at the table, shook hands with John Brannigan.

The two exchanged pleasantries, with Brannigan inquiring about James' recent travels. "Well, I haven't made it to Fredericksburg yet. Got to Manassas and then on up to Gettysburg. But now that you brought me back here, I will likely take in the aerospace museum. Maybe go down to the Lincoln Memorial."

"You know there's a nice museum under that memorial," Brannigan offered.

James' antennae were up, since that is where he observed Brannigan, Loren, and Schmidt meet in secret many months ago. Not knowing whether Brannigan now remembered seeing him there that night, James cautioned himself to be alert. "I had heard that. Now that you mention it, I seem to remember an elevator down to it."

"Yes. But you don't have to walk up all those stairs. There's an entrance on the ground level—little modest black door."

"Really?"

"Yeah. With my gimp leg here, I don't go up all those stairs, just to take an elevator down." He laughed. "It doesn't look like an entrance to anything, but it is the museum. Saves a lot of walking."

Thanking him for the tip, James decided to be the first boxer to make a move. "So, what was it you wanted to run past me, John?"

"It's a little delicate, James, but it has to do with McCoy and Rodriguez. Since you introduced them to me, I just wanted to get a little more information on how well you know them."

"Sure. I hope they have done a good job for you…"

Before he finished his sentence, Brannigan interrupted. "They have—or at least I think they have. How well do you know them, really?"

James knew that honesty in such a conversation would be necessary. And since he did, in fact, not know them well, he answered truthfully. "Not well. As I mentioned some months back, they were referred to me to help a friend of mine get his fiancé back. That's all. Other than the day they brought her back, I had not seen them."

"And what friend was that, James?" Brannigan asked as he pretended to be focused on buttering his bread.

"Andy Weir. He helped me years ago on a project when I was still with the Agency." So far, everything he had said was true. But he knew Brannigan was just setting him up.

Brannigan nodded, ate a bit, and then asked, "So, you are close with Weir then?"

"Yeah. I don't get to see him much. But we have always stayed in touch. That's more than I do with most people. So, you could say we are close."

Brannigan chuckled. "Well, I understand that one, James. One of the liabilities of our trade, I'm afraid."

Brannigan then turned the conversation to Carver & Weir and the new game, wondering if James was familiar with it. "I know they launched one. But I am not a gamer. Haven't played it. Have you?"

The sparring between both men went on for a while. Brannigan was probing to see just how tight the links were between James, Vince, Hector Rodriguez, Andy Weir, Jessica Ranger, and Bud Walker. He had hoped that James' reactions might give him a clue how to connect the dots—if there even were any to connect.

Finally, James had had enough. "John, I don't know what you are trying to explore here, but you might want to tell me. Frankly, there can't be much of a connection between Weir and McCoy. Andy was the client, and as far as I know, that was a one-time shot. I don't think anyone else has been kidnapped," he joked.

Brannigan smiled. What James had told him about how he had been connected to each of the parties Brannigan had mentioned seemed plausible to Brannigan. He still had some nagging doubts as to whether these alliances were, in fact, just a coincidence or whether they represented something more sinister. However, his main interest now was in who had set up a loop of surveillance on himself and Peter Loren.

His unexpected decision to bring James into the loop for an analyst's viewpoint opened the door for James to create a second diversion. The first one would be accomplished at the end of their meeting, but a new crack in the door opened, and he decided to walk through it.

Dropping the sparring, James put on his analyst "hat" and resumed conversation just as normally as he would had the two of them still been at the Agency, trying to solve a problem. "Okay. You hired McCoy and Rodriguez to surveil this guy Peter Loren. I'm not going to ask why. That's your business. Now, you find someone is surveilling you both and made it look like you are each surveilling the other."

"Yes."

"And you need to find out who is behind it in order to know who you can trust."

Brannigan barked a laugh. "Blunt, but accurate." Brannigan remembered now the reputation Mikolas had had with the Agency once he became an analyst. Spot on but, sometimes, insubordinate. He still had his guard up, but there was nothing in the conversation so far, or in Mikolas' body language, that suggested deception.

"We can remove one unknown." Brannigan's raised eyebrow caused James to elaborate. "You know why you put surveillance on Peter Loren. Now, you just need to find out who is behind Loren. Wittingly or unwittingly, someone is. So, the real question is, who is using Loren to surveil you?"

Brannigan was chewing on that. He had kept his analysis to Peter, and whether or not he could trust Peter, but Mikolas' last statement opened the door for sure for a third party. He considered now who would want to spy on Loren, and on Brannigan at the same time, yet make it look like they were spying on each other if the surveillance was detected.

At that moment, Brannigan made a supposition—that it would make sense, actually, for Ernst Schweiner to have set up something to keep tabs on him and Loren, and possibly even Serge Pilaf, since all three had just been given their seat at the table. He could be checking them out. That didn't let McCoy off the hook, but he expected a report soon on what Rodriguez had done with the two new cellphone numbers he had given him as bait.

"John," James continued, "I don't know who that might be. But I am pretty sure you can rule out McCoy and Rodriguez."

"Why's that?"

"Because those guys are mercs. This thing you described—this loop—that's way above their pay grade. Look for who has a connection to you and Loren. That's where I would look."

Brannigan nodded and seemed to accept that. Whether he did or not, James decided it was time to end the lunch/interrogation and leave Brannigan to his doubts. James had been in the game a long time, and he knew that in psychological warfare, anytime you can get your opponent to doubt his own reality, or the veracity of a colleague, that doubt gnaws away and produces a degradation of thinking and of the relationship. He always thought of it as the Iago Effect from Shakespeare's "Othello." Iago, as a trusted adviser, manipulated Othello into believing his faithful wife was cheating on him, and that nagging doubt had festered until Othello eventually killed the person he loved. *Let's hope the same thing happens here with these bastards,* James thought as he smiled and thanked Brannigan for lunch.

Telling him he was headed to the Smithsonian National Air and Space Museum, he left.

Brannigan had just entered his home and was descending into his basement office when a call came in from his source at the Agency. He had put a tail on Mikolas, to see what he was doing in D.C. and who he met with. He was also waiting on the report on what had transpired with the new cellphones. Had someone hacked in and set up surveillance in the last four days?

"Yeah," Brannigan answered, without giving his name—an old habit from his Agency days.

"I have some information for you." That was all the male voice at the other end said.

"Shoot."

"First, there is nothing set up on the phones that you and Loren are now using—at least not up to this point." Brannigan was relieved to hear that. *Four days have gone by, and that's ample time for Rodriguez to do something—if he had done it in the first place—and if he still has an interest in either me or Loren,* he thought.

"Good. Stay on that. Let me know if anything changes."

"Roger that. The second one, though, you may want to look into. When the 'subject' left lunch with you, he did not head into the National Mall. He went to the Israeli embassy and was seen entering. He is still there at this time."

One of the phenomena of those who trade in secrets, who live in the shadow world, is that truth and lies can often become blurred to the point where the person can no longer differentiate because he has participated in too much of both. Such was the case with Brannigan that day. John Brannigan had many secrets, and he automatically assumed that there must be some secret thing occurring between Mikolas and someone in Israel's intelligence community.

He was greatly relieved about the first bit of information and diverted his attention away from McCoy, Rodriguez, and phone surveillance. Now he put it on Israel. His attention went to what menacing things they might be doing to him and also to whether or not Peter Loren might be working for the Israelis, and they were using Loren to get to him. That created more questions than answers, and his mind started to grind along that path.

He had taken the bait. And he had no idea that James Mikolas had just successfully planted the seeds of doubt. As they took root, John Brannigan started down the same path as the legendary Othello.

CHAPTER FIFTY

*E*rnst Schweiner stood looking out his office window to the lake below. At this time of year, sailboats dotted the lake, and colorful beach umbrellas lined the shore like a garden of flowers. It was a beautiful day in Geneva, Switzerland, but Schweiner's mind was mired in gloom and apprehension. Though the day was clear, he was not. In a few moments, a phone call would begin that he hoped would shed some light and, hopefully, some reassurance.

Sitting calmly down, he watched as Rutger opened up the call with the Americans, as they referred to them. On short notice, Pilaf, Brannigan, and Loren had been summoned to an urgent call. Rutger could see by their faces that they did not seem to know why the call was happening. That alarmed him even more.

Schmidt wasted no time. "What the hell is going on at Walker News Group?"

"Which part?" Peter asked, betraying his lack of awareness even more.

"The cable news network, Peter. Are none of you aware that they have canceled all the advertisers on all their shows?"

News like that was shocking, frankly, and Loren leaned into the screen. "Did you just say they have canceled all advertisers?"

"I did. And Ernst and I are, frankly, a little dismayed that none of you seemed to be aware of it."

To say the three were astounded was an understatement, and only Brannigan had the immediate presence of mind to start analyzing. "Now, Bud Walker has always been a maverick. True. Even self-destructive over the years. But for him to do away with advertisers, means his network could collapse. He knows that. We all know enough about advertising and business to know that if you don't have advertisers, you can't broadcast...."

Before he finished the sentence, Serge Pilaf quietly inserted a comment. "Which means he is doing a preemptive strike."

"Against whom?" Rutger snapped.

"Against me—well, not me personally, but against the Big Tech companies that could harass the advertisers so much that they would cancel their ads, thus causing a disruption. He is taking that control out of their hands."

Brannigan continued, "Which also means he is doing a preemptive strike against me—also, of course, not me personally, but against the 'revelations' that might come out about him that would cause all advertisers to turn on him and justify bailing on his network. My content. Serge's distribution."

That hung there for a moment as Rutger struggled to think this through. Emotionally, he was much more flamboyant than Ernst when need be. And today, he felt he was missing something. Sitting in his glass conference room in the Manhattan skyscraper, pissed off about having to do yet another early-morning call, he could not refrain from demonstrating his pique.

That afforded Schweiner the opportunity to be the mediator and to step into the conversation. "All right, gentlemen. Something clearly unusual is happening, and we need to assess whether this does, in fact, have anything to do with us and our plans or whether this is just the flailing of a demented media mogul."

"So, John, what you are saying is that he may have concluded that you are going to manufacture some dastardly information about him and leak it in such a way as to spook his advertisers. Or to provoke Serge and those he represents to just outright declare war and cancel him. Is that right?"

"Well, it's just a hypothesis I was expressing, Ernst. I just checked in with my network—who, by the way, must have been blindsided by this, too, because they did not even call me. They would have called to get my comments and opinions. Anyway, they are befuddled, and I can see ANN has decided to ridicule. Sharks in the water now. Changing channels, I can see all the networks are seizing on this rather gleefully."

"So, before his advertisers can be impacted by your propaganda, he has made that a moot point," Peter said. "Is he actually tanking his network or doing something far bolder?"

Schweiner was listening closely now. "Peter, explain what you mean, please."

"Absolutely. But first, Rutger, is he making any unusual financial moves other than the apparent suicide of his network?"

"Yes. I was just informed by people in investments that he appears to be liquidating all his assets. What do you make of that?"

The group concluded that Walker was getting his hands on as much cash as possible, but they remained mystified as to why—until Brannigan asked one question. "So, there are no ads at all? Just dead air in those ad blocks?"

"No, not really," Rutger responded. "There are ads but from just one company. All ads are from this one company."

"And who is that?" Brannigan asked, knowing the answer before he even asked the question.

Turning on the television in the conference room, Rutger said, "Well, let's see for ourselves."

Though this did not mean anything to four of the five on the call, it certainly meant something to John Brannigan. All ads were from Carver & Weir, and they all were promoting its newest game. Changing channels, to subsidiary WNG programs, they, too, were promoting this game.

Brannigan decided not to reveal his knowledge of Carver & Weir or his involvement with any of the players who might be party to what Bud Walker was doing. *Clearly, someone is messing with me right now,* he thought. Whether it was his narcissism that caused him to bring this back to some plot against him or whether it was his survival instinct to cover his own behind, he said nothing.

But Ernst Schweiner was watching all the men on the call. The only one whose behavior seemed odd to him was Brannigan. However, Schweiner had no knowledge of Brannigan's surveillance activities and had no reason to doubt the man. Wisely, he said, "All right, I see this has caught all of us by surprise. Let's not get into recrimination now. Let's just look at what Walker has done. Well, he must have a reason for doing it. If he, in fact, is doing a preemptive strike to prevent someone from doing something to him, I think the more relevant question for us is what is he planning to do to someone else? Don't you think? And he needs protection from a retaliation. Let's see if we can't figure that out. John, you can work on that. We will all speak further, I am sure."

And with that, the call ended for everyone except Rutger and Ernst. "Are we free to talk?"

"Yes, Ernst," Rutger said.

"I have a most uneasy feeling about this, Rutger. Most uneasy." Rutger nodded. "I don't know this man Walker, and frankly, we have mostly ignored his news agency. I do not know if this means anything or if, in fact, he has lost his mind and is foolishly touting some new wunderkinds. But what I am quite certain of is, whether it has anything to do with Walker or not, there has been a momentum shift relevant to our plans. I feel it." He paused for a moment, and Rutger could see that Schweiner was looking out the window, as if to try to bring something into focus. Turning back to the camera, Ernst continued, "We are going to need an all-hands meeting. Please set it up—all parties, classified. You know the procedure."

"Here in New York?"

"No. Like before. If momentum is shifting, then time is of the essence, and I don't want precious time wasted on travel. We will do the meeting like the last one."

"Just tell me when you are ready, Ernst, and I will set it up."

"Thank you, my friend. Now, if you will excuse me, I think I will take Bruno for a walk. It's a lovely day in Geneva."

Chapter Fifty-One

*R*eagan approached the door to Andy's office reluctantly. He had been working almost 24 hours a day readying the server farm that could handle the needed game players in order for their plan to work. That pressure was compounded by his simultaneous creation of a QR code that would have a video link in it—to not just a short one-minute promo video, but the entire day's meeting of the men seated by Ernst Schweiner in his secret inner circle.

To his knowledge nothing quite like that had ever been created before, let alone tried on a scale this immense. The challenge was daunting, and the workload was crushing. After a few days, Brian and Andy had brought in a team of engineers to create the servers for millions to play a game and the platform the gamers would purchase the game on. That, too, had to be huge, and the ability of the players to play the game had to be protected. Fortunately, since there was nothing confidential in the development of a massive server configuration, they were free to choose top-level engineers who liked a challenge.

That part had been easy. The prospect of working with Andy Weir was enticing, the pay Carver & Weir offered was irresistible, and, since many of these engineers liked games themselves, they felt honored to put this project on their resume.

Andy's part was the make it or break it, and no one but Andy had the skills. More importantly, no one but Andy could see the content. Success or failure in this Stone Age Viral project depended completely on the surprise attack. And on a platform "strong" enough to sustain the pressure of millions watching a long video.

As Reagan opened the door, and gingerly walked in, she quietly said, "Andy, there is a call coming in for you from the office in Kalispell. When he turned to look at her, it was all Reagan could do to hold back a gasp. He was pale, and there were dark circles under his eyes. Always slim, he seemed thin and exhausted. To her, his unkempt appearance made her think of someone recovering from a major illness who is just getting his act together, where appearance was not yet a priority.

But she knew how vital this was for everyone. Though this was the first time she was personally witnessing a weight of this magnitude on his shoulders, Reagan remembered Andy had looked like this a few years before when he trusted Brian to rescue her, while he created a game that could stop a financial Armageddon planned by some of the world's top banking people. He had done his part, and so had Brian.

So, though he looked terrible, Andy's extraordinary ability to focus and to deliver under pressure was part and parcel of who he was. It was that ability that had touched and impressed James Mikolas so much, and had caused him to love this man as a son. Project Stone Age Viral, however, was the most difficult, the most risky, and the most dangerous task this MIT grad would ever attempt.

He managed a smile for Reagan, fending off an apology from her with, "It's not a problem. My eyes were getting a bit blurry anyway. I'll take a break, and maybe you could make me some breakfast, please."

Handing him the phone, he said, "Weir here."

David Hower, his gaming project manager, shouted into the phone, "You'd better get over here right away, Andy. Something important, I think, is happening!"

"David, it's probably an hour drive. Just tell me what it is."

"Can't, Andy. You got to see this for yourself. I know you don't want to come, but you have to."

Sighing deeply, Andy said, "All right. I'll be there as soon as I can."

"Good. Make it quick, though, Andy. I don't know what this means."

Andy had no idea what Hower was talking about, and frankly, had he not been so tired and hungry, the "mystery sandwich" his manager offered up would have been rebuked. He knew, though, that David would not have called if it were not important.

Heading back to his shower, he called out to Reagan, "Can you make that a breakfast sandwich or burrito, sweetie? I'm taking a shower, and we have to get over to the office right away. I need you to drive. I'll eat on the way."

An hour and fifteen minutes later, Andy and Reagan's SUV pulled into the parking lot of Carver & Weir—or, at least, Reagan tried to pull in. The entire parking lot, and most of the highway before and after the entrance, was taken up by coach buses.

"What the heck is this?" Andy asked, scarfing down the last of a protein shake Reagan had added to his breakfast sandwich. "Park across the highway, and we'll walk across."

The two were headed into the main entrance and could not help but notice crowds of people standing outside each bus, waiting. Just then, David Hower threw open the doors and raced out. Right behind him was DeShawn Williams. Brian, too, had been called and had joined them.

Andy was speechless. He just stood there with his jaw wide open. DeShawn shattered the moment by coming up, giving him a huge bear hug and then a fist to Andy's right shoulder. Before Andy could even wince from DeShawn's version of affection, DeShawn Williams looked at Andy and said, "Jesus, bro, you look like hell!" Turning to acknowledge Reagan, he playfully scolded her, "Woman, you need to feed and rest this guy!"

Reagan embraced him, kissing him on his cheek. "It's good to see you, DeShawn."

Recovering from the surprise, Andy added, "It sure is. But what are you doing here? And who are all these people? The buses…?"

DeShawn Williams had risked his life to take Andy's game out for a test drive in the gang-controlled areas of Los Angeles. He had turned in his initial report of getting the generals and their lieutenants of the major Black and Hispanic gangs to participate in the test market research. Statistically, Brian and Andy knew that the gang members had played the game and had done well. Not knowing any player by name, however, they really did not understand what Williams' presence here meant.

"This is a real mixed bunch, isn't it, bro?"

Andy merely nodded as he surveyed the odd collection of men who would normally be committing crimes against one another. Each bus seemed to have a captain, and upon his signal, the passengers waved and shouted greetings from their bus.

Turning back to DeShawn, his unlikely friend said simply, "Every man here played your game. The bus captains are their generals and lieutenants. As you can see, no one is wearing colors today. And nobody's armed. They've dropped all rivalries, for the time being, and they have come as a group."

"Why?" Andy's question was totally sincere.

"Well, simply put, it seems that game of yours had the same effect on them that Brian's first one had on Hector Rodriguez—and me and my crew."

"Well, that's great, DeShawn. I just don't get why they are on a bus caravan to Montana."

"We are not headed for Montana, Andy. We just stopped by to let you know what we were up to. We are headed to Portland."

"Portland?"

"Yeah, bro. Me and the brothers, and these other mixed-breeds, got word that some bad guys—armed and financed—are planning to cause a whole world of hurt again in Portland. It's a second wave, and the word is that whether citizens are deliberately in the way or not, they are going to beat those citizens down."

Andy nodded. DeShawn continued. "We don't like paid agitators. We don't like mercs. And we don't like anarchists. We are no choir boys—as you know…" he poked Andy. "But we got our standards, and we pay our debts."

Andy responded very earnestly, "I know you do."

"So, these guys here feel they owe you a debt, Andy. We're going to Portland, and we are going to stop those bums from terrorizing those citizens and cops. They go low, we go high." Turning suddenly to Brian, he barked an order. "You just make sure your friend Bud has a film crew on the ground. This will look real bad for Antifa—or whatever these hooded warriors call themselves. We're gonna stop them. And you will be proud of how we do it." He just stood there now, grinning.

It was all Andy Weir could do to keep his eyes from sweating. *All the work, all the sacrifice, all the hope…we may just make it. We may just make it,* he thought.

Turning to Brian, Andy softly said, "Fighting chance, right, Brian?"

DeShawn broke it up, taking control once again. "Anyway, we gotta roll. Your crew fed us and let us use the restroom. Much obliged." Signaling to each of the captains, he yelled in a way reminiscent of wagon masters from years past, "Mount up, men. We got a riot to stop! We got people to save."

At that moment, the crowd in front of each bus erupted into a cheer. Loudly, and almost in complete sync, they shouted, "Free Portland!" Twenty minutes later, the last bus in the caravan rolled out. David Hower, Brian, Andy, and Reagan stood by themselves in the parking lot.

"Something, wasn't it?" Hower commented.

Chapter Fifty-two

A ndy was napping when Brian arrived with a handful of what looked like email printouts. Reagan was guarding access to him since he had not had much rest. A few hours earlier, he had stuck his head into Faith's room, where Reagan was reading to her, and said he was going to take a nap. He seemed pretty normal, so Reagan had assumed he was at a good place to stop and rest. And she was going to make sure that rest is exactly what her husband got.

"I have to see him, Reagan," Brian said firmly.

"Can't it wait?" She knew the answer even as she asked the question because Brian was jumping back and forth from one foot to the other, and she knew that was good news of some kind. "All right. But don't spook him, please."

"Me? Nah. I'll be gentle as can be!"

At that moment, Brian turned, ran down the corridor toward the master suite at the back, shouting, "Hey, Weir, wake up!" She could only shake her head as he bellowed, "I got something real interesting for you." He didn't wait for Andy's response. Brian opened the door and disappeared inside.

"Bro, if you thought DeShawn's bus tour was something, get a load of this!"

"What?" Andy asked. He had just been awakened, but Brian's enthusiasm was infectious, and he hoped this was really good news. It was.

"Do you remember that group of gang members years ago who dropped their gang activities, disarmed themselves, and decided to help and protect the people they used to prey on?"

Andy nodded, sitting on the edge of the bed now. "I do. I remember it started back east, and people really started to feel safer with them around. Didn't they franchise into other cities?"

"That's right. They franchised into almost every major city in the country. Along the way, I met the founder of the group. I really admired them going unarmed and, instead, they became highly trained in martial arts. To me, since they had once been on the streets, they really know what to look for."

"Agreed. But why am I sitting on the edge of the bed rather than lying down for my nap?"

"Hah!" Brian laughed. "Because I just got a call—followed by these emails confirming what he told me on the phone—from the head of their whole operation. He says the number of members in their group has tripled in the last few weeks, and they are doubling their training programs to get these new recruits ready to deploy."

"Where are they headed?"

"New York City, Baltimore, Minneapolis, Kenosha, Los Angeles, Seattle, Atlanta, Oakland, and D.C. They are going to keep the peace. And they are going to every city that defunded police in some way. He's convinced that really jeopardizes the safety of people he already felt responsible for."

"All right, so he would have done this anyway, right? He just has, thank God, more manpower?"

Brian grinned and bounced back and forth a little bit. "That was just the appetizer!" He winked and continued, "Here comes why I woke you up. He's going there to keep the peace because they are going to be protection for all the 'Moms and Ministers' rallies that are scheduled."

It took a moment for Andy to get what Brian was saying. He was not familiar with any "Moms and Ministers" groups, let alone rallies. He must have looked puzzled because Brian again smiled and said, "Yeah, bro, they been forming up all over the country. They plan to take back the streets and their cities. Moms in the actual neighborhoods pair up with local ministers, and some big guns for sex appeal, and they are rallying in every city. Our man is going to be there to support them."

"Moms, ministers, and reformed gang members…" Andy's voice trailed off as he looked at the picture his mind was creating of this counterforce against violence and lawlessness. And he couldn't help but realize that their wives, too, had answered the call. "Well, Brian, sit down here with me for a moment."

Brian did. He said nothing, just waited for his friend to take the lead. "Looks like our game is producing results. People empowered to create their own solutions. It comes from their own innate goodness, you know?" It was more of a rhetorical question. Brian just waited until Andy finished his thought. "Some of them are going to get hurt, you know."

"I know."

The two friends sat quietly side by side, listening to a gentle rain that had started falling. "Well, here's another bit of news. I think I am about ready to give Bud the 'go' sign on the pamphlets."

Brian's face said it all. Andy continued, "The toughest part was the length of that video. Geez, those bastards were long-winded. But I think I figured out how to do it. There will be a lot of failures out there in the field—you know, people trying to watch with varying versions of phones, and incomplete updates, and printing anomalies from one printer to the next, which may blur some of the QR code…Our servers overloaded on the front end…outages, even with the hot mirrored sites for both the game and the video."

"With all that, you are still going to tell him to 'go' on the pamphlets?"

"Yeah, I am. Because time is of the essence, and I realized something else just before I lay down for the nap."

"What's that?"

Andy laughed for a moment. "I realized this pamphlet is not like us releasing a game, where everything has to work, every time, or we would be putting out a corrupt product. This is war, and this is a war game we are playing for real. So, to me, this is more like D-Day. Eisenhower had a plan. There were a ton of things that could, and did, go wrong. The casualties, he knew, would be extreme. But he had the element of surprise and chose to risk it all." Andy paused for a moment. "My mom told me how much Dad admired the courage it took to do that."

Rising, Andy tucked in his shirt and said, "I'm going to tell Bud to print 10 million pamphlets."

"How many 'casualties' are you expecting?" Brian asked easily, though he was not prepared for the answer.

"About 90 percent."

"Did you just say 90 percent?"

"I did. Some will be total failures, just not able to get in at all. A lot will be partial failures—you know, the person was able to watch part, but not all, of it. But that leaves 1 million who will have been instructed in the pamphlet to stay off any social media, but to show this to 10 others instead."

"Ahh, I get it," Brian said. "With those 1 million—assuming at least half of them do follow through—you will know it is watchable. And if each of them takes the pamphlet that is working to 10 others and they do 10 others, in about 10 days 50 million people could have watched it. Cut that in half, and it's 25 million."

Andy just nodded. "Whew," Brian whistled. "That's going to be a lot of pissed-off citizens!"

"Awake—and pissed off! Good thing Bud plans to provide the link to the game 'Hate' in every pamphlet, too." Andy started to laugh. The combination of fatigue and irony just overtook him, and he released weeks of the frustrating programming where he had been probing into unknown territory.

After they sobered a bit, Brian went philosophical again. It was a trait he had always had of looking at some dimension of their various problems and projects with a distinctly human eye and a keen spirit. "So, is this what it felt like for him, do you think?"

"Who?"

"Eisenhower. I'm feeling fear but also a sense of resignation. It has to be done. The goal is imperative, and the risk is huge. I feel that. Did he?"

"I am sure he did, Brian." Andy paused to think about that himself. In his mind, he could see that photo taken of General Eisenhower near a window on the day he had to make the fateful decision. Lonely. "He knew the goal. He just didn't know the outcome. That was in the hands of his troops, and the peoples of the countries that needed to be freed, don't you think?"

"And God." Brian said, "My mama would have added that."

Bud's pamphlet was written testifying to the veracity and to the importance of what they were about to view. The instructions were clear. No social media. Just neighbor to neighbor. Good old-fashioned grassroots. And he included the free game called "Hate." When he got the word from Andy and the document with the QR code inserted, Bud Walker started the printing presses he had been buying up all over the country.

He called his sports editor, telling him to let James Mikolas know the "fishing trip is back on" and that it would start in three days. Dispatched at the same time was an overnight delivery to the P.O. box in Arlington.

Having done that, knowing that the "go" order was issued, Bud suggested that the Montana team meet at the ranch. He had them join him at a campfire and barbecue. Instead of hosting major media personalities and prominent government people as he had in decades past, that night, and in the following nights, he assembled his brilliant but "amateur" crew to wait this out together. They had done their part. Soon, it would play out in different arenas.

The sky in that sector of Montana was known for nights so clear and star-studded that you could put your finger up and almost touch the Milky Way. The entire sky was filled with stars to the point the observer had the sense of an immense and unknown space and power just above— yet, it seemed so close and accessible that one could almost join in.

And that night, the Northern Lights decided to appear and dance. Only Bud and Jessica had ever seen them before. Mesmerized by the gossamer green phenomenon, they all hoped this was a good omen. If the squeals of laughter and delight from Faith and Hope were any indication, the night lights were just that.

CHAPTER FIFTY-THREE

*T*he drop began before dawn. In every major city in America, vans—driven by game players who wanted to engage in the real-world game—used geolocation technology and a QR code Andy had provided to locate their van, secure the van, and drop off mass pamphlets at the locations specified in the QR code. The generation that had grown up chasing a cute creature into real-world situations was now following a QR code directional system to locate for them all their drop-off points. That alone had been a monumental task for Andy. But Alicia Quixote had indeed delivered on her promise to organize the transportation and distribution.

Eager drivers, along with one helper in each van, had started arriving at their van locations before midnight. On command, the vans were released at different times in the night so as to adjust for different time zones. 6:30, 7:30, 8:30, and 9:30 AM were the destination times in each different time zone. That was risky, but Bud Walker had felt it was even riskier to have the East Coast get these first and then warn the West Coast to be on the lookout. The entire event had to come off like a well-strategized, and well-executed, surprise attack.

The instructions in the pamphlet were clear, and the "marketing" message, which would draw even the casual reader into a "desire to read further" mentality, had been written by Bud Walker. Using "come on marketing," whereby you create a mystery and reveal something enticing in order to inspire the buyer to come in and look at your product, his pamphlet was a teaser. To get the whole story, the person had to scan the QR code. His message was designed to appeal to anyone who wanted to "protect our democracy." Knowing that catch phrase would transcend party, and attract even the most virulent of both, he then addressed "freedom dying in darkness" and who was doing it to them. The QR code could be scanned and would take them to a website.

In reality, large amounts of his fortune had been spent not only on printing presses, vans, airplanes, paper, personnel, but also on a massive server farm—owned exclusively by him and housed near Helena, Montana. Bringing the power and delivery capability into that remote area had been daunting and expensive, especially given the short timeline. But Bud Walker knew it would be protected by the Montanans he knew were in support of him.

More importantly, he had adopted the philosophy of "go big, or don't go at all." No one could have guessed how many servers he had set up—each one to handle the lengthy multimedia video experience those who read the pamphlet and scanned the QR code were about to witness. It was the unedited entire meeting of the group of men who would rule us all. And Bud Walker knew he had one shot at this.

Andy had assured him that the QR code, when scanned, would use a smartphone's app the person had probably already downloaded in order to use the camera for viewing menus and ordering or for watching promotional videos. It would take them to the URL he had programmed in. Inside that website, a second QR code also allowed entry into the game "Hate" for free. He and Brian had decided to create as much sanity and awareness as they could in one blow—no matter the lost revenue to either of them.

And, like Bud Walker, they also understood that they had just one shot at this. Americans would be watching, and then—following instructions to stay off social media—they would go grassroots to friends and neighbors to help them watch it. The media empires and those in Schweiner's crew who controlled all of those media people would be stunned and disoriented, and it would take them a few days to figure out who had done this, let alone how to debunk it. Meanwhile, WNG's reporters were to be in the field interviewing and livestreaming citizens' responses to what they were watching. All WNG shows and all hosts would devote their entire timeslot to the coverage.

They were gambling that the intelligence community that still was honest and intelligent would validate the authenticity of the video and verify it was not an edited or deepfake video. Though no communication could occur with anyone in that governmental community, everyone on the team in Montana had concluded there were still enough brave men and women who would do the right thing. Recognizing this was their chance at freedom, too, they would perform their duty.

At least, that was the hope.

The banners were printed and attached to the planes. Once the vans had made their deliveries and the sun had risen, an armada of signage planes took to the air—dragging this message behind them: Scan the QR Code. With an arrow pointing down, and a picture of the pamphlet and code on the banner, they knew the viewer on the ground would recognize the meaning.

Planes were swarming everywhere in the United States that morning. They flew for 10 hours. The chosen locations filled up with the people who would normally arrive for work or school, and the millions of pamphlets disappeared into anonymous crowds. What Bud could not see, and Ernst Schweiner could not know, was that hopeful people were hiding in restrooms scanning the QR code and, seeing what it appeared to be as the video started to play, they put it on pause and returned to their office to suddenly take a "sick day." Once home, in the quiet of their homes, husbands and wives sat down and watched.

Bud and Jessica sat quietly at home, too. Bud got reports that the vans had dispensed all he had printed. Making the executive decision to print even more, in case he still had time to get them out, the presses fired up again. Meanwhile, Andy and Brian were at the server farm. Neither of them, nor any of the engineers they brought with them, had ever seen anything like this. The number of people linked to the website by the QR code was staggering. It kept climbing throughout the day. If one server crashed, it rolled to another, and another.

Andy knew that millions were probably failing to make the link. He knew people's various cellphone cameras might not be good enough, or they might not be able to download the app that would allow them to scan the code. But he was heartened by the constant increase in people entering. "Wouldn't you love to have been out there where the planes have been flying?" Brian commented almost wistfully.

"Yeah. I am sure somebody is filming this, though."

In fact, James, Vince, and Hector were in the District. Not knowing what their next move would be, they didn't want to get caught with a two-hour trip to get into town. Hector had his "gear," and the three were prepared for anything. On the way in, they had stopped to film some of the planes.

However, that morning, eight men and one woman were completely unprepared for what was about to happen. A battle had just begun, and the outcome would determine whether the Great Reset would continue or whether it would end in this century, in this decade.

CHAPTER FIFTY-FOUR

Operation Stone Age Viral launched in the morning of the last Monday in August. The construction of the technology to accomplish it all was done at warp speed. Before the day was over, Andy Weir had lost over one-third of his servers—not to hackers trying to take them down, but to crashes produced by the increasingly heavy traffic as the day wore on. He and his team of engineers knew they would be working 24 hours at a time.

Cots had been rolled in. Jessica Ranger was catering food and moving money wherever it was needed to keep the attack going. Bud suggested having WNG's evening anchors announce that the creator of the pamphlet told the viewers to photocopy someone's pamphlet if they had not been able to get one that morning. Explaining that the QR code might not be brought into focus sufficiently to link to the website, each anchor could scroll on the chyron on their screens the website address they could use, if need be. Risky as that was, he felt the more people who got their hands on a pamphlet in the first day or two, the better a chance they had of stopping Schweiner's table mates.

Fortunately, Andy nixed that idea. Knowing it would open up the main website directly to hackers, he couldn't risk it. Preferring to suffer the losses of people who tried to open the QR code unsuccessfully, he needed that separation from the code to the website to delay a Big Tech counterattack as long as he could.

It would not prove necessary.

Ironically, Ernst Schweiner had also convened a meeting of all eight men at the table, as well as the Kitchen Cabinet woman, Svetlana Carolina, for the morning of the last Monday in August. They were all sequestered in their secure locations on an encrypted video call. Svetlana Carolina was masked as usual. Ernst wanted to review some recent occurrences Schmidt had been monitoring that alarmed them both. He intended to advance the timeline of completing a coup in the United States and was prepared to inform each one of them to be ready to launch the simultaneous assault in order for the new world government to emerge and assume supremacy.

He was bolstered somewhat by a communique Schmidt had just received. Top U.S. military officials had been purging what they referred to as "extremists" for several months. That had played well in the press and had given them cover for what they planned next. The communique simply signaled Ernst Schweiner, and the GCF, that the U.S. military was prepared to be defunded, just as their counterparts in local law enforcement had been. Ernst knew that meant they would stand down, if need be, and be prepared to fold into an international military force as the means of protecting their citizens. That was good news. Notwithstanding the assurance that a coup would go essentially unchallenged, Schweiner was consumed now with a sense of impending doom. Nothing extreme had changed in the United States really. It was not like their plans were imploding. The good news from the military was a real win. But he was very sensitive to a shift in momentum. And he knew enough about psychology to recognize that if the minds of Americans were shifting, any slowing in his momentum could eventually lead to a collapse and a balk by the American people.

When he came on the call to assume control, and to lay out his perceptions and new objectives, he was immaculately dressed. The others might be dressed more casually, given the hour this started in Silicon Valley, but he maintained the discipline and decorum he had for more than 40 years. He appeared calm. The only thing that might have revealed his uneasiness was the fact that he seemed to purse his lips more often than usual, and he clearly was drinking more water from his crystal goblet.

"Gentlemen," he began, "welcome to this call. I appreciate you joining me, given the time." Turning to the representative from the Chinese Communist Party, he joked, "I don't even know what time it must be for you. But welcome."

Mr. Koo bowed slightly in acknowledgment.

"I don't know if you saw what happened in Portland yesterday and the day before. If you did, I expect you are somewhat concerned that the order given by our 'wealthy friend and investor' to the anarchists who have been deployed around the country for more than a year was received, taken up, and then stalled."

A few men at the table had seen something on the news, but the story had been spun so much under the careful tutelage of Peter Loren that the significance had escaped them. It had not escaped Schmidt, Schweiner, or Loren, though.

"Peter, would you like to describe what happened, even though you have successfully made the story into a nonstory and one that has been relegated to almost no coverage?" Ernst tossed the ball to Peter.

"Yes." Peter was eager to engage. "In short, the anarchists prepared to attack the courthouse once again, this time escalating the 'tools' that our man had provided. But they were met by a completely unexpected, and surprisingly effective, counterforce." Seeing that some in the meeting were about to ask if it were law enforcement, or perhaps National Guard, he continued, "A mysterious caravan of buses from Los Angeles arrived. Hundreds of gang members from that city poured out and stopped the anarchists."

He let that sink in for a moment. "It appears serious gangs in the United States really know how to scare the fool out of our pansy anarchists—who only prevailed because, before, the local residents did nothing when violent riots occurred. Their local government leaders did nothing before. Their governor did nothing before. But this crew really knows how to counterpunch. Given that, in the past, they just spent their time shooting one another, it is odd that they banded together to caravan to a distant city to prevent destruction." He could not conceal the contempt he felt for the citizens from the inner city who had decided to neutralize his paid and supplied anarchists. "Don't you think, everyone?"

Schweiner resumed control. "Well, I do, Peter. And that is why I convened the meeting with the level of urgency each of you experienced. I have concluded—and Rutger concurs—that this is a harbinger of things to come. Peter did a marvelous job of sidelining this one occurrence. But before this mysterious caravan moves on to another city like some kind of perverse gang vigilantes, protecting the people they normally would exploit—and before we lose any real momentum and start sliding backward—we are going to launch our final takeover now."

No one revealed any emotion. However, there was a silence, pregnant with unspoken communications. "I did inform you, you will remember, that we were going to move the timeline up before more than 100 million Americans awoke from the hypnotic spell our mind guys have put them under." They all nodded.

"So, here is the plan. We will launch riots simultaneously in 150 U.S. cities, whether justified or not. John and I will inform the members of the U.S. military that are with us, and who would welcome a new and better form of government where they will have more influence and control, to be ready to deploy. We will make Washington, D.C. ground zero on the riots, and it will be so severe that the military will be called out again, in even greater force. I want the Capitol and the White House completely surrounded by senior officers whose men will follow an order to occupy.

"John and Peter, you will be needed here, and Serge, you will be both the vanguard and safeguard as we have discussed often. Peter, as this is unfolding, you are to persuade every network to miss the significance of what is actually happening. Get them to take the bait that a bunch of ruffians are destroying our democracy and that the people are rioting in the streets—not just anarchists and Marxists, but the people themselves, and the military needs to bring order."

Peter knew exactly what to do with this. "What do you want us to do if any of the networks refuse to cover this story the way we want them to?"

Ernst Schweiner had a ruthlessness in him, which rarely displayed itself publicly, but this was his core group, and without hesitation, he said, "Serge, you can take down the networks' satellites, can you not?"

"I can, indirectly. And I am sure Mr. Koo can be of assistance, if need be."

Realizing that Serge was referring to the time the Chinese had hacked into a major network's satellites to obtain workflow related to an international incident they were involved in, Mr. Koo simply smiled and said, "Of course. Between Serge and myself, all satellite means of communication will be neutralized."

"Good. Good." Ernst exuded pleasure. "And the content of any that are broadcasting will be determined and controlled—and I do mean controlled—by John and Peter. Use whatever means necessary, John, to extort compliance from the corporate owners and network heads. You should not really meet resistance. After all, they have long been part of our plan. Always remember, they know a new world is coming. And they can be counted on to do whatever is necessary to remain at the table."

Turning to Cedric Cornell and Rudi Iseli, he softly said, "And, going forward, you know what to do to frighten the people, to force them to stay inside rather than come out and participate in any insurrection not created by us. And to sedate any who are unruly, right?" Both men nodded.

And, last, our representative from the International Currency Fund will be prepared to put pressure on all government officials—whether they be in the executive branch or the legislative branch—to submit and to surrender their government to the international body that is prepared to really care for the citizens of this planet. Given the choice of financial Armageddon, and the enslavement of their population, they will resign and will assist in the transition out of their republican form of government."

"And if they do not submit?" the ICF representative who was not visible, as usual, asked an audio-only question. She realized full well that it was possible that the President, even when confronted with an apparent military coup, might resist. And she needed clarity on what might come next.

"In that unlikely event, you push them back into the Stone Age, my dear. Present company exempted, of course, and the business and government members of the Global Commerce Forum as well." Ernst spoke with no lag in the answer—and with no uncertainty. If anyone had had any doubt about the sincerity of his commitment to the world of the future, it was removed then.

He was just about to suggest that the woman with the lovely voice who had inserted herself into their meeting come and be introduced to the others when Rutger stopped him. Rutger Schmidt was clearly shaken by something. All color had drained from him, and he was shaking his head back and forth, saying, "No. No. No!"

Seeing the confused expressions on the faces of everyone else in the meeting, he recovered his composure and his voice and said, "I think you should see this. You all should see this."

Bringing up on the screen a QR code from the pamphlet he had been handed by his assistant, he explained that something had happened while they had been in their meeting. Millions of these pamphlets were circulating all throughout the U.S. At that very moment, the cellphones of the others present exploded with urgent messages from people trying to reach them. No one acknowledged their phones, however.

Rutger first brought up on an adjacent screen a network whose field journalist was filming planes flying with banners waving behind the planes, exhorting the people on the ground to open the QR code. Then, the journalist filmed groups gathering, with people peering at something on their phones, something that was clearly shocking to them. The journalist could not get his camera close enough, and a group shoved him aside when he tried to inch in. The men in the meeting had no idea what this was about or what it signified. Not yet anyway.

Rutger Schmidt's assistants were better paid and more industrious than your average TV journalist. They were aided by the fact that Rutger's building was one of the ones where pamphlets had been dropped for all the offices of some the most influential firms in New York City. His aide had snagged one and brought it directly to Rutger. Now, every one of the conspirators' eyes were riveted to the screen as Rutger opened the QR code—and the video commenced flawlessly.

They were witnessing their own encrypted meeting where they had each painstakingly laid out how they were going to bring about the Great Reset within a year and that the linchpin would be the end of the United States as the world's most dominant power. Watching themselves on video explaining to one another how they were going to collapse America in the process—rendering the people of the United States powerless and ready for subjugation—left each person speechless. They were personally devastated. The wind seemed to have been knocked out of them, as they realized that not only were they exposed, but the top-secret plan had been "declassified" in a horrific way by some unknown adversary. All that they had planned, all that they had done, might just have been exposed.

Finally, John and Peter looked at each other. They were the professionals in the art of information warfare, and they knew the game had changed and that they were going to have to do the heavy lifting on this one.

Ernst was the first to speak. "Rutger, I have seen enough for now, if you please." He signaled to stop the video. Rutger complied immediately, and everyone's attention returned to Ernst. "Clearly, we have a great deal to uncover here. But if this is being watched around the country..." before he could finish his sentence, Rutger nodded that it indeed was, as far as his intelligence was conveying. Schweiner stopped and then almost immediately pivoted. "Therefore, I want you all to put a hold on all the activities we have discussed here this morning. Though I was prepared to give you all your marching orders, with the end of the task at hand, I can no longer do that." If Ernst Schweiner was personally devastated by this turn of events, he did not show it. "I need to investigate and assess some things. If you are in agreement, I would recommend that each of you hunker down, ride this public relations fiasco out, and we will redo our plans once I know more."

No one disagreed with that. Brannigan's private thoughts reflected those of every other person there. *Get me the hell out of here, so I can find one of those pamphlets!*

CHAPTER FIFTY-FIVE

*T*he first indicators that Bud Walker's strategy might be working came at the end of the first day. The major networks were in complete disarray, not knowing what to do with this shocking video and its content. That night, however, the point was moot. The overnight ratings showed a nationwide drop in viewership in all categories, and in all delivery systems, of 10 million viewers. It was like everyone had turned off their televisions, abandoning their normal broadcast watching or streaming.

While other network executives scratched their head wondering why no one seemed to be watching, Bud knew in his gut what those millions were doing. They were watching the video. He and his team knew how long it was. Ernst Schweiner and his team did not. That night, Americans sat down to watch, and becoming engrossed, it took up the whole night.

Serge Pilaf was getting reports that there was no chatter at all on social media. It wasn't just that people weren't talking about the pamphlets and what it all meant. It was as if the social media giants had gone dark—as if people had censored themselves. No one was engaging. How could they if they were watching a video?

That changed the next morning, though, when a New York City resident ventured out onto the street in the Upper West Side of Manhattan. What startled him, causing him to get out his cellphone camera and start filming his neighborhood walk, was a phenomena the individual had never witnessed. In multiple windows in various apartment buildings, the American flag was on display. In Manhattan, that alone was an anomaly, but the reason the person was videoing and taking photos was because the flag was upside down. The picture taker had no idea why— and posted it on his favorite social media site to have someone explain why the neighbors were flying the flag like this.

The response was explosive. As social media saw it and shared it, the hapless citizen learned that morning about what the symbol of the flag being flown upside down meant. It was a distress symbol. Universally recognized, an upside-down flag means there is distress and help is needed. Though there was a lot of the usual inane chatter and opinions, as the photos went viral, the new viewers weren't reading the comments section. They were riveted to photos of an entire New York neighborhood signaling the country was in distress.

Not even the social media's algorithms, which were created by ignorant millennials, knew what to do with it, so people all over the world saw it as well. The AI that had been dictating to citizens for years—and which had been recently turned into a 21st-century form of inquisition, with banning, pillorying, and outright cancellation—completely missed the symbol of the flag. Bud learned of it when his network manager called from his home in New York City to report the phenomena and to get instructions on what to do that day.

That answer was simple. His instructions were to recommend all news shows, and their anchors, keep attention on the "man in the street." Interview them. Get a handle on their reactions to this pamphlet. Given that the American people had had the previous evening to view it, things started to shift.

In the ensuing days, by the weekend, the New York Stock Exchange was grateful for the weekend break. All Big Tech stocks collapsed. The money taken out appeared to be redirected into American companies only—and not technology companies or pharmaceuticals. That sudden change was hastened by the fact that, near the end of the week, the advertisers for all network news—especially opinion shows—canceled their ad buys. That created a programming nightmare in all the high-rises of power in media. Since most of the advertisers were pharmaceutical companies, whose motives had been impugned in the video, they ran for cover and tried to keep as much daylight as possible between themselves and any of the people in, or mentioned in, the video.

The founders of the Democracy Preservation Project were perhaps the most alarmed. Knowing that investigative journalists would be emboldened now by this release, they recognized that people would trace Brannigan and Loren back to them for sure and start snooping around into all their "opposition research" projects. They would be caught with their hand in the cookie jar, spreading misinformation to distract and manipulate the American public.

Their fears were confirmed when members of Congress and law enforcement that would normally welcome their calls, and any "information" they could provide, refused to speak with them. Likewise with their favorite network shills. No one wanted to hear from them. And they knew their influence in Washington, D.C. was coming to an end.

The International Currency Fund knew to just stand firm. Every move they made was to stabilize currencies and appear to be totally supportive of the United States in this moment. The goal now was to come out of this intact. Not knowing what was happening, or how it would play out, the ICF decided wisely to just sidle up to the United States and bet on her. Since Svetlana Carolina had never appeared on camera, and she had only asked one question on audio, she was not in anyone's crosshairs. She took comfort in her certainty that no one would try to do a voice match. Her "Kitchen Cabinet" designation had saved her.

China, of course, was caught red-handed, and though a powerful adversary, they were momentarily blindsided by the horrific implications of what they had done to the world and what they might do in the future. In the tradition of anyone running a true con, they simply stood in place denying everything. Not only did they deny what they had done, they denied the video. They denied their seat at the table. Their voice of denial was insistent and incessant.

But the worst blow for Ernst Schweiner was the phone call he received from the members of the Global Commerce Forum canceling their upcoming meeting in Switzerland. They all had many secrets of their own, and some were, in fact, part of what Schweiner had been setting up. They wanted to just lay low and assess. They were clearly shaken by the revelations in this universally leaked video, and many were jealous that they appeared to not have a seat at this special "table" he had created. So, the meeting where Schweiner had expected to triumphantly inform the Global Commerce Forum of the successful culmination of their Great Reset—and rise to power and control—was put on hold.

Sitting at his desk in Geneva, he looked down at his right hand and could almost see his decades-long dream dissolve and escape between his outstretched fingers. He reached for the phone and made a call he had never expected to make. "Rutger, my friend. We have much to survey and much to discuss. But for now, I think it is wise if you return to Geneva."

Giving him no argument, Rutger responded, "I think, Ernst, that is prudent. We do have much to discuss and obviously fix. For me, it is better to be where you are. I will see you in a few weeks."

After hanging up, Ernst Schweiner took his attention off what he had lost—permanently. And he put his attention squarely on who had done this. *Clearly, one of the men at the table betrayed us.* Removing his spectacles and cleaning them thoroughly, as if that would enhance his sight somehow, he locked his jaw—for he believed he knew who it was.

James knew it was a waiting game now. His countrymen had clearly been shaken. And the enemy had gone into cover mode. James Mikolas had always believed in the American people, and he was counting on them now to do their part in the continued rollout of the truth and their creativity in handling it.

Hector was the most distressed and agitated of the three of them. Since James had left the farm and gone back to the hotel, Hector convinced Vince to go into the city with him and to meet with James. Sitting in James' modest hotel room, Hector said, "So, this 'reality TV show,' is it working? Are people watching?"

"It appears they are, Hector, and the numbers after the first week are going exponential now. Andy is optimistic."

"Andy is always optimistic!" Hector shot back sarcastically. "I watched that thing as they were plotting. I did not have time to really stop and take it all in. The mission, you know." He said it quietly, turning to Vince. Vince nodded. "But I watched every damned word of that again this week. Even took a QR code and opened it to watch it."

James was a little surprised by that. "Why? May I ask?"

"I wanted to see if it was as bad as when I watched them in real time."

"Was it?" James asked.

"It was worse, man! I started to look over my whole life, and I could see their handiwork in all that I have lived through, and my people." He stopped, and his voice cracked.

James reached over and slapped him on the knee. "I completely understand, Pal! But we can't change what is. It is what it is. And thank God you did what you did. Do you understand that without you and your 'skills,' as Vince describes them, none of this would have come out?"

Hector dropped his head down into his hands and started to weep. That made Vince uncomfortable, but James waved off any attempt to jog

Hector out of this moment. James knew that his emotion was a release, a natural release. So, he let him cry, just like many years earlier he had let Brian Washington Carver weep when he had made his crucial discovery about the loss of his family to pharmaceutically- induced suicide.

Sometime later, Hector's shoulders stopped heaving, he gulped some air in and some water down, and said, "I was just so sad, for my country." Looking at the floor a while longer, he then raised his head and said, "Thanks, though, for what you said about me. It makes me feel better."

James decided to change course a bit and said, "Hector, do you remember when I asked you to cut out in a separate flash drive the material you took from Brannigan's transmitter and hard drive at the storage?"

"Yep."

"Do you have it with you?"

"I do. There is a backup secured at the farm, but I have this one on me." He offered it to James.

"Thank you." James turned the flash drive over and over in his fingers.

Vince suddenly stood up and said, "Well, Hector wants to continue surveillance on Loren—you know, see what he does after the extremely important covert role he played in this. And I want to follow Brannigan or at least stay close."

"That's fine. Just not too close on Brannigan. I mean don't show up at the house for dinner!" he joked.

"Well, I do want to see what shows up at Loren's for dinner or if he goes somewhere else now that he is not such a hot commodity, if you know what I mean," Hector said.

James could see that each of them had to have a role now. Maybe Bud, Andy, and Brian could just wait this out, to see if they had somehow pulled the country back from the brink, but both Vince and Hector were more action heroes, and they wanted to get back out to see what they could see.

"That's fine by me, guys," James said. "There's somebody I gotta see myself. One more video to deliver. Return a favor, if you will."

He stopped first at a local drug store to buy a greeting card. Not long after, James Mikolas arrived at the Israeli embassy and presented his former credentials to the guard. "These are expired, sir," the guard said officially. Then he winked and added, "But I know who you are and who you want to see."

Ari chose to meet James outside the embassy. Both knew cameras would be recording everything anyway. Ari seemed a bit surprised to see James. "James, I would have thought you would have a lot on your hands right now. We're watching in the embassy what I assume is your handiwork." He smiled.

James smiled, nodded, and said, "I have something I want to give you for a change." He handed Ari a greeting card and encouraged him to open it. As Ari pulled the card out of the envelope, a flash drive slid into his hand, hidden from view of any cameras. Pausing, taking his cue from James, he read the card. "I owe you, Ari, for what you have done for us all along here. What's on this flash drive, I believe, will be of interest to your government."

James could see by the raised eyebrow that Ari was a bit confused. "What is this?"

"It's the Bethesda location you have been looking for—and the person." Instantly, Ari looked up at James. There was a grin and expectation on his face. Like James had done so many times in the past when Ari had a folder or information for him, now Ari just stood there, silent.

James said simply, "My government—or at least someone in the Intelligence and Justice departments—should be interested in the content of the hard drive. Coming from me, it means nothing. Probably end up in some middle manager's desk drawer. But coming from your government—and I expect you will know exactly which person should hand it over to the United States—it will be received, looked at, and acted upon." Ari understood and pocketed the flash drive, along with the greeting card.

He added, "An 'exclusive,' you might say?"

"Yes. Secured during our operation but immediately actionable. It exposes a Chinese spy." With that, James embraced his friend and walked away.

A few hours later, a special envoy from the government of Israel secured a meeting with his counterpart in the State Department, with the U.S. Attorney General attending. The flash drive was transferred to those who had the authority to have the appropriate law enforcement and intelligence agencies take action. The Israeli envoy had no idea if the U.S. would act upon it. But he knew they should. And he knew also they would implicitly understand Israel had kept a copy as leverage in the event anyone wanted to deep-six this revelation.

The Attorney General looked at it in his office and summoned his most trusted U.S. Attorney. And for the first time in a long time, proper search warrants were secured and executed.

CHAPTER FIFTY-SIX

*T*he only light visible on the block in Georgetown was the one in Brannigan's front hallway. While others were sleeping, and while Ernst and the rest of his cohorts were trying to figure out how to ride out this debacle, John Brannigan had come to a conclusion. *I have to be brought in!*

Over the last few days, Americans seemed to be having watch parties of some kind in their homes—10 people at a time—and then 10 more with 10 people. Jesus, it's like a goddamned cancer metastasizing and duplicating. As his face started to flush with anger, he now shouted, knowing no one could hear him.

"Ernst may delude himself into thinking we can ride this out. The fool! This isn't going away." And one thing John Brannigan could be counted on was to look out for himself and make sure he did not get caught. All of his other covert propaganda operations for the last five years had worked. Smart law enforcement might have looked at him a time or two, but, in the end, they had nothing and had given him a pass.

He was determined not to be around in case the heat got turned up to the point that Schweiner and Schmidt were looking for someone to scapegoat to save their decades-long conspiracy. So, for the last two days, he had copied electronically everything in the file cabinets—knowing the content would afford him ample blackmail and get-out-of-jail-free opportunities. He was confident of that. After each file was copied, he destroyed it completely. Without a trace! He smiled, becoming calmer with each permanently destroyed file and, ultimately, the hard drives.

His office was as clean as a whistle now. If any search warrants were issued, they would find nothing. Not even John Brannigan. For he had decided to have his handlers bring him in out of the cold. "Hah! I haven't used that term since the '70s. But...I have served them well, and I am sure they will provide handsomely for me," he told himself.

Exiting the basement, he packed just one bag. It held several different passports and identities, casual men's attire and hats, ladies' heavy stockings, a frumpy blue-print dress, coat, and head scarf. He closed and locked the back door, got in his car, and drove off.

"Ari, what's up?" James asked as he answered Ari's call.

"I'll keep this short. I know it's late. Just wanted to thank your man for the great referral on that storage unit. It proved to be perfect for our needs."

Though a casual observer might not have gleaned much from that statement, if he had overheard it, James knew Ari was thanking him for the video exclusive he had handed to Ari—exposing the U.S. end of the mysterious satellite communications between Beijing and the United States.

"He's right here, Ari. Do you want to thank him yourself?"

"No. No. But you might tell him he may want to check out his storage unit tomorrow morning, early. I hear there are going to be some very interested other parties following his 'referral.'"

"Will do. I'll let him know."

Before Ari hung up, he added, "That's something you should skip, James…" And the call ended.

James reflected on that short call for several minutes. Then, he went to Hector and told him he might want to witness some activity at the storage facility in Bethesda. He didn't know what it would be. "But my guess is the Israelis successfully handed off the material you grabbed from that hard drive."

"You think?" Hector and Vince both perked up on that. They were camping out in James' room so as to facilitate any needed action.

"Just a hunch. Anyway, be there early, and you can let me know later what happens."

That same evening, a Petra 2001 Restaurant delivery van pulled up in front of a townhome in Dupont Circle. The driver who regularly delivered food to Peter Loren got out of the car and went into Loren's house. He had no food to deliver, and he appeared to bypass knocking.

A few minutes later, Loren and the driver got back into the van and returned to Petra 2001. Peter Loren entered the restaurant, acting as if he would be dining in. He carried nothing other than his sport coat and a man purse. Peter Loren never came out of the restaurant that night.

It would be some days before anyone noticed his disappearance. No one occupied his offices either. PL & Associates appeared to have closed its office, sold its furniture, and sent whatever clientele it had elsewhere. Hastily, his townhome was rented to someone else. And no one at the Democracy Preservation Project cared to even inquire as to his whereabouts.

Their entire world was beginning to feel like a trap, and they were scrambling themselves to destroy any and all incriminating material so that it would not be available if subpoenaed. In fact, no warrants or subpoenas had been issued. But after years of gaslighting the unsuspecting public, and leaders in Washington, they appeared to have gaslighted themselves—each person there sitting at home in absolute paranoia.

Brannigan knew he had early-morning access to his storage unit, though he had never come out there that early. He drove up Wisconsin Avenue, expecting to slip into his unit and send a communication to the satellite, telling his Beijing handler to bring him in and provide instructions as to where to go and what to do. He expected to be there no more than 30 minutes.

Just as he turned into the driveway that led to the storage buildings, he slammed on the brakes, frozen in horror. The place was swarming with FBI who were easily identified by their lettered jackets, which must have been unbearable in the late-August heat. Thankful that he had donned one of his Irish hats with a brim he could pull down slightly, he peered into the crowd of men and women who were clearly going in and out of his unit, carrying bags and—worst of all—his transmitter and related gear. He also spotted some personnel from the CIA and a U.S. Attorney he had often maligned when functioning as a commentator on the network. "God damn it!" he cursed to himself.

Knowing that his only ability to communicate with Beijing quickly and secretly had just been compromised, he felt he was witnessing a dike, when the proverbial finger is removed and the water rages through, sweeping everything in its path downstream. Brannigan could only concern himself now with how to get off of the storage facility's property without being detected and, once clear, how to make an escape from the United States.

John Brannigan was, in fact, a very bright man with an amplified survival mechanism. It took him only a minute to have a plan of escape. The big thing was to back up and get out without attracting the attention of anyone at the facility.

He saw his opportunity when a car that had been inside the property came to the gate to exit. The hapless citizen had apparently been caught inside as the place was suddenly swarmed by armed men in suits. *I bet that schmuck peed his pants when this circus arrived!* he thought. *I'll let him pass me, and then I'll turn my car around and follow him out onto Wisconsin.*

It wasn't long before Hector Rodriguez's car cleared the gate and drove toward Brannigan's. As Hector approached the car parked in the driveway facing toward him, he didn't recognize Brannigan with his dapper hat. Hector had just been so relieved—when he opened his own storage unit and waited inside for whatever Ari had alluded to—to see U.S. law enforcement confiscate what he knew to be the transmitter a spy had used for a long time to undermine American interests.

Eager to get back and tell James and Vince, Hector smiled and motioned as if to tip his hat to the other driver. That man reciprocated. And right after the exiting car passed him and turned south on Wisconsin, Brannigan remembered the other driver was the man who had a unit near him and who was there the last time Brannigan had transmitted a message to China. Additional memories cascaded as he remembered now that the same man was apparently renting a unit the time before when he had gone to Bethesda to transmit to the satellite.

That's three times now. That's no coincidence.

Gently turning his car in order not to attract attention, he, too, exited the driveway and turned onto Wisconsin. "You son of a bitch. Who are you?" he asked himself as he turned north, away from the mystery man. He had a plan. He had a fallback location if things went south. Ernst himself had offered it months ago. John Brannigan headed north and kept driving. Just before the Canadian border, he changed into the frumpy woman's clothing and left his car on a quiet street, knowing it would be a long time before anyone who might be looking for him would find it. He knew they would be looking for him. To have seen his storage unit raided, and the equipment confiscated, meant he was now the target of an investigation. He had no intention of being arrested and standing trial. Now, by his own choice, he would become the target of a manhunt.

Today, however, he carried a grocery bag, limping like an elderly woman who had crossed over the border to buy less expensive groceries and who was now heading back to Canada—presumably to catch a bus to her humble dwellings. He offered her Canadian passport, smiled at the border agent, and exited the United States into Canada. The only thing the border agent would remember later was that she had an odd gait, as if one of her legs was shorter than the other. Given her age and grizzled appearance, he figured she was a Canadian citizen from one of the western provinces and gave her no more thought until the U.S. marshals showed up to inquire.

CHAPTER FIFTY-SEVEN

*T*he following morning, James heard a knock at his hotel room door. Thinking it was housekeeping, he opened the door. Ari was standing there. Knowing this was completely unusual, James motioned him in and, once the door was closed, asked, "What's up, Ari?"

First, Ari apologized for arriving unannounced but said he felt it best to deliver this to James in person—and privately. James demurred. He, frankly, did not care much how Ari communicated to him, but he knew that something must have changed.

"Brannigan is in the wind."

"What the hell? How could he have known?" James was frustrated that Brannigan might have slipped the clutches of law enforcement, just as they were seizing the proof of his betrayal of his country.

Ari sighed. "We don't know. Timing may have just been off is all. My thinking is that he had already decided he needed to leave, even if he had no idea we were onto the espionage aspect. The good news is our embassy understands from the FBI that his storage unit produced the equipment and the proof they needed. It is being examined forensically as we speak."

Judging by James' silence, Ari just waited. James was formulating a question. "So, when did they discover he was gone?"

"According to my source, it was late yesterday." Before James could start cussing at alleged incompetence, Ari reassured him, "Now, hold on, they didn't delay. The FBI went to his residence in the late morning and were prepared to execute the search warrant."

Before he could finish, James interrupted. "Any media there to cover this?"

"What do you think?"

"Bastards!"

"Well, James, given how incestuous these relationships have become, the FBI didn't care. They planned to do it properly and, given his long-standing service in government and his prominence in the eyes of the public, they planned to tell him to get his lawyer and meet them at their headquarters."

"All right. All right," James grumbled, but he knew that was not a bad sign.

"Anyway," Ari continued, "when they got to his home, no one was there. His car was gone, but nothing seemed out of the ordinary at the house. So, they kept a car there, with the agents ready when he would return. Except, he didn't return."

James scoffed and laughed. "And how long did it take this bunch to figure out he was in the wind?"

"Late last night. They issued a bulletin for his vehicle but have not located it yet."

"They are not likely to either, Ari, you know that." Ari nodded. "Please tell me they at least prevented him from using that equipment."

At that, Ari grinned. "Absolutely, my friend. My government can confirm that the satellite did not fire up yesterday at all—no communications to or from Beijing. It is in your government's hands now, James. Once they have assessed the forensic analysis of the transmitter and gather the exact conversations from the hard drive, they may be able to counterfeit him and see if they can fake out the Chinese. You know, see if they can precisely identify who he has been communicating with."

"Yeah, well, don't hold your breath."

"Agreed." Deciding it was best to break all the bad news at once, he said, "There's more. Loren has also vanished."

James was completely silent. He had no idea what to say to that. He just sat there on the side of the bed. He knew the Israelis felt Loren was dirty somehow in relation to Al Qaeda, and that added a whole other complicating aspect to this Schweiner team.

"Both gone, huh?" James repeated trying to analyze this himself.

"Yes. Both."

"FBI interested in Loren?"

"Not as far as I can tell, James. But give it time. The team handling this is bright, and this U.S. Attorney is very thorough. We can help him connect some dots. But right now, for the United States, the priority is Brannigan."

"Agreed." James frowned, almost wincing, and asked his friend, "If he gets out of the country, what do we do? The FBI doesn't have jurisdiction."

Ari leaned over and patted James on the hand. "Don't you worry about that, James. We—meaning my team—have some experience at locating people hiding in plain sight and seeing that they get back to their rightful home." He let that subtle reminder of the raid in Argentina that had captured Adolf Eichmann decades earlier just simmer for a bit. "Right now, my job is to find him. Yours is to have on hand those 'amateurs' you used in Venezuela a few years back. You will have a role in this. I promise."

CHAPTER FIFTY-EIGHT

*A*ri Ben-Gurion did not like having to keep his old friend and colleague in the dark. But he knew James would not fail to take the recommendation to have Hector Rodriguez and Vince McCoy standing by. Ari did not initially know their names, but he knew from his own country's intelligence of two mercenary "white hats" who seemed to have taken an unusual assignment.

Video surveillance of Peter Loren had revealed an unknown male entering the New York headquarters of the GCF many months earlier. A trace on the unknown person with John Brannigan that day turned up the fact Brannigan had a bodyguard named Vince McCoy. Ari easily was able to link McCoy back to Mikolas and knew Mikolas was running his own operation. Thank God for those three, Ari thought. The hack into that classified meeting with Ernst Schweiner and the others was a godsend for Ari's government.

He was also very confident that, given a few hours, James would figure out that his mercenary friends might be needed for what was their known specialty—extraction.

Ari Ben-Gurion had a theory about where he felt John Brannigan would go, now that his cover was blown and he was about to be exposed as a mole inside the U.S. intelligence community. Though all of the members of this elite GCF group were disgraced, and persona non grata in all the circles they had previously dominated, Ari knew that each was still a force to be reckoned with and that they would likely stick together—or, at least, provide support if they could.

So, he had concluded that Brannigan would not try to get to China or to a Chinese embassy. Brannigan would still try to keep himself in good standing with the Chinese and would not do anything to compromise their relationship. Further, Ari had to assume Brannigan knew his storage unit in Bethesda had been compromised. There was only one other safe place he knew of for Brannigan, where no one other than himself, and James Mikolas' trio, would even think to look.

Ben-Gurion had concluded that John Brannigan would go to Dinkelsbühl, Germany, to the house where he, Loren, and Schmidt had first met with Schweiner. It was the one meeting place where there had been no electronic spying or recording. They had started their global plan in the security of the Schweiner family home. That is where he is going, Ari told himself. He was so confident of this that he had a man on the ground in Dinkelsbühl keeping an eye on the house, prepared to notify him if someone showed up unexpectedly.

A few days later, while the Stone Age Viral video was spreading like a prairie fire, unstoppable by any of the technology companies or media giants, conversations were occurring over dinner tables and in backyards throughout the country. People who had not spoken to each other for months—who had been consumed with the hatred for one another that had been so carefully planted and nurtured—were now talking with one another about issues of common ground that exceeded their divides.

An ocean away, it was a crisp morning in early September when a man, presumed to be a European tourist who had spent the spring and summer in Dinkelsbühl, seemed to be taking a nostalgic walk around town. He had become a familiar face to the citizens of the town, especially in the area near Schweiner's house. So, no one thought anything of his walking the parapet, snapping photos of the scenery inside and outside the walls, and sitting on benches reading. Today was no different for the locals. But it was different for the "tourist." This pleasant man was, in fact, a member of the Mossad, the most feared and perhaps most informed intelligence agency on the planet.

And he had just sent a message to his partner: "One lonely duckling just arrived."

Not long after, James, Hector, and Vince boarded a plane for Zurich, Switzerland. They had been briefed on the location. Operating as private citizens, they hoped to snag this "lonely duckling." They were on their own.

CHAPTER FIFTY-NINE

*E*ntering the home had been relatively easy. Brannigan remembered well the second day when Rutger had escorted Peter and him through the kitchen, into the butler's pantry, and behind a secret panel stocked with canned foods and baking supplies. He had joked to himself that at least he would not run out of food while he was assessing how to make a better escape.

John Brannigan needed rest, however. And the tower attached to Schweiner's family home was just the place. Suspecting that it had played a bigger role in the '40s than Ernst had let on, he explored the "keep," as he thought of it. Since there were no windows, he was able to have lights on, with no fear of anyone outside seeing it.

And, just as he had guessed, he found the floor above the meeting room they all had convened in months before. It had a clean and meticulously made single bed, a washstand, and toilet. The plumbing drained to the main house and, from there, merged with the normal water flow of the household, so one could remain hidden, yet be sanitary. And no one would guess.

The room was provisioned also with drinking water and food. *These are far more appetizing than the MREs I have had!* he joked to himself. Schweiner had, in fact, taken advantage of the latest technologies in the freeze-dried-food packaging of totally sustainable meals that could last for more than 25 years.

Not that I expect to be here for 25 years, he sighed. *A few days of rest and planning, and I will make connection somehow with Mr. Koo.* Brannigan believed that Mr. Koo knew who John Brannigan was when he took his own seat at the table. It seemed inconceivable to Brannigan that the Chinese—happy as they were to have him as a spy—would have allowed one of their men to be at that table without being aware there was another man who had China's back.

With that in mind, Brannigan believed his best chance was to reach Koo in Beijing and let Koo figure out the best way to bring him in. Confident with this conclusion, he fell asleep, enjoying the silence and remoteness of the keep.

A few hours later, he arose and went down to the main room.

While Brannigan was getting himself situated, another team was also engaging. Unbeknownst to him, a phone call was taking place. "Are you sure of that?" Ari asked his partner, Aaron.

"Yes, Ari. Brannigan was disguised when he entered—looked rather dapper, actually—but the man who went into the house is a man with a gimp leg. He has a very quirky walk, almost like a left to right wobble."

Ari smiled.

"And he is not particularly tall."

"Thank you, Aaron. Three Americans are likely to show up there. I'll convey to them that you see no lights and assume he is in the tower."

"Very good."

"And Aaron, I want you to stand down. Stay in the area, but do not engage the Americans. This is their party, and I don't want to get involved."

"Understood. But you should alert them they are likely going to have to find the passageway into the tower. I hope they have the equipment…" he offered.

"They will." Then, Ari added, "I will be enroute as well. You will see me when you see me."

That old joke between two partners put them both at ease.

Ari Ben-Gurion then called James. Knowing that he and the other two were likely already at the Zurich Airport, he gave them the necessary information. He knew James would have rolled just on the first call he had placed to tell him his theory of where he expected Brannigan to show up. James had not disappointed him and was already on the ground in Switzerland.

"Let's roll," James said, picking up his briefcase. The papers and passports that might be needed to re-enter the United States were inside.

"Hector, you got all your equipment?"

"Yeah, boss. The Swiss are a little sloppy in their inspections. Guess they thought it was all camera equipment. And you should have seen Vince here explain his thermal equipment!" He rolled his eyes. "The guy bought it that Vince was a medical equipment salesman, hoping to make a sale of his thermal imagery equipment to a major cancer institute or two. Beautiful!"

James chuckled. "All right."

Two hours later, they had entered Dinkelsbühl, well before the drawbridge would come up for the evening. The house was easy to locate. It appeared no one was home. In fact, they guessed that Schweiner had closed the house for winter now and that no one was regularly on the premises. James' assumption was correct.

Stepping back, James told Vince and Hector that he would be at the coffee house at the next corner. They all were ready. James would have eyes on the house, but he was distant enough to maneuver around or warn them if he spotted any unusual activity. The plan was that when Hector located the entry to the tower, James would join them. Given the age of the tower, and the fact it was a private residence of Schweiner, Hector assessed that the entry itself would be something mundane and not difficult to find or unlock. To him, it was more likely Schweiner would have concentrated any security measures inside the keep and not have bothered about the entrance, other than to mask it somehow. His instincts proved correct.

Brannigan heard the pantry door sliding open. Startled, he dropped the magazine he had been reading and stood up just in time to see Vince McCoy enter the room. Before he could even ask why his former bodyguard had just entered the secret tower room, James Mikolas entered, followed by Hector Rodriguez.

It was when Brannigan saw Hector, remembering him from the storage unit and the raid that occurred there, that he put two and two together. His mind was flooding with images of James and Vince and the "chance" meeting at the Mayflower that had led to Vince's being hired; of conversations with Hector about Peter Loren; of James' quirky wanderings in the D.C. area. *My God, it was them!*

He realized he had been outsmarted by these three and that they had hacked into the meeting—creating the video that was now going viral— and further that James must have been the one to get it to Bud Walker. He was wincing almost in pain as the tapestry of the Carver & Weir game, the QR code drop, the electronic loop, the discovery and ultimate exposure of his transmitting equipment unfolded before him.

Like an old bull moose that realizes it is encircled by a wolf pack, and that there is no escape, he just slumped into the chair and submitted to what would come next.

"John, we are here to take you back to the United States. You can do this hard or easy," James said.

"Easy, James." His voice was barely audible in the silent keep as he officially surrendered.

Before Brannigan could add anything else, the ornate decorative wall tapestry that he was sitting in front of moved suddenly and violently. Emerging from behind the tapestry, through a seamlessly concealed door in the wall, Peter Loren strode in. He held a handgun with a hefty magazine in it—which he aimed immediately at the trio of Brannigan's captors—and warned them not to reach for any concealed weapons they might have. "Especially you, McCoy. I see you even move those hands, and you are done."

"Peter…" Brannigan exclaimed. As he rose, he believed that he was being rescued and started to proclaim a victory. Loren gave him no time to finish. Unceremoniously, he shoved Brannigan over to where the other three were standing. There was now a healthy distance between Loren and the other four. He could cover them all. Brannigan stumbled from the ferocity of the shove, almost falling. James reached out to steady him, signaling, at the same time with his other hand, that he was not going to threaten Loren.

"Well, well, this is a surprise!" Loren laughed. "McCoy, I remember you, of course. It seemed odd to me that John here really needed a bodyguard, but then, to each his own…" Without taking his eyes off Vince, he totally shocked them with his next words. "You two," he pointed to James and Hector, "I have not met before. But…I can only surmise all three of you are behind this unholy debacle of a counterattack. And you were also involved in Venezuela, huh?"

No one said anything. James was trying to assess as quickly as possible why Loren would be referencing their covert operation in Venezuela. *Who is this guy, really?*

"In any case, I am happy to see all of you and to get all of you! Quite a coup, actually—and totally unexpected." A sinister and fleeting smile crossed his face. "It was John I came for."

In the world of propaganda and manipulation, Peter Loren may have been a brilliant protégé of Samir Taghavi, but there was one key difference between them. Taghavi, as a top Al Qaeda operative gifted in terror, knew to shoot first and talk later. Loren, on the other hand, was more of a talk first, shoot later guy. He wanted to make sure his victims were tortured by his words before he took them out. Taghavi had always understood that the ones who die are not important. Rather, it's the ones who witness it or hear about it later, and are terrorized, who are important.

That difference in training and ego would make all the difference. Loren said, "Just so you understand, I am not here because of Schweiner, the Great Reset, or the colossally incriminating video you guys captured and released. No. However, the serendipity, McCoy, is that you—and your compadres—will die because of Samir Taghavi and your mission that killed him."

James did not even blink. He was relying sheerly on his training. He knew now he was face to face with the current propaganda chief for Al Qaeda and that terror group was renowned for its long arm of retribution. Loren smiled again, letting them stew in it for a bit, and then turned to Brannigan. "And you, John, will die for Usama Bin Laden."

John Brannigan was shocked and speechless. He had not even been the head of the CIA when Bin Laden was killed. Loren sensed the disconnect and explained further. "*You*, you arrogant bastard, appointed yourself the representative of your entire intelligence community as far as the rest of the world is concerned. Nightly, on television, you have pontificated and bragged—and deceived. Well, here's the thing, John," he snarled. "That self-aggrandizing braggadocio—which will now lead to your death—will hold great significance for others from your country who might dare come after us."

Apparently satisfied that he had informed each man why he was to die that day, regretting only that he had no way of videoing it, he aimed the weapon specifically. Knowing that the other three men would likely charge him, he decided to start with Brannigan, in the hopes that his falling body would block or interfere with their charge. Just before he could execute his plan, he was struck from behind by another man who seemed to simply materialize from behind the curtain. A second commando simultaneously burst through the hidden door and grabbed the weapon, just as Loren's unconscious body slipped to the floor.

"Sorry about that, sir," the first commando said to James. "We couldn't risk the gun going off and spoiling your fun today."

James stepped forward. "Thank you. But where the hell did you come from?"

"Same place as this swine, sir. These places are always full of 'back doors.'" Turning to Brannigan, he added, "And you should have known that, Mr. Brannigan." Picking up the still-unconscious Loren, the two men pulled the tapestry back, revealing a dark hole that obviously led in and out of the tower. "We are taking him with us, if you don't mind."

McCoy stepped forward as if to protest, but James raised his hand and stopped him. "Be my guest."

The men disappeared down into a subterranean passage. Shortly after, McCoy escorted Brannigan back through the pantry into the main house and out into the late-afternoon sun. Emerging right behind him were James and Hector. They said nothing for the longest time, each reviewing the extraordinary peril they had been in and the surreal rescue that had saved them all.

"Well, it looks like that went off pretty well, even if you are a bunch of 'amateur Americans,'" Ari Ben- Gurion said, as he stepped down off the parapet steps, walking briskly to his friend. His familiar grin said it all. Tipping his hat sarcastically to Brannigan, he said, "Good day to you, sir. I wish you a good trip back to the United States." Brannigan scowled, knowing the Mossad had, once again, lived up to its reputation. And he frankly didn't know which would have been better, to have been killed by Peter Loren or to endure the trial he would likely be facing.

"Were you here all along?" James asked Ari.

Ari chose not to answer that directly. "Well, it was your party, James. My people had no plans to crash it until Loren showed up uninvited. So rude!" Letting that hang in the air for a moment, he added, "We missed Peter Loren once, if you remember." James did indeed remember how the Israelis had given Loren a pass when they were hunting down Taghavi at his Paris offices. How could he forget? It was likely the reason his counterpart had been so accommodating throughout this whole ordeal.

"Just so I am clear," Ari said to James with a professional formality, "Peter Loren stays in Europe, in the custody of the Israeli government. And John Brannigan is extracted and handed over to what I am told is a very anxious, and now-grateful U.S. Attorney."

James nodded, extending his hand.

Realizing by the position of the sun that the bridge would soon come up, all parties prepared to leave. "Just one thing, Ari…how did you know how to get in that way?"

Ari snorted. "That's going to cost you a big piece of pie, James! My friend, you did not think we would miss a tunnel, did you? These terrorists always have tunnels. Where do you think they learned it, huh? There is always an escape tunnel. And we had a few months to find it." He paused and then said, "You really should take a walk along the moat before you leave. There is a particular bench down there, near the house. People stop often to feed the ducks. The tunnel runs under the moat to the woods on the other side." With that, he winked and got into a car that had just driven up.

"Tell you what, John," James said, "Let's walk up onto the parapet and see what he is talking about. They climbed the stairs and walked along the rampart to the point where Brannigan had spotted Peter Loren, months earlier, sitting, feeding the ducks. Brannigan's stomach wrenched as he remembered his suspicions about Loren that morning. The two of them, like knights of the past, had been jousting ever since.

Grateful that McCoy's intrusion had saved his life—knowing now that Loren had come for him and had just been waiting for the right moment to strike—Brannigan straightened up. *I'll take my chances with that U.S. Attorney they keep touting!*

CHAPTER SIXTY

*J*ames didn't know exactly what he expected now that he was finally bringing John Brannigan to justice. But what he was experiencing didn't match any possible expectation. He had thought there might be exhilaration, certainly relief. But when he looked at Brannigan when they surprised him in the keep, the man seemed powerless and small. *More like a gnome,* James had thought.

So, on the plane on the way back to the United States, Brannigan meant no more to him than any other person on board. James did not feel hatred toward him. He just felt calm that this man's reign of terror and extortion would be coming to an end.

Perhaps it was the looks other passengers on the plane gave Brannigan. Vince and Hector were seated together just behind the door to the cockpit. James was with Brannigan a few rows back. He had chosen not to handcuff him, as he knew Brannigan had no place to go. And given the dirty looks the others gave him, James had more concern about needing to be a bodyguard for Brannigan than being his captor. Seeing that the man was intimidated by the proximity of the people, and their hostility, he offered, "Do you want to take the window seat, John?"

With no hesitation whatsoever, Brannigan answered, "Yes. Thank you." He spent the rest of the trip back to Washington, D.C.'s Dulles International Airport looking out the window into the sky above the clouds. James could only guess what must have been going through his mind, for John Brannigan—if the Justice Department followed through—would be facing perilously serious charges. His life, as he knew it, was over.

Two days later, John Brannigan, escorted by his attorney, turned himself into the FBI. Brannigan could not know it then, but Ari Ben-Gurion did, in fact, know who in the FBI would not turn a blind eye, nor could he know that things would not go his way with that U.S. Attorney. The public had not heard the content of the storage room computer, let alone heard the contents of his transmissions with Beijing. At his trial, however, the already-disgraced man who once held a "seat at the table" would have to listen quietly as his perfidy was revealed.

James Mikolas would not attend that trial.

Meanwhile, back at home, while James had been out of country, an orderly but determined mass of "peaceable assembly" events were occurring across the country. Whether it was the game that had produced the shift in citizens' minds or viewing the disgusting future those eight men and one woman had planned for them and their children—or both—there was a palpable shift.

Schweiner had been correct in his perception that the momentum had slowed. After the release of Operation Stone Age Viral, there was a collapse backward, and Schweiner's plans were stopped cold by the various marches.

Perhaps the most impactful group that had sprung up all over the country, with franchise-like extensions into all major cities, was the group of "Moms and Ministers," accompanied and protected by reformed gang members. They had demonstrated in front of all major city school board meetings, held rallies in every state capital, and were leading a massive march of 100,000-plus people to the Supreme Court.

Though the Capitol was still surrounded like a besieged building, and there were still thousands of totally bored military personnel guarding the place, the space near the Supreme Court was open. Antifa was stopped cold in all the cities where this group marched because Antifa's handlers and financiers could not envision maiming and beating moms of all races and ages and ministers of all ages, religions, and races who had joined arms with them.

Only WNG and a handful of other news agencies covered the "Moms and Ministers March" to the Supreme Court. But inside the Supreme Court of the United States, and inside the halls of Congress, it was obvious by the quantity of people outside that this group meant for the men and women in both buildings to do their job.

The people were speaking. And they stood on their constitutional rights to do so. The rally lasted all day, tied up traffic everywhere in the city, and offered speeches by civil rights leaders and citizens alike.

Down the mall, opposite the Washington Monument, the occupants of the White House could easily see the massive size of this protest march. Politicians can be counted on for one thing, for sure—they like to live to fight another day. So, wherever this crowd of "Moms and Ministers" went, the men and women who were supposed to serve them, and serve every other American as well, started to listen. And ask questions. Whether they had played the game called "Hate" or not, they had stumbled onto the first step of the reconciliation of viewpoints in the country. They asked questions, and they listened. It made all the difference.

Elsewhere in the country, people were coming up with their own solutions to each of the dots in the four connecting spider webs Andy had located. Disgusted and shocked by the usurpation of their rights as citizens by the cabal planning the Great Reset, and by the complicit media, they, too, were just talking to each other and finding their own solutions. Ironically, in trying to break down the individualism that characterized America, the backlash against the cabal was actually strengthening it. It would not be possible for the United States to succumb and become just another nation on Earth headed and governed by a superior breed of men in Europe. The United States would not look for the trans-human, not look to separate men by those worthy and those not worthy of a seat at any table.

A Great Reset in reverse was happening. The country was resetting itself on our foundation—and not on a new world order.

It was the prayer of the ministers that the United States' "great experiment" would continue, moving inexorably along its path—imperfections and all—learning from its mistakes, picking itself up, dusting itself off, and proceeding with the firm belief in their fellow man and in potential.

Reagan and Alicia had pledged themselves to make certain that the United States—no matter what it took with unions, school boards, and courts of law—would teach its own history, not the pernicious and distorted, hate-driven history a few had driven into the culture.

No matter the issue, those tackling them knew they were in for a fight. The difference was they now knew they were at least in a fight. They were communicating—and that is the entry point to all understanding.

Back across the pond, isolated and depressed, Ernst Schweiner had recalled Rutger Schmidt to Geneva. Within days, the two had driven to Schweiner's home in Dinkelsbühl, where they set up a private, confidential residence away from all the global economic and scientific projects they intended to continue.

It was not so much to lick their wounds, but rather to assess the damages in all the arenas where their tentacles had extended, and to decide the future. Men with the intention these two had would not give up easily.

One evening, on the rooftop of the keep, the two were enjoying a sherry. Ernst Schweiner was no quitter. Pursing his lips and looking down his glasses to his crystal sherry glass, he said with an almost poignant tone, "Well, that certainly did not turn out as we expected, did it, my friend?"

Shaking his head, Rutger barely verbalized, "No. Indeed."

"I don't know how far the fallout will go on this, Rutger. But we have to assume that all of our key players may fall, all of our plans may collapse, and we will have to redo it all."

Rutger looked off into the forest, contemplating that horrific task.

"I will likely not see our beautiful future world emerge, let alone our dreamed-of superhuman, given my age. Rutger, you, however, still can. We will simply need to recruit and select a new team, that is all. Surely, someone will emerge and rise like the mythological phoenix from the ashes of the Great Reset. That new responsibility will be assumed by a new generation, and it will fall to you to teach them our history."

"I understand, Ernst. This began in this place more than 80 years ago. It is fitting that we will reside here for a while."

With that, Ernst offered his glass in a toast.

CHAPTER SIXTY-ONE

*E*arly autumn in the farmlands of the East is resplendent with color as the leaves change, in the process of dying and falling, all part of the process that would lead to rebirth in the spring. James, Vince, and Hector had remained at the farm to wrap up their operation and to ensure that anything needed from them could be supplied.

Actually, Vince and Hector were scouting out their next rescue assignment in Central America. Waiting for the phone to ring, they were enjoying their time on the farm, using it to climb down off the tightrope they had been walking for nearly a year.

The low-lying fog that fills in the valleys of hill country, almost caressing the ground in its slow roll across it, was just lifting. James liked that time of day. It seemed to him the fog was holding the Earth, forcing the dew to remain on the grass. Once it lifted, the dew could escape. This morning, however, it was frost that was burning off. The previous night had dipped to freezing, and frost had formed in the areas of the farm that got less sunlight. What pleased him was the diamond sparkle he was witnessing as the frost crystals were exposed, released from the smothering fog.

"Hey, James." Vince came up behind him. "Let's get down to the air strip. The jet will be landing any minute."

"Sure." James zipped up his jacket and followed Vince to the back part of the farm. On board were Bud, Jessica, Brian, Alicia, Andy, Reagan, and the two girls. So much of what had occurred happened from the remote locations in Montana. Once the game operation and Stone Age Viral had settled into a rhythm, the Montana contingent wanted to visit Manassas one last time.

Though Hector and Vince did not know it, the trip was not a nostalgic one for Bud and Jessica. They wanted to personally see these two men before they took off into the isolated world they worked in. Later that morning, they were all on the porch, sitting on the steps, in chairs, or on the railing. It was quite a crowd.

Hector and Vince were just walking back from the hangar, carrying their duffel bags and backpacks. A call had come in, and they had to roll. Packing was easy for these two. Neither had roots. They had each other. As they walked toward the others, Jessica said to no one in particular, "Those two are two peas in a pod, aren't they?"

"You got that right, Jessica," James laughed. "They have to be the two quietest men on Earth. Do you know, they almost never talk? All the time I was here with them, it was like they made no noise—and even less conversation."

It had not been said critically. The others nodded because he had just articulated what their own experience of Vince McCoy and Hector Rodriguez had been. Two silent warriors, Andy thought.

Suddenly, Bud got up and went into the house without explanation. Vince and Hector dropped their duffel bags and plopped down onto a free spot on the steps. Saying nothing, they just smiled. Before any other conversation could resume, Walker came through the screen door, carrying what looked like a picture frame in his hands.

He stepped off the porch, where he could stand in front of the whole group. Looking at Hector directly, he said, "Hector, I know this was especially hard on you." Hector looked straight at Bud, not knowing, for sure, where he was going with this.

"I guess."

"I just want you to know that, in my opinion, we could not have been victorious had you not developed those 'skills,' son, and had you not used that incredible talent to break into those meetings. I can't even imagine where we—and our country—would be today without you."

Hector looked down to the ground, clearly a little uncomfortable. Undaunted, Bud continued, "I know you were scared, Hector. We all were. But you did your job. Plain and simple." Looking over to Vince and to the others, he said, "Son, I have a gift for you. Nothing of much value, except hopefully to you. These are words from the past, from another man who helped citizens and generals alike face fear and do their job. We inherited what they began."

He handed Hector the picture frame. Hector took it and started to read what was written and had been framed. It read: "Tyranny, like hell, is not easily conquered; yet we have this consolation with us, that the harder the conflict, the more glorious the triumph."— "The American Crisis," Thomas Paine, December 1776.

Bud then handed him a small pocket-sized card with the same message on it. "The quote is from my favorite journalist, Hector. I want you to have it because I believe you just lived it. But you can't carry the plaque around with you, so here is something you can keep close by as you and Vince head off to save somebody else."

"Thank you." That was all he said. He handed it over to Vince, so he could read it as well. Vince smiled. Not knowing what to say, Hector did the only thing that felt right. He jumped up and gave Bud a giant bear hug. Given his size, it could have been bone-crushing. Bud was startled but seemed to handle the sudden affection and exuberance fairly well.

"You are welcome."

Hector grinned. It almost masked a single tear in his right eye that was sliding out the corner. "You called me 'Son.'"

The whole gang spent the rest of the day relaxing, enjoying each other's company and a little peace in the quiet countryside. Bud, Andy, and Brian were cooking up something. Given they had this huge server farm they had created for Operation Stone Age Viral, they were figuring how they might use that for some independent future business projects— with emphasis on the word **independent**.

Walker thoroughly enjoyed the irony that he now owned most of the printing presses in the United States. His keen business head—which had allowed him to become not just a billionaire, but a highly respected businessman—was filling with ideas. With those printing presses, instead of being put out of business, he could, if he chose to, develop a newspaper division of Walker News Group and challenge the New York and Washington, D.C. establishment papers. He had to admit he was tempted.

At one moment, he told Andy that WNG was still standing— bloodied, but still there. And it looked as if necessity had truly been the mother of invention. With that quantity of servers, and with Andy's prowess, they talked of having their own tech platform. It had cost him most of his fortune, but—instead of perishing—his empire was poised to flourish using these new innovations.

When James inquired as to whether the boys would stay in Montana, the response was a resounding yes from them, their wives, and the little girls. Not long after, a car came for Hector and Vince, and they departed for their assignment. The rest crammed into the farmhouse for an overnight visit, and the next day, Brian, Alicia, and Hope joined Bud and Jessica, who were eager to return to the ranch.

Remaining with James, Andy and his family made some special plans. They had some unfinished business—their own family tradition.

CHAPTER SIXTY-TWO

*T*he fence around the Capitol had just been taken down. Military officers who had been identified as sympathizers to Ernst Schweiner and the others—who had been prepared to step up and stage a military coup, if necessary—had been rooted out. The code of secrecy had been broken, and, once outed as men and women who placed themselves and other global entities above their loyalty to their own country, there were mass resignations. Each was allowed to depart with pension and due respect for their service.

There was almost a collective sigh of relief, however, as the U.S. military attempted to get back to its own job. Protecting our citizens was a tall enough task. And most remaining high-ranking military were happy not to have to deal with this quasi-insurrectionist group that had been progressively taking hold.

Today, Andy, Reagan, and Faith went to Arlington National Cemetery to place a traditional memento on his parents' graves. James joined them. Though Faith was likely too young to understand, she seemed to have a keen interest in all the grave markers and in the two names carved on the Weir headstone. Normally very chatty, she had fallen silent and seemed to be studying the scene.

She slipped her hand into James', and stood close to him, as if she sensed somehow that they both were somewhat outsiders at this scene. Faith had never known grandparents. Today, she seemed content to lean against Unka James, as she called him.

A short time later, as she and her parents headed down the hill, James lingered for a moment by himself, placing a yellow rose on the grave. It was for Kelly Weir. Looking straight ahead, he could see the Lincoln Memorial, the National Mall, and the Capitol, and he hoped Reagan and Andy would enjoy their stop with Abe as much as he planned to.

Once across the Potomac, they came to the foot of the stairs that led to Abe. Andy picked his daughter up, so she could go with them. James knew that Hector and Vince were likely in Honduras by now. *I sure wish they could have joined us,* he thought. James wondered if Hector had any real idea of what his "skill sets" had pulled off. There was such an irony—in his mind—that the "least of them" had toppled the "mightiest of them." *Still, that was a nice thing Bud did for him, he reflected on the special moment at the farm.*

His thoughts turned to Brian and Alicia. "Hey, Kid, what do you hear from Brian? They all get home OK?"

"Yeah. He just texted me that they are sorry they couldn't join us, but Alicia felt she needed to get back to set up the next round of public appearances for her and Reagan." Andy felt he needed to explain the rest of the text, too. "Brian says he is celebrating Kelly's life by himself."

"He said that?" James asked.

"Yep." He paused for a moment then decided to add, "James, he has always been very private about honoring her—and his family. You know him. He's a real mensch of a guy—emotion, you know."

James thought about it a moment and appreciated the odd reference to a very honored Hebrew designation—especially as it related to a boy from the southeast side of Washington, D.C. He nodded.

Reagan jumped into the conversation. "Oh, James, there is one more thing, though, from Bud. You'll get a kick out of this. He called from the plane before we left the farm and told me to tell you he's toying with the idea of putting WNG, the whole thing, on subscription. That way, the public is truly in control, not advertisers and bullies."

Hah! That sounds like him, James thought. *He's a wily bugger. Last-laugh type of guy!"*

Reagan added with more than a hint of pride in her voice, "He called because he had a big realization about something on the plane on the way home to Montana. He wanted to tell Andy that he felt the game had done it. Getting hate to evaporate, it opened people's eyes and minds. And he realized something Brian had discovered—that if you hate, you cannot look. If hate goes away, you can look. We enabled them to look, that's all."

"That's cool. Thank you." James sat now on the top step of the memorial, gazing down the mall. They had the whole place to themselves. It was still too soon for people to have returned en masse to the famous sites they had grown up admiring and visiting. Each day, more and more people were venturing into the mall, though, hoping that it was safe and that somehow it would be the same as they remembered.

It was not, of course. It was up to the visitors now—the rightful inhabitants of that National Mall and all that it held—to make it into something new. If the lessons stuck, their choices would not be driven by hate. James Mikolas was not a religious man, but if he prayed, he prayed for that.

Andy sat down next to James. While the two enjoyed the quiet moment, Reagan walked Faith around with her, as she gazed up at Lincoln and then went to each side of the statue to read his Gettysburg Address and his Second Inaugural Address. It was the latter that struck her the most. For in her heart, she knew that they had each passed through such a time, and such a dilemma, as Lincoln had faced then.

Suddenly, Faith broke loose and scampered to her daddy, tackling him from behind and clinging to his neck. "Loot, Daddy, loot. The big man!" Her green eyes sparkled and grew big, along with her grin, as she pointed to the larger-than-life sculpture of the 16th president of the United States. Joining them, Reagan sat down on Andy's right side. Her gaze, too, went forward to the mall and to the Capitol dome that appeared so inviting at the end of the expansive park.

James remembered the story Andy told him about his little helper, his "code writer." It tickled him how Faith's mischievous desire to help had led not to disaster, but to a solution in the game. It was her blunder and erasure of all the "identities" of the players that had opened the door to a better game—and to a solution. He smiled, then chuckled. "Do you think she will ever know the part she played?"

Andy turned to pat her head, but she was not there. Like parents of any first child, Reagan and he both went onto high alert. She was not with them. Andy could almost taste the adrenaline as he leaped up, not knowing where to turn first. They spotted her quickly, however. "Thank God!" Andy exclaimed.

She had gone back to Lincoln, apparently very enamored of him. The adults had been reminiscing, and she took advantage of that. She was in the process at that moment of climbing up onto the statue.

"Oh, my," Reagan said, as she went to retrieve her little girl. "That's the tomboy in her, Andy. How on Earth did she get up there? Oh, my…"

Faith had crawled up as far as his foot. She used that to stand up, clinging to his leg. She was, in fact, very high up, but her attention was totally on Lincoln, and she appeared to want to get into his lap. Breaking all rules, Reagan climbed up onto the base of the statue and got close enough to reach up and bring her daughter down.

At first, Faith pouted a bit, but as she was carried down, she turned to look up at him and said, "Bye, nice man!"

"Judging by *that*, James," Andy said, shaking his head, then tilting it back toward the Lincoln statue, "I think she does know. I think she does." Then, to reassure James, he said, "But when she is older, we will tell her—just in case she gets any 'woke' ideas in her pretty little red head." Andy winked, knowing James would flinch at that idea.

James thought about that for a minute. Then he laughed. It was a private joke. *I think I have a future companion when it's time to visit my old friend Abe. And given all the museums I visited this summer, I should have plenty to show her.*

He reached out and stroked her copper hair. "What do you say we all go get some pie? I know a lady who makes the best lemon meringue pie in the country."

Acknowledgments

Since the publication of the first three "White King" novels, many friends and professional colleagues have continued to support the books—and their message. They have supported me and encouraged me. And that means more than one could imagine. I do not really have words to express how much it means to have people who help you keep a dream alive. There are also men and women who had a profound influence on me in my willingness and ability to face these issues. They, in their own rights, were warriors and were so gifted in their arenas. Everyone here—directly or indirectly—made this book possible. Many are now deceased, but their legacy endures.

Let me mention them now, in no particular order. You are all simply the best: Mark Nathan, Tom and Jan Solari, Paul Vallely, Jerry Molen, Eileen Batson, "Sam" Warner, Vince Rush, Tanii Carr, Marcy and David Sanders, Bill and Peggy Britt, Gary and Mary Kanady, Tanya Meyers, Rex and Judy Nichols, John and Martha Stevens, Jeff Moore, Ivan Passer, Barry Farber, Verna Sabelle, Steve and Jeannie Luckey, and CJ and Sharon Johnson.

Lastly, heartfelt gratitude to the creative team who produced such a quality book: Linda Gipson of www.gipsonstudio.com, who created the internal design and the stunning cover, and Kelly Lutterschmidt, whose editing helped bring the book to a stellar level. You both are a joy to work with.

Thank you, all. Here's to the White King!

ABOUT THE AUTHOR

*L*ee Kessler is a television actress, screenwriter, playwright, stage director, and e-commerce business owner. Her career in Hollywood and New York spans 40-plus years and includes dozens of guest-starring roles in episodic TV, mini-series, and movies of the week. She had reoccurring roles in the series "Hill Street Blues" and "Matlock" and was submitted for Emmy nominations twice for her starring roles in the movie "Collision Course" and the ABC special "Which Mother Is Mine?" She co-starred with Peter O'Toole in the movie "Creator."

Lee became the first actress in the world authorized to portray the legendary diarist Anaïs Nin when her play "Anaïs Nin—The Paris Years" was produced in New York and Los Angeles, with a subsequent tour on the West Coast. She also directed the West Coast premiere of A.R. Gurney's "Who Killed Richard Cory?"

Since the publication of her suspense novels, "White King and the Doctor," "White King Rising," and "White King and the Battle of America: The Endgame," she has made numerous radio and TV appearances discussing the books' relevance to the events we have all witnessed and experienced in the first two decades of the new millennium and has spoken often at book signings and private readings in New York and Los Angeles.

In 2008, she was inducted into the Dazzling Daughters of the American Revolution—becoming, at that time, one of only 121 women in American history to be selected for this prestigious group, which includes luminaries Susan B. Anthony, Eleanor Roosevelt and Clara Barton.

In 2014, Lee was chosen by the Secretary of the Air Force to participate in the Air War College/National Security Forum—to engage with top U.S. and foreign military officers in strategic analysis and discussions focusing on national and international security issues.

She has a passionate commitment to the youth of today, known as Generation Y, and speaks to them often about their role in keeping America free. Further, she vigorously challenges them to make the journey from being the Trophy Generation, which is their current mantle, to the Hero Generation, which she believes they can become.

CPSIA information can be obtained
at www.ICGtesting.com
Printed in the USA
LVHW040606020723
751240LV00001B/47